THE CAMELOT WARS - BOOK II

CAMELOT
RISING

MICHAEL CLARY

A PERMUTED PRESS BOOK

ISBN: 978-1-68261-156-2
ISBN (eBook): 978-1-68261-157-9

Camelot Rising
The Camelot Wars Bok Two
© 2016 by Michael Clary
All Rights Reserved

Cover art by Dean Samed

PERMUTED
PRESS

Permuted Press, LLC
permutedpress.com

Published in the United States of America

♣ MERLIN ♣

Things were not perfect, but they could certainly be a lot worse. Then again, things could always be a lot worse. Arthur wasn't coming along. He wasn't willing to change. Our king drank all day and whored all night. We did our best to keep him from the populace.

That was my decision.

The tales of Arthur's deeds had spread far and wide. A leader who rode out on a massive black horse and took on an entire army of Death Reapers in defense of his wife and child's graves.

It was the stuff of legend.

It caused people to believe in him. Image what their reaction would be if they saw Arthur stumbling off a bar stool or groping some random young lady. Let's just say he wasn't big on impressing people. Still, the legend spread and the people came. The first of the large groups of people to reach us didn't stay long. That's when we realized it was best to keep Arthur away from others.

The people wanted the legend. They needed the hero. Arthur wasn't fit for the job. He wasn't motivated to lead. He wasn't motivated to do much of anything unless forced to do so.

Enough about Arthur.

It was plain enough to everyone that the man couldn't be counted on to do his duty. That wasn't a problem. Arthur created the spark and the spark created the fire. People came to Camelot and Camelot took them in.

Our numbers grew and spread out over the course of three years. New towns sprang up within a few days ride. Our armies grew, and our knights became warriors and leaders without peer. We were doing just fine. This was our land. Morgana and her forces, for the most part, stayed far away.

Yes, there were skirmishes. Every now and then our people would run into a small battalion of Death Reapers. The battles weren't much. We outnumbered them too greatly.

Gwen was my student. She'd been my student for a while now. Magic and sorcery isn't exactly easy to use. Three years into her training and Gwen still wasn't able to pull off the simplest of spells, at least not to a reliable degree, but I could sense the power inside of her. Someday, she'd rival even my greatness. In the meantime, she cursed a lot.

Her relationship with Arthur never improved. On the contrary, it sort of went south between them rather rapidly. Arthur ignored her, and she in turn, seemed to regard him as something she might have been unlucky enough to have stepped in.

I'd really missed the boat with the two of them.

Dellia was doing fine. She helped run the hospital. We'd found more doctors and that was great. Healthcare wasn't something to be overlooked and, even though we lacked the technology we once possessed, we all got along just fine. Dellia and Gwen had become very close. They respected each other, and often spent time together.

Wayne was still an asshole. I loved the guy, he was dependable, loyal, fierce, and brave, but the son of a bitch could get on my nerves like no other person in the world. That being said, we'd have lost much without him. He was necessary.

Reynolds and Bedder were also incredibly valuable to our cause. Reynolds was an incredible strategist, and Bedder, though strange and often angry, was a skilled combatant.

Lancelot didn't have much to do anymore. His job was to protect our king, and since our king never left our town, he wasn't often put in danger, excluding an angry father or husband wanting to pummel his face for what he'd done with their daughters and wives. Arthur's ability to seduce wasn't something he could control. Acting upon the urges this ability could cause however, made him guilty as sin.

There came a knock on my door. That was odd. It was rather early for company. Was it an emergency? I wasn't exactly known for my hospitality so early in the morning.

2

I opened the front door and saw nothing, but I felt a presence by the bushes.

"Yes," I said. "What's happening, Lancelot?"

"He's at it again," Lancelot answered.

"Does anyone know it's him?" I asked.

"No," Lancelot answered. "He borrowed armor from Wayne's wife. The helmet is covering his face."

"Is he riding Goliath?" I asked.

"Yes," Lance answered.

"It's like having to raise a baby dragon," I mumbled. "Every time I turn around he's getting into something."

Lance giggled from outside my house, and I turned grumpily in his direction.

"We should ban the entire sport," I said.

"I don't think that would be a good idea," Lancelot argued. "The men seem to enjoy it."

"Of course they do," I said and walked outside into the bright morning sun.

The air was cold and dry. Not yet, but soon, the snow would begin to fall. Camelot was beautiful in the winter time. Well, this wasn't exactly Camelot. I was referring to the kingdom of old.

Much of this new Camelot had been damaged by fire when the Black Knight made his attack. What could be salvaged afterwards was repaired, but many homes had been destroyed in the attack, and an open field now resided where families once flourished.

It was prime real estate located just outside and to the right of the town square. It wasn't long after all the repairs were made that a few young men took to riding their horses in the field. At first they'd tried the football field by the high school, but were told to find another place to ride that wasn't so close to the students.

Well, a farmer's field certainly wasn't an option so they moved their activities to the field in which I was currently headed towards. At first it was simply a group of young men that practiced their horsemanship, but young men, being young men, soon began racing their horses against one another.

Then came the jousting.

Yes, the jousting. The greatest of all sports had been rediscovered. I myself helped outfit the competitors in proper protection. I myself gave advice to the riders. It was fun. I probably shouldn't have encouraged them, but what can I say, I love the sport.

The popularity caught on like a wildfire. Soon a small stadium had been erected around the field complete with bleachers, tents, and a few buildings.

Every weekend would draw a large crowd. It was great. The sounds of pounding hooves, the applause, and the snort of an adrenaline charged horse. It was a blast from the past, and I loved every second of it.

Unfortunately, so did Arthur.

He routinely took a break from drinking and bedding women to compete. That of course couldn't be allowed. Jousting was dangerous. Our figurehead king couldn't be allowed to risk himself in such a needless way.

We did our best to distract him, but Arthur was a tricky man.

I entered the stadium and immediately lost track of Lance. Two armored combatants faced each other, one at each end of the field. One of them sat upon a massive black horse that scratched at the ground and made shrill angry noises out of his nostrils.

Goliath.

Arthur sat impatiently upon his back waiting for the flag to drop. His wooden lance was held straight up while his opponent's lance was already pointed in his direction. Arthur was too cocky. Eventually he was going to be hurt.

The flag went down.

I could hear and feel the pounding of Goliath's hooves as he bore down upon the smaller horse. Arthur repositioned his lance. Man and animal crossed the midway point of the track and lances crashed together before their opponents managed to get up to speed.

The poor man fell from his horse amidst an explosion of wood. Our king then circled and rode back to the stables without removing his helmet or acknowledging his victory.

I made my way to the stables.

By the time I got there, Arthur had dismounted and was busy feeding him an apple while he himself drank happily from a flask. Excalibur was on his hip in its scabbard. At the moment I sensed that the sword was resting and unconcerned with the current goings on. I shouldn't have worried; Arthur had learned on his own how to deal with the sword.

"Drinking and jousting?" I asked.

"The jousting part's over," Arthur answered. "Maybe you were watching?"

4

"I saw the ending," I answered.

"When my opponents get better, maybe I'll sober up," Arthur laughed.

"I need eyes in the back of my head if I'm going to keep you out of trouble," I said.

"What trouble can I possibly get into?" Arthur asked. "I'm the king and you're overreacting."

"What good are you as a king if you get killed in a joust?" I asked. "You don't want to be a leader, fine we can't force you, but we need you to be a figurehead. We need you to pretend that you're capable of looking after Camelot."

"I'm glad you brought that up," Arthur said. "Who in the hell started calling this town Camelot? This is Mill Ridge. I never gave anyone permission to change the name."

"Camelot is the name," I answered testily. "It's the place where Arthur lives. It's where his court resides. It's a safe place and the epicenter of your kingdom."

"It's pretentious," Arthur said dismissively.

"It sure is," Wayne agreed from the depths of the barn with his loud booming voice.

"Wayne," I said. "I should have known you'd be a part of this."

"Well we can't keep him confined to his house all day," Wayne said. "A little activity is good for him."

"Are you kidding me?" I asked. "Do I really need to explain the dangers of jousting?"

"How'd you find out, anyway?" Arthur asked abruptly.

"What do you mean?" I asked in return.

"You know what I mean," Arthur said. "Who told you I was jousting?"

"I'm a wizard," I said. "Nobody had to tell me anything."

"Lance!" Arthur shouted. "Where are you?"

"Dude," Wayne said. "Did Lance rat you out? Oh man, that's harsh."

"You think?" Arthur said.

"I don't need Lance to tell me when you're up to no good," I said.

"Lance," Arthur continued. "I know you're here, say something."

"I'm here," Lance said from somewhere in the rafters.

"You're supposed to be my bodyguard," Arthur complained.

"I am," Lance said.

"No," Arthur said. "You're my tattletale, and that I don't need."

"My duty is to protect Arthur," Lance argued. "If you're doing something stupid, and I can't stop you, I'll go to somebody who can."

"I'm not sure how a teenager can stop two full grown men," Wayne added with a laugh. He was of course referring to my youthful appearance. I still hadn't aged a day since I over exuberantly used magic to reduce my age. Wayne was trying to get me riled up.

"I can show you," I said in my most sinister voice.

"Bring it on, whippersnapper!" Wayne bellowed.

I snapped my thumbs and a bucket from a nearby shelf leapt into the air, flew across the room, and lightly smacked Wayne in the back of the head.

Wayne yelped loudly and rubbed the back of his head.

"That's not fair," Wayne said. "I'm not using magic."

"That sucks for you," I said.

I was acting ridiculous. The age reduction spell I'd used on myself was way too strong, and unfortunately, it also affected my maturity. To my great embarrassment, a halfwit like Wayne was now in fact able to rile me up.

"Arthur," I said. "Can I assume that you're finished for the day?"

"I believe I am," Arthur said agreeably...too agreeably.

Arthur wasn't looking at me. He was looking outside the stables at a couple of twenty-something girls walking by.

I sighed deeply and hoped that they didn't have boyfriends or overprotective fathers.

"Try and stay out of trouble," I said.

"Trouble's just what I'm looking for," Arthur said with a smile. "Wayne, can you brush down Goliath for me?"

"No," Wayne answered.

"What?" Arthur asked. "What do you mean, no?"

"Goliath doesn't like me," Wayne answered. "I'm not going near him."

"You'll be fine," Arthur said. "Goliath is just a bit shy."

"Fuck that," Wayne said. "I'm not doing it."

The relationship between Arthur and Goliath had changed dramatically since the graveyard battle and the search for Excalibur. Arthur showed a level of love towards that horse that I'd not have thought possible if I hadn't seen it with my own eyes. Goliath returned the affection equally. The two of them were damn near inseparable and fully devoted to each other.

That however, didn't mean that Goliath had gone soft. On the contrary, in developing a soft spot for Arthur, the great horse took even greater pride in harassing others. Many a stable boy had been bitten or kicked by the foul tempered animal. His nastiness was legendary.

"I'll take care of Goliath," I said.

"Thanks," Arthur said and quickly vanished from sight.

"You think you can handle that horse?" Wayne asked.

"Of course I can," I answered.

"Only because you're magic," Wayne said.

I laughed and approached Goliath.

The horse's eyes went wide.

He gave a low snort, and scratched at the ground.

"Don't you dare even think about it," I whispered right before he tried to bite me.

Goliath snorted in response, dipped his head low, and nudged my shoulder.

"That's more like it, my friend," I said while brushing his long mane. "Don't let Arthur influence you."

"Speaking of Arthur," Wayne said. "You should probably ease up on him a bit."

"You think he pays attention to anything I say?" I asked.

"Probably not," Wayne admitted, "but he hears what you say nonetheless."

"What are you telling me?" I asked.

"When's the last time you gave him a word of encouragement?" Wayne asked. "When's the last time you said something other than criticizing him?"

I didn't like where Wayne was going.

"It's like this," Wayne continued. "We know now that Arthur isn't going to be some great leader, but that doesn't mean you're no longer his grandfather and it doesn't mean that I'm no longer his best friend."

"That's where you and I differ, I'm afraid," I said. "You've given up on him. I haven't. Arthur will one day rise again. You saw him in that graveyard. You've fought beside him. You know what he's capable of."

"He's a fierce fighter," Wayne said, "but he's no leader. We should let him be who he is."

"Trust me when I say that I'll never force Arthur into anything," I said. "Yet, I will be there to light the way when the night grows darkest."

"I don't even know what that means," Wayne said. "Anyway, those were only my two cents on everything. You can take it or leave it."

"I appreciate your two cents," I said as Wayne walked out of the stables.

I continued brushing Goliath, lost in my thoughts and enjoying myself. I'd forgotten that Lancelot was still nearby.

"I believe in Arthur," Lancelot whispered.

"I know you do," I said.

"I've seen him looking at Gwen," Lancelot continued.

"Really?" I asked. "I had no idea."

"They don't often see each other," Lancelot said, "but if they happen to cross each other's paths, his eyes linger."

"Then perhaps their paths should cross more often," I said.

"I'm not so sure that's a good idea," Lancelot said. "Sometimes they call each other names."

I sighed deeply.

It's never easy.

I'm a horrible matchmaker.

I should cast a love spell.

Would it even work on Arthur?

Probably not with Excalibur on his hip, Excalibur could block unwanted magic.

"I'll think things over," I said. "Maybe I can come up with something that won't end with the two of them yelling at each other."

I spent another hour with Goliath. He demanded it. After that, I asked a stable boy to take him on home. The poor child didn't seem to appreciate the suggestion, but children tend to not disagree with me. I think I frighten them. It's probably because of my appearance combined with the way I speak.

I walked slowly around the town. In the distance I could hear Reynolds screaming out at the training soldiers. That man knew a lot about warfare. I was glad that he was on our side.

The fields on either side of Main Street looked healthy. The farmers were already out and going about their daily routines. The shops on either side were just opening and children could be seen playing games on the sidewalks.

Camelot was a town of happiness and peace, but how long would it last? I had a training session scheduled with Gwen in a few hours. She'd be early, but that wasn't a problem. I had nothing else scheduled for the day.

Bedder came out from behind a building, riding straight towards me.

"Good morning, Bedder," I called out as he approached.

"Maybe not," Bedder said. "Malcolm and his bunch were scheduled to return at first light. We haven't seen them yet."

Malcolm and four other riders were one of the many scouting groups that road far and wide throughout the land. They kept an eye out for trouble, and thus kept all of Camelot and the towns residing nearby safe.

"It could be that he's just running a bit late," I said.

"He's never been late before," Bedder said. "He's due for a few days off. He'd want to see his girlfriend."

"How long's he been gone?" I asked.

"Two weeks," Bedder answered.

"Yes," I admitted. "He'll probably be looking forward to seeing his girlfriend. What do you want to do?"

"I can find him," Bedder said. "All the scouts leave a map in case something like this happens."

"I'll come with you," I said. "Find Wayne and Tristan as well. They'll be useful if things get rough."

"I'm expecting rough," Bedder said. "It's been too quiet lately."

"I hate to agree with you," I said.

"I'll grab another ten soldiers as well," Bedder said. "If we need any more than that, we'd best come back for Reynolds."

I went back to the stables. Gwen was there brushing down her horse when I arrived. She smiled at me, and the world became a much brighter place. The woman grew more beautiful by the day. Men would fight wars just to receive a smile from her.

"Are we still on for later?" Gwen asked.

"I'm afraid not, my dear," I answered. "Something has come up."

"What?" Gwen asked.

"A scouting party was due back at first light," I answered. "They haven't returned yet."

"Is it something we should worry about?" Gwen asked.

"Not at this point," I answered. "We'll follow their return route and see if we can't track them down. It should only take a few days or so."

"Who's going?" Gwen asked.

I told her what Bedder and I had come with.

"I should go as well," Gwen said.

"You and Reynolds should stay here," I said. "Just in case."

"We have too many scouting parties out there," Gwen said. "Nothing's going to sneak up on us."

"It's still best to have strong people in charge when I'm not here," I said.

"But I'm bored," Gwen said. "All I do is practice magic. I want to get back out there. I want to be useful."

"Have you already mastered magic?" I asked.

"Not even close," Gwen answered honestly.

"You would be useful out there," I said. "That goes without saying. Your archery skills are second to none, but imagine how much more useful you'll be when you've mastered what I'm teaching you."

"I'm a leader," Gwen said with a roll of her eyes. "This makes me feel useless."

"Your time will come once again, my dear," I said. "In the meantime, today's lesson is in my home on the front desk. You can go through this one without me."

"When are you going to move out of that old police station by the way?" Wayne asked from the open doorway.

"I hadn't realized it bothered you so much," I said without answering him.

"It's just weird," Wayne said. "Who wants to live in a police station? There has to be an empty house around here somewhere. Or maybe we can find you some surrogate parents. That might help fill out the teenybopper illusion."

"You're too funny," I said.

Gwen was trying not to laugh.

"You're sarcasm isn't very polite," Wayne added. "If you were my kid, I'd ground you."

"If I was your kid, I'd suffocate you in your sleep," I said.

I was acting like an annoyed teenager again.

I should have been embarrassed with myself. How could I let him get a rise out of me again and again? My fingers twisted without my consent. A bit of concentration later, and I'd stuck his tongue to the roof of his mouth.

It was excessive.

It was also funny.

Wayne would not agree with that assessment.

"Relax," I said. "You'll have your tongue back in an hour or so."

Rude gestures immediately came my way.

Gwen lost the battle and started laughing.

"I can't believe you just did that," Gwen said between giggles.

"Really?" I asked.

"Well, okay maybe I can believe it," Gwen said, "but still..."

"I could have pulled his ears off," I said.

"Can you teach me how to do that?" Gwen asked.

"As soon as you learn to summon magic when you need it," I answered. "It'll be your first lesson."

"Merlin," Gwen said. "I've never asked you. Have you trained others?"

"Yes," I answered.

"Are they still around?" Gwen asked.

"Unfortunately, they are not," I answered truthfully. "Magic isn't an end all be all. Wizards still die. I wish it were otherwise, but there you have it."

The sound of approaching horses could be heard from outside. I grabbed a nearby horse for the journey and went out to meet Bedder. Wayne followed angrily behind me.

"All is ready?" I asked the spooky knight with the pitchfork-like dagger for a left hand.

"We've got provisions and mounted soldiers," Bedder answered. "All of them are battle tested."

"Hello Tristan," I said to the androgynous youth riding next to Bedder. "I'm sorry to disturb your morning so early."

Tristan yawned and gave me a non-committal wave; the meaning of which I could only guess was that all was fine.

We rode out immediately.

Chances were that Malcolm and his men had just gotten tied up with something, but we didn't like to take chances. Hopefully by heading out in the direction the scouts intended to use on their return route we'd be able to find them sooner rather than later.

I wasn't overly concerned, but despite that Morgana and her Death Reapers were not a force to take chances on. We had to check under every stone.

An hour went by on our journey. We'd entered the forest which despite the chill was still green in abundance. The forests around Camelot always stayed green. I had a cloak wrapped around my shoulders, not because I was cold, but because it felt so comfortable.

Wayne was talking once again.

"That was not cool," Wayne grumbled next to me.

"Admittedly, it wasn't," I said. "It was excessive. I apologize."

"Really?" Wayne asked.

"Yes," I answered.

"That easy?" Wayne asked.

"You bet," I answered.

"What are you planning?" Wayne asked.

"Nothing," I said with a smile.

"This is bullshit," Wayne complained. "It's no fun hacking on each other if you're going to use magic on me all the time."

"Wayne," I said.

"What?" Wayne asked.

"Be afraid," I said. "Be very, very afraid."

Tristan who had overheard everything started laughing, and that's pretty much how the first day of riding went. When it got dark, we made camp and lit a fire. The men passed around a flask of whiskey, but I abstained. At night they fell asleep in makeshift tents and I rested my back against a tree.

In the middle of the night I was awakened.

A rumble came from far off. I couldn't pinpoint the direction of the sound, not with all the trees around. I needed a higher elevation for that. Perhaps I hadn't even heard it. Had the sound wakened me from my sleep or had I dreamt it?

I felt ill at ease.

I felt threatened.

I said nothing to the men in the morning. There was no use in alarming them over nothing and I had no evidence to the contrary. I certainly didn't hear another rumbling sound again.

I rarely feel ill at ease in the forest.

The men drank coffee and ate a simple breakfast before packing up the horses and setting off once again. Bedder was his usual stoic self, but the rest of our group was in good spirits. Laughter and jokes bounced from rider to rider.

The day was uneventful and the tension I was feeling began to ease a bit. It didn't vanish, but it began to ease with inactivity. We took breaks every few hours and the men complained of sore asses. A light lunch came around midday, and we were off again until sunset.

The tension and the ill feelings returned with a vengeance as we made camp.

This was too much.

There could be no mistake.

We were in danger.

I told the men to remain on guard. I wanted two of the soldiers watching over us at all times. I myself would stay awake during the night as well. This made the men a bit nervous. They knew better than to doubt me. I only wished I knew what was in the forest with us.

The night was deathly quiet.

With the exception of the crackling fire and the occasional snore from Wayne all was silent. Not even the animals were about. That was unusual to say the least.

Daybreak came and things had not improved.

"Should we go back and get more men?" Wayne asked.

"That'll take too much time," Bedder argued. "We have men in possible danger out there. We can't wait for reinforcements."

"I can travel pretty fast," Tristan added. "Just say the word, Merlin, and I'll bring back our whole damn army."

"We may be in above our heads," I said. "Perhaps it would be better if I went alone."

"That's not going to happen," Bedder growled. "We won't be leaving you."

I sighed deeply. I expected that answer. Bedder was creepy and definitely not the most entertaining person to be around, but he was loyal.

"Tristan," I said. "Ride ahead and scout for us. Keep quiet and be safe. Don't create too much distance between us."

Tristan nodded in response and saddled his horse.

"This would be a lot easier if we knew what we were up against," Wayne said. "Will the attack come from the forest? Will it come from the air? Will it come from under the ground?"

"If I had to guess, I'd say the forest," I answered.

We rode out about an hour after Tristan departed us. We took our time and we constantly checked our surroundings. The forest was thick. An ambush would be easy to pull off. We were following a rough trail, our horses moved in single file, and the forest rose up on either side. An attacker could be five feet away from us and we'd never know.

It started to rain.

It wasn't too heavy a rain and all of us were used to the sudden showers, but at this time of year, the rain was cold and it made riding uncomfortable for the men. Worst of all, the sound of the falling rain hitting the leaves would provide enough noise to cover up someone or something moving through the forest.

That latter part wasn't something I had to remind everyone of. They'd had their training. As soon as the rain started everyone fell silent. Our ears were straining to pick out any sound that didn't belong.

Two hours later the rain had let up.

The ground around us had grown muddy, perhaps a little bit too muddy.

"Bedder," I said. "Is there a body of water somewhere nearby?"

"There's a large pond around the next bend in the trail," Bedder answered.

"Tristan will be waiting for us there," I said.

"Are you certain," Bedder asked.

"Be on the lookout for trouble," I answered.

The pond was a water source. Malcolm and his scouts would have stopped there. I was sure of it. It would also be a great place for an ambush.

Bedder signaled for the soldiers to dismount and spread out through the woods in two different directions. The rest of us stayed on our horses and followed the trail.

The mud got a bit worse as we rounded the bend and came to the pond. Tristan was at the water's edge waiting for us. He shouldn't have been in the open like that. He knew better.

I passed Bedder who was in the lead and rode over to Tristan.

"Why aren't you being careful?" I asked.

"I couldn't stay anywhere nearer to the forest," Tristan answered. "There's something foul in there. You can sense it. You can even smell it."

I followed his gaze and realized he was correct.

We were in trouble.

"I found some footprints," Wayne called out.

"I found a dagger," Bedder added.

A fluttering cloth at the tree-line told me that I'd found the remains of a tent.

"Are the tracks human?" I asked.

"Looks like it," Wayne answered. "I think there might have been a battle of some kind, but it's hard to tell with all these big puddles around."

"I've found a body," Bedder announced from close to the tree line. "He's sunk into the mud, but it's one of Malcolm's scouts. I'm sure of it."

Puddles.

Wayne said puddles.

Why was that bothering me so much?

What caused the puddles?

I left Tristan at the water's edge and rode over to Wayne.

"Do you see all the disturbances on the ground?" Wayne asked.

I didn't answer him right away. I was too busy looking at what Wayne thought were large puddles.

Half of our soldiers emerged from the forest on the other side of the pond. I waved them to come forward quickly.

"Wayne," I said calmly. "Get back on your horse."

Wayne moved at once, but remained calm.

"How bad?" Wayne asked.

"Very," I answered.

Bedder rode over to us. He knew something was going on. The soldiers had rounded the pond and were cautiously approaching us. I motioned for them to mount their horses.

"What is it?" Bedder asked.

"We need to leave immediately," I said. "I'll explain everything after we've gained some distance."

"We'll wait for the rest of the men to come back and we'll be off then," Bedder said.

"The other men aren't coming back," I said. "We need to be off immediately. Move slowly until I give the word."

"I can't do that," Bedder said.

"Bedder, I need you to trust me," I said. "The men are dead. We need to leave."

"We're brothers-in-arms," Bedder said. "That means we owe something to our soldiers. It means we don't turn tail and abandon them at the first sign of danger."

"Listen…" I tried to say before a deep roar sounded out from the forest and abruptly cut me off.

"What was that?" Bedder asked.

"Something horrible," I said. "Hopefully there's only one."

Another roar sounded out from a different area of the forest as if mocking my hopefulness. The volume and the power of the roars would be impossible to describe, but the very air vibrated under their onslaught.

The men drew their swords.

A body flew out from the forest before us and landed with a sickening thud in front of our horses. The body was contorted and the poor man's limbs were twisted at unnatural angles and broken. He must have suffered terribly.

Wayne had an axe in his hand. He was scanning the forest furiously, looking for a threat, but coming up empty handed.

"Merlin," Wayne said. "Are they ghosts? Why can't I see them?"

"You will see them soon," I answered.

"How do we fight them?" Bedder asked.

"We fight them with hundreds of men," I answered. "So we're a little short at the moment."

The sound of trees snapping echoed out of the forest.

"Shields up!" I shouted. "The attack is beginning!"

The men did as I asked. Sadly, it was probably a futile effort. What we needed was a fair amount of cover, and that wasn't available so close to the pond.

The tops of the trees began to sway back and forth as something large moved closer to us underneath the dense canopy of foliage.

The horses were frightened. Two of the animals bucked up, knocking their riders out of their saddles.

Rocks about the size of my fist began to rain down on us. They bounced off the shields in a riot of sound. The men instinctively moved their horses closer to one another and created a shield wall of protection.

It worked well enough in the beginning, but the small rocks were only a distraction.

"Stay together!" I shouted. "Weather the storm!"

More thunderous growls came from the forest. The horses panicked. More riders fell. The shield wall started to break apart. A second body flew through the air.

This new mangled body landed on top of the remaining shields, stunning several of the men. The rocks grew larger after that. The unharmed soldiers immediately were forced to spread out.

The injured soldiers weren't so lucky. Too disoriented to move, they were left at our attacker's mercy.

I twisted my hands together, and the sand and pebbles on the ground rose up and solidified in their defense. Broken trees flew at us as if they were spears. Rocks the size of large shrubs rolled past us.

"What the hell are we up against?" Wayne asked.

"Giants," I answered.

The forest grew suddenly quiet.

The men were confused. They looked around at each other and didn't know what to do. Luckily for them, I knew what must be done.

"Grab the injured," I said. "Get back on your horses if you've fallen off. We're leaving this place now."

To give them credit, the soldiers immediately went into motion. Bedder and Wayne even dismounted in an effort to help the injured.

I unhappily patted my horse from the saddle.

A large creature stepped out of the forest blocking the route we'd used to get here. He was spotted immediately and a great wave of panic washed over our small party.

I couldn't blame them.

The giant stood naked to the world. Its entire body was covered in a reddish brown hair. The head seemed too small for the massive shoulders and the large black eyes showed a cruelty beyond measure.

Its arms hung below its kneecaps. There was very little neck for the head, and its overall proportions were unbelievable. The creature was simply too thick and muscular even with its incredible height. An average man would barely stand up past its kneecaps if he were stupid enough to get to close.

Giants eat men.

Another giant, just as grotesque as the first, emerged from the forest on our opposite side. We were trapped. Giants blocked the way to and from the pond on both sides. Our only options would be to jump into the pond, or head directly into the forest in front of us, the same area the rocks, bodies, and trees had been hurled from.

Everyone was once again mounted.

I looked at the first giant. Its face was the only part not covered in hair. It appeared in my eyes to be a misshapen mask of a human face. The eyes were too far apart. The forehead was too small. The mouth was an ugly pit filled with blocky yellow teeth.

The giant stared back at me, a gleam of evil intelligence shone from its eyes and made the hairs on the back of my neck stand up.

"Merlin," Bedder said. "What do we do?"

I had to give him credit. He sounded calm.

"We ride," I answered. "I'll clear the way."

I twisted my hands. A large ball of fire grew between them. My hands moved back and forth and the fireball grew larger and larger. When it was the size of a beach ball, I released it into the air and sent it towards the giant.

The giant smiled.

The fireball collided with its hairy chest and exploded. The giant was pushed backwards a few steps by the explosion, but other than that he was unharmed, due to his tough skin.

I rode towards him as he stepped forward to meet me.

Little did he know, the fireball was only a distraction. I twisted my hands as I rode. I concentrated my effort and will.

The same sand and pebbles I used to protect the stunned soldiers once again rose from the ground, but this time, they shot directly into the face of the giant.

The giant roared in frustration.

He swung his arms towards me in anger, but the sand and pebbles had temporarily blinded him. Before he managed to recover, I was past him and fleeing for my life.

Bedder, Wayne, and the soldiers were directly behind me. I screamed for them to ride faster. Giants were quick, but they tired easily. We needed to gain some distance.

I heard a scream, looked over my shoulder, and saw a soldier in the hands of the second giant. I stared in horror as the man pounded his fists on the gigantic hand holding him tight. I wanted to go back for him, but the first giant, still rubbing sand and pebbles from his eyes appeared next to his fellow giant.

Together, they pulled the soldier into two pieces, stuffed the pieces into their mouths, and began chewing.

"Son of a bitch!" Wayne shouted.

The men had all unconsciously slowed their horses as they watched the macabre scene behind them.

"Keep riding!" I shouted. "Don't slow down."

The two giants began pursuing us and soon after that they began catching up to us.

"Merlin," Bedder said from my left hand side. "Can you do something?"

"Not really," I answered. "They're too close and too fast. I don't have time to concentrate. Well...maybe...just possibly..."

"What?" Bedder asked.

Another soldier screamed out. Both he and his horse had been smacked off their feet. The horse screamed out in pain. The man screamed out for help.

"Damn it!" Bedder shouted in frustration.

18

"Ride ahead of me," I said. "Everyone ride ahead of me."

Nobody was happy with that idea, but what choice did they have. We were being picked off one by one.

My hands twisted and my concentration flowed into a large tree between the giants and our fleeing party. I took control of the tree. Under my will, the roots began to swell and lengthen.

The giants were slowed only briefly as they devoured the soldier and his horse. My horse came to a stop as they advanced towards me. I spared a brief glance at them. They both wore sadistic grins on their faces.

I pulled the trigger on my sorcery as they passed the tree at full speed. The large roots blasted up from underneath their feet and tangled around their legs. Both giants fell to the ground with an earth trembling thud.

"Wizard," the giant said as he looked up at me. "I'll soon dine on your flesh."

"Not today," I said.

I focused even more on the roots until they wound up to the chests of the giants, and then I rode away. All I had done was slow them down. The roots wouldn't hold them forever. The giants were too strong for that.

Less than a mile away, I caught up with my group. They had slowed down a bit, but they'd never stopped moving.

"Did you get them?" Wayne asked.

"No," I answered. "I only slowed them down."

"Why didn't you kill them?" Wayne asked.

"I wish it were that easy," I said. "All things considered I think I did a pretty good job since most of us managed to get away."

"We need to kill them," Wayne said. "Imagine the damage those bastards can cause."

"Imagine the damage a small army of them can cause," Bedder added.

"Wait a minute," Wayne said. "You don't think..."

"I do think," I interrupted. "Camelot is under attack."

"But there's only two of them," Wayne said. "Surely with enough people we can take down two giants."

"There are more than two of them," Bedder said. "The rest were in the forest."

"Holy shit," Wayne said. "What do we do?"

"We ride home," I said. "We prepare for battle."

♣ GWEN ♣

I have a strong dislike for magic, and to be completely honest I feel that magic has a strong dislike for me as well. I'm not sure what it is, but the two of us don't seem to work very well together.

My hands ached terribly. Twisting my fingers into strange symbols over and over could have that type of effect on somebody. Merlin didn't care. Over and over he made me concentrate and twist.

I was developing a strong dislike for Merlin as well.

A snide and sarcastic teenager that never failed to laugh at me as I botched one spell after another, that's all he was.

"I've been practicing and pushing myself for three years," I would complain. "When is something going to happen?"

"It'll happen when it happens," Merlin would answer. "Don't be impatient."

The laughter would come after that. That annoying teenage laughter that made me want to throw something at him. What I wouldn't give to feel my bow in my hand. I should be leading soldiers, not hiding away and practicing magic.

Merlin wasn't around.

Why in the world was I still practicing this crap?

I was never going to get it. There were other more important things I could be doing. I left Merlin's little home and entered the town square. People smiled at me as I walked by. I smiled in return.

Where was I going?

I had no purpose.

I had nothing vital to attend.

I walked to Dellia's house.

I came upon Arthur when I was halfway up the dirt driveway. He was handsome, very handsome, but completely unpleasant. His reddish-blonde hair had grown slightly longer, as had his beard. He was scruffy, but somehow it worked on him. Other men had picked up on his style and did their best to copy Arthur, but it was never the same.

I wondered how he could inspire anyone. Despite his features, he wasn't a good man. He wasn't a nice man. I didn't like him. I didn't like his grey eyes and the way they sneered at me as I got closer.

"Good morning, Arthur," I said in an effort to be polite.

"Yup," Arthur answered without the slightest bit of friendliness.

I didn't care. I had no respect for the man. Everyone who knew him made excuses for his behavior, but excuses were only excuses. We've all had a rough time. We've all lost people. Now get back on the horse and start living.

I think...

I think what upset me most of all, was that Arthur had the potential to truly be somebody. He had an aura that made others want to follow him. With a single word he could inspire the entire kingdom, but that word would never come.

The king was a disappointment.

My father told me to find him. My father told me that Arthur could cleanse the land. He told me that I should stay by his side. I was finding that impossible. My deceased father came to advise me in a dream, and though I was here, I doubted that I'd ever bother to be there for Arthur even if he did need me.

Dellia was sweeping her front porch.

"Arthur's up early," I said by way of greeting.

"He's yet to go to bed," Dellia said.

"I see," I said.

"It's the same old story," Dellia said sadly.

"I understand," I said.

"I wish you could have seen him before he lost his wife and child," Dellia said. "You wouldn't have even recognized him. There was a joy in his eyes. He was so kind and happy. I miss that part of him so much, but he loves me still and I love him."

"Of course you do," I said. "He's your son. You don't need to explain anything to me."

"No," Dellia said. "I guess I don't. I don't need to explain anything to anyone, but I feel compelled to do so anyway. I guess it's a bit of a habit for me."

"You want a subject change?" I asked after a brief moment of silence.

"Yes please," Dellia said.

"I'm giving up on magic," I said. "I'm not getting anywhere with it. I'm going back to leading the soldiers."

"Does Merlin know about this?" Dellia asked.

"Not yet," I answered. "I'm going to tell him when he gets back."

"He won't be happy," Dellia said.

"Nope," I agreed, "but he'll have to learn to live with it."

"Have you ever argued with Merlin?" Dellia asked.

"All the time," I answered.

"He doesn't intimidate you?" Dellia asked.

"It's hard to be intimidated by a nerdy teenager," I laughed.

"You've got a point there," Dellia laughed.

"Besides, I'm sure he'll find someone else to torture eventually," I added.

"Is it really that bad?" Dellia asked.

"I broke a finger a few months ago," I said.

Both of us laughed, and I ended up spending a few hours sitting on Dellia's front porch drinking tea and gossiping about the town.

Eventually a young boy came running down the driveway looking for me. Apparently Merlin had just gotten back and he was calling for a meeting.

"Are you going to tell him now?" Dellia asked as she stood up with me.

"I guess I better wait and see what's up," I answered as we walked towards Merlin's house, which wasn't really a house at all, considering it used to be the Sheriff's station. I think Merlin liked it because it was located in roughly the center of the town square, and it kept Merlin in the middle of all the comings and goings.

Dellia and I arrived at the station to find Tristan, Wayne, Merlin, and even Reynolds waiting for us. All of them looked alarmed. It was unsettling.

"Better get on with it," I said. "If things are as bad as I'm guessing there's no use in beating around the bush."

"Morgana is leading up for another attack," Merlin said.

"How do you know?" I asked.

"There are giants in the area," Bedder answered.

"What do you mean giants?" I asked.

"Large, wide creatures that are covered in hair and have an appetite for human flesh," Merlin answered. "They're tough to kill. We lost some good men out in that forest."

"How big are they?" I asked.

"I came up a little past their kneecaps," Wayne answered, "but they're also wide like a small mountain."

"How many are there?" Dellia asked.

"Enough to cause us serious problems," Merlin answered.

"Do we know for certain that they're going to attack?" I asked.

"Giants don't group together for any other reason," Merlin answered. "They're normally solitary creatures."

"Will there also be Death Reapers in the attack?" I asked.

"I would assume so," Merlin answered. "Morgana will also need someone to lead them all, but whoever that is hasn't arrived yet. That's why we didn't see any Death Reapers."

"She can't do it alone?" I asked.

"She's not shown herself yet," Merlin answered. "I see no reason for her to change things up, but the new leader will be fierce. Giants don't respect much of anything except death."

"So you think she's found someone to replace the Black Knight, and that person will be leading the giants in an attack upon Camelot?" Bedder asked.

"Yes," Merlin answered.

"Don't forget about the Death Reapers," Wayne added. "He'll probably have an army of Death Reapers with him."

"How could I forget," Bedder said moodily.

"How are the town's defenses?" I asked.

"Better than they used to be," Reynolds answered. "We could hold off a considerable amount of Death Reapers. Our soldiers are better trained and there are plenty of them, but..."

"But not giants," Merlin continued. "Giants will prove too much for our defenses. Stronghold Wall isn't powerful enough to stop that kind of attack."

"So what are our options?" Wayne asked.

"Remember when I told you that I was going to resurrect the Camelot of old?" Merlin asked.

"Yes," Wayne answered. "You said you were going to pull it from the ground."

"If I can do that," Merlin said. "Camelot will be indestructible."

"Okay," Dellia said. "Let's resurrect Camelot. What do we need?"

"We need Arthur," Merlin said.

Everyone grumbled and shifted uncomfortably.

"Yes, I know what everyone's thinking," Merlin said, "but a lot of the magic in this ever growing kingdom depends upon Arthur. Resurrecting the old Camelot is no different. I need Arthur's help to find the key."

"The key?" Bedder asked.

"A simple key will unlock the spell," Merlin said.

"You want to send Arthur out on another mission?" Wayne asked. "I'm not sure he'll go. The last mission almost killed him."

"I won't be sending him alone," Merlin said. "I'll be going with him. He'll need me to find our guide."

"What guide?" I asked.

"I entrusted the key to an ancient race of magical beings," I said. "They will lead us to the key, but only Arthur can touch it."

"Why only Arthur?" Bedder asked.

"The key holds all the magic of Camelot," Merlin answered. "Only the true king of the land can withstand its power and use it correctly."

"How do we convince Arthur?" I asked.

"We tell him that we'll all be killed if he doesn't help out," Bedder said.

"I doubt that'll bother him much coming from you," Wayne said.

"I'll talk to him," Merlin said.

"It won't work," Dellia added. "You and Arthur have grown distant. I'll need to be the one that speaks to him. He'll listen to me."

"Fine," Merlin said. "We'll set out tomorrow. In the meantime, I need to work on a potion that'll help me get into contact with our guide."

"How dangerous is this going to be for Arthur?" Dellia asked.

"It may not be dangerous at all," Merlin answered. "Then again, I have no idea. It all depends upon where the key was hidden."

Dellia frowned.

"He'll have me and Lancelot there to look out for him," Merlin continued. "I can't do it without him."

The crowd left silently.

None of us were happy to be relying on Arthur. He'd come through before, but most of the people that knew him figured he'd just gotten lucky. The Arthur of the cemetery, the warrior, the destroyer, well, that was just a once in a lifetime miracle; a miracle done for the sake of revenge and not for the sake of others.

I waited outside of Merlin's house for Dellia.

Inside I could hear them arguing. Dellia didn't want Arthur placed in danger. Merlin needed him. It was an old argument. Normally Dellia won, but not this time. Poor Dellia, she loved her son. Arthur was all she had left in the world. My father had also tried to keep me safe. Undoubtedly, if he were still alive, he'd still be trying to keep me safe.

Dellia finally came out of the house.

I could tell by the expression on her face that she was worried. I walked next to her without saying a word.

"I'll talk to Arthur tonight," Dellia said as we came upon her long driveway. "He's coming over after sunset to watch the stars with me."

Dellia and her stars, how she loved looking at the stars. Arthur's mother could sit outside on her porch all night and gaze at the stars. I knew that Arthur often joined her, and wondered if he also loved gazing at the stars or if he only pretended to be interested out of kindness to his mother.

He must have enjoyed stargazing, because I couldn't imagine Arthur doing anything out of kindness.

"I'm sure everything will be alright," I said.

Dellia looked over at me.

"You're sweet," Dellia said. "I'm so glad you found your way to us. I can't imagine a life without you."

She patted my cheek.

I smiled and turned away before she saw the tears in my eyes. I missed my mother. Dellia was a lot like her. Maybe that's why I enjoyed spending so much time with her.

I went home for the evening.

Tara, my friend and roommate who insisted on taking care of me, already had supper prepared. It smelled and tasted delicious. The two of us ate quietly.

"Are you going to tell me about what's bothering you?" Tara eventually asked.

"There's going to be another attack," I answered.

"Oh, shit," Tara said.

"Yes," I agreed. "It gets even worse."

"Oh no," Tara said.

"There are giants," I said. "And the giants will be joining the Death Reapers."

"What do we do?" Tara asked. "What can we do?"

"Merlin wants to bring back the Camelot of old," I answered. "If he can do that, we'll be safe."

"Why do you look so worried?" Tara asked.

"Because we need Arthur's help," I answered.

♣ DELLIA ♣

My son, my beautiful son, how would he react? Would he laugh at me? No, that wasn't in Arthur's nature. He was never cruel or angry, especially not towards me.

Would he help?

Would he help if I asked?

He didn't really have a choice if he wanted to live. We were all in danger, but he wasn't going to be happy about things. He wasn't going to be happy at all.

I was also worrying about his relationship with his grandfather. Arthur seemed to avoid Merlin as much as possible, and when the two of them were together, Merlin often nagged at my son. Arthur was learning to dislike his grandfather, and that was terribly sad. The two of them used to be so close.

I made dinner.

I cooked enough for four people. Arthur probably wouldn't eat much, but Lance was a growing boy. He gobbled up my cooking.

I took Lance's meal outside so that he could eat on the roof as he preferred, and saw Arthur walking up the long driveway about two hours after sunset. To his right, I could see the tall grass moving. Arthur had a smile on his face for me.

"Lance," I said to the open air after Arthur reached the porch. "Here's your dinner. You just let me know if you need anything else, okay hun?"

"Yes, ma'am," Lance's voice answered from the tall grass.

Arthur gave me a hug and followed me inside. When we were both seated at the table and Arthur was nibbling on some bread, I started talking to him.

27

"Why do you eat so little?" I asked.

"My stomach is always queasy," Arthur said.

"Why do you think that is?" I asked. "Should we get you to the doctor?"

"No," Arthur answered.

"You've lost a bit of weight," I said. "I can see it in your cheekbones."

"You have anything to drink?" Arthur asked.

"I have tea?" I answered.

"You have anything to put in it?" Arthur asked.

"Of course not," I answered. "Maybe you should..."

"Mom," Arthur interrupted. "Let's have a good night, alright?"

I sighed. If I pushed anymore, Arthur would leave. I didn't want that. I needed to talk to him. I also wanted him to stay. I enjoyed spending time with him, especially when he was in one of his better moods.

"How's Lance been lately?" I asked.

"Lance is Lance," Arthur answered. "He seems pretty good to me."

"I've been worrying about him ever since he stopped eating inside with us," I said.

"I think he just likes his space," Arthur said. "He's getting older. He's got a girlfriend now. Did I tell you that?"

"You didn't," I said. "Who?"

"The grocery store's daughter," Arthur answered. "I think her name's Cindy."

"I know Cindy," I said. "She's a lovely young lady. When did this happen?"

"Sometime after the battle," Arthur answered. "Or maybe during the battle, I forget what he told me. I only found out about it last week."

"Arthur," I said. "The battle was three years ago. Are you telling me that Lance has been dating a girl for three years and you've only now just found out?"

"Yes," Arthur answered.

"Son," I said. "Lance is a young boy. You need to take an interest in what he does."

"Mom," Arthur said. "I'm not his father. Our relationship isn't like that."

"God help that poor kid," I said, "but you're the closest thing he has to a father."

Arthur looked at me and laughed.

"You find that funny?" I asked.

"I think I was a pretty good father back in my time," Arthur said.

"You were a wonderful father," I said.

"Well," Arthur said as pushed away his plate. "Times change, are you ready?"

"I am," I answered. "I'll clean the dishes later. Don't you worry about a thing."

The two of us walked to the barn and climbed up to the second floor. Arthur unlatched the wide swinging doors to the outside sky in the front of the barn, and gently swung them open.

I grabbed the ancient brass telescope we'd been using for years and removed the soft tarp covering the old looking glass.

"I've always wondered why this thing still works," Arthur said as he placed the telescope in front of the open doors.

"Well," I said. "I suppose this is technology that could have existed back in medieval times."

"You're probably right," Arthur agreed. "After all, it's just brass and glass."

I focused the telescope and the two of us took turns looking at various constellations. I could name over a hundred of them. Arthur never bothered with the names, but he seemed to enjoy having me point them out to him.

Stargazing was something we'd done since Arthur was a boy. His father was the one that got the two of us interested in the hobby, and we still enjoyed staring at the heavens even after he was gone. It almost felt like the three of us were once again together. Maybe that's why we enjoyed it so much.

Arthur was laughing as I reminisced about the time I'd told him all about Perseus and his winged sandals. Arthur used to love those old stories, and Perseus was his favorite. He spent the next several weeks trying to attach paper wings to his favorite pair of sneakers. Eventually the sneakers had so many holes in them from the experiments that I had to throw them away. Arthur wasn't happy.

"I was a child with an active imagination," Arthur said.

"You loved the old myths," I said. "Perseus was your favorite."

"He's the only one that didn't die a painful death," Arthur said.

"He's not the only one," I said. "There were others."

Arthur shrugged next to me. We had long since abandoned the telescope and were sitting on the edge of the open doors with our legs hanging off the side of the barn.

"We need to talk," I said after watching him for a bit.

"Please don't start on me," Arthur said.

"It's not about your drinking," I said.

This got my son's attention and he turned to look at me. Just then I noticed the smell of hay in the barn, felt the cool air on my face and realized I was about to ruin a perfect moment.

"What's going on?" Arthur asked.

"There's danger coming," I said. "There'll be another attack."

"Well," Arthur said with another shrug. "We've got a sizable army now. We should be good."

"No," I said. "This new army is different. They have giants. They'll be able to breach our defenses."

"Giants?" Arthur asked.

"Yes," I said. "And between them and the Death Reapers, well...Camelot can't survive."

"So what do we do?" Arthur asked with very little concern on his face.

"We need you," I said in a quiet voice.

"No," Arthur said immediately.

"Arthur," I said. "Listen to me. We need to resurrect the Camelot of old. If we can do that, we'll be safe from the giants."

"So do it," Arthur said, "but do it without me. I'm not interested. I've done my part. I didn't like it."

"You have," I agreed. "You did what no one else could have done. You found Excalibur and you killed the Black Knight, but we need you one more time."

"What for?" Arthur asked.

I was speechless for a moment. I had just realized that Arthur wasn't carrying Excalibur. I hadn't seen the sword all evening.

"Where is Excalibur?" I asked thinking the worst.

"Over there in the corner," Arthur answered while motioning with his arm across the room to where the sword was leaning against the wall.

"Why aren't you carrying it?" I asked.

"I don't need to," Arthur answered. "It follows me around."

"I understand that," I said, "but what if..."

"Mom," Arthur interrupted. "I have it under control."

"I suppose you do," I said.

"Well anyway," Arthur said as he stood up. "I have plans tonight, so I'll stop over tomorrow."

"Wait," I said standing up as well. "We haven't finished talking."

"I'm not going to go on some dangerous quest for Merlin," Arthur said. "He needs to get over that shit. I'm not playing his games anymore."

It bothered me that Arthur called him Merlin. I was sure he'd done it before, but never with so much disdain.

"This isn't for Merlin," I said. "This is for Camelot. This is for me and everyone that seeks refuge on your land."

Arthur cursed.

"I'm sorry," I said. "For what it's worth, Merlin will go with you. He'll keep you safe."

"Merlin?" Arthur said. "Merlin can't even keep himself safe. He can't keep this town safe. I don't need him. Where was he when all those Death Reapers were chasing me down? He didn't help me. The Gods of the Forest helped me."

"Will you go?" I asked.

Arthur glared at me.

"We need you," I said. "I know you hate it, but there is a key that will unlock the spell to resurrect old Camelot and only you can touch the key."

"Of course," Arthur said. "I just love how his stupid little spell needs to involve me."

"Arthur," I said in a firm voice. "You need to do this. You need to. There are too many people depending on you. I know it's not fair, but you're going. You are going to save this place once again."

"Well there ya have it then," Arthur said.

"I'm sorry," I said.

"So am I," Arthur said.

♣ LANCE ♣

Arthur was far from happy when he got home. I've seen him irritated before, but this was something else. I shouldn't have left him at his mother's, but I figured he'd have a date afterwards and I certainly didn't want to be around for that.

I went to see Cindy.

Her home was close to the high school, but I covered the distance easily and quickly enough by going over the rooftops like I always do.

She was expecting me. I visited her almost every night. Sometimes I was even brave enough to touch her hand. Lately, she'd been wanting to kiss me.

I crawled up to her second floor window carefully, so as not to awaken her parents. A lantern was burning softly, and I could see her at her desk. She was reading a book, and her dark hair curled down to the middle of her back in brown waves.

She was wearing a tank top and a pair of pajama bottoms. She looked beautiful, and someday soon I was positive that she'd end our relationship.

The thought of that coming day broke my heart prematurely, but I knew that I could never give her what she wanted. A kiss, I was incapable of giving her a simple kiss. Aside from Arthur and a few others, she was my life. I needed to try harder. I needed to force myself.

I tapped on the window.

Cindy turned with a smile and opened it for me.

"I didn't expect you so soon," Cindy said. "I was just reading."

"What were you reading?" I asked.

She told me the name of the book. I'd read it as well, but I didn't stop her when she started telling me all about it. I wanted to hear what she thought of the book. I wanted to experience it from her point of view. I wasn't disappointed. Cindy never disappointed me.

After talking for a bit at the window, Cindy went and shut off her lantern. I crawled in silently and perched myself on a chair in the corner of her room.

"I can see your outline," Cindy teased.

"I should find a better place to hide then," I said with a smile.

"No," Cindy said. "I like seeing you. Even if it's just your outline, I like seeing it."

My heart was pounding in my chest. I felt unprotected. I felt vulnerable. I was failing her, and I was failing myself.

"Talk to me," I said. "Tell me about another book that you've read."

Cindy began to talk. She kept her distance and went on and on about another book she'd recently read with cowboys. It sounded like a good tale. I'd have to borrow it from her sometime. Most importantly, her storytelling distracted me. Her voice calmed me down.

Sure I noticed every single time she stole a glance in my direction, but I wasn't jumping out the window or anything.

If I pushed myself, could I keep her?

Could I push myself?

Cindy yawned.

"I should go," I said. "I don't want to keep you up too long."

"You did really well tonight," Cindy said.

"What do you mean?" I asked.

"This is the longest you've ever stayed," Cindy explained.

"I'm working on it," I said.

"I know you are," Cindy said.

"I'm worried about disappointing you," I said.

"Can I have that kiss?" Cindy asked.

I panicked.

Cindy heard me move and stood up. She was too late, I was out of her window and three houses away before she'd even realized I had left.

I hated myself for doing that to her. I hated myself for doing that to me. I was losing the battle, and eventually I'd lose the girl.

I didn't go straight home. Instead, I stayed on the rooftops and headed towards Shakey's Tavern. I did that sometimes, it was fun to hang out on the roof and listen to all the drunken conversations.

I was a bit shocked when I heard Wayne's voice. He normally spent his evening's home with his family unless something was going on.

Something was going on.

Wayne wasn't out having fun, he was speaking to the bar. I thought I heard the word giant. I definitely heard Arthur's name. I listened more intently, couldn't hear everything too clearly, and decided to wait.

It only took another thirty minutes before Wayne left the tavern. The big man was completely sober and very worried.

"Wayne," I whispered from the rooftops as I followed him from above.

I scared him and he jumped. I normally enjoyed this type of activity, and it normally upset Wayne. Tonight however, I didn't want to pick on Wayne. I just wanted answers.

"Is that you, Lance?" Wayne said after he calmed down.

"Yes," I answered as he looked around for me.

"You're a bit of a prick," Wayne complained. "Are you aware of that?"

"No," I answered.

"Well, what do you want?" Wayne asked.

"What's going on?" I asked in return. "Does it concern Arthur? I thought I heard you say his name."

"Arthur has a mission," Wayne answered. "Merlin's going with him."

"Then so am I," I said. "What's the mission?"

Wayne gave me the details and I could scarcely believe him. When he was finished, I thanked him and took off towards Arthur's house.

It was a bit of a journey, but I covered the distance pretty quickly. I knew the best tree's to climb on through the forest. I knew the best places to leap through the air.

Arthur's house, which was also my house, was the same cabin by the lake. We'd never moved out after the Death Reapers attacked. We just cleaned it up and continued where we'd left off. Was it dangerous? Yes, it probably wasn't the safest place for the king to live, but Arthur didn't want to be in the middle of things. He didn't want neighbors. Merlin threw a fit, but Arthur kept his cabin.

From the nearest tree, I sailed through the air, dove in the window to my bedroom, and came to my feet after the softest roll across the floor.

I called for Arthur.

He gave me no answer, but I could hear him moving around downstairs. I quietly entered the kitchen and found him sitting at the table drinking from a bottle. He looked pale and sweaty in the dim lantern light.

"I heard about the mission," I said.

"Yeah," Arthur said. "I heard about that myself."

"Are you going to do the mission?" I asked.

"I don't have much choice," Arthur said.

"Why are you drinking so much if we're leaving tomorrow?" I asked.

"Lance," Arthur said. "Leave me alone."

I left without another word. When Arthur drank like that, I didn't much like to be around him anyway. He wasn't much of a conversationalist during those times. Heavy drinking brought back memories that made him sad.

I moved back to the forest.

What to do with the remaining night?

I thought about Cindy. I should go to her. I needed to apologize and say my goodbyes. She was going to worry about me. Would she be angry that I was leaving? Surely she'd understand. My sacred duty was to protect Arthur. I had to go.

I went back to Cindy's house. Her light was off, but I didn't need a light to see in the dark. I found her quickly. She was in her bed, but her eyes were open. She was awake and alone with her thoughts. At least she thought she was alone.

I knocked very gently on her window and watched her turn her head in my direction. There were tears in her eyes.

I smiled at her under my mask as if she could see the loving gesture. She made no move to open her window, so I slid it open myself.

"I'm sorry," I whispered.

"I know," Cindy said.

"Don't give up on me," I said.

Cindy smiled and I entered her room.

I kneeled close to her bed. I rested my arms near her pillow and whispered in her ear.

"I'll do better when I get back," I said. "You mean the world to me. I won't let you down. I just need you to be patient."

Her hand reached out to touch me, and I moved away.

"Where are you going?" Cindy asked.

"I'm leaving with Arthur and Merlin," I answered. "We're searching for a magic key that will somehow rebuild ancient Camelot."

"Is that possible?" Cindy asked.

"I guess so," I answered. "I leave the magic stuff to Merlin. I'm just a fighter." Cindy sat up.

"Will it be dangerous?" Cindy asked.

"Nothing's chasing after us," I said. "So I wouldn't worry too much. I'll be back before you know it."

Cindy rolled over and gave me her back.

"Will you stay with me until the sun comes up?" Cindy asked.

"Yes," I promised as her eyes closed and she drifted off to sleep.

I kept my promise. I felt exposed and extremely uncomfortable, but I stayed by her side. When the sun came I watched the window. The light grew brighter and brighter and the familiar tingle began to trickle down my spine.

I lightly touched Cindy's hand, and I was gone before she ever woke up.

♣ MERLIN ♣

"This doesn't look good," Wayne complained a couple of hours after sunrise. "I don't think he's coming."

"He'll be here," Dellia said. "He's probably just running a bit late."

"Lance," Wayne called out. "Are you around?"

"I am," Lance answered from the top of my home.

"Was Arthur drinking last night?" Wayne asked.

"Yes," Lance answered.

"How much was he drinking?" Bedder asked.

"He was drinking," Lance answered.

"This is ridiculous," Bedder said. "He's endangering the entire town."

"It's fine," I finally said. "Lance can go and collect him."

"He may be in no shape to ride," Wayne said.

"Then I'll tie him to his horse," I said without humor.

It was late morning before Lance returned with Arthur. The king entered the town square wobbling back and forth slightly. He was still drunk and reeked of alcohol. Fortunately Dellia had packed for him, because he showed up empty handed.

Wayne had to help him onto Goliath's back. It wasn't pretty, and when Wayne got a little bit too rough with his inebriated friend, Goliath promptly bit him on the shoulder.

"What the shit?" Wayne screamed.

"Don't fuck with me around my horse, asshole," Arthur said.

I rode out ahead of Arthur without another word. What could I say? I'd expressed my disappointment in the man too many times. He wasn't going to change and we were stuck with him.

I was in a foul mood.

I sensed that Lancelot was close by. That meant that he was keeping an eye on Arthur. That was for the best. Without Lancelot close by, Arthur stood a decent chance of falling off his horse and hurting himself.

I caught a glimpse of Gwen as I exited the town square. She waved, but there was something about her wave that gave her away. She was planning on quitting. Well, it was about time. Most wizards quit a lot sooner than she did.

The woman was tenacious, good for her. Now it was time for the next phase of what I had planned for her. Not that I was entirely proud of myself. I certainly wasn't, but things needed to be pushed along, and nothing would be accomplished until they were. There were risks involved, and things may not even work out, but I was left without another option.

Enough about that.

I was looking forward to entering the forests and speaking to our guide. It had been centuries since I last spoke to one of their kind.

I felt a slight weight land on the back of my horse.

"Already tired, Lancelot?" I asked.

"No," Lancelot answered. "Arthur reeks of whiskey.

"I see," I said. "Where did you find him?"

"He was still at the cabin," Lancelot answered. "He wasn't alone."

"He never seems to be alone," I said. "It even gets worse when he's upset. Do you know who the girl is?"

"I've never seen her before," Lancelot answered.

"Lots of new people in town these days," I said.

"He's very upset," Lancelot said.

"I know he is," I said. "He'd rather stay home and drink himself to death than be out here risking his life for others."

"You don't like him anymore," Lancelot said.

"I love him dearly," I said. "He's my grandson, but I don't like what he's become."

"He's getting worse," Lancelot said. "He needs help."

"What happened at the graveyard was difficult for him," I said, "but Arthur can only help himself."

The slight weight on the back of the horse vanished, and I was once again left alone with my thoughts.

We rode until midday. Arthur slept the entire time. Goliath would fuss and make noise every time Arthur started to slip off his back. At that point Lancelot would right him again, and we'd continue.

Inside the forest, with the green leaves blocking out the sun it was cold. I lit a fire and Arthur stumbled off his horse to join me in sitting next to the warmth. Arthur was shivering, and looking rather pale.

"Are you ill?" I asked.

"Duh," Arthur answered.

"Would you like something to eat?" I asked.

"No," Arthur said. "I'd like to set up camp right here until I feel better."

"That's not an option," I said. "Time is of the essence."

"Well I feel like shit," Arthur complained.

"I'll give you something for your hangover," I said, "but only because we need to get moving."

"Whatever," Arthur grumbled.

I went over to my horse. I patted her on the mane and reached into my saddlebag. There I had a large pouch filled with different potions. I grabbed an empty tube, poured in a touch of this and that, and walked into the forest.

It took me almost forty five minutes before I found the correct mushroom. I was in a bad mood by the time I came back to our fire.

Arthur was sound asleep.

I woke him up roughly, received a warning sound from Goliath, and gave him the drink. I could sense Lancelot high in the trees above us. He was watching with interest.

Arthur grimaced from the taste.

"Son of a bitch," Arthur complained. "I'm going to be sick."

"No you're not," I said.

"That didn't make me feel any better," Arthur continued to complain. "The taste alone is going to make me...I feel better."

"We should get going," I said. "We'll stop again in a few hours. You should be hungry by then."

"Well, I'm still freezing my ass off," Arthur said.

"Your mother packed for you," I said. "Look in your saddlebag."

Arthur was wearing hiking boots, cargo pants, and a thick long-sleeved shirt with a v-neck. He definitely needed to warm up a bit, and that was funny coming from me. I was only wearing hiking boots, jeans, a t-shirt, and a hoodie. Then again, I was never really bothered by the cold.

Arthur found a pea coat stashed inside his saddlebags and a large cloak with thick white fur around the collar. He put both of these on. I thought it was a bit excessive, but what do I know.

I looked at the sky above us as soon as we hit a clearing. It was a turning grey. At first I thought rain might be coming, but the clouds were different. They were tinged in cold.

It was going to snow.

Did Arthur know something I didn't? It wouldn't surprise me. Arthur was in touch with the land. The land and the king were as one.

When next we stopped, Arthur was indeed hungry. His color had also improved, but only slightly. He wasn't talkative, not that that bothered me.

"How's it taste?" I asked as the first of the snow started to fall.

"Don't give up your day job," Arthur answered.

"How are you feeling?" I asked, already knowing that the potion I gave him would carry him through the entire hangover.

"I'm good," Arthur said.

"I'm thinking we should ride until nightfall," I said. "Then we'll make camp."

"Do we have any camping supplies?" Arthur asked.

"Yes," I answered. "There's a pack horse following us."

"No, there isn't," Arthur said.

Excalibur had appeared next to the campfire. Without thinking about it, Arthur reached out and took a hold of the sword. It was then that I noticed he'd already had his dagger strapped onto the back of his belt.

"Are you expecting trouble?" I asked.

"I'm expecting anything," Arthur answered.

"You do realize that I'm here to look after you?" I asked.

"If you were any kind of beneficial, I wouldn't even need to be here," Arthur said.

"I see," I said.

"Why do you need me to find this key?" Arthur asked. "Why can't you handle the giants?"

"Giants are remarkably resistant to magic," I answered. "I could perhaps handle a few of them, but a few isn't going to help us much. I need to be able to stop them. I need to work my magic from a safe distance and use the defenses of Camelot."

"What else is resistant to magic?" Arthur asked.

"Excalibur," I answered.

"I figured," Arthur said. "How would Excalibur do against a giant?"

"Excalibur will cut through a giant just as easily as it cuts through anything else," I answered, "but don't worry about giants. We're going to stay well away from them now that I know they're here."

After Arthur stretched his legs, we rode on. The snow continued to fall. It wasn't a heavy snowfall, but it was consistent.

"I'm going to need to stop for a bit," Lance stated from the trees above us as the sky began to darken.

"Yes," I said. "This will be an excellent spot for us to camp for the evening."

"We're kind of off the normal trails here," Arthur said. "Are you sure we're going in the right direction?"

"I have no idea," I said. "Only our guide can tell us that, and in order to make contact with him, we needed to be a day's ride from the world of men."

"I'm not even going to ask," Arthur said.

"It'd be easier if you didn't," I said.

"So where's that pack horse you were talking about?" Arthur asked.

"He'll be here in an hour or so," I answered. "I had forgotten a few items, and had him sent after us."

Arthur stopped talking after that and went to work on a fire.

The fire was burning and the food was finished cooking by the time the pack horse arrived. The real reason the pack horse had been delayed was due to a potion I had brewing. It hadn't been finished when we left, so I let it simmer and had Dellia send it on out with the pack horse when it was ready.

Arthur noticed me fiddling around with the glass jug.

"Is that moonshine?" Arthur asked.

"Sort of, but not really," I answered.

"Give it to me," Arthur said.

"This is for our guide," I said. "Not for you."

"Give me a little bit," Arthur argued. "It's cold out here."

"Put your gloves on," I said. "We can't afford to lose any more time while you go on another bender."

"I just want a sip," Arthur said.

"Not going to happen," I said. "Now stop bugging me please."

"I knew this was going to suck," Arthur said.

"So did I," I said.

I walked away from the campfire, pulled out a wooden mug the size of a thimble, and filled it with the alcohol. Next to the mug, I placed a tiny red hat, and a soft grey cloak. I also lit a small fire with a bit of magic. The fire would burn all night long.

I walked back to the pack horse and removed two rustic tents. One was for Lancelot and the other was for Arthur. I was going to use magic to set them up, but Arthur rudely grabbed his tent from me and set it up by himself. When he was finished, he went to bed without another word.

I stared up at the nighttime sky after sitting by the fire. The snow was still falling, but it was gentle. The air smelled pure and fresh. A soft thud next to me told me that Lancelot had returned. With a wave of my hand, his tent jumped into the air and began setting itself up.

"The cold doesn't really bother me," Lancelot said. "You should do something for the horses."

"You're right," I said.

I waved my hands again, and the tree's leaned towards each other, creating a roof over the heads of the horses. I twisted my hands and the shrubs nearby responded instantly. In no time at all, I'd created a three-sided barn for all three.

Goliath wasn't happy being so close to the other two horses. He growled and stomped his hooves whenever they bumped into him.

"How's that look?" I asked.

"Good," Lancelot responded.

"I was hoping to get a little more conversation from you since Arthur doesn't want to speak with me," I complained.

"Arthur's nervous," Lancelot said.

"Is he?" I asked. "Why?"

"I don't know," Lancelot said, "but he told me to keep an eye out for an attack."

Was Arthur once again sensing something that I wasn't? I know that he's in tune with the land, but if he was sensing danger in the forest his connection must be stronger than I thought.

I reached out with all my senses.

Nothing.

I tried again.

Nothing.

At the very least, we were going to be safe from attack this evening. Of that I was certain. What would come our way in the future was unknown, but Arthur was making me nervous.

"We'll be safe this evening," I said to Lancelot. "Feel free to get out of the snow."

Lancelot went straight to his tent after grabbing a bite to eat. No wonder the two of them got along so well. Neither of them spoke very much. I was beginning to miss Wayne.

I ate what was left for the pure enjoyment of eating, put my back against a tree, and closed my eyes.

Three hours and twenty minutes later the snow had stopped falling, and the land seemed just a bit brighter than it had been. Our guide had arrived.

I stood up slowly, breaking through the snow that had swallowed me up. My eyelids had been crusted over with ice and my skin had turned a silly blue color. I found that funny.

I walked away from the camp, past the horses, and over to where I had placed the mug of moonshine and other items. The small fire was still burning brightly, but the hat, cloak and mug had vanished.

"Bit of a fire hazard, wouldn't you say?" Came a small voice from behind me.

"Not with me around," I answered.

"Well, let me get a look at you," the small voice said.

I turned around slowly and saw a tiny humanoid only six inches tall. He was wearing the pointed red hat and cloak I had given him, and his wiry grey hair blended in quite nicely with the grey cloak.

"Well," the gnome pondered. "Who might you be?"

"I'm Merlin," I stated.

"Now that's a name my kind hasn't heard in quite a long while," the gnome mused. "Let me see, you certainly don't look like Merlin, but I do sense the magic in you. Could it be?"

"Yes," I said patiently.

The gnome came forward, stood right in front of me and stared at me long and hard. I waited patiently for him to complete his inspection. There was no use in hurrying a gnome, not if you needed his help.

"I see a boy," the gnome said, "but I'm not sure."

I didn't say a word.

"Why did you summon me?" The gnome asked after taking a swig from his mug.

"I seek the key," I answered.

The gnome's eyes went wide and he took an involuntary step backwards.

"In whose name do you seek the key?" The gnome asked.

"I seek the key in Arthur's name," I answered.

"Is Arthur here?" The gnome asked.

"The king is sleeping in one of the tents over there," I answered while motioning towards our campsite.

Now the gnome's eyes went even wider.

"Say the words," the gnome commanded.

Speaking the tongue of gnomes wasn't easy. In fact, it was ridiculously difficult, and very few creatures with the exception of the gnomes themselves had ever mastered their language. I always thought a password would be a good idea so the gnomes wouldn't be tricked into surrendering the key to an enemy. Saying the password in their own language made it that much more difficult.

"I seek the key," I said in gnomish. "I seek to bring forth that which was lost through treachery and deceit. I seek to resurrect the great castle. I seek to resurrect Camelot."

"My name is Toad Winterstool," the gnome said. "I shall be your guide."

"Thank you Mr. Winterstool," I said. "Your help will be greatly appreciated."

"Call me Toad," the gnome smiled. "And don't thank me just yet. We hid the key in a most perilous place. Only danger awaits you, danger of the worst kind."

"Why place the key in such a place?" I asked.

"My people have long since given up on Arthur's return," Toad explained, "but we still felt obligated to protect that which you asked us to protect. We hid it where no one would ever dare look for it. A place no one ever returns from."

"How far away is this place?" I asked.

"For me, a few hours," Toad answered. "On horseback, much longer."

"Okay," I said. "We'll set out tomorrow morning."

"Sounds excellent," Toad said. "I'm excited to meet the king. Would you mind letting him know that I'm here."

"This king isn't the most pleasant of people," I said. "Perhaps introductions can wait until tomorrow."

"Ah," Toad exclaimed. "Typical angry humans, if you've met one of them, you've met them all. What a disappointment; alright then, how about some more of this delicious drink to fight off the nights chill?"

"That I can arrange," I said with a smile.

Relocating ourselves back at the tents, we drank the night away. A part of me worried about Arthur waking up and joining us, but he appeared to be thoroughly finished with me for the evening.

As dawn approached, one of the tents flapped with movement.

"There's something fouled with magic in that tent," Toad said.

"He's on our side," I said.

The opening of the tent burst open and an indistinguishable shape darted into the forest. Toad watched the shape for a brief moment.

"You created that magic?" Toad asked.

"I did," I answered.

"You created a monster," Toad said.

"Not quite," I said. "That's Lancelot. He's happier this way."

"I'll never understand humans," Toad said. "Pass me a final drink, please."

Another hour or so passed, and I cooked breakfast. Arthur woke up when the smell of bacon drifted into his tent.

"Hungry?" I asked.

"Yes," Arthur answered grumpily.

I made him a plate of bacon and biscuits. He ate them slowly as I poured him some coffee. I noticed that he was shaking, and it didn't seem to be from the cold.

"Are you feeling okay?" I asked.

"Don't worry about it," Arthur said.

"That young man needs himself a drink or my names not Winterstool," Toad said from a nearby stump. Arthur hadn't even noticed him until that moment.

"What the fuck?" Arthur asked.

"This is Toad Winterstool," I said. "He's our guide."

Arthur started laughing.

Toad didn't seem to appreciate his rudeness.

"A king should have manners," Toad said.

"A guide should be longer than my penis," Arthur retorted.

"Arthur!" I snapped.

"This just keeps getting better and better," Arthur said. "What the hell are you dragging me into? What the hell is that thing?"

"Toad is a gnome," I answered. "His people hid the key for me. They have a knowledge of the forest that you'd scarcely believe. We are in the best of hands with him as our guide."

A rustle in the trees around us let me know that Lancelot had returned. Arthur noticed him as well.

"Lance," Arthur shouted. "I'm turned around. Can you get me out of here?"

"I don't think we can leave," Lancelot argued from above. "We need the key."

"Can you get me out of here or not?" Arthur demanded.

"Yes," Lancelot answered.

"This man is no king," Toad said sadly. "He cannot retrieve the key. The danger is too great for him."

"I'll be by his side," I said.

"He's sick," Toad said.

"He'll get better soon," I argued. "I have potions that can keep him going through the worst of it."

Toad scratched at his long grey beard and considered the situation.

Arthur glared at the both of us.

"We need this," I said very calmly to Toad. "Without a true Camelot, we will all soon fall."

"Without a king you'll fall as well," Toad said.

"I'm working with what the world has given me to work with," I said. "I have plans. I'm not without options if things get critical."

"This isn't the Arthur of old," Toad said. "This Arthur is broken. What plans you have are ill advised. Change your course."

"You know I can't do that," I said. "The giants are coming. I don't have the time. Your place is not to advise me. You place is to lead me to the key."

"Really?" Toad asked.

"Remember who you're dealing with here, Mr. Winterstool," I said. "I'm not the boy you see before you. I'm the wizard of legend."

"I have offended you?" Toad asked.

"You have," I answered.

"My counsel is sound," Toad said, "but you're correct. It's not my place to give you counsel."

"Excellent," I said. "Let's all pack up and be on our way."

"Who said I was going?" Arthur asked.

"You're going," I answered. "You're going because you have no choice. You can't return home because if you don't find the key you won't have a home to return to."

"You think I won't leave?" Arthur asked.

"I definitely think you'll leave," I answered. "And you'll return home to panic. Panic throughout the entire town because you turned your back on everyone. This time however, your mother won't try and leave with you. Wayne won't try and leave with you. You'll watch them all die."

Arthur said nothing.

"Go ahead, Arthur," I said. "Go home and watch the few people you actually care about die."

Arthur said nothing.

"You're a coward," I continued. "How could someone like you ever be king? How could someone like you—"

"Enough!" Lancelot shouted from above me.

A great sense of menace washed over my shoulders and the back of my neck. Was Lancelot preparing to attack me?

I realized I was breathing heavily.

I was embarrassed at losing my temper.

My words were unforgivable.

"Make your decision," I said quietly.

Without a word, Arthur started packing up his tent. I could have done it with magic, but he didn't seem to want my help.

Toad let out a low whistle. The gnome couldn't possibly understand all that had led up to that moment, but he nonetheless took everything in stride.

In half an hour we were on the move once again. Strangely enough, Toad rode on the top of Goliath's head. Arthur was drinking again. I had no idea where the bottle had come from, but he boldly carried it in his hand and sipped from it frequently.

Toad seemed to be talking at a mile a minute. Arthur didn't respond much to him, but he didn't tell him to shut up either, so I figured his mood had improved at least a bit.

Lancelot moved through the tree's around us. He was so good at concealing himself; even I could barely keep track of him.

I rode forward a bit to see if he would speak to me. It was best not to have both Arthur and Lancelot against me. Luckily, Lancelot wanted to speak to me as well.

"What was that about?" Lancelot asked when I rode close to the wall of forest on our right hand side.

"I lost my tempter," I answered. "It was a mistake on my part."

"You're making him hate you," Lancelot said.

"Our relationship has been damaged for a while now," I said. "I don't have the luxury of repairing it. I need him to do certain things."

"He'll get there on his own," Lancelot said. "He's not going to let anything happen to his mother or Wayne. You don't have to confront him like that."

"You're absolutely correct," I said. "The mistake was mine. I won't let it happen again."

"I hope not," Lancelot said before vanishing.

Arthur was drunk by the afternoon. Toad finally seemed to be drunk as well because he was singing loudly from the top of Goliath's head.

Lancelot started laughing.

Arthur started laughing.

Their humor made me relax somewhat. We needed something to break the mood. If it took a drunken gnome with a horrendous voice to do it, well, that was fine by me. I'd grin and bear his rowdy songs.

Goliath stopped.

It took me a moment to notice they were no longer following since I was a bit ahead of them. Arthur was turning his head from left to right as if he were trying to see through the thick forest surrounding us.

"What's happening?" I asked after I rode back to them.

"We're being followed," Toad answered.

"Are you sure?" I asked.

"Arthur's sure," Toad answered. "I can't sense anything."

"Neither can I," I said. "What are you thinking Arthur?"

"There a ways away," Arthur answered.

"Can you tell if they're friend or foe?" I asked.

"No," Arthur said.

"Tell me how you're feeling," I said.

"I feel uncomfortable," Arthur said. "I don't know how to explain it."

"Can you tell how many are following us?" I asked.

Arthur looked around some more. He was definitely experiencing a growing relationship with the land. That was good; the land was filled with magic. The land would tell him things. Of course, it could be only the alcohol talking to him.

"It's a small army," Arthur said.

"I can check it out and be back within the hour," Toad said. "Just point me in the right direction."

"They're too far off," Arthur said. "It'll take hours to reach them, maybe even an entire day."

"Gnomes are capable of great speed, Arthur," I said. "Point him in the right direction."

Arthur did as I asked.

"Just continue down this trail," Toad said. "I'll be back before we need to turn off."

I nodded and set off along the trail. Toad jumped off of Goliath's head and walked into the forest. Arthur and the pack horse followed behind me.

Arthur was still looking tense thirty minutes later.

"Tell me," I said.

"Death Reapers," Arthur said. "I'm almost positive. It's as if the land itself dreads their touch, but I don't understand how they found us."

"We'll know soon enough," I said.

Lancelot was above us. I could see the branches sway slightly at his touch. I gave him a motion with my hand, certain that he'd see it.

"Yes?" Lancelot asked.

"Keep an eye out just to be safe," I said.

"Done," Lancelot said.

Arthur had his left hand resting on the hilt of Excalibur, which hung on his hip. His right hand still held the bottle. I noticed that at some point he'd put his gloves on.

We rode on in silence as the snow fell gently around us.

Time passed. We didn't stop for lunch. We wanted to create as much distance as possible. Shortly before nightfall, we moved away from the trail and camped at the edge of a lake.

"No fire tonight," I said as I magically erected the tents and a shelter for the horses.

"What about food?" Lancelot asked.

"There's dried meat and the biscuits from this morning with the pack horse," I answered.

I placed myself under a tree as Lancelot tried to convince Arthur to eat something. Arthur wasn't interested. He was content to drink from his bottle.

"Lancelot," I whispered after it was obvious that his attempts were doomed to fail. "Come here please."

There came a soft rustle in the branches above me.

"Yes," Lancelot said.

"Stay close to Arthur tonight," I said.

"You don't want me in the trees?" Lancelot asked.

"Not tonight," I said. "I have that covered."

The sky grew darker, but the bright moon kept us from pitch blackness. My senses were cast out all around us. If need be, I'd set up some magical defenses, but I didn't want to catch Toad with them upon his return. Toad was running very late.

I joined Arthur who had positioned himself right at the water's edge. He was drinking from another bottle.

"You should get some sleep," I said.

"There's danger all around us," Arthur said. "I can't sleep."

"There's no danger near us at the moment," I said. "Of that I'm sure. You should rest while you can. You should eat something as well."

"You don't get it," Arthur said. "There are Death Reapers following us, and if I'm right we're headed someplace even worse than what's creeping up behind us."

"What do you mean?" I asked.

"I can't really explain it," Arthur answered, "but up ahead in the distance is something truly evil. I can sense it. I have a feeling that Toad is taking us there."

"I'm here with you," I said. "You'll face nothing alone."

"I face everything alone," Arthur said quietly. "It makes no difference how many people are with me."

Toad appeared behind us.

I noticed him no more than I'd notice a chipmunk. That's how harmless he registered on my defenses. Then again, Gnomes weren't known for their fighting prowess.

"Death Reapers," Toad said. "Lots of them, and they're definitely following us."

"What took you so long?" Arthur asked.

"I wanted to find out how they latched on to our trail," Toad answered.

"How?" I asked.

"Rotten luck," Toad answered. "A much larger band of them ran across our tracks, and sent out this group to take care of us."

"Why chase after a few horse tracks?" Arthur asked.

"Because of you," I answered. "The last time you left Camelot as an attack was underway you came back with Excalibur and the Gods of the Forest."

"And Tristan came back with an entire army," Arthur agreed. "The Death Reapers are covering their bases."

"How much time do we have?" I asked Toad.

"They aren't resting," Toad answered.

"We're in trouble," Arthur said as he took a large swig.

"Can we outrun them?" I asked.

"Any attempts could be in vain when we reach the key," Toad answered.

Arthur let out a low curse. We had no other choice. A fight was headed straight towards us, and we were grossly outnumbered.

"I wish we had the Gods of the Forest with us now," Arthur said. "We should have contacted them before we left."

"The Gods of the Forest have gone back to their own land," I said. "I have a feeling that we'll see them again, but not anytime soon. It isn't their duty to fight in this war."

"I'm sure they'd have come if I'd asked them," Arthur said.

"Do you forget who your Grandpa is?" I asked. "You do remember that I'm Merlin, don't you?"

"Well, you haven't done much so far," Arthur argued. "Hell, you didn't even know we were being followed."

Arthur was correct.

I was off my game. I was getting emotional in arguments and I was missing things. I should have sensed the danger that was pursuing us.

"We need to prepare," I said. "This area right here is the perfect place to set a trap. I can even call for a bit of help."

I walked to the water's edge and placed my hand on top of the rippling water. I uttered a few words of greeting. I created a summons and focused my will. After that I stood back and waited.

Arthur and Toad were staring at me. Arthur looked confused, but Toad looked uncomfortable. Moments later my summons was answered. A mournful horn blew an eerie note across the lake.

"Did you just do what I think you just did?" Arthur asked.

"It'll be fine," I answered. "The dead are no friends of Morgana."

"They're not necessarily friends of ours either," Arthur said.

"You keep dangerous company, my friend," Toad said.

A shape emerged from the far side of the lake. I couldn't make out any details, but it had a canoe like shape with ends that rose up high into the sky. We waited silently as the boat quickly made its way over to us.

The tortured woman carved into the front of the boat became visible, and I heard my name being whispered across the lake. Shapes began to emerge on the deck of the boat only to vanish before my eyes could focus on them.

A squared structure was in the middle of the boat. Standing on top of that and turning a great wheel was the Ferryman. I waved a greeting. The Ferryman didn't return the wave. The boat came to a stop twenty feet away from the shore.

"I seek your help," I said without raising my voice. "We are being pursued by the forces of Morgana."

There was no answer.

The lake became still.

Shadows stretched and churned on the deck of the boat.

The Ferryman was no longer at the helm.

I watched. I couldn't see much of anything. I was about to use magic in order to improve my night vision, but right as my fingers started to twist and turn the boat began to rotate on the water until we were facing its side.

The drawbridge like door on the side of the boat lowered into the water. I watched the Ferryman descent into the black lake.

"This is new," Arthur grumbled.

"This is not good," Toad said as he climbed up on Arthur's shoulder.

A cloaked head emerged from the water, followed by cloaked shoulders, and the rest of the Ferryman. He didn't walk, he glided and moved towards me with a purpose. His movements were menacing. I couldn't see his face, but one of his armor encased hands clenched an ancient grey sword.

The Ferryman stopped about five feet away from me. Freezing water dripped from his cloak.

"Merlin," The Ferryman said in a dry and scratched voice. "Why would the dead help you?"

"Because I'm with the king," I answered.

The Ferryman turned his covered head towards Arthur and sized him up.

"I owe this king nothing," The Ferryman said.

"Don't you?" I asked. "He freed the sword. He brought magic back to the world. The great power you now possess is because of him."

"I ferried him to Excalibur," The Ferryman said. "I kept him safe. I owe him nothing."

"Then perhaps I can owe you something," I said. "After all, what is defending us to you? It would be so simple an act."

In the blink of an eye the Ferryman glided over to Arthur.

"Why are you here, king?" The Ferryman asked.

Arthur looked at me before answering. I nodded that it was okay.

"I'm here to find the key," Arthur said. "We need to raise the Camelot of old before giants attack."

"There are giants?" The Ferryman asked.

"I guess so," Arthur said.

"There will be no bargain, Merlin," The Ferryman said without even looking at me. "I'll aid you without payment."

The Ferryman turned and glided back into the water without another word. Arthur looked even more confused than before. Toad climbed off Arthurs shoulder and stood between us.

"Giants are a plague," I said. "The reproduce quickly and kill for the sake of enjoyment. Within a few years, if gone unchecked, they'll destroy the land and pollute the lakes. The Ferryman doesn't want his lake polluted."

"I didn't realize this was the same lake that I travelled before," Arthur said.

"This lake travels far and wide," I said. "It may not even have an end."

"Well that makes no sense," Arthur said.

"It's magic," I said. "Now gather around everyone. We need a plan."

"We're on a pebble beach," Arthur said. "The beach is surrounded by forest. When the Death Reapers enter the beach, use your magic on the trees so that they can't exit. Meanwhile, the Ferryman and his group can attack from the water."

"That'll work," I agreed.

Voices drifted across the lake. They sounded like whispers to Toad, Arthur, and Lancelot, but to me they were clear.

"Not all the Death Reapers will enter the beach," I said. "The Ferryman wants you to stay behind in the woods to pick off any stragglers."

"That's not part of the deal," Arthur said.

More voices drifted towards us.

"The Ferryman isn't giving you a choice," I said. "If we leave behind any stragglers, we'll soon have more Death Reapers pursuing us."

"We'll have more Death Reapers pursuing us either way," Arthur argued. "When this group doesn't make it back to the others, more will be sent out after us."

"I'd rather have them sent after us later than sooner," I said.

"Then send some of the Ferryman's ghosts into the forest," Arthur said. "Let them pick off the stragglers."

"The ghosts can't venture that far from the water," I said. "They need to stay on the beach."

"Well shit," Arthur complained as he took a pull from his bottle. "You're just determined to get me killed."

"Arthur," I said. "It makes sense—"

"I haven't fought anyone since the damn graveyard!" Arthur shouted. "How do you suggest I handle this?"

"You handle it with the skills I made sure you learned," I answered. "You are a warrior, you wield Excalibur. This will be easy for you."

"Anything can happen in a fight," Arthur said in a menacing tone as he walked away.

♣ ARTHUR ♣

This just kept getting better and better. I knew this was going to be a bitch. I knew I was going to be in danger. Merlin...what the hell good was Merlin? He wasn't along to protect me. That asshole was the person who kept pushing me into danger.

I was storming off. It felt like a temper tantrum, and it probably was, but I didn't care. I headed towards the forest. I needed to find a good place from which to attack.

We'll kill them all

Excalibur; the sword hadn't spoken to me in so long I'd thought that it no longer could. It was a surprise, but a welcome one. I'd need Excalibur. There was no telling how many Death Reapers I'd be facing.

Stop drinking

That wasn't going to happen. I appreciated the sword's advice, but drinking was the only reason I didn't hop up on Goliath's back and ride the hell out of here.

"Where are you going?" Merlin asked.

"I'm going into the woods," I answered. "Where do you think I'm going?"

"Take Goliath with you," Merlin said. "You'll have an advantage that way."

"No shit," I grumbled and changed direction.

Goliath was happy to see me. I rubbed his nose, gave his neck a hug, and prepared him to ride. It took a bit, I wasn't exactly an expert on putting a saddle and bridle on a horse, but I managed.

I rode into the woods.

In just a few moments I found a thicket of bushes and trees off to the side a ways away from the trail. It would provide the cover I needed. At least

I hoped it would. A small shower of snow fell from a branch above my head. Lance was with me.

"I'm glad you're here," I said.

"I had nothing better to do," Lance said.

I smiled and drank some more.

The evening grew colder and colder. The snow began to fall a little bit harder, yet there was no wind. I pulled my cloak tight around my body and pulled my hood over my head. A part of me worried about Lance, but weather didn't seem to bother him or Merlin.

At some point I fell asleep in my saddle.

Goliath made a low grumble and rocked back and forth until I woke up. The bottle fell from my right hand, and I reached for Excalibur. A green fog was drifting in around me.

"Not yet," Lance whispered from above me.

I was breathing heavily. In my own mind, it was too loud. The Death Reapers were sure to hear us. I was going to ruin the plan and then I was going to be stuck in the middle of the forest with an army of enemies trying to kill me.

My hands were shaking. Was it the cold? I didn't think so. The cloak kept me plenty warm. I was nervous. No, nervous wasn't the right word. I was terrified. I clearly remembered all the Death Reapers chasing after me as I went to retrieve Excalibur. How many times did they almost kill me?

I heard the sounds of footsteps crunching through the crust of snow.

I heard the sounds of chainmail scraping against branches.

Whispered voices.

"Not yet," Lance whispered.

My head was spinning. I felt faint. I felt sick to my stomach. My bottle was on the ground. I wanted a sip. I contemplated retrieving it, but I was worried about making noise.

A group of soldiers brushed past my hiding place. Did they stop? Did they hesitate because they heard something? Maybe they smelled the horse smell of Goliath. They were looking around. No, they were moving on.

"Now," Lance whispered.

I couldn't move.

The soldiers weren't anywhere near me. I could hear them, but I couldn't see them. The shouting began. Orders were being shouted out. Men began screaming.

I couldn't move.

Lance was gone in a puff of snow.

Goliath started to growl and scratch at the ground.

Now

"I can't," I told Excalibur.

You have no choice

A sword jabbed at me through the branches, narrowly missing Goliath. My horse spooked, bucked up, wheeled around, and charged out of my hiding place.

I was surrounded by panicked Death Reapers.

I drew Excalibur and charged straight for them. I didn't mean to do it. It wasn't an act of bravery. It was instinct.

I swung my sword and blocked an attack. Goliath spun and I swung out, taking the head off of an enemy. A brilliant blue flame burst out along my blade.

"It's Arthur!" A Death Reaper shouted in fear. "It's the king!"

The Death Reapers around me froze.

I didn't.

I swung and hacked at them.

Excalibur sliced through shields and limbs with ease. My fear melted away. This was easy, not difficult at all. I was the greatest swordsman in the world. I wielded the greatest sword. How could I have been so afraid?

Lack of action breeds fear

That made sense, and it was good to hear from Excalibur. It was good to know that I wasn't alone. Merlin put me in harm's way. Maybe he even wanted me to get killed. Well, I'd show him.

I saw five Death Reapers running along the trail. They didn't want to fight. I gave Goliath a nudge and he galloped after them. Cowards, they deserved what I was going to do to them. I felt good. I felt alive. Goliath weaved in and around the trees. Snow sprayed out from under his powerful hooves.

The first Death Reaper I caught up to was no problem. I took his head with the lightest of swings. The next one fell just as easily. The flame on my sword lit up the night.

The final three Death Reapers decided to meet their fate head on. I stopped Goliath before them. One of them had a light axe. The other two had rusty swords. I hated their soggy hair and silver eyes. I hated the black tunic over their worn chainmail. I hated the white drawing of a dagger piercing a heart.

They were ready to fight.

So was I.

I dismounted my horse with a smile on my face. A Death Reaper with a sword ran at me. His attack was clumsy. I deflected his sword and opened up his back as I passed by him. He screamed out in pain and fell to the ground. I enjoyed the look of fear on the faces of my two remaining enemies.

"I'm enjoying this," I said to them.

My words forced them into motion. They came at me as a team. This would be interesting. I dodged one swing, kicked out with my leg, and blocked the axe swinging at me from behind.

I was in a dance and I knew all the moves.

Finish them

I ignored the sword. I was in my element. I was doing that which I enjoyed so much. The Death Reaper with the sword stabbed out at me. I blocked his thrust and pushed his arm above his head before swinging down at his exposed leg.

The Death Reaper screamed out a horrible sound as he fell to the ground and realized I'd removed his leg. The axe swung at my head. I stepped backwards to avoid it. The Death Reaper swung again and again. I easily avoided his attacks, waiting for the right moment, which came in an instant. He swung just a little too hard and I stepped inside his arc, piercing his sternum with Excalibur.

He fell to the bloody snow gasping for air like a fish out of water.

There were more screams coming from the direction of the lake. There was movement all around me. My job was basically to make sure none of the Death Reapers escaped. I went to work.

I jumped back on Goliath's back and we rode through the trees looking for victims. Goliath was screaming and snarling. The blood scent in the air excited him. He was the perfect war horse.

I soon found a target. His bravery and ferocity had vanished. He was reduced to a frightened child as I rode him down. He even tried to plead with me as my blade swung out and cut him in half. As I rode away, he was still babbling as he bled out.

More and more Death Reapers fell around me. Lancelot was helping. He was probably killing even more than me. I didn't like that. They were mine. I didn't need his help.

"Go away," I snarled. "They're mine."

In the distance, I saw four Death Reapers escaping down another trail on horseback. I rode after them. Their horses were no match for Goliath. Together we closed the distance almost instantly.

A large tree hung over the trail right before the riders. I threw Excalibur at the trunk of the tree. My aim was perfect. My sword sliced through the thick trunk of the tree as if it were paper. The tree fell in front of the path, blocking the Death Reapers' escape.

I pulled my dagger and jumped from Goliath's back onto the back of the nearest horse, right behind its rider. I grabbed a hold of the Death Reaper and stabbed him repeatedly in the neck, before throwing him off the horse.

I charged his horse straight into the bodies of the other horses, knocking all of us to the ground right before the fallen tree. I freed myself from the tangle of horseflesh and chainmail instantly.

Once free I began to stab and slice. My dagger was sharp. I rarely used it and when I did, I made sure to sharpen it back up afterwards.

The final Death Reaper backed away from me enough to draw his sword. Excalibur appeared in the midst of the blood and torn flesh. I picked up the sword without hesitation and charged my foe.

Our blades clanged out in a series of strikes and blocks. He was a trained swordsman. I appreciated that. I wanted that.

I let him push me backwards. I let him think he had the upper hand, then I sidestepped, and slashed open the backs of his legs. The Death Reaper screamed out and cursed. I laughed as he spun around and attempted a clumsy thrust.

Too many fighters lose their discipline when they're injured. This idiot was no different. He was no longer calm and calculating. He was panicked and becoming frenzied. I backed away, toying with him. He ran straight at me, swung his sword out, I blocked with Excalibur, moved in close, and plunged my dagger into his neck.

Blood splashed out against my face as I removed my dagger. The night was deathly quiet. Even the soldiers that had made it to the lake had stopped screaming.

I was breathing heavily, but I wasn't tired. I could fight like this for an eternity. I enjoyed this work. How could I have stepped away from this for so long?

"Arthur?" Lance said from somewhere above me. "Are you okay?"

I had forgotten I wasn't alone.

"Are there anymore?" I asked.

59

"No," Lance said. "We got them all."

Excalibur was burning brightly. I didn't want to quench those flames. I wanted to feed them. A brief thought crossed my mind. Attack the orphan, but that wasn't right. It wasn't what I wanted. Lance was an ally. Lance was a friend. The idea vanished almost immediately.

I sheathed my sword.

It felt as if I'd lost a part of my soul.

It took a moment to readjust.

A quick whistle and Goliath was beside me. I mounted the horse quickly, and rode him back to where I'd been hiding. I needed my bottle. The alcohol would numb me up good and proper. The alcohol would get me through the evening.

I rode back to the edge of the lake after I'd reclaimed it.

Ghosts with a slight bluish tinge were making their way back into the lake. The water barely rippled as they entered. I sneered at them. No longer did they make me uncomfortable. Now they were simply pathetic.

The bodies of Death Reapers littered the pebble beach. Goliath stepped over them. The horse didn't seem to want to touch their cold and clammy skin. I patted his neck and laughed a bit.

The green fog had long since evaporated.

Merlin was right at the water's edge. He and the Ferryman seemed to be arguing as the snow fell all around them. The image was odd. The Ferryman was cloaked and menacing. Merlin was young, short, and nerdish. Yet, there he was, having an argument with something that should have been giving a boy not much younger than him nightmares.

I rode over to them.

"You'll get him killed," the Ferryman said. "What will happen to the land if the king dies?"

"You're not worried about the land," Merlin said. "You're worried about the magic. You need the magic to stay strong."

"What pain the land experiences will hurt the lake," the Ferryman said. "Your way is fraught with danger. The Camelot of old is gone. Let it rest in peace."

"There are people that depend upon us," Merlin said.

"They don't matter," the Ferryman argued. "All that matters is the life of the king. Arthur cannot die."

"Your advice has been heard," Merlin said, "but we'll continue on our journey."

"Then at least allow me to give you safe passage," the Ferryman said. "I can get you there by late afternoon."

Toad appeared as if out of nowhere.

I took a swig from my bottle and watched him approach Merlin and the Ferryman. Merlin turned patiently, but the Ferryman ignored the little gnome.

"The Ferryman has the right idea," Toad said. "The forests are becoming dangerous. The boat will give us quite an advantage."

"Arthur," Merlin called out to me. "What do you think?"

"Let's take the boat," I said.

At my words, the lake began to recede from where the boat rested. It wasn't anything too dramatic. It sort of looked as if the water of the lake was merely evaporating. I looked at Merlin. He seemed transfixed, as if studying the magic being used to shrink the lake.

The way to the boat was suddenly clear.

"Even with me here," the Ferryman said. "It's best for any of you not to enter these waters after the sun has fallen."

We gathered our supplies quickly, made our way across the muddy floor of the lake, moved up the ramp, and entered the boat, which was resting at an odd angle after being beached.

Once all of us were aboard, the lake began to fill up once more. When the boat began to float, we were all rocked against its sudden buoyancy, except for Merlin. His balance remained perfect.

I took another swig from my bottle.

"Well," I said. "That was fun."

"How was the fighting for you and Lancelot?" Merlin asked.

"Nothing we couldn't handle," I answered.

"What about Excalibur?" Merlin asked.

"What about Excalibur?" I asked.

"Did the sword...behave?" Merlin questioned.

"It wasn't too bad," I answered. "Nothing to worry about."

"I see," Merlin said.

"Once again, Arthur," the Ferryman interrupted. "You may sleep in my quarters."

I left Merlin without another word.

The cabin was exactly as I remembered it, a bed, a mirror, a painting of a woman, two cabinets, and a window. It was rather empty, but more than I needed.

"I'll be sharing the bed with you," Toad said from behind me. "All those ghosts make me nervous. I'm a part of the natural world, and they certainly aren't there with me."

Truth be told, I barely paid attention to the ghosts. They didn't bother me, and I had no interest in them. I saw them of course. They were all around us, but as far as I was concerned they were Merlin's problem.

"Don't crawl up in my ear or anything when I'm asleep," I said.

"You're a rude cuss when you want to be," Toad said.

"That's what I've been told," I said. "Now why don't you tell me where we're headed."

"Get a good night's sleep first," Toad said. "I'll fill you in on everything tomorrow."

"Why wait?" I asked.

"Right now," Toad said. "Sleep is more important than knowledge."

The gnome didn't want to tell me. I found that a bit odd. After all, I was the one that was retrieving the damn key. Didn't I have a right to know where I was headed?

I took another massive swig from my bottle, took off my boots and gloves, and fell into a deep sleep. I didn't wake up until late morning.

I felt refreshed as I climbed out of the bed. Toad was nowhere to be seen, and neither was Lance, though I distinctly heard him enter the room late at night.

Breakfast and coffee were waiting for me on a small table that had been brought into the room. I ate out of necessity, but what I really wanted was another swig from my bottle.

My bottle had been refilled.

The morning was turning out to be pretty decent. It had even stopped snowing sometime during the evening.

I put my boots back on, and went outside with my bottle.

Merlin and Toad were standing at the front of the boat. Actually, Toad was standing on Merlin's shoulder. I patted Goliath as I passed him and went over to Merlin.

"I want to know where we're headed," I said.

"Of course," Merlin said. "Toad, would you be so kind?"

"We're going to the house," Toad answered. "I believe that you're slightly familiar with it, though you had enough common sense not to enter."

"You're not talking about that spooky house that Lance and I passed on our way to find the Ferryman?" I asked.

"Yes," Merlin answered. "It's a dangerous place, but that is where the key has been hidden."

"I need to go into the house?" I asked.

"Yes," Toad answered. "Had my people known that this day would come, we never would have hidden it in such a vile place, but we never dreamed that Arthur would be reborn."

"Let's just burn the house down and find the key in the ashes," Lance said from behind me somewhere.

"The house won't burn," Merlin said. "It can't be harmed by ordinary means."

"Do you know how many Death Reapers got killed inside that house?" I asked. "There's something very wrong with that place."

"Indeed there is," Merlin said. "Indeed there is."

"Well what's in there, then?" I asked.

"Something ancient and evil," Merlin answered. "Perhaps Toad can shed more light on the house's occupant?"

"I can't," Toad said. "My people refuse to speak of it. Like the animals, we keep far from that house no matter where it ends up."

"Do what?" I asked. "The house moves?"

"It does," Toad answered. "Not often, but someday it will vanish only to reappear in some other state, perhaps some other country."

"Toad," Merlin said. "I understand your people don't speak of this, but I'm going to ask you to break protocol and tell me what we'll be facing."

"I can't," Toad said.

"Why not?" Merlin asked.

"Because we don't speak of it," Toad answered. "I have no idea what's inside that house. We don't speak of it."

"I'm going with you, Arthur," Merlin said.

"I don't think that's a good idea," Toad said. "This is Arthur's duty, not yours."

"I'm going as well," Lance said from over by the horses.

"Merlin," Toad said. "I don't think your magic is going to save you in that house."

"Arthur will not go alone," Merlin said. "Lancelot, I don't want us to be crowded inside the house. It'd be best if you waited outside and kept watch over the horses."

"My job is to protect Arthur," Lance said.

"And you do a wonderful job," Merlin said, "but this time I think he would be best protected under my watch."

"I disagree with this Merlin," Toad said. "I think you're adding more danger to an already dangerous situation. Your presence just might enrage what lives inside that house."

"We'll soon find out," Merlin said with a smile.

I went to top of the boat where the Ferryman was steering us. I didn't care if Merlin went with me or not. I knew he was powerful, but he was also the one that kept forcing me into dangerous situations. If he wanted to help, that was fine, I'd let him go first.

"Your mission is a dangerous one," the Ferryman said as soon as I was standing next to him.

"It always is," I said.

"You have no faith in your comrades," the Ferryman said.

"I have faith in Lance," I said. "I have faith in my horse."

"You need to have faith in Merlin," the Ferryman said. "He'll keep you alive."

"I'm more interested in that key," I said. "Can that key really be used to protect my people?"

"As far as memory can recall," the Ferryman said. "No enemy has every breached the walls of Camelot."

I nodded my head and watched the scenery as we drifted down the lake. A few hours later some birds began to fly around the boat. Toad went and stood on the front railing, and I became worried that the birds would gobble him up. Instead, they landed next to him as Merlin looked on.

Toad began to pet the bird and inspect its wings. He also began speaking with it in a weird language that made absolutely no sense to me. When the bird finally flew away, it made sure to circle me a few times before departing.

"What was that about?" I asked.

"You're the king," the Ferryman answered. "Merlin is summoning you."

"Is he?" I asked looking down towards him on the deck of the boat.

Merlin motioned me to him. I didn't like it. I didn't like him taking charge of things. I didn't like him telling me what to do, but I went back down and joined them anyway.

"What's going on?" I asked.

"The birds say that the Death Reapers we killed last night were missed," Merlin answered. "They've sent more soldiers into the forest."

"We expected that," I said.

"We didn't expect them to react so soon," Merlin answered.

"So we'll go in," I said. "We'll find the key, hop back on the boat, and get another head start on them by traveling over the water."

"That's the plan," Merlin said, "but we'll need to be ready for anything. We'll also eventually need to travel on land once more. The boat unfortunately can't take us the entire way."

"You sure about that?" I asked. "This lake is pretty mysterious. I'm not even sure how it connects to the house we're headed towards. It's not on any maps, and it seems to grow as needed."

"This lake is very mysterious," Merlin agreed, "but it still has its limitations."

Noises came at us from the shore over to our left. All of us looked in that direction. A primitive looking type of man was standing there with a crude spear in his hand and shouting something at us.

"What's he saying?" I asked.

"Nothing good," Merlin answered.

More primitive people emerged from the trees all around him. There were men, women, and children and all of them were shaking spears at us.

"When the red fog came," Toad said. "Many humans vanished into the forests never to return. My people have run into them from time to time. We believe that they lost their minds and turned into savages."

"Duck!" Merlin shouted.

All of us did as he asked, and the spears flew all around the boat. I was worried about the horses. Until I realized that the spears never even came close to them. Savage or not, our attackers had good aim.

"Ignore them," the Ferryman called down to us. "They'll give up very soon. This isn't the first time I've encountered them. They won't give chase either. They know what will happen if they enter the water."

I watched them as we passed by. They were dirty and covered in animal skins. Was Toad correct? Were they really modern humans that entered the forest and lost their minds? I could hardly believe it, but surely they didn't exist before the red fog. Someone would have noticed them.

"Someday," Merlin said sadly. "When all is said and done, and Morgana is a faded memory, we may need to return and deal with these unfortunate people."

"Why not leave them alone," I said. "They're far enough away from civilization. They shouldn't become a problem."

"You must not have noticed the human skulls they carried," Merlin answered. "They had them hanging from their belts."

"They're cannibals," Toad said. "They go out hunting every full moon."

"Oh," I said.

"We could have the Ferryman and the ghosts deal with them," Lance added.

"They'll flee as soon as the ghosts leave the water," Toad said. "They're a superstitious bunch. Ghosts terrify them. It'll take a group that can pursue them on land."

The primitive people had disappeared back into the forest. I wasn't afraid of them; instead, I felt pity for them. If our soldiers went after them it would be a massacre. That wasn't the way to deal with people that had lost their minds. Still, it wouldn't be right to let them continue preying on people. I took a large swig from my bottle and stood up.

"Another few hours," the Ferryman announced.

That made me nervous. My stomach clenched up in anticipation. In order to calm it back down, I took an even larger swig from my bottle.

"Don't get drunk," Merlin said testily. "You'll need your wits about you."

"The joke's on you," I said. "I'm relatively witless."

Lance and Toad laughed.

Merlin didn't.

Feeling the need to be alone, I went back inside the cabin. In a short amount of time, Lance entered as well. I saw the door open and close. I also saw a vague shape move to the top of one of the cabinets.

"I really wanted some alone time," I said.

"Don't mind me," Lance said. "Outside makes me a bit uncomfortable. Not a lot of places for me to blend in to."

I gave up. There was no use in trying to find some privacy. The boat simply wasn't big enough. Then again, the entire planet probably wasn't big enough.

An hour later, I was getting sick off the side of the boat. Maybe it was just a case of the nerves. Perhaps I was getting a bit seasick. It was probably the alcohol.

Merlin who was still standing at the front of the boat was giving me dirty looks. I'm not sure what he was so pissed about, if anything I'd at least be a bit more sober going into that house.

I laughed at my own joke and took another swig from my bottle.

That was apparently enough for Merlin. He immediately stomped his way over to me. I did my best to ignore him and kept my head resting on my forearms which were on the railing holding me up.

"You've got to be kidding me," Merlin said.

"If there's a joke I'm not aware of it," I said.

"What the hell's wrong with you?" Merlin asked.

"I might have had too much to drink," I answered.

"You realize we're soon going to be in danger, don't you?" Merlin asked.

"I'm not really worried about that," I said. "I've got a badass wizard in a teenager's body there to protect me."

I finally looked at Merlin. There were tears in his eyes. I could have cared less. My life would be infinitely better if he up and disappeared.

"I never wanted to believe it," Merlin said. "I never wanted to give up on you, but now I can see...there's nothing left of the man you used to be."

Merlin walked away.

I got sick again.

An hour later and the pier was in the distance. Beyond the pier was the house. It seemed as if it was closer to the water than I remembered. Could that be possible?

I looked at the house long and hard. It wasn't a large home by any means. The faded grey paint looked the same as the last time I saw it. There were no lights on at the moment. Nah that would come at nighttime, and I had a feeling that whatever was in that house slept during the day.

The boat bumped into the pier gently.

I jumped up on Goliath's back. Merlin mounted his horse, and the drawbridge type deal of the boat lowered towards the dock.

I went first. I wanted Merlin to know that I didn't need him. Toad was on top of Goliath's head. Lucky for the gnome, Goliath seemed to like him.

I enjoyed the sound of hooves against the wood of the pier. It was a soothing sound. Goliath grunted his frustration at being near the house once again.

"You'll need to wait until sunset," Toad said. "You won't be able to get inside until then."

"Are you sure the key is still in there?" I asked.

"Definitely," Toad answered. "You'll find it in one of the upstairs rooms. It'll be in an old jewelry box covered in seashells. Just grab the jewelry box and get out of there."

"You think it'll be that easy?" I asked.

"I certainly hope so," Toad said.

"Well, I have Excalibur with me," I said.

"You also have the greatest wizard this world has ever seen looking over your shoulder," Toad added.

I snorted, but didn't say anything.

A hundred yards from the house we dismounted and set up a little camp. There was snow on the ground, and that made finding a dry place to sit difficult. I was getting grumpy, so I took another swig from my bottle which had somehow filled up once again.

The first swig wasn't good enough, so I took another one. Merlin refused to even look at me. I was fine with that. At least I didn't have to listen to him complain.

It was my life. If I wanted to drink and be stupid that was my right. I didn't ask for any of the things Merlin was trying to thrust upon me. I didn't want involved in things. I didn't want anything. I just wanted to be left alone.

I resented Merlin.

I did. I resented my own grandfather. I understood that I was a loser. I understood that I was a failure at life. So what? Just leave me be. There wasn't anything that I wanted. There wasn't anything that I desired. Life had lost its flavor a long, long time ago. All I did was go through the motions.

Was I depressed? I didn't think so. Depression would take too much energy. Occasionally I could have fun. The women, the jousting, the alcohol... sometimes I enjoyed those things.

I fell asleep sitting on a log.

Maybe I passed out.

Perhaps it was a combination of both.

I think I snored.

Toad shook me awake. He was pretty strong for such a little guy.

"Arthur," Toad said. "It's nearly time."

"Yay," I mumbled as I lifted my head.

It had started snowing again. It was also pretty damn cold. I was shivering and almost anxious to get inside the house on the off chance that it'd be warm inside.

I stood up.

Merlin seemed comfortable in his hoodie, even though his eyes were rolled back into his head. I worried about him briefly until I remembered that he was Merlin and the cold didn't really bother him.

"What's he doing?" I asked Toad.

"He's preparing," Toad answered.

"Preparing for what?" I asked.

"To protect you," Toad answered.

"Whatever," I said. "Where's Lance?"

"He left when the sun started to set," Toad answered. "Hopefully he'll be back before the two of you venture into that house."

"Don't worry," I said. "We'll wait for him."

The sky grew a grayish color. I became impatient. I wanted to get this over with. My left hand was holding onto the hilt of my sword. Excalibur was awake. The sword wasn't speaking to me, but I could just about feel the pulsating energy.

Merlin stood up.

I saw him out of the corner of my eye. I didn't really pay attention to him. I was busy watching the house. This was my mission. It was an unwanted mission, but I wasn't going to rely on Merlin for any help.

A light inside the house turned on.

"Are you ready?" Merlin asked.

"I'm waiting for Lance to return," I said.

"Arthur..." Merlin tried to argue.

"I'm waiting for Lance to return," I interrupted.

The three of us stood in silence. The sky hadn't grown any darker. It seemed as if it were stuck in that eerie grayness. The snow continued to fall. None of it stuck on the house. Would a door open like it did last time? Would I get another invitation?

The light moved from the upstairs window down to the first floor and then back again. Was the inhabitant of the house watching us? Did it know that we were outside? I think it did.

"I'm back," Lance said from inside the line of bushes on the one side of our little campsite.

Merlin looked at me.

"Lance," I said. "Take care of Goliath. If I don't come back, get him to my mother."

Lance didn't answer. He didn't need to. I knew he'd do as I asked. I also knew that he was pissed to be waiting outside. He wanted to go with me. My protection was what gave meaning to his life. Not the greatest way for a kid to grow up, but despite my best effort, that was how he felt.

I walked towards the house.

Merlin was right behind me. An ancient wizard trapped inside the body of a teenager. It was ridiculous to think that he was so powerful. It angered me that I was relieved to have him with me.

I moved in an ever-widening circle to the front of the house. The front porch was just as crooked as it was before. That was to convince people that the place was neglected. A safe place to pass away the night, it even had a warm light that moved from room to room as if a little old lady lived there, just waiting to bake cookies for a visitor.

The front door opened.

"There goes the element of surprise," I grumbled.

"We might be okay," Merlin said. "That could be a something like a reflex, like lights turning on due to motion."

"I wouldn't count on it," I said. "Now how do you want to do this?"

"We go in as fast as we can, grab the jewelry box and run like hell," Merlin said.

"Bad idea," I said.

"You have a better one?" Merlin asked.

"Not yet," I admitted.

The two of us walked closer to that crooked front porch. I could see the dust and cobwebs on the windows, but I couldn't see through them into the house. Merlin moved in front of me and stepped onto the first step. It creaked loudly, but held his weight.

I pulled my dagger.

At the top of the porch, Merlin motioned to me as he looked inside the house where he'd wiped the window clean. I joined him and took a look. All I saw was a sparsely decorated living room.

"We should do this quickly," Merlin said. "I'd like to be finished before the sun sets and it gets dark inside the house."

"It's already pretty shadowy," I said.

We stepped inside.

The smell was musty. I didn't like it. Something in the air was foul, but I couldn't put my finger on it. The musty smell wasn't natural.

70

The front room had a fireplace, a large couch, and a rocking chair. In the middle of the room was a small wooden table. Other than a painting that I couldn't really see in the shadows, the room was empty.

The stairs were a bit to our right.

"Let's do it," Merlin said.

"No," I said. "We need to check out this floor first. I don't want something coming up the stairs behind us."

Merlin considered my advice.

"You have a point," Merlin consented. "I'll lead the way."

I followed my would-be protector past the stairs into the adjacent room which turned out to be a kitchen. There was a sink, another table, cupboards, and a few pots and pans. Aside from the faded wallpaper there was no other sign of decoration.

I went to the sink.

"Don't touch anything," Merlin said.

I ignored him and turned on the water. Nothing came out of the faucet. The pipes didn't even rumble. Merlin gave me a questioning look. I smiled at that. It was funny to see a bit of confusion on his young face. Too often he had an arrogant look that irritated me.

Unfortunately, I myself didn't know what I was up to. Something about the house just seemed off. I tried the cupboards next. None of them opened. They weren't real.

I looked at Merlin again.

He didn't have an answer for me, but we were standing in a fake kitchen and I didn't understand why someone would bother creating a fake kitchen.

Merlin moved on and I followed him.

The next room we came upon was a dining room. Here there was a large wooden table covered in nicks and scrapes. There were no chairs, and only a single painting on the wall. This painting I could see clearly due to the large window in the room. It was the image of a man bound to a rock at the edge of the sea. The man was terrified and his mouth was open in a silent scream as he stared off the painting at whatever horrors were headed his way.

There were blood stains on the wooden floor.

I didn't bother pointing them out to Merlin. I was positive that he'd already seen them. Merlin missed nothing.

There was one more room left to investigate.

The door was in the middle of the short hallway. I was pretty sure it'd only turn out to be a non-functioning bathroom, and went to turn the handle.

Merlin stopped me.

"There's something off about this room," Merlin said.

I put my hand against the wood of the door. Of course, I felt nothing.

"I don't think there's danger behind that door," Merlin continued, "but whatever it is, it'll break the illusion of this house."

I opened the door.

I couldn't make anything out in the darkness. There were no windows to this room. Merlin snapped his fingers in a strange way and produced a small fire on the palm of his hand. He entered the room and raised his arm.

The room was empty with the exception on an old broken mirror on the wall and a large pit about three and a half feet wide.

An odd bathroom.

I walked over to the pit, and couldn't see how deep it went in the darkness. I waved Merlin over to me and a small spark jumped off his hand and floated down into the pit, lightening the contents. I placed my head directly over the pit in order to see.

The pit turned out to be about fifteen feet deep. Inside were a grayish sludge and numerous dried out bodies. I backed away as the stench hit me full force in the face.

The second I was away from the pit, the stench was gone.

"Why's it only smell if your face is right over the pit?" I asked.

"If that smell penetrated the house, no one would ever enter," Merlin answered.

"This is a latrine of some sorts, right?" I asked.

"I'd say so," Merlin answered. "And more."

"What do you mean more?" I asked.

"Those remains haven't been eaten," Merlin said. "They've been attacked, but they haven't been eaten. In addition to being used as a latrine, this pit is also a convenient place to throw the bodies."

"Why kill them if you aren't going to feed off of them?" I asked.

"I didn't say they weren't fed on," Merlin answered. "I said the bodies weren't eaten."

"They were sucked dry," I said. "Are we dealing with a vampire?"

"I wouldn't think so," Merlin said. "I've dealt with vampires before. This isn't something they'd be interested in. They also produce no waste."

72

"So what are we dealing with?" I asked.

"That remains to be seen," Merlin said as he backed out of the room.

I followed him and his little fire. I had no desire to be stuck inside that room alone. For all I knew, something could come crawling out of that pit after me.

Merlin walked over to the stairs.

The two of us stared long and hard, but saw no danger.

"This is starting to weird me out," I said. "Where's the attack?"

"I don't think we've been playing by the proper rules," Merlin said. "The evil in this house is waiting for us to make a mistake."

"Then let's not make one," I said.

We went up the stairs. Merlin went first and I followed closely behind him. The wooden stairs creaked ominously with every step we took. The weird musty smell was even stronger on the upper floor.

At the top of the stairs was a hallway that went to our left which ended at a window and a curved staircase that probably went to the attic. In between were three closed doors and an old fluffy armchair that still looked pretty comfortable.

Merlin led the way.

He opened the first door, and there wasn't much to see aside from a comfortable looking bed and another fluffy armchair.

The second room was the same, another relaxing chair and a bed. The only difference between this room and the last was a painting on the wall. A spider. Why would anyone want a painting of a spider hanging over their bed?

There was only one room left and after that, we'd need to go up into the attic. Merlin put his hand against the door and closed his eyes. After a moment, he pulled his hand away.

"I don't sense any danger in there," Merlin said.

"Then open the door," I said.

I needed a drink. As soon as I was out of this house I was going to chug about half my bottle. I didn't give a shit about how Merlin would react. If he gave me any problems, I was going to throw the bottle at him. On second thought, that'd be wasting good alcohol.

Merlin opened the door.

This time there were two fluffy chairs, a nightstand, and a nice comfortable bed, but no jewelry box covered in seashells. I went over to the nightstand as Merlin got down on the floor to look under the bed.

I opened the drawer of the nightstand and found the jewelry box. Little tiny seashells had been glued to the outside like something you'd find in a trinket shop near a beach.

"I found the box," I said.

Merlin put his hand on the bed and looked up at me.

"Are you sure?" Merlin asked.

I showed him the box.

"Should I open it?" I asked.

"Not here," Merlin said as he stood up. "Wait until we're outside."

I stuffed the little box into one of the pockets of my cloak and made my way towards the door.

"Alright," I said. "Let's get out of here."

"I can't," Merlin said.

"Why not?" I asked looking back at him.

"It appears that I've made a mistake," Merlin answered.

"What mistake?" I asked not seeing a problem.

Merlin hadn't really moved at all. He was still leaning over like he'd just stood up, and his hand was still on the bed.

"My hand is stuck," Merlin said calmly.

"What do you mean stuck?" I asked.

"I'm not sure how to explain it any more clearly than I already have," Merlin answered like a smartass.

"To the bed?" I asked.

"Yes," Merlin answered.

"Well, pull it really hard," I said.

"I don't think that'd be a good idea," Merlin said.

"Then how are you going to get free?" I asked.

"I'm trying to think of some spells I can do with only one hand," Merlin answered. "It's not going to be easy. Most larger spells require two hands."

I walked over to Merlin, knelt down, and took a look at his hand on the bed. It didn't appear stuck. It just appeared to be a normal hand on a normal bed.

"Wiggle your fingers," I said.

"I don't think it's a good idea for me to move," Merlin said.

"Just do it," I said leaning closer.

"Don't touch the bed!" Merlin shouted.

His warning came too late. The tip of my beard was stuck firmly. I pulled my head back, until it hurt. Not even the covers on the bed moved.

"Stop moving!" Merlin yelled.

I did as he asked.

"How badly are you stuck?" Merlin asked.

"Just the tip of my beard," I answered. "No big deal."

Merlin wanted to say something, but before he could I used my dagger and cut through less than half an inch of beard. If the bed wanted my beard so much, it could have it.

"Well, that's good for you," Merlin said, "but I'm still stuck."

"I could cut your hand off," I suggested with a smile.

"You're very generous," Merlin said. "And you're also an asshole."

I smiled.

"I've got it," Merlin said. "I know a bit of magic that will release simple magical traps."

"Is that what this is?" I asked.

"I'm assuming it's a magical trap," Merlin said. "I've never seen one quite like it, but I don't know what else it could be."

Merlin closed his eyes and moved the fingers of his free hand around, but nothing happened. He tried it again and again, but he was still stuck to the bed.

"Damn it!" Merlin growled. "Of all the things to go wrong."

"I bet you were thinking I'd be the one to make a mistake," I laughed.

"Oh shut up," Merlin said.

"Try another spell," I said.

"I already have," Merlin said. "Nothing's working, whatever this trap is, it's not magical."

"What else could it be?" I asked.

"That remains to be seen," Merlin answered.

"What if I cut the material around your hand?" I asked.

"Your dagger will become stuck," Merlin answered.

"What if I use Excalibur?" I asked.

"That would work," Merlin answered after a moment's consideration, "but it might also cause some repercussions."

"Just yank your hand off of there, then," I said. "This is getting ridiculous. The great Merlin, trapped by a bed, I can't wait to tell everyone."

That did it for Merlin. He yanked is hand. He didn't do it all gently like I had when I pulled on my beard. Nope, he yanked like a madman, and then he pulled and twisted.

"It's coming," Merlin announced.

The cover on the bed began to twitch. It was subtle at first, but the harder Merlin struggled the more the cover began to twitch.

Merlin hadn't noticed.

"I think you better stop," I said.

"I've already gotten most of my palm free," Merlin argued.

"Look at the cover," I said.

Merlin stopped struggling and took a look. His jaw dropped at the sight of the writhing cover. It looked like large worms were underneath it and squirming around.

"Oh my," Merlin whispered.

We both looked upwards at the ceiling after we heard a large thump coming from above us. After that, we looked at each other. Merlin's eyes were as big as saucers. I looked at his hand. His palm was reddened by the struggle, but free. Four of his fingers were not so fortunate.

There was a scurrying sound on the wooden stairs that led to the attic. I gripped the handle of my dagger just a little bit tighter.

"I think it's time to leave," I said. "Yank like hell, and I'll go check out that noise."

"Right," Merlin said as he began to free himself.

I went to the doorway of the room and looked towards the stairway that led to the attic. The scurrying sound was just out of sight behind the wall and getting closer and closer. At any second whatever was making the noise would appear.

The noise stopped abruptly.

Whatever made the noise was just out of sight and waiting for me to make the first move. I stepped partially out into the hallway, keeping my dagger hidden inside the room behind me.

I gave a low whistle.

Nothing.

"Hello?" I called out.

Nothing.

I looked back at Merlin. He was still struggling to free his hand.

"I can't see anything," I said.

"Probably a good thing," Merlin said between grunts.

I looked back towards the attic stairs and saw a quick movement. Something had taken a look at me while I was talking to Merlin.

"Listen," I said. "I'm not sure who or what you are, but don't worry about us. We're leaving, so go ahead and stay where you are and nobody needs to get hurt."

The face of an old lady suddenly popped out from behind the wall. She didn't look mean or anything. She just looked like a little old lady with her grey hair up in a bun, but her eyes were a little too black and her face had absolutely no expression.

"We'll be leaving very soon," I said.

The old lady continued to stare at me. Her expression was hollow and empty. I began to wonder if she was perhaps insane. Maybe there wasn't any true evil in this house. Maybe it was just a crazy old lady.

I took a slight step back inside the room.

More of the lady popped out from behind the wall as I stepped backwards. She was wearing a blue nightshirt with little white patterns on it. Around her neck was a pearl necklace. I was starting to relax.

"Who are you talking to?" Merlin asked.

"There's an old lady," I answered.

"Don't take your eyes off of her," Merlin said.

I looked back at the old lady. More of her body was peeking out. I could now see her shoulders, and her hands were resting on the side of the wall.

"What's she doing?" Merlin asked.

"She's staying put," I answered, "but more of her body is sticking out from behind the wall."

"Don't move," Merlin said. "Don't back up and don't take your eyes off of her."

"I'm not," I said.

The old lady continued to stare at me without expression. I could see the lacy white frills on the cuffs of her nightshirt. The musty odor was getting stronger. It was the kind of odor that wasn't horrible at first, but after a while it became almost unbearable.

One of her fingers began to tap against the wall as if she were impatient.

"Just keep calm," I said. "We're on our way out. No need to get excited."

The old lady had no reaction to my words.

She was seriously starting to creep me out.

"What's she doing?" Merlin asked.

"She's tapping her fingers," I answered.

"I'm almost free," Merlin said.

I looked over at Merlin and saw that he had managed to free all but two of his fingers. I'm not sure why I turned to look at him. I didn't exactly mean to. It was more of a reaction to his words. The old lady pushed more of her body out from behind the wall. If she hadn't looked sinister before, she certainly looked so now.

She was now showing herself all the way down to her waist. One of her hands was on the ceiling and the other was still on the wall. Her body was perfectly sideways, and I couldn't understand how she could be holding herself in that position.

I stepped completely out into the hallway.

I let her see the dagger in my hand, but I didn't threaten her with it.

"Just stay right there," I said. "Don't come any closer."

"What's she doing?" Merlin asked.

"She's coming out from behind the wall," I answered. "She's also a bit sideways or something."

"Shit," Merlin mumbled.

Fingers on both her hands began to tap against the wall. The tapping was faster than before, almost frantic in its impatience.

I heard a snapping sound coming from the bedroom and Merlin was standing next to me. The old lady turned her head slightly to look at him, and a strand of dark drool poured out of her mouth.

"Get behind me," Merlin said.

I did as he asked.

"Stay where you are Widow Queen," Merlin said. "I am the wizard Merlin, and I know of your kind."

I'm not sure what Merlin said to piss her off exactly, but a skinny, ebony colored leg came out from behind the wall.

"Run," Merlin whispered in an urgent voice.

I didn't listen to him. I was frozen solid. Not necessarily out of fear, I was stuck by a morbid fascination. Every sense in my body told me to run, but I just had to see the rest of the nightmare hiding behind that wall.

More legs came forward and fastened on the walls. They were so black they almost shined in the dim hallway. I opened my mouth and tried to say something. I think I was going to warn Merlin that we should both run, but the words never came.

The old lady had reveled herself.

From the waist up, the creature had the body of an old woman. From below the waist she had the body of a large black spider. On her spider belly, which I only saw briefly as she moved into the hallway, was a bright red hourglass.

I found my voice.

"Let's make a run for it," I said as I stared at the creature before us.

The Widow Queen had never touched the floor. Her legs pressed against either side of the hallway, and her body was suspended in the air high enough to make her back scrap against the ceiling. Midway between floor and ceiling, was the large black orb of the spider's body that hung below the human anatomy.

"Both of us will never make it out the door," Merlin said. You run and I'll hold her back for you."

Merlin's fingers started to twist and contort. In a less than a second the hallway became unbearably hot.

The Widow Queen charged towards us.

"Nice fucking move, asshole," I shouted at Merlin as I took involuntary steps backwards.

Merlin held his ground, clasped his hands together, and when he pulled them apart a great burst of fire shot out from his palms and bathed the hallway.

The Widow Queen slowed down a bit, but kept coming.

"Down the stairs!" Merlin shouted.

I obeyed him immediately.

When I was at the foot of the stairs, I looked back up. Merlin was only halfway down and the Widow Queen was only a few feet away. I moved to get a better angle, intending to throw my dagger, but Merlin unleashed his next attack before I could do so.

The air around me instantly turned bitter cold. So cold that it became difficult to even move. The Widow Queen froze almost instantly, and Merlin slowly backed away until he was standing next to me.

"You did it!" I said happily.

"That's because I'm a badass," Merlin said. "Now let's get the hell out of here."

We both ran towards the front door. Four hands fumbled at the knob when something large and heavy landed on top of us.

I twisted underneath the weight, looked up, and saw the bright red hourglass of the Widow Queens stomach. I panicked, but she wasn't after me. It was Merlin that held her attention.

I scurried out from underneath her, and backed into one of the couches as Merlin struggled to keep the fangs in her wrinkled mouth from piercing his flesh.

I needed to help him.

I couldn't.

My back was held fast to the couch just as Merlin's hand was held to the bed. I struggled, but in my panic, I only succeeded in trapping my left arm as well.

"Arthur!" Merlin shouted. "Get out of here!"

"I can't," I said. "I'm stuck."

Merlin chanced a look at me and the effort cost him. The Widow Queen threw him across the room, into the rocking chair.

I'll give him credit; he wasn't dazed by the impact. He didn't even knock the rocking chair over, but he was just as stuck as I was. The Widow Queen had no use for webs. Instead, she used the furniture inside the house to trap her prey.

She came towards me.

I swung at her with my dagger. The blade didn't penetrate what I could only guess was the exoskeleton of her spider leg. She backhanded me with her human hand and left me dazed.

I knew I should be freaking out. I knew I should be fighting, but the blow I had just received made me pretty much incapable of doing anything in the cause of self-preservation.

Her old wrinkled face came to within a few inches of mine as she sized me up. I watched the lips on that expressionless face draw back and bare the almost delicate fangs that filled her mouth. The fangs dripped with venom.

"Over here, bitch!" Merlin shouted. "I'm not through with you yet."

The Widow Queen jerked her face towards Merlin, reared up to her full height, and rushed across the room to the rocking chair.

Merlin was brave, there was no doubt about that. Both his hands and both his legs were firmly stuck to the rocking chair. He was defenseless.

I shook my head in an effort to regain my senses.

I heard the sound of the rocking chair scraping across the floor and turned my head to get a better look. Another mistake, now my cheek was stuck to the couch.

Take me up

Excalibur.

The sword was speaking to me. The sword was giving me directions. Could I reach Excalibur? I tried, but the weapon was twisted beneath me. I couldn't reach far enough with my right hand.

Instead of reaching for the handle, I moved my hand directly behind me and carefully felt for the scabbard. I found it in no time at all, and pushed it, inch by inch out from behind me.

I reached for the handle once more. My fingers grasped the golden pommel. My fingers rested on the silver wrapped grip.

Pull

With only my fingers, I pulled the sword from its scabbard. Again, I had to do this inch by agonizing inch. When the sword was finally free, the scraping sound of Merlin's chair against the floor abruptly stopped. The sound was replaced by the by sounds of a struggle.

Merlin was putting up a fight.

My fingers grabbed at the blade. I slowly lifted the sword from the ground and angled it towards the couch. I pressed as hard as I could and heard a crunching sound as Excalibur bit deeply. I pushed harder, which really wasn't hard at all. The angle was all wrong for me to do much good, but Excalibur was sharp. Just the weight of the sword was doing all the work for me.

My back was free. Soon after, my left arm was free as well. Freeing my cheek was easy. Freeing the tiny bits and pieces I hadn't noticed before was even easier.

Merlin's struggling ended with the heavy thud of a body slapped on top of a wooden table.

The dining room.

I picked up my dagger, placed it back into its sheath, and moved down the hallway towards the dining room.

I moved as quickly as possible, but I was still cautious. I didn't want the creature coming up from behind me. I held Excalibur forward. The sword was all that could keep the Widow Queen from pouncing on top of me.

Would the sword cut into her?

Yes

I entered the dining room. Merlin was on top of the table, the Widow Queen was above him, forcing every inch of him to make contact with the

81

wooden surface that held him fast. Merlin was struggling, but his fate was already sealed.

Or was it?

"Widow Queen," I said.

The giant spider-lady twisted in my direction. Her face was just as expressionless as before, but her fangs were noticeable as was the dripping venom.

"I am, Arthur," I said. "I wield Excalibur."

With a motion of her many legs, the Widow Queen dropped from the ceiling and stood over Merlin on the table.

"This is your final warning," I said. "Go back to your attic or die."

"Arthur..." Merlin said.

The Widow Queen lunged towards me. I rolled clumsily away from her, swinging as I moved. The sword connected, and the tip of one of her spider legs fell to the floor with a heavy thud.

The Widow Queen screeched out a terrible noise. Her many legs stamped and slapped at the table and nearby walls. I got to my feet and noticed the flicker of sparks moving up and down the blade of Excalibur.

The sparks ignited.

I attacked.

I swung to the left and right. I used no skill. I tried no technique. Excalibur was a club. A dangerous club and I was out to kill a spider.

The Widow Queen backed away.

I pushed her into a corner, and moved in for the kill, when one of her pointed spider-legs came out like a sword thrust. I barely dodged in time, but after I did, I swung Excalibur out and removed the leg.

The Widow Queen screeched out again, and climbed backwards up the wall. I swung at her, and she stabbed at me with her dangerous legs. There was still no expression on her old face.

"Arthur!" Merlin shouted. "Can you free me?"

"Not at the moment," I answered.

The Widow Queen spread out from the corner. Her remaining legs were all dangerous, and it seemed she needed only the back two in order to stay on the wall. I couldn't get to her. Every time I tried, she'd attack me with a different leg.

She was fast. No doubt she'd been in this position before. I'd injured her, which meant I was dangerous, so she wasn't taking any chances.

Then what was she doing?

Merlin said something else, but I didn't hear what it was. The Widow Queen stabbed at me again. I moved and swung at empty air, and in that moment I understood everything. She was wearing me down, making me tired. She knew I couldn't leave. Merlin wasn't going anywhere. She could come at me over and over again until I got tired. I was in a bad spot.

I backed away.

I needed to force her to move. I needed an opportunity to hurt her. With her many legs spread out, she moved to the ceiling and followed me.

I swung out at her and missed. She thrust at me and cut through a piece of my cloak. She was still making me move. I was still expending energy.

I almost bumped into Merlin's table. That would have been a disaster if I became stuck to something while trying to fight her.

"Arthur," Merlin barked. "What are you doing?"

"Shut up," I said as I suddenly stopped backing away.

The Widow Queen hesitated when I stopped moving. Then she surged forward in an effort to force me into contact with the table. I rolled out of the way, came up, and slashed at her abdomen, right on her red hourglass.

The wound opened up, and a dark green fluid splashed onto the floor. She'd overcommitted to her attack. She wasn't as skilled as I thought she was in a fight. Then again, she probably didn't need to be. Not with all her sticky furniture.

The Widow Queen dropped to the floor, rolled around in agony, and rushed out of the room. I moved to Merlin as soon as she was out of sight.

Excalibur was burning brightly as I hacked at the wooden table. In moments, Merlin was free, but pieces of the wood were still clinging to his clothes.

The sight made me smile.

"Yeah," Merlin said. "It's easy for you to laugh. You weren't the one stuck to her table. She was about to eat me, you know?"

"Have you never lost a fight before?" I asked.

"Not in a long, long time," Merlin answered. "She's immune to most of my elemental magic, and I can't work a lot of other things inside this house."

"Good thing I have Excalibur," I said. "My dagger was useless."

"Yes," Merlin agreed. "Now let's make our way out of this house. How badly did you hurt her?"

"I slashed her open pretty good," I answered. "It might be lethal, but I have no idea."

"Then we'll move cautiously," Merlin said.

"I should probably go first," I said after Merlin attempted to get in front of me. "You're kind of useless here."

My words stung him.

They were meant to.

I walked out of the room. Dark green blood was all over the floor and the lower parts of the walls. The Widow Queen was staying on the ground, probably too injured to climb. The blood smelled sickly sweet. The odor was worse than the musty scent, and it was making me nauseated.

I could see the blood spatters leading out of the hallway and dripping off the stairs. It looked as if the Widow Queen had made her way back up into the attic. Would she die there? I hoped so, but I also knew I wasn't going to go up there and make sure.

It was time to go.

Let somebody else finish her off.

Merlin was right behind me. I passed the kitchen, headed to the front door of the house when the old lady part of the Widow Queen reached out from the doorway of the kitchen ceiling and grabbed hold of Merlin.

I cursed out loud, and chased after them.

I ran into the room, heedless of danger. The Widow Queen was hanging from the ceiling, and young Merlin was hanging below her. He struggled mightily, but he was held fast between her spider legs.

The old lady face watched me enter the room without expression. The great body turned as I tried to find an angle from which to attack.

Merlin worked something with his fingers and a brisk wind started blowing inside the house, but the spell was never finished. Upon feeling the wind, the Widow Queen reached down with her human arms and brought Merlin up to within an inch of her face.

Her bite was quick.

Merlin screamed out, and then he was thrown to the floor.

I hacked off another leg amidst the distraction. The Widow Queen was not amused. She moved towards me rapidly, but I held my ground and swung Excalibur. The blade bit deeply into one of her human arms.

The Widow Queen backed away from me cradling her now disfigured limb. I pressed the attack, wondering why Merlin wasn't backing me up.

A black spider leg jabbed out at my face.

I hadn't expected that while she was backing away, and the leg sliced open my cheek. Due to Excalibur's scabbard, the wound didn't bleed, but I knew that I'd be needing stitches if I ever made my way out of this house.

The Widow Queen made her way to the stairs, and for a brief moment took her eyes off of me. I hacked away another one of her legs.

The Widow Queen screamed out in pain and fury. She twisted and turned, splashing her green blood everywhere.

Another one of her legs jabbed out at me, but it was clumsy and easy to avoid. The monster no longer desired to feed upon me. I'd wounded her too much. All she wanted to do was escape the encounter.

I hacked at her spider body the second she turned around to crawl up the stairs. The cut was deep, and I could see her internal organs.

"Arthur," Merlin called from the kitchen.

Ignore him

I placed my foot on the stairs, intent on finishing the creature.

"Arthur," Merlin called again. "I need you."

Finish the creature

I looked from the kitchen doorway back to the wounded Widow Queen. She was crawling slowly up the stairs. Her spider body was no longer elevated. Instead, it was dragging on the steps as blood poured from the wound.

Merlin called once more.

I went to the kitchen. Merlin hadn't moved from where he'd been dropped. His skin was chalk white and he was sweating terribly.

"You're poisoned," I said.

"I can barely move," Merlin said. "My muscles are breaking down. I need you to get me out of the house. I can make an antidote."

I leaned over and picked up his dead weight, shocked to feel how light he was in my arms. I threw him over my shoulder and made my way to the front door.

I went about things slowly. I needed to make sure the Widow Queen wouldn't jump out at us again. The last I saw of her, she crawling off down the upstairs hallway and out of my sight.

Merlin and I exited the front door.

The sky was much darker than when we'd entered the house, but full darkness was still a bit away. I whistled as loudly as I could after I'd gotten some twenty or thirty feet away from the porch.

Goliath came running. I climbed on his back and rode us back to our little camp.

"Gather my leather bag from the pack horse," Merlin said as I helped him off of Goliath's back and sat him by the fire.

I did as he asked. Toad was watching silently from a log, the horses seemed panicked, and I could hear Lance moving closer to the fire.

Merlin was shivering uncontrollably. His youthful face was swollen beyond belief. He was shaking horribly, and his fingernails were bleeding. I didn't think he was going to make it.

I watched as he began gathering things from his bag of potions. I wanted to help him, but I had no idea how.

He collapsed.

I dropped down on the ground next to him and started shaking his body.

"He's not dead yet," Toad said.

"We need to wake him up," I said. "He needs to make the potion."

"What potion?" Toad asked. "What happened to him?"

"He was bitten by a Widow Queen," I said.

"Oh dear," Toad said. "We don't have much time, not even a wizard can withstand the venom of a Widow Queen for very long."

"No shit!" I shouted. "Now help me wake him up!"

"He won't be waking up," Toad said. "His insides are liquefying. Not a problem, though. I can make the potion."

"You can?" I asked.

"Certainly," Toad answered. "Now sit by the fire and calm yourself. Merlin will be out of danger by morning."

I watched as Toad rummaged through Merlin's bag. The gnome worked quickly. In no time at all, he had his ingredients all stuffed in a glass beaker. He then poured some liquid into the beaker and held the glass over the fire until it boiled.

An orange smoke began floating out of the beaker. It smelled like candy. I drank from my bottle. I drank a lot. I drank until I stopped shivering. I drank until I stopped looking over my shoulder.

"Lift his head," Toad said after the beaker had cooled down.

I stumbled over to Merlin and did as he asked.

Toad poured the water colored liquid down Merlin's throat and checked his pulse.

"He'll survive," Toad said. "That was a close one though. Another five minutes, and he might not have been so lucky."

"What's a Widow Queen?" Lance asked from somewhere behind me.

"A nasty predator," Toad said. "They have the torso of an old lady on top of a spider's body. Their venom is potent. They are almost impossible to kill, and fortunately they are extremely rare. I bet she's the only one you'll even find on this continent."

"Not anymore," I said.

"Did you kill her?" Toad asked.

"Oh yeah," I said. "I sliced her up real good."

"Did you see her die?" Toad asked.

"No," I answered honestly, "but she was in pretty bad shape when I left. There's no way she'll survive."

"Don't bet on it," Toad said.

I sat up quickly, upset with myself for getting drunk.

"We should leave," I said.

"It's too dark," Toad argued. "And Merlin needs his rest. Don't worry. A Widow Queen won't leave her house."

"We're too close to the house," I argued.

"We're fine," Toad said.

"How could you not have known she was in there?" I asked.

"I apologize for that," Toad said. "It's unfortunate, but I've already explained to you that my people don't speak of it. It could have been one of a hundred different things lurking in that house. A Widow Queen was the last thing I expected. They really are extremely rare."

"Are you positive she won't come after us tonight?" I asked.

"Widow Queens don't leave their homes," Toad said. "Now tell me, how did you survive?"

"Excalibur," I said.

"Ah," Toad said. "The magic sword, I should have known it would be able to cut into the Widow Queen. Excalibur is rumored to be able to cut through anything."

I didn't bother replying.

I also didn't sleep that night. I stayed by the fire and watched the house until dawn. No light shined from behind the windows.

Merlin awoke at dawn.

"What the...how did..." Merlin stammered.

"Toad made the antidote for you," I said. "You were lucky."

"I don't feel lucky," Merlin said.

In truth, he didn't look very lucky either. His skin was still pale, though not as pale as the night before, and his eyes had dark rings underneath them. All in all, he looked like a teenager with a pretty severe hangover.

"How long until you're ready to move?" I asked.

"I can move now," Merlin said as he sat up.

"Ah," Toad said as he walked out of the forest from where he'd disappeared a few hours ago. "Glad to see you awake. I've been out collecting some things that'll further your recovery."

Merlin took the twisted ball of leaves and weeds that Toad handed him, looked at it briefly, smiled, and began chewing on it.

The snow was falling down around us lazily, and I was thankful that it hadn't snowed much during the night. I would have frozen my ass off. At one point I wanted to get Merlin inside a tent, but Toad wouldn't let me. He thought the cold would be good for Merlin's fever.

Merlin wasn't very talkative as he chewed his pick-me-up. He was also wearing a very moody expression as I went about making breakfast.

"Are you going to pout all day?" I asked.

"Yes," Merlin answered. "Are you going to drink all day?"

"Probably," I said. "What's your problem anyway? We got the key. We did it."

"I got my ass kicked," Merlin answered honestly. "I'm not used to that, and I don't like it."

"The Widow Queen was immune to your magic," I said. "Not much you could do about that."

"Not inside that house anyway," Merlin grumbled.

"Well Toad isn't quite sure that she's dead," I said. "Apparently they're pretty hard to kill."

"They're also quite rare," Merlin added. "I doubt there are more than ten of them on the entire planet."

"Toad said they were pretty rare," I agreed.

Merlin was staring at the house angrily and not paying me the slightest bit of attention. Getting his ass kicked really did a number on him.

"You want a drink?" I asked.

"No," Merlin answered.

"It might help you wash down that humble pie," I said.

Merlin gave me just about the dirtiest look he could muster and stood up slowly. There was no doubt he was in pain. It seemed as if his entire body was sore, but he was on a mission of some sorts.

I watched as he pulled the hood of his hoodie over his head, and broke off a branch from the nearest tree. He seemed cold as he used a knife to shave down the branch and that was unusual. Merlin didn't really seem to get cold.

"Do you need a cloak or something?" I asked.

"I need you to be quiet," Merlin barked. "I'm working."

After he had the branch shaved up into a nice staff, Merlin then began carving symbols into the wood. I watched him with interest, wondering what he was up to.

"This is going to be good," Toad said as he took a seat next to me.

When the staff was finished, Merlin took a rough cloth and rubbed it smooth before rotating it slowly over the fire. The staff didn't burn, but it took on a reddish-brown color.

Merlin then walked back over to the house.

I stood up.

"I don't need you," Merlin said.

A rustle of branches over my head marked the arrival of Lance.

"What's he up to?" Lance asked.

"Revenge," Toad answered. "Wizards tend to have egos. Wizards like Merlin tend to have gigantic egos. I doubt he's been beaten by anything in centuries."

"Should we try and stop him?" Lance asked.

"Only if he tries to go inside," I said.

When Merlin reached the house, he stood outside and stared at it for a long time. Toad and Lance packed up the camp while this was going on, and I climbed up on Goliath's back and moved into a position that would allow me to see what Merlin was up to.

Merlin began walking towards the house.

I slumped in the saddle. I was tired. I was drunk, and I had no desire to fight the Widow Queen once again. She almost killed both of us already. If it wasn't for Excalibur...

Merlin didn't enter the house.

Instead, he came to a stop right in front of the crooked front porch, rammed his staff into the ground, and began dragging it around the house in a complete circle.

"What's he up to?" Toad asked after the camp was packed up and he ventured over towards me with the horses.

"I'm not sure," I answered. "He just drew a circle around the house with that staff of his."

"You know," Toad said. "It normally takes a wizard about three months to make a staff. That should give you an idea on how powerful Merlin actually is."

"How do you know about that?" I asked.

"Know about what?" Toad asked.

"Magic and stuff," I answered.

"My people use a fair bit of magic when we need to," Toad answered. "Nothing like what a wizard can do, but effective nonetheless."

Merlin stood in front of his completed circle and raised his staff towards the sky with both hands. After a few moments, his hands began to vibrate.

"Well, something's happening," I said.

"Indeed it is," Toad said.

A white streak of lightening flashed down from the grey sky and struck Merlin's staff with a deafening crack of thunder. The staff flashed with electricity. Merlin held it aloft for a moment longer, and jammed its tip into the ground once more.

The world around us went completely quiet.

I looked towards Toad, but he didn't return my gaze. He was too busy watching Merlin work his magic.

The ground began to tremble.

Smoke began to rise from the chimney of the little house. A few seconds later, I saw flames behind the windows.

Merlin twisted his staff.

The outside walls of the house began to buckle and warp. The loud sounds of snapping wood echoed forth, and the crooked front porch collapsed upon itself.

"Damn," I said.

"Just wait," Toad said.

Following the porch, the left side of the house began to tear and collapse. Thick dark smoke poured into the sky. The other side of the house began to fall as well. It looked as if an invisible giant was kicking in all the walls.

All that remained standing was the center point of the house. The front door blew off its hinges, and I could see the stairway beyond.

Merlin gave another twist of his staff.

All that remained standing was squeezed inward with a vicious implosion. The house fell, and the fire raged forth. I heard screams at that moment. They were the sounds of the Widow Queen as she met her death.

"I don't think she'll be surviving that," I said as the rubble continued to burn.

"Wow," Toad said. "Just wow."

Miniature explosions burst out of the burning rubble. They sounded as if the place were littered with small bombs that guaranteed not even the slightest piece of wood or spider would escape the flames.

The grey smoke looked unhealthy.

It looked unnatural.

The fire went out.

Nothing was left behind aside from ash. Merlin had wiped the very existence of the Widow Queen from the face of the earth. I had no idea he was that powerful.

I rode up to him.

"You feel better now?" I asked.

"Most certainly," Merlin answered in a happy and agreeable tone, "but I still don't feel very well."

"I guess now would be the time to tell you that I still haven't looked in the jewelry box," I said.

Somehow, Merlin turned even whiter.

"You haven't looked in the jewelry box?" Merlin asked.

"Nope," I answered.

"Why not?" Merlin asked.

"I was a bit distracted," I answered.

"Open it now," Merlin said.

I pulled the box from my cloak, turned it around so that the hinges were pointed towards Merlin and opened the lid. We were lucky. Inside was a heavy and rusty, iron key.

"It all worked out in the end," I said nonchalantly.

"I can't believe you never checked the box," Merlin said. "How could you be so—"

"Watch your tongue," I said. "I'm sick of listening to you. I'm sick of you putting me in dangerous situations. I saved your life in that house. I don't need you. So you can stop relying on me. If you have anything else that requires me risking my life, don't bother sending my mom after me. My answer's, no."

I rode away from him.

♣ LANCE ♣

Arthur and Merlin were getting ridiculous, but since the mission was over, they finally seemed content to ignore one another. Merlin didn't understand Arthur. It was really that simple. The king Merlin used to know was no longer.

I wasn't happy about that bit of knowledge, but there wasn't anything I could do about it. The best thing for everyone would be to leave Arthur alone. Whatever path his life was going to take, it wouldn't be the path Merlin desired for him.

Arthur drank heavily on the way back to the boat. Once we boarded, he drank even more. Toad kept filling up the bottle for him. I tried to ask him why, but Toad didn't seem to have a good answer.

Merlin sat on a crate at the front of the boat. He didn't look good. He looked as if he was sick, and he was using his staff to walk around.

"I thought the antidote was going to make you better?" I asked.

"It did make me better," Merlin answered.

"You don't look good," I said.

"I'm not good," Merlin answered. "The Widow Queen has a dangerous bite. It'll take some time for my body to recuperate."

"I see," I said. "Has your magic weakened?"

"No," Merlin said.

"Then why the staff?" I asked.

"A wizards magic is more powerful when they use a staff," Merlin said. "They can also conjure quicker and use less focus. It'll come in handy now that I'm not feeling so well."

"You've never used one before," I said.

"Not in a couple centuries," Merlin said. "I haven't needed to."

"I see," I said.

"Don't worry, Lancelot," Merlin said. "Injured or not, I'll still manage to do my part."

"Does that include riding?" I asked.

"Yes," Merlin answered.

He looked tired, but I knew he wouldn't allow himself any rest.

"What'll happen with that key?" I asked.

"Magic," Merlin answered. "Incredible magic created at the height of my power. As impressive as I can currently be, there was a time in which I was much greater. I'm not back to that level yet. I'm not even close, but in time..."

"Will you have the magic to make that key work?" I asked.

"Oh, the key has nothing to do with me anymore," Merlin answered. "I worked that magic a long time ago. This is all about Arthur now."

"What does Arthur need to do?" I asked with a tremor of worry in my voice.

"Nothing dangerous," Merlin answered. "He only needs to find the lock. The key will show him the way don't you worry."

Toad appeared next to me and smiled in my direction. His close proximity made me uncomfortable, so I moved away a bit.

"Don't worry about me, young Lancelot," Toad said. "I'm only a harmless gnome that's had a few too many drinks."

Merlin looked over at him.

"Stop filling up his bottle," Merlin said.

"You knew it was me?" Toad asked.

"Of course," Merlin answered. "How drunk is he?"

"Drunk enough to pass out," Toad said. "That's a good thing you know. He hasn't rested. He stayed up all night and watched over you and the camp."

Merlin looked a bit shocked at that information.

"First he saves your life, and then watches over you," Toad said. "I bet you didn't expect that to happen."

Merlin stared out impassively at the lake.

"He saved my life twice inside that house," Merlin said. "His skills are incredible. He's even managing to keep from being overwhelmed by the sword. It's such a waste. Imagine all the good he could do if he just had the desire."

"Rough talk about the man who saved your life," Toad said. "He'll come around, or he won't. There's nothing you can do about that except drive a wedge between the two of you."

Merlin didn't reply, but there was something in his eyes, something that made me uncomfortable.

The boat ride was uneventful.

The Ferryman took us to within a day's ride back to our town. The snow was falling hard as we disembarked the boat, and Merlin wasn't looking any better. He still hadn't yet gotten any rest.

"I thank you for helping us," Merlin said to the Ferryman.

"I took you as far as I could," the Ferryman answered, "but you aren't out of danger. Morgana's forces are still looking for you."

"Of course they are," Merlin agreed.

"If you camp here, I'll stay nearby and watch over you this evening," the Ferryman said. "Set up your camp near the dock."

"We should probably keep moving," Merlin argued.

"You won't survive a battle in your current state," the Ferryman said.

Arthur was listening to their discussion. He was unbelievably drunk, and could barely stand. Fortunately, Goliath was next to him and he could lean on the horse to keep from falling over.

"Why don't we just sleep on the boat?" Arthur asked.

"It's not good for you to spend too much time amongst the dead," the Ferryman answered. "The lost souls of the lake are developing an interest in you."

"That sucks," Arthur said.

Merlin looked long and hard at Arthur. Arthur laughed in his face and threatened to throw the key into the lake.

"We should camp here," Toad said. "You need to rest and Arthur needs to sober up a tad."

"He wouldn't be drunk at all if it wasn't for you," Merlin snapped.

"No," Toad agreed, "but he'd be going through withdrawals and that would set us back more than his drinking."

Merlin looked in my direction, shook his head, and waved his hand dismissively.

"Fine," Merlin said. "We'll leave at first light."

The camp went up quickly. Merlin used his magic, but I noticed that he was leaning on his staff harder than ever.

"Why aren't you resting?" I asked Merlin.

"There's too much at stake," Merlin answered. "I was worried about the ghosts in that lake. I could sense their interest in Arthur. Things were becoming dangerous. The dead often envy the living."

"You can rest now," I said.

"Yes," Merlin agreed. "The boatman took us farther than I thought possible. We've saved a lot of time."

Merlin made his way towards the fire and spread out a blanket on the snow. Arthur had already gone into his tent. Toad was sitting on a stack of wood by the fire on the opposite side of Merlin.

"Do you know where we are?" I asked.

"I'm pretty certain this dock didn't exist until we arrived," Toad answered.

"You didn't answer my question," I said.

"The trail we'll need to travel lies a few hours in that direction," Toad said as he pointed. "It'll be easy to find."

"I think I'll go scouting," I said.

"No need," Toad said. "We're very well protected."

"You trust the ghosts?" I asked.

"The Ferryman has offered his protection," Toad said. "His word is good. You should get some sleep. You'll need your energy tomorrow."

I told the little gnome goodnight and went into my tent. It was warm in the tent. I think Merlin must have used his magic on them somehow. Whatever, it was comfortable and I found myself quickly relaxing.

I awoke to a commotion early the next morning.

Merlin was still looking ill, but he was cleaning up our campsite anyway. Arthur was getting sick over in some bushes. Toad was supervising from the top of Merlin's shoulder, and the snow kept coming.

"Are we going to eat anything?" I asked.

"No time," Merlin said. "The attack could start at any moment."

I felt a tingling around my neck and shoulders.

"I need to go and do my thing," I said. "Will you wait for me?"

"No," Merlin answered. "Just catch up to us when the hour is up."

"What if there's an attack?" I asked.

"I'll handle it," Merlin said.

I ran into the forest, found the nearest tree, and climbed. I was high up in the sky when my power vanished, but I was still nicely concealed. Twenty minutes later, I saw tree's moving not far from my position, and watched as Merlin, Arthur, and Toad moved into the forest.

I wasn't worried about losing them. I knew where they were headed, but I wasn't without worry. Merlin looked horrible. Arthur was sick. The only one doing well was Toad, but Toad wasn't going to be much help in a fight.

I should be there with them. I hated my condition. I should be following them through the woods, but right now I was stuck high up in the trees. Climbing down without my powers would be suicide.

Thirty minutes or so later I saw trees swaying towards my left. I could also hear dogs barking and Death Reapers shouting. They were far enough away from my group, but seeing and hearing them made me nervous.

I looked for other signs of activity in the forest. Far off in a clearing was a band of about twenty Death Reapers. I watched as they gathered water from a stream, and then something large stepped out of the trees and joined them.

A giant.

My first look at a giant, and even from a great distance it looked impossible to defeat. How were we going to beat such a fearsome enemy? Its height and width were frightening. The hair covering its body gave it a wildness that I'd never seen before. It walked on bent legs. It slouched terribly, but a single blow from one of those creatures would kill a normal man.

More trees swayed in the forest.

Our enemy was numerous.

If so many of the Death Reapers and giants were in the forest looking for us, how many were going to be attacking Camelot? Their army must be massive. Not even the Gods of the Forest could bring down an army of giants.

I was scared.

The Black Knight was fearsome enough. These creatures were on an entirely different level. Even if Merlin managed to recreate the Camelot of old, how could anything withstand an assault by an enemy so large?

I waited for the change.

When the tingling sensation finally came, I smiled in relief. When I was back to my usual self, I leapt into the air. The free-fall was glorious. I caught a branch ten feet from the forest floor, and took off in the direction of my friends.

I moved silently.

In no time at all, I encountered another group of Death Reapers. They weren't exactly quiet. The two giants with them ripped trees from the ground as they pushed into the forest. The Death Reapers were laughing and having a good time. Clearly, they weren't intimidated by the prospect of running into an attack. Why would they be? They had giants with them.

I decided to do something about that.

I dropped to a low branch as soon as the giants passed underneath me. I waited until the entire group passed by, and silently jumped on the back of the last Death Reaper's horse.

I pulled the twin blades from the scabbards on my back, and went to work. The first Death Reaper dropped lifeless from his horse without a sound. I moved on to the next Death Reaper and removed his head.

It was easy work.

I killed five of them before a horse spooked and burst into a run with a headless corpse still somehow clinging to his saddle. The Death Reapers went berserk after that. It didn't help them much though. I still took out another three before the giants turned around and noticed my attack.

"What?" Shouted a giant. "What's happening?"

"Help us!" Shouted a Death Reaper.

"What's happening?" Asked the giant.

They weren't the sharpest. That was easy enough to see. I kept them in the corner of my eye as I moved from horse to horse. The giants couldn't understand what was happening because they couldn't see me.

"The little bush is attacking them," the other giant said.

"Little bush?" The first giant questioned.

In no time at all, all the Death Reapers were dead. They should have spurred their horses and made an escape. Instead, they were hoping for the giants to rescue them.

I stopped moving.

The giants were scratching their heads.

"Now what?" The second giant asked.

"Let's stomp," The first giant said.

I briefly wondered what he meant by that, but when he raised his leg high in the air and stomped down on the dead Death Reapers with his foot, I understood him very quickly.

Both of the giants began to pound the ground with their feet like a human would step on a spider. However, the giants weren't anywhere near me. They were just stomping the corpses. The scene was grisly in no time. The smashed remains and their bloody feet were disgusting.

Everything went downhill the moment one of the giants started stomping in my directions. I suddenly felt very foolish. I waited until the last possible second, but I had to move.

"The little bush," the giant said. "It's running away."

"Smash it!" The other giant shouted.

They chased after me and I ran. I couldn't vanish high up in the trees. The giants were too tall for that nonsense. I could only run, but as long as I was moving, they'd be able to catch glimpses of my movement and give chase.

I needed to get some distance.

I moved faster in the trees.

I leapt to a high branch, and immediately jumped to another tree. I spun around the trunk of the tree, and set off in another direction. I planned on losing them with distance and direction changes.

The giants pursued. They smashed trees and roared out in anger, but eventually I lost them. They couldn't destroy the entire forest. They had to give up.

I let out a sigh of relief as they vanished back into the trees almost without noise. They could be stealthy themselves when the need arose.

I set out after Arthur.

On the way, I came across some more groups of Death Reapers, but I didn't bother them. I didn't want to deal with the giants again.

I was moving quickly through the trees. Nothing was slowing me down, but it still took some time to catch up to my friends. They'd covered a lot of ground very quickly.

Neither Arthur nor Merlin looked very good.

Arthur was still drinking.

I made some noise as I landed into a thicket of bushes behind them. Merlin looked over at me. Toad gave a little wave, but Arthur didn't even turn in my direction.

"This forest is filled with Death Reapers and giants," I said.

"We've been avoiding them all morning," Toad said.

I found that strange as well. It was almost as if Toad had taken over the leadership of our little group. Merlin was normally the one who answered questions, and prepared the food. I hoped Toad was a decent chef, because he was busily preparing a meal without any kind of fire to warm it up.

"I'm not hungry," Arthur said as he got up and walked over to the bushes to get sick.

"Is he still throwing up?" I asked.

"He's been doing it all morning," Toad said.

"How are you feeling, Merlin?" I asked.

"About the same," Merlin mumbled.

"I'm going up into the trees," I said. "I'll keep a lookout while everyone rests."

"Good idea," Toad said.

I climbed until I broke past the tops of most trees. I could see in all directions. Snow covered trees were swaying all around us. That meant giants. The trees here were too old and thick to be moved by regular sized people. One such group was headed towards us, but were still a ways off.

I kept an eye on them from the trees until a low whistle from Toad told me they were ready to ride once again.

Arthur had started drinking once more, and the snow was falling harder than ever.

"This isn't good," Toad complained. "We're leaving tracks. Merlin can you do anything?"

Merlin looked up from where he was slumped over his saddle. His hood was covering most of his face. He never gave a response, just a slight side to side shake of his head.

I landed on the pack horse behind Toad, who was standing on the horses head. He started at my sudden appearance.

"You're gonna scare me right off this horse, demon-child," Toad said.

"Can we move any faster?" I asked.

"I'm not sure Merlin would be able to stay mounted on his horse," Toad said. "He's much worse off then he's letting everyone know."

"There are Death Reapers and giants headed towards us," I said. "And we aren't moving fast enough."

Toad looked concerned. He looked from left to right, and pointed to some bushes.

"Grab some of those long leaves," Toad said. "Cut them into strips, and use them to tie Merlin to his saddle."

I was off in a flash. I gathered the long leaves Toad had pointed to, and jumped from a tree onto the back of Merlin's horse.

The cutting went quickly, and I was left with a strong fibrous rope like material. I used the material to tie Merlin's hands to the horn of the saddle, and his feet to the stirrups.

I jumped back to Toad's horse.

"What about Arthur?" I asked.

"I good," Arthur slurred out in a drunken voice.

Both Toad and I gave him a funny look.

"I'm serious," Arthur said. "I feel better now. I can do this."

"What do you think?" Toad asked looking back at me.

"I've seen him ride in worse conditions," I said.

"Then let's pick up the pace," Toad said.

A lone Death Reaper stepped out of a thick tangle of trees directly in front of us. He smiled and his silver eyes glinted. He pulled his sword from its scabbard slowly as the green fog flowed out through the trees behind him and reflected off the pure white snow.

"I can take him," Arthur said as he nudged Goliath into a gallop.

"Wait!" I shouted out. "There's too much fog. There are more of them."

Arthur either didn't hear me or chose to ignore me. Before he reached the Death Reaper, a dozen more stepped out of the trees. Arthur didn't stop. Instead, he drew Excalibur and charged straight into battle.

"Take Merlin and get going," I said to Toad. "I'll help Arthur."

I leapt from the horse, grabbed the nearest branch, and took off into the trees. I was above Arthur in only a few seconds. He'd already killed three Death Reapers. We were lucky that this group didn't have any giants with them.

They did have some dogs, but Goliath would kick out at any of them foolish enough to get too close while Arthur hacked away at the enemy soldiers.

I dropped into the battle.

I hacked and slashed as the snow fell heavily around us. The splashes of red blood stood out starkly against the white background. The screams of the injured and dying broke the relative quiet of the wintery forest.

"Arthur," I said in the midst of battle. "We need to run. We're making too much noise."

"Shut up," Arthur growled, his eyes red as blood.

Excalibur had a hold on him. I'm not sure if it was the stress and fear, or if it was the alcohol, but Excalibur had found a way inside of Arthur.

I stood back from the battle and watched my friend go to work. He was as deadly as a snake. The Death Reapers looked like amateurs against him. Blood was flying everywhere, and trees were tumbling over as the magical blade cut straight through them.

I jumped on the back of Goliath.

"Arthur," I said. "More Death Reapers will be coming. We need to get out of here."

Arthur ignored me.

The last of the Death Reapers dropped into a puddle of his own blood and gore. Arthur was breathing heavily. He was also smiling.

He yanked Goliath from left to right looking for anything else worth killing. Excalibur burned brightly from all the blood.

"There's no one left," I said. "We need to get out of here."

"I'm sick of you," Arthur said. "I'm sick of all of you."

I was about to say something back to pacify him, but the very ground began to tremble all around us.

"It's too late," I said.

Loud roars came from the forest behind us. We could feel the vibrations inside our chests. I took a look. More Death Reapers had arrived. I could see them running towards us through the snow. I watched as they weaved around the trees with their rusty blades held high over their heads.

Arthur turned Goliath towards them and charged.

"No Arthur," I said. "They aren't alone."

My words fell on deaf ears. All Arthur cared about was death. He was in his element. My friend was gone. All that remained was a red-eyed, bloodthirsty monster.

Goliath twisted and turned around the trees. The Death Reapers tried to use their superior numbers against us, but they couldn't pin us down. Everywhere I looked I saw blood and death as Goliath moved and Arthur struck. The blood stood out starkly against the snow.

That's when the trees before us parted in a sudden and violent ripping sound that brought Goliath to a halt.

Two giants stood before us.

They had snow on their shoulders.

They looked at all the blood and licked their lips.

Goliath was making odd noises, and backing away from them.

"Kill him!" One of the Death Reapers shouted to the giants as he pointed his finger towards Arthur.

The hunched giant leaned forward to get a better look at Arthur, and Arthur charged straight for him. Goliath began screaming out angry noises, but he followed Arthurs command. The massive leg of the giant rose into the air, but right as it came crashing down towards us, Goliath veered out of the way.

Arthur wasn't finished. He rode immediately for the other leg, and slashed out with Excalibur. Blood splashed and the giant screamed. I looked behind us as Arthur rode away. I watched as the giant fell to the ground with a slashed tendon.

The other giant reached out for us from the side. More blood splashed out as Arthur swiped at the giants fingers, and kept riding.

Goliath came to a stop about forty feet away. Arthur turned him and faced the Death Reapers and the still standing giant. Goliath reared up in challenge. The giant roared in anger.

I heard the crinkle of leather gloves as Arthur tightened his grip on Excalibur, and more giants stepped out from behind the trees all around us.

"There's too many!" I gasped.

Goliath shifted back and forth wondering what to do as Arthur cursed under his breath. With a growl of frustration, Arthur spun his great horse around, and retreated into more trees.

The giants were right behind us. So were the mounted Death Reapers. The snow was getting deeper and deeper, which served to slow down the small horses of the Death Reapers, but the giants were unaffected. Goliath himself was a bit slower than normal, but not nearly as much as the enemy horses.

We rounded a small hill, and leapt over a frozen stream. I couldn't see Arthur's face, but I could see the clouds of steam from his breath. He was breathing hard as if he himself was the one running.

"Should I get off the horse?" I asked.

"Stay where you are," Arthur said.

We moved down a hill, just as a giant broke through the trees behind us. Its large hand reached for us, and I slashed at it with my knife. My blade bit deeply, but I severed nothing. The giant roared in confusion and anger.

Goliath made a sharp turn towards the left as a rock flew at us, and very quickly we were surrounded by denser forest.

Arthur didn't slow down. He pushed Goliath harder than ever, and found a stream to follow. We moved slowly after that, and the giants crashed around in the forest surrounding us.

"We're going the wrong direction," I said.

"Are you sure?" Arthur asked.

"Yes," I answered.

"What we need is a good trail," Arthur said. "If we can find one I'm positive Goliath can outdistance them."

"The trail we need is in that direction," I said as I pointed behind us, "but that trail leads us back to town."

"It'll work," Arthur said.

"We'll be leading them right to our doorstep though," I argued.

"They'll be there soon enough anyway," Arthur said.

He spun Goliath around and moved slowly in the correct direction. We climbed up a short hill that bordered the stream, and moved cautiously back into the forest.

The sounds of crashing trees and cursing Death Reapers were everywhere. We'd freeze if they seemed too close and wait for them to pass by. Excalibur was back inside the scabbard. Arthur was once again in control.

"Keep us pointed in the right direction," Arthur said as the enemy got closer and we were forced to change directions. "I'm lost in this forest."

"Head towards your right," I said.

Arthur did as I asked him. Goliath was picking his steps carefully. He too seemed to understand our need for stealth.

From our right, we heard the roar of a giant. Goliath froze. From our left, we heard the sounds of approaching Death Reapers. The green fog was all around us. Arthur looked back the way we'd come. His eyes were no longer red. He was thinking about backtracking.

"Don't do it," I said. "They could be following our tracks."

A group of Death Reapers came forward in front of us. They weren't mounted, but they blew a horn to summon reinforcements. Arthur didn't skip a beat, he charged Goliath straight towards them.

Without even needing to draw his sword, Arthur charged through them and broke freely into the forest.

Our moment of triumph was short lived. At least ten giants were gaining on us. As Goliath weaved around the trees, the giants charged straight through them. Goliath began to whinny in fear.

I kept a lookout behind us and let Arthur worry about what was in front of us. The giants got closer and closer. I readied one of my knives. Behind the giants was a growing group of mounted Death Reapers.

Goliath jumped over an embankment, and took a sharp right turn that almost knocked me off his back. The ride became smoother, and much faster. I quickly realized that we'd finally come to the trail.

The giants were too close.

Soon they'd be on top of us. Goliath couldn't outrun them. I could only do so much with my throwing knives. I wasn't going to be able to save us. I was going to fail.

That's when I noticed that the mounted Death Reapers were beginning to pass by the giants. I also noticed that the giants were falling behind all of us.

The giants could no longer match our pace.

They didn't have the endurance that Goliath had. Now all we had to contend with were the Death Reapers, and Goliath was proving to be much faster than their horses.

"We're doing it!" I shouted. "Don't slow down!"

"I don't plan on it," Arthur laughed with relief.

"Do you think we can keep this pace until we get home?" I asked.

"No," Arthur said. "We'll need to slow down a bit, but that's not a problem, the Death Reapers will need to slow down as well."

"Horses can't run forever," I said.

After a while we could no longer even see the Death Reapers following us. We still continued to ride hard. Goliath let us know when he needed to slow down, and that was fine by us. The Death Reapers were almost a forgotten memory.

We let the horse relax into a quick walk. That seemed to be enough for Goliath. That animal had no problems letting us know when he was unhappy about something, and so far he wasn't complaining.

The forest around our well worn trail was quiet. As if all the falling snow had a muffling effect.

I didn't like it a bit.

"Do you think I should climb up a tree and scout ahead?" I asked.

"Yes," Arthur said.

I jumped for the nearest overhanging branch, moved through the closest trees until I found a tall one, and climbed as quickly as possible. I could see no signs of our enemy in all the snow covered forest, but I could see up ahead on the trail and I could see familiar landmarks in the distance.

I smiled.

I dropped from my high branch and fell almost to the forest floor. At the last possible second, I reached out for a low branch and grasped it with one hand. The branch bent under my slight weight, but held up without difficulty.

Then I really started moving. From tree to tree, and from branch to branch I travelled. Finally, I had passed Arthur and waited for him to arrive on another branch that hung low over the trail.

As Arthur passed, I dropped behind him on Goliath's long back.

"Did you see anything?" Arthur asked.

"Nothing bad," I answered.

Arthur didn't ask any more questions, so he was surprised when we rounded a corner and came up upon Merlin and Toad. Being reunited with the two of them didn't exactly make Arthur happy, but at least it didn't put him in a bad mood.

Merlin looked shrunken underneath the blanket wrapped around him. I couldn't see his face beneath the hood, and he gave us no acknowledgement that he was aware of our arrival.

"Any problems?" Toad asked.

"Yes," Arthur answered. "We're being pursued."

"How far behind us?" Toad asked.

"We have a decent head start," Arthur answered, "but we should pick up the pace."

"I don't know that we can," Toad said. "Merlin isn't doing so well."

Arthur looked over at Merlin. I couldn't read his expression as he studied the injured wizard. Was he worried? Was he indifferent? I hadn't a clue.

"Camelot is less than an hour away. Perhaps Merlin and I should hide in the forest," Toad said. "At least until he feels better. That way you can make your way back home safely."

Arthur continued to stare at Merlin.

"I'm not leaving him," Arthur said.

"There's no reason to risk yourself," Toad said.

"He's the only one that knows what to do with the key," Arthur said before riding off and ending the conversation.

I moved over to the pack horse and sat next to Toad. Underneath the gnome's bushy beard, I could see the concern etched throughout the wrinkles in his face.

"We aren't far from Camelot," Toad said.

"That's a good thing considering we're being followed," I said.

"We'll be leading the enemy to your home," Toad said. "Our actions could start the battle prematurely."

"The battle has already started," Merlin said. "It started about an hour ago."

Merlin's sudden announcement caught the both of us off guard. First of all, we didn't really even think he was awake, and also because we had no clue that the battle had commenced.

"Are you sure?" I asked.

"The land cries out in protest," Merlin answered. "I can feel it all around me. Stronghold Wall is being threatened."

"Is it a frontal assault?" I asked.

"Yes," Merlin answered. "There's no need for trickery, not with the giants on their side."

"We'll use a rear entrance to get into Camelot," Toad said.

"No," Arthur said from up ahead on the path. "We're going to charge right through. It's the fastest way, and just because the Death Reapers are attacking from the front doesn't mean they won't have men waiting in the forests around Stronghold wall."

"How do you plan on charging through an entire army?" I asked.

"That's easy," Arthur answered. "They won't expect a single rider to come at them from behind, and besides, I have the fastest horse."

"That's a horrible idea," Toad said. "Tell him, Merlin."

Merlin had once again passed out.

"Arthur," I said. "Merlin can't ride through that kind of chaos."

Arthur came to an abrupt stop, turned Goliath around, and rode quickly up to Merlin. A few slashes with his dagger and Arthur had pulled Merlin onto Goliath with him. He situated the unconscious teenager on the saddle in front of him, and wrapped an arm around his chest.

"I'll be taking the wizard," Arthur said. "You and Toad hop on over to Merlin's horse. Lance, your job is to protect Toad. I doubt much will come your way. The Death Reapers and giants probably won't even notice him, and there's no reason to attack a riderless horse."

I didn't like Arthur's plan.

I thought Excalibur had burned away most of the alcohol in Arthur's system. Had he started drinking again without me noticing? The plan was insane; hopefully it was insane enough to work.

✤ ARTHUR ✤

The sun was setting as we rounded a hill and had our first clear look at our home. The lanterns and torches had already been lit around the town. What was once a beautiful forest in front of the gates of the town had all been cleared away. In its place was a snow covered battlefield. Our forces fought against the Death Reapers and the giants valiantly, as small fires burned all around them, and a green fog drifted lazily throughout.

Giants pounded against Stronghold Wall, not on the wall itself, but upon the magical shield that rose up from the wall and protected the town. Horses and riders rode aimlessly around. I thought I could hear screams drift across what was left of the forest.

Men beat their swords against the shields of the enemy. Archers shot their arrows. Hundreds of small battles raged around a much larger frontal assault.

A small gasp came from behind me.

"We'll do what we can," I told Lance.

"Look what they did to the forest," Lance said. "Look at how many of them there are."

Lance was right to be shocked. We'd been in this position before, but even then the enemies hadn't been so numerous. This current army dwarfed what had attacked us last time, and that wasn't even counting the forty of fifty giants that I could see.

"Can the key...?" Lance tried to ask.

"Merlin says it can," I answered. "We'll take his word for it and do our part. What do you think, Toad?"

Toad took a while to reply.

"In all my days," Toad said. "I've never seen destruction like this. I've never seen this kind of brutality."

"It'll get worse," I said.

We waited for Lance to undergo his change, but as soon as he was back, I rode forward along trail and the others followed me.

Our home was under siege, and even though I really wanted no part of any of this, I had no other choice. I had to act. If I didn't, I'd have no home to return to. I motioned to the others to stay quiet and rode off the trail.

Inside the forest, we made our way to the battlefield. From our position right at the edge of the clearing we got a close up look at the battle. Our soldiers were tough, but the odds were horribly stacked against them. A single giant caused death with each savage blow he struck.

The main body of our enemy's forces was off towards our left. Their leader wore blood red armor. He was sitting boldly on top of a reddish colored, armored horse that was almost as big as Goliath. He issued commands and sent forth battalions as needed.

Who was he?

Why did his armored form bother me so much? He wasn't nearly as big as the Black Knight. What had he done to become the leader of this vile army?

I could pick him off from my position if I had a bow. Gwen could do it for sure. She was an excellent archer. I stopped that line of thought immediately. I never entertained any thoughts that concerned Gwen.

"Who is he?" Lance asked.

"No clue," I answered.

We couldn't help but watch him for a bit. There was something scary about him. Something about the way that he moved as he calmly ordered his army out into the battlefield to kill our neighbors.

"We should do this now," Lance said. "I'm not sure how much longer our people can hold out."

"Alright," I said tearing my eyes away from the Red Knight. "Let's go."

I grabbed Merlin just a little bit tighter and gave Goliath a nudge. We stepped out into the clearing, and gained speed. Lance, astride Merlin's horse wasn't far behind. We weaved in and out of the enemy soldiers. In the beginning, none of them bothered to attack us. We weren't wearing the tunics or armor of Camelot, and that seemed to confuse them.

I rode past a battalion of reinforcements on horseback, and our luck abruptly changed. A horn blew from somewhere behind me, the Death Reapers turned around at the sound and saw me galloping past them.

They gave chase.

Goliath swerved around a burning stump, and within a second, I had Death Reapers all around me. I pulled Excalibur free, and casually cut down the nearest of them with a single backhanded swing. The blade sparked into flames, and the gig was truly up.

Shouts rang out all over the battlefield.

"The king has entered the battle!"

"Bring down the king!"

"Beware Excalibur!"

In mere moments, I was the most popular person out there, and I wasn't liking that one bit. I slashed and hacked at any Death Reaper foolish enough to get too close, but it wasn't easy, I was still holding on to Merlin with my left hand.

Groups of Death Reapers crowded around me. It was all I could do to keep from being pulled off of Goliath's back.

"Arthur's here!"

"Protect Arthur!"

"Protect the king!"

The cries from the soldiers of Camelot began to reach my ears, and I urged Goliath to move faster in an effort to keep the enemy forces from slowing our momentum any more. In the distance, I saw our soldiers begin to surge forward in an effort to reach me. If I could get to them, I was confident that I could make it, but Goliath was tired. He'd been traveling all day and hadn't eaten a thing.

Excalibur sizzled and crackled as the snow fell upon the burning blade. I wheeled Goliath in circles, looking for a way to break through the growing numbers of Death Reapers.

All I could see was snow, blood, swords, and men.

"Arthur," Lance shouted. "Where do we go?"

I couldn't answer him.

I could only slash and hack.

Blood and snow.

My world had become blood and snow. Excalibur wanted back in. I could feel the sword scratching around inside my mind. My stomach was sick. I was tired. Goliath was slowing down. The growing number of bodies pushing against him had finally gotten results. It was a miracle that I was still alive.

In panic, I struck out harder and faster knowing that the strike which would end my life was only moments away. I hammered the Death Reapers away from me, but I couldn't keep them back. They came from all sides, and seemed endless in number.

Goliath reared back in fear, and I almost fell off his back.

"Arthur!" Someone shouted over the furious sounds of battle. "I'm coming!"

I knew the voice, thought it currently sounded strained. I knew the voice. Could he get to me in time? A spear shot out and sliced open the side of Goliath's neck before penetrating my upper thigh.

Both of us screamed out in pain.

I cut the spear in half, but part of it was still in my leg. I chanced a glance at Goliath's neck. It was bleeding, but he'd survive.

A sword stabbed at my face, only luck prevented it from piercing underneath my chin. Hands grabbed at my cloak, and Goliath went insane. He bucked up and kicked out. The great horse spun in circles creating a distance from our numerous enemies.

I chanced a glance back towards Lance.

All was well with him. As I figured, the Death Reapers paid no attention to what they believed was a riderless horse. Nonetheless, he too was trapped inside all the commotion.

And then it was over.

A group of mounted soldiers charged into the Death Reapers all around me. Their shields deflected the enemy swords and by pure might and surprise, they dispersed the crowd enough for the foot soldiers to come in and surround me.

Wayne, in full armor, rode into my circle of protection.

"Are you hurt?" Wayne asked from beneath his helmet.

"I'm fine," I answered. "I have the key. I need to get inside the gate."

"Is that Merlin?" Wayne asked.

"The gate!" I shouted. "I need to get inside the gate!"

Wayne stared at Merlin for just a moment longer. His two axes were dripping blood.

"Follow me," Wayne said as he made a circling motion with his hand to the other mounted soldiers nearby.

A group of maybe ten of us galloped away from the skirmish. Lance was following closely behind. I blinked snow out of my eyes. All I could see were fallen bodies from both sides of the fight. Blood, blackened by the night was everywhere.

We charged forward.

Giants were still pounding against the barrier. Waves of blue energy reverberated up into the night sky. I quickly noticed that the waves of energy were being distorted. The giants were distorting the magical defenses.

Sooner or later, they were going to break through Stronghold Wall. I needed to move quickly, but I wasn't sure how we were going to get around them.

That's when Wayne took over.

He shouted out orders to his fellow soldiers, and they split up into two groups. Each group rode directly towards the two giants on either side of the large stone entry way. Each group attacked. One after another they hacked and stabbed at the legs of the giants as they rode by.

The two giants roared out in pain and immediately gave chase. The way had been cleared. Without slowing down, I charged Goliath towards safety.

Out of the corner of my eye, just as I passed the safety of the stone gate, I saw one of the groups get trampled by the stomping feet of one of the giants. Was that Wayne's group? I didn't know. I was panicking. A part of me wanted to ride back out and try and help.

Merlin put his hand on my arm.

"We must save everyone," Merlin said in a weak voice.

Goliath came to a stop. He was breathing heavily. The snow was building up inside the gates. It was over two feet high in some places. I saw archers scattered around the length of the wall. From their position, they could fire endlessly and not have to worry about enemy attack...at least while the protection of Stronghold Wall lasted.

Lance rode up behind me.

"Now what?" I asked as I yanked the remains of the spear still stuck in my leg free.

"Take out the key," Merlin said quietly.

I did as he asked. The key was warm in my hand.

"Where does it lead you?" Merlin asked.

"Get the fuck out of here," I said. "It's not leading me anywhere."

"It will," Merlin said, "but you must pay attention."

"Then we're in trouble," I said. "Because this key isn't talking to me."

Goliath shifted at a sudden noise from the battlefield. The key grew warmer in my hand. Wait a second, was it that easy? I moved the key back towards the battlefield. It grew colder. I then moved it towards town, and the key grew warmer.

"I think I got it," I announced.

Using the key as a compass, I rode towards where it was warmest. My leg was throbbing in pain, as were numerous other places that I hadn't noticed when I was in the thick of things.

"You must hurry," Merlin said in that weak voice. "The magic of Stronghold Wall is beginning to fail."

"I'm going as fast as I can," I said.

I needed a drink. I didn't care about the cartwheels inside my stomach. I needed a drink. Nope, scratch that. I needed a lot of drinks.

I rode down the road. I passed snow covered farms and homes. I passed groups of soldiers running towards the battlefield. I saw the people who weren't fighting, standing alongside the road and watching the battle.

I passed by a wagon filled with injured soldiers. I saw medical tents set up, and I saw more blood on the snow leading up to the entrances.

In a short amount of time, I had entered the town square. The key was growing warmer and warmer as I passed the shops and entered the wooded park.

Eventually, I came upon a stream inside the park. The stream was only about two feet deep and five feet across. In the summer, the kids like to feed the fish that swim in the stream.

"We're here," Merlin said. "I can feel it. The land is ready. Camelot is ready."

I heard screams coming from behind us, and then I heard people shouting that the giants had broken through.

My heart sped up inside my chest.

"Calm yourself," Merlin whispered. "Every key has a lock. Find the lock."

I hopped off Goliath's back, and walked over to the stream. The stream stopped flowing as I approached. The surface of the water began to bubble. A part of me was a bit worried about what might be coming out to meet me.

I shouldn't have worried.

A three foot column of rock silently emerged from the water. I touched the surface of the wet rock, wondering what to do. The key was almost burning my hand through my glove. I wiped the stream sludge off the top of the column and found the surface of a circular key hole.

Was it really that simple? Well, why wouldn't it be? It wasn't exactly hard to pull Excalibur from the stone. Why would it be any harder to find the lock?

I looked back at Merlin for some guidance. Merlin appeared to have passed out.

"Lance?" I asked.

"Do it," Lance said from a tree above me.

"Toad?" I asked.

"Do it," Toad answered from just a few feet behind me.

I placed the damn near burning key inside the lock. It fit easily as if it were oiled, but nothing happened.

"You need to turn the key," Lance said.

"No shit," I said. "I'm just being careful."

"This isn't Raiders of the Lost Ark," Lance said. "Don't worry about booby-traps."

I turned the key until I heard a loud click and stepped back. Toad moved with me, I also heard a soft noise that meant Lance moved away as well.

More bubbles popped at the surface of the stream around the base of the column as we watched, but nothing else happened.

"Did I do something wrong?" I asked.

"I don't think so," Toad answered.

We watched in silence a bit longer. From the direction of the front gate, I heard shouts and screams. I even heard the roar of a giant. We were definitely being breached.

"Well, fuck this," I said as I pulled my bottle out and took a swig.

"What are you doing?" Lance asked.

"Having a drink," I said.

"Now?" Lance asked.

"Don't you get it?" I asked in return. "It's over. The enemy is getting past Stronghold Wall. We've lost. I'm going to have a drink, find Wayne if he's still alive, find his family, find my mom, and make a run for it."

"Where will you run?" Toad asked.

"Far away from here," I said. "Far away from Merlin."

The column slid back into the water with a slight grinding noise.

"Maybe it's working," Lance commented.

The shouts and screams were getting louder. I could now hear people running past the park. I could even feel the slight tremors as the ground shook beneath the feet of the giants.

As the column vanished beneath the water, the water once again began to flow.

"I don't know..." I said.

I was watching the water. I didn't know what else to look for. I was hoping that something would happen. We needed something to happen.

"The fog," Toad said.

I looked over at him.

"What about it?" I asked.

"The fog is dissipating," Toad said.

He was right. There was a low level of green fog surrounding everything, and now we appeared to be in a clearing, away from the fog. It seemed as if some invisible force was holding it back.

People began running through the park.

"I need to find my mom," I said. "She'll be in one of those medical tents near the front gate."

"What about the key?" Toad said.

"What else can I do?" I asked. "I put the key in the lock, nothing happened."

"Something will happen," Toad said. "Something is happening."

"It's taking too long," I said. "Maybe we were too late. I can't wait any longer. I need to find my mom. I need to—"

"Look at the stream!" Lance announced.

Toad and I both looked. The running stream was running a bit too fast, and only getting faster.

"Uh oh," I said under my breath.

"What do you mean uh oh?" Lance asked.

"We probably need to take a step back," I said as the water began to overflow the edges. "There was a lot of water when I freed Excalibur. This could go very badly very quickly."

"This was supposed to help us," Lance said.

"Magic sucks," I said as I took another drink.

"What should we do?" Lance asked.

"Find my mother," I said as water began to flow past the snow and threaten to soak our feet.

Without waiting for another word from Lance or Toad, I moved towards Goliath and mounted his back behind Merlin.

"Let's go," I said just as small explosions began to happen under the surface of the stream. Water was shooting high into the air.

Toad ran towards me, leapt in the air, climbed up my leg, and we were off.

"I don't understand this magic," Toad shouted from Merlin's shoulder.

"It's Merlin's magic," I said.

"His level of skill..." Toad said. "I can't even comprehend his ability."

I looked over my shoulder. Merlin's horse was following us, but Lance wasn't riding him. Instead, Lance was in the trees above us.

I rode Goliath through the park. I didn't bother sticking to any of the paths. Instead, I jumped over bushes and skirted trees in an effort to create as much distance as possible from the stream.

The green fog had all but vanished from the park. I noticed that it was also missing from the street as well when we emerged from the park, and instantly came to a sudden stop. The town square was filled with people.

Frightened people.

Screaming people.

I looked for the cause of their fear.

A giant was making his way down Main Street. There was another behind him, heading off towards a large section of homes, but this one was headed right towards the town square.

Behind both of them, far in the distance, I saw yet a third giant climbing through a large hole in the magical barrier above Stronghold Wall.

"Damn!" I shouted as Goliath twisted and turned amongst all the people pushing and shoving against him.

I needed to move quickly. If Goliath got freaked out enough, he was sure to start kicking at people. He wasn't exactly the friendliest horse in the world.

I moved Goliath back into the park. The ground was already wet and splashing as I maneuvered Goliath back through the trees.

"What are you doing?" Toad asked.

"I'm going to try and go around all these people," I said.

"Those people are in danger," Toad said.

"I'm looking for my mother," I said.

"You are Arthur," Toad said. "You are the king. You must aide those people. They need you."

Goliath stopped.

I took another swig from my bottle and suppressed a gag as the harsh liquid hit the back of my throat.

Everything sort of went into slow motion. I closed my eyes and concentrated on my breathing. I didn't want to be here. Everything was supposed to be finished.

I drew Excalibur from the scabbard on my hip and turned Goliath around. I was going to get killed. I just knew it. I was going to get killed.

I pushed my way back to the street. I shouted at people to let me pass. I heard them calling my name. I heard them asking for help.

When the way was clear, I charged towards the giant. The monster didn't even notice me till I was right on top of him and slashing at his leg. He was too busy smashing some poor bastard into the road with his feet.

He sure as hell noticed me after I cut open his leg though. Unfortunately, the cut wasn't severe enough to cripple him. I'd have to do better on my next attack.

Nope, scratch that. The giant was chasing after me and way too close for another attack. I slid Excalibur back into its scabbard and kept riding. At least he'd forgotten about entering the town square. I now had his full attention, lucky me.

Goliath sped up, so did the giant. We only needed to maintain our distance for a little while. The giants weren't great over distance, but as mighty as Goliath was, he'd been on the move for too long, the horse was tired.

I turned on a street and entered a section of homes. After that, I turned again in an effort to lose the giant. The furry idiot was starting to slow down, and Goliath was gaining more distance. A quick turn through a front yard, a sprint through three backyards, and before I knew it we'd lost the giant and found refuge next to a large tree between two homes.

Goliath was breathing heavily, but he never gave up on me. I was proud of my horse. I patted his cheek and scratched at his thick mane. Goliath in turn reached over, grabbed me by the ankle and pulled me out of the saddle.

I hit the snow covered ground with a thump.

Miraculously, Merlin and Toad didn't fall with me. Merlin was still out of it, but Toad was looking at me with the weirdest expression on his face.

"What was that?" Toad asked in a whisper.

"Goliath's pissed at me," I answered.

I got to my feet. Goliath was staring at me. I reached over to him and hugged his head. The horse made a low noise and then nuzzled into my neck. I was forgiven.

Footsteps.

Very heavy footsteps.

I looked towards the back of the house, another giant. He was leering at us from a distance. A huge club was in his right hand and dragging through the snow.

I jumped on Goliath's back and dug my heels in. Goliath reared up, and sprinted towards the street. The giant started out slow with a fast walk, but quickly gained speed in that hunched-over awkward way that they run.

Goliath slipped on a patch of ice in the street. His legs kicked out furiously beneath him in an attempt to keep from going over, and luckily he stayed on his feet. The giant was right behind us. He reached out with his left hand, and I swung Excalibur at his finger.

I cut him deeply, and Excalibur ignited furiously.

The giant roared, and his roar was answered by another. The first giant that was chasing us rounded the far corner of the street and suddenly we were trapped between the two of them.

Well, trapped is a strong word.

With the snow falling all around me, I shoved Excalibur back into its scabbard, and darted between two houses. Both giants were in pursuit. Both of them were barreling down on me. The roads that hid me earlier were suddenly slowing me down.

I needed a long stretch of road. I needed to get back to Main Street. Once there, I just hoped Goliath had enough energy to outdistance the two giants. Not that getting there was going to be easy. I was weaving around houses, but I wasn't gaining any distance on the giants.

Actually, the giants seemed to be gaining on me.

Goliath was too tired. The giants were too fast. They clumsily crashed into homes and pushed at each other as they chased after us. People were going to be pissed at me for the property damage.

I briefly wondered where Lance was. He had to be near me somewhere, but he'd been so quiet. I was worried that he'd do something foolish in an attempt to help me.

Main Street wasn't far away.

One last bit of road, and I'd be there. Now was the time to start gaining some speed. I whispered into Goliath's ear. The horse growled in response, but he sped up regardless.

I smiled as we hauled ass down the street. I laughed when I looked over my shoulder and saw that the two giants pursuing us were falling behind.

Right up ahead was Main Street.

One hundred feet to go, and we'd be out of danger. Seventy-five feet remaining and the giants were falling even further behind. Twenty feet away, and Goliath started making a wide turn in order to keep from slowing down.

I was still laughing as we finally hit Main Street and started riding towards the front gate, and then I began cursing.

Blocking the street, not fifty feet in front of us, were another three giants. Goliath came to a stop. He was breathing too heavily. I was running him to hard. I had nowhere to go. Giants behind me, giants in front of me, the town square in one direction, and a bunch of shops in another.

The only way open was towards some shops, but that wasn't going to work. There weren't any places to hide in that direction. I'd be cornered almost immediately.

We'd come to the end of the road.

Goliath was too tired for this. I wasn't going to put him through any more. I dismounted, and drew my sword. Goliath made a high pitched noise, and nudged me from behind. I shoved him away, and the giants charged towards me.

Goliath didn't want to leave my side.

"Go on you stupid horse," I said. "Get out of here."

Toad was screaming something, but I couldn't hear what he was saying over the pounding footsteps of the giants. From somewhere off to my left, I also heard Lance begin to scream out something as well. I couldn't hear what he was saying either.

I did however notice the green fog moving rapidly through the air as if a giant fan were pushing it away from out town. The sight caught my attention because it was so dramatic. I even felt the cold air, as if from a breeze, but felt no actual breeze.

The two giants from behind us entered Main Street and came to an abrupt stop. They screamed out, teetered and fell as this strange magical wind began to push on the two of them with a mighty force. I watched in amazement, not sure of what to do.

The giants in front of me were already on their knees when I turned to look at them. Their hands were clawing into the ground, tearing out great chunks of earth, as they tried desperately to keep from being blown away.

"What the shit?" I asked.

"Welcome to Camelot," Merlin said in a weak voice from atop my saddle.

The wind grew fierce, and the giants were blown down Main Street. I watched as they tumbled into one another and were forced towards the front gates.

One of the giants in front of us fought against the wind, and his grip on the ground was just strong enough to hold him in place. He grinned at me.

"Magic won't save you," the giant growled. "I'll destroy this town. I'll crush every last one of you beneath my feet, and then I'll sup on your—"

His face split down the middle and the giant screamed. Large chunks of fur and skin began flying off his body. His eyes were squished inside the sockets of his skull. Fur and skin gave way to blood and meat. The giant was being ripped apart in front of us. The screams had stopped. Only slight gurgles of anguish came from the ruined form blocking the center of Main Street.

Before the bones became visible, the giant finally released its grip upon the earth and the tattered remains of its body tumbled away towards the front gate.

The night became deathly quiet.

I never once felt the slightest bit of the wind that wreaked so much havoc on the giants.

Snow fell from the sky. Everywhere I looked was covered, and the people were no longer panicking.

I mounted Goliath, and walked him down the road, towards where I saw the medical tents. Our soldiers were rushing back through the front gate. A full retreat had been sounded, but people were also cheering.

I came to a stop at the tents and dismounted.

"Look at Stronghold Wall," Lance said.

I looked towards the wall. It was growing. How could a wall be growing? I had no answer, but I could see the wall growing right from the ground as if it were a plant that had just been fed some miracle growth serum.

Soldiers were still coming through the front gates which were also growing. People everywhere were staring at the wall in disbelief.

I entered the nearest tent and looked for my mother. She wasn't there. I asked where she was, and got directions. Three tents down. I didn't like being in the tents. The moans of the dying and the smell of blood was everywhere. I couldn't shake it from my nostrils.

I finally found my mother. She was fine. She was safe. She didn't have time to talk, just a quick hug and she was back to work on a patient. They were lucky to have her. When I walked outside the tent, people began cheering me.

What'd I do?

"You saved Camelot," Merlin said from atop Goliath as if he'd read my mind. "You're a hero once again."

I took a drink, and then I took another.

From somewhere close by I heard Lance giggling.

Everyone was touching me.

Everyone was patting me on the shoulders.

Women started hugging me.

I was beginning to like this.

I saw Reynolds and Gwen walk up to the edge of the crowd. Both of them were covered in blood. Gwen had her bow in her hand. Her eyes were narrowed as she looked at me. It wasn't a kind look.

I gave her the finger.

She grinned without a trace of true humor and vanished into the growing crowd. I wasn't sure what her problem was, and I really didn't care. She always had a stick up her ass.

A large hand grabbed onto my shoulder and spun me around.

Wayne.

I was glad to see him. I was glad that he was alive. We hugged each other as the crowd grew even larger.

"You did it!" Wayne shouted. "You found the key!"

"You're damn straight I found the key," I said. "Somebody had to save your ass."

I took another drink and looked back towards Stronghold Wall. It had grown to about twenty feet tall. The old rocks that made up the wall seemed to be crumbling away, and underneath the façade was clean and white stone.

The ground around Stronghold Wall began to grumble and shake. The people around me started getting nervous. Hell, I was a bit nervous myself, but it turned out to be nothing worth getting freaked out over.

Stronghold Wall was simply widening in the middle.

"Holy shit!" Wayne said. "I hope my kids are watching this!"

I looked around at the crowd. Magic was nothing new to a few of us, but some of these people had not yet seen Merlin do his thing.

Merlin.

I went over to Goliath. Merlin was still on his back. He was awake and watching the wall. I gently grabbed his arm to get his attention.

"Yes?" Merlin asked.

"You should go lie down in the tent," I said. "Let somebody look at you."

"A doctor can't help me," Merlin said. "Only time will do that. I just need to rest for a few days."

"Then go rest," I said.

"I plan on it," Merlin said. "Just as soon as my living quarters arrive."

"Your living quarters are down the road," I said.

"No, dear boy," Merlin laughed. "My living quarters are on the side of the castle."

"Castle?" I asked.

Merlin laughed.

"Surely you didn't think the magic would stop at Stronghold Wall?" Merlin asked. "Camelot is rising. Just you wait and see. The best is yet to come."

Toad shrugged his shoulders as if to say he didn't have a clue. I smiled at that. The alcohol was warming my belly and putting me in a good mood.

Stronghold Wall was continuing to widen. It was more than a wall now. I think the name of what it was turning into was a rampart, but I'm not exactly up on the technical words for medieval walls.

I laughed when I saw the pack horse we'd been using walk up to Goliath along with Merlin's horse. We'd lost Merlin's horse in the crowd when we left the park and entered the street. We'd lost the pack horse a long time before that. It couldn't match our speed when we passed through the battle. Well, I was becoming rather fond of horses. I was glad that they were both alright.

More noise from Stronghold Wall. It seemed as if something were happening every fifty feet or so. The rock seemed to be breaking apart and then rearranging.

"Those are towers," Wayne said. "It's creating towers along the wall. Now we'll be able to post sentries."

"I believe the wall is now called a rampart," I said.

"Really?" Wayne asked. "Are you sure?"

"No," I admitted, which brought out a hearty laugh from Wayne.

Loud pops began to echo out not far from us. A few screams echoed out, followed by laughter. Main Street was changing. Cobblestones were popping out through the asphalt.

"How far is this going to go?" Wayne asked.

"All the way," I answered.

"We'll probably never see another thing like this for the rest of our lives," Wayne said.

"Might as well enjoy the view," I said.

"I plan on it my friend," Wayne said as he put a big arm around my shoulders.

"I'm not going to have sex with you," I said.

"Sure you are," Wayne said.

I was about to respond when the farm house nearest to us crumbled upon itself and sank into the ground as if were swallowed up by a gigantic sinkhole.

"Woah," I said. "That doesn't look good."

"Should we worry?" Wayne asked.

"I'm not sure," I answered.

The ground trembled again, and the top of a large stone structure rose slowly from the surface of the earth. The farm house was being replaced.

"It's safer," Wayne said. "A rather vintage look, but quaint."

Things went into overdrive at that point. Other farm houses in the distance began crumbling as well, only to be replaced by the slow rise of a new stone dwelling.

"Our houses are falling apart!" Someone shouted from the far end of Main Street.

A crowd of thousands had gathered in the middle of the changing street and were watching the scene unfold. One by one people's homes were crumbling into the earth. I could hear the screams and angry shouts.

Camelot was rising.

Stone cottages grew from the earth where the homes once stood. It was unreal. It was magic. It felt as if we were time traveling into the past.

"Arthur!" Tristan shouted. "Arthur!"

"He's over here!" Wayne answered.

Tristan and Izzy rode up to us through the massive crowd. The two of them looked pretty rough. Tristan, like Wayne was in full armor. Izzy was dressed in chainmail and a tunic. They were covered in smears of drying blood.

"What is it?" I asked.

"You need to see the stream," Tristan said.

I whistled for Goliath, and mounted behind Merlin when the horse made its way over to me. Toad was riding in the saddle of Merlin's horse which followed Goliath. This gave Wayne quite a start when he climbed the saddle and almost sat on top of him.

"Toad," I said. "Meet Wayne. Wayne, this is Toad."

We rode down Main Street into the town square. The shops and buildings inside the town square were in the process of crumbling and being sucked into the earth. The stream had turned into a small river and was flowing from left to right in front of us.

"Where's the water coming from?" Wayne asked.

"I guess we have a new river," I answered. "I'm going to miss this place. I'm not sure what's going to replace all of this, but it had better be good."

A roar sounded out in the night.

Wayne and I exchanged brief glances of concern until we realized that the roar was the sound of rushing water, and watched as a great wave pushed its way past us, and enlarged the river even larger.

The river grew and grew. It pushed away earth and rocks and formed a winding path in which it could flow freely. The shops all around us that made up the square of the town square had vanished and the growing river forced us to retreat or go swimming in the swift current.

In no time at all, we were standing outside what used to be the town square and watching the river flow by in amazement.

That's when it happened.

That's when things truly became magical.

After a good twenty minutes, the river slowed into a soft current. It was a peaceful sight. It was a relaxing sight, and then a great flag emerged from the center of the river. I knew the flag. It was my flag. It was red with a white circle in the center. Inside the circle was a dragon.

There were sounds of amazement coming from the people all around me. I took another long pull from my bottle.

Underneath the flag was a great tower with a red, conical rooftop. It rose high into the sky, and it was followed by many other towers as well. All of them had the same red, conical shaped roofs.

The ground rumbled, and the water churned as more parts of the enormous castle rose high into the night sky. It was amazing, it was beautiful. The castle just kept growing and growing out of the river.

"Ah," Merlin said from behind me. "Not much longer now. Good thing, I'm in need of a rest. Arthur, I'll need some privacy for a few days. Do you think you can manage?"

"I think so," I answered sarcastically.

I didn't want to talk to Merlin. I wanted to watch the castle rising out of the river. I wanted to see how big the castle grew. Already it was the largest castle I'd ever seen. Not that I'd visited many castles, but I used to watch TV back in the day. I'd seen a few of them, and this one was big enough to get lost in.

"Those are the battlements, I believe," Wayne said.

"What are?" I asked.

"That big fence that's rising up right now," Wayne answered.

"Are you sure?" I asked.

"Does it matter?" Wayne asked. "We've got a freaking castle!"

I smiled at that. Wayne was right. We had a freaking castle. It was a definite upgrade from my little place by the river. I was going to enjoy myself. I took another swig of alcohol as I thought about inviting certain ladies to my new residence. Being a king was finally going to be entertaining.

Underneath the castle was a low island of rock that came up around what Wayne believed was the battlements. In front of us was a drawbridge big enough to drive at least three semi trucks through side by side.

The drawbridge was closed.

"That doesn't seem very inviting," I said to Wayne.

"Not at all," Wayne answered. "Merlin, how do we get inside?"

"The drawbridge will open only for Arthur," Merlin answered.

"So how do I get it to open?" I asked.

Merlin wasn't answering. He looked as if he were on the verge of death. Toad was looking at him worriedly.

"You okay?" I asked the little gnome.

"I'm just worried about the wizard," Toad answered. "He needs his rest."

Merlin stirred and pointed to a small little wooden dwelling on the left side of the castle, right next to the water.

"That's my home," Merlin said. "Arthur, if you would be so kind as to call down the drawbridge."

"How?" I asked.

Merlin seemed asleep once again. This was getting ridiculous.

"Go call it down, dude," Wayne said.

"How?" I asked for the billionth time.

"Just call it?" Wayne laughed.

I rode up to where the drawbridge would rest when opened. I drew Excalibur as if the sword were proof of my identity.

"I am Arthur!" I shouted. "I seek to enter!"

With a loud creak of moving chains, the drawbridge began to lower. The people all around me began to cheer. Bedder came out of the crowd, and walked over to Wayne.

"The Death Reapers have given up," Bedder announced. "They're leaving."

"All of them?" Wayne asked.

"No sense in any of them staying," Bedder said. "They seem to know the capabilities of Camelot."

"That's not too surprising," Wayne said. "They've probably dealt with this place back in the day."

I was getting bored of their conversation. The danger had been over for a while now.

"So post some men on Stronghold Wall and have them keep an eye out," I said. "Let us know if anything happens."

"Your concern is overwhelming," Bedder said.

"And your voice is annoying," I said as the drawbridge finished descending. "Get out of my sight."

I rode Goliath to the center of the bridge, noticing that the front of the castle was not over the water. That seemed a bit weird to me, but then I remembered that all of Camelot was magical and normal precautions probably weren't very necessary.

So, no river-moat, instead the river flowed from left to right underneath the castle. I jumped off Goliath, and gave him a little smack on the butt while pointing towards a little trail that led to Merlin's house. Goliath walked away slowly so as not to disturb the wizard. I looked behind me at all the people. There were a lot of them.

"Anyone care to join me?" I asked.

A loud roar came up from the crowd, and they followed me into the castle. Past the gate was a great market place just waiting to be filled up with vendors and their goods. I saw empty stables; I saw fountains sputtering to life. Lanterns were lighting up all around us.

Everything was made of stone. The battlements were a grey color, but the actual castle was white. Everything was also clean and dry. The ground beneath our feet was cobblestone. How a castle that had just emerged from a river could look so good was beyond me, but I certainly wasn't complaining.

I didn't explore the grounds outside, I mean I saw what I saw, but my priority was the castle. I wanted to see the castle. The red double doors were fifteen feet high and decorated with metal furnishings. They swung open as I walked towards them.

That's when I damn near pissed my pants.

There was a ghost waiting just beyond the doors. He was bluish and transparent. A portly, balding man that probably died in his mid-fifties.

My hand went to Excalibur as the ghost gave a low bow. Beyond him, I saw other ghosts flitting around the inside of the castle. Many other ghosts.

"My lord," the ghost said. "We've been waiting for you."

"What's going on here?" I asked. "I didn't know this place was haunted."

"We serve the king of Camelot," The servant said. "We've stayed on to maintain the castle."

"They're your servants," Wayne whispered in my ear.

I nodded my head in understanding. I had ghosts for servants. That was easy enough to follow. Sort of weird, but at least I wouldn't have to keep the place clean on my own.

"What's your name?" I asked.

"My name is Wendell, my lord," Wendell answered. "I'm in charge of all the others and we won't disappoint you with our service."

Wayne tried to whisper something else into my ear, and Wendell politely interrupted him.

"Your majesty," Wendell said. "If I may, I see that you have guests. Might I suggest a celebration? The ballroom is nice and warm at the moment. I'm sure your guests would enjoy themselves."

"A party," Wayne said.

"I'm in the mood for a party," I said.

I looked behind me at all the anxious faces. I smile crept over my lips.

"Lead the way Wendell," I said.

The ghost did indeed lead the way. The ballroom, like everything else in the castle was gigantic. It could easily fit the entire town, maybe even the soldiers as well. More importantly, there was a lot of alcohol. The ghostly servants knew how to keep their guests happy.

I was led to a throne at the far side of the room. I was a bit embarrassed to be sitting there, but everyone kept cheering me on. There was a smaller throne next to the one I was sitting on. I knew immediately who that was for, and I was about to ask the servants to take it away, when she just happened to enter the ballroom.

Everyone began to cheer for her. Apparently she did some amazing things in the battle. The soldiers and citizens alike loved her dearly...and then they led her right to the other throne.

Damn it!

This was no good!

I didn't want her next to me. I didn't even like her.

Reluctantly, she took her seat. Everyone was clapping and cheering. Gwen was smiling happily at them, and fortunately they were soon distracted when the servants began bringing in big plates of food.

"What the hell are you doing?" I asked Gwen.

"Don't for a second think I'm happy to be here next to you," Gwen answered.

"Then leave," I said.

"That would make you look bad," Gwen said. "These people look up to you. They think you're a hero. I'm not going to do anything to shatter that illusion."

"I'm pretty sure I can take it," I said. "You're cock-blocking me."

"I'm what?" Gwen asked.

"You're cock-blocking me," I repeated. "I'd like to get laid tonight, and that's not going to happen if every woman in this place thinks I'm with you."

"You're so vulgar," Gwen said.

"Well, I've earned that right," I said. "I did save everyone."

"You didn't save anything," Gwen said. "You had people help you and push you every step of the way."

"And what did you do?" I asked. "Sit there and look pretty while men fought for you?"

"Nobody fights for me," Gwen said. "I was right there in that battle with them."

"Yeah," I said. "I'm sure you were beneficial. More likely you had twenty soldiers around you at all times to make sure you didn't break a nail."

"I really hate you," Gwen said.

"I don't even think about you," I said.

"Well, you win," Gwen said as she stood up to leave. "There are more important things to do tonight than argue with you. Enjoy the alcohol and women."

"I plan on it," I said.

That was apparently the last straw as far as Gwen was concerned. She stopped walking away and turned back to face me. We'd argued before. That was nothing new, but I'd never seen her so angry. Her eyebrows were arched and her eyes were fierce.

"You could have been really special," Gwen said. "You could have been an inspiration. A simple word from you could lead our people into an age without Death Reapers and giants. A simple word that you refuse to give because you only care about yourself, I pity you."

Gwen stormed off after that.

I let her have it. I didn't want her coming back. I didn't consider her words either. I didn't care what she had to say. I just wanted her to get away from me.

Immediately I caught the eyes of a group of women in their mid-twenties that were standing not too far away and sipping wine. I smiled at them and three of them smiled back. Gwen was instantly forgotten.

"She was wrong," Lance whispered from above me.

"Where the hell are you?" I asked.

"I've been hanging out in the rafters," Lance answered.

I looked up. High above the party all along the sides of the pitched ceiling were ornate wooden beams. It was the perfect place for Lance to kick back and enjoy the evening.

"You really think she was wrong?" I asked.

"Yes," Lance answered. "She doesn't know you at all."

"Then why didn't you say anything?" I asked with a smile on my face.

"I have a rule to not get between you and an angry woman," Lance said. "I'd never be able to relax if I did that."

I laughed. He wasn't too far from the truth.

"Go away," I said. "I don't think I'll be needing any protection tonight. Go find your girlfriend, or go explore the castle."

"You sure?" Lance asked.

"Yup," I said as I stood up to go introduce myself to the three interested ladies.

Even though they weren't very far away, it took a bit of effort to make my way over to them. Every single person I passed wanted to shake my hand, hug me, and have a few words with me. I couldn't catch a break with any of them.

Finally I arrived at my destination.

"Are you ladies enjoying yourselves?" I asked.

"That we are," one of them answered. "This is a very nice place you have here."

"Thank you," I said. "I built it myself."

"Did you now?" Another woman asked.

"Yes," I answered. "Did you not see me raise it from the water?"

The woman laughed at my joke. I smiled in return.

"Are you really a king?" The third woman asked.

"That's what they tell me," I answered.

"Can you prove it?" The first woman asked.

"Definitely," I answered.

More laughter.

The second girl noticed the few cuts and scratches on my body.

"I think you might need some medical attention," she said. "Some of those cuts may need stitches. The one on your leg looks especially bad."

"Nah," I said. "I'm not even bleeding."

"How are you not bleeding?" The third girl asked.

"I'm magic," I answered.

They laughed.

"I can prove that as well," I said.

More laughter.

"I've stitched up more than my fair share of wounds, Mr. King-of-the-world," Would you like me to help you out?" The second girl asked.

"First I better get a few drinks in me," I said. "Then maybe we can all go somewhere more private and take care of me."

All in all, the evening wasn't too bad. Wendell led me and my new friends to my bedroom. The bedroom was incredible. It had old hardwood floors, rock walls, dark wooden rafters, and giant candelabras hanging from the ceiling. The bed itself was gigantic and had thick drapes hanging above the three sides not backing up against the wall. A large burning fireplace was against one wall making sure the room was at a comfortable temperature.

"Thank you Wendell," I said. "Can you please make sure we're not disturbed until tomorrow?"

"Of course, my Lord," Wendell answered. I'll set up guards at the door.

What came after the stitches was an epic party. I just wish I remembered all of it. Sometime shortly before dawn, I found myself underneath the warm covers of that big bed. I fell immediately to sleep.

I needed that sleep.

Wendell woke me up sometime in the late afternoon. I was nursing an incredible hangover and didn't want to get out of my bed. I also wasn't alone.

Wendell escorted my company to the door.

"Where did you send them?" I asked.

"One of the servants is waiting to lead them out of the castle," Wendell answered.

"I was having fun," I complained.

"Yes, my lord," Wendell sympathized, "but your friend is here, and he'd like to speak with you."

Wayne came in immediately after I asked the question.

"Looks like you had an interesting night," Wayne laughed.

I shrugged by way of a reply.

"How's Merlin doing?" Wayne asked.

"No clue," I said. "He wanted to rest up. Where's Toad? I haven't seen him since we entered the castle."

"He wandered off after Merlin," Wayne answered. "I guess he wanted to stand guard."

I laughed at that.

"He'll make a great bodyguard," I said. "So why are you bothering me?"

"We should probably talk," Wayne said. "The Death Reapers and giants may have left the immediate area, but..."

"Why are you telling me this?" I asked.

"What do you mean?" Wayne asked. "Who am I supposed to tell?"

"Tell Merlin," I grumbled.

"Merlin is resting," Wayne said.

"Tell that Reynolds guy," I said.

"We've already discussed it," Wayne said. "We thought you'd like to know what we came up with."

"I don't give a shit about what you came up with," I said. "Wendell, bring me something to drink, please."

"Yes, my lord," Wendell said before bowing and walking away.

"Wendell," I called out. "Make sure it's whiskey."

❧ DELLIA ❧

I had barely gotten any sleep for the last three days. There were too many injured and dying that needed my help. Now, after the tireless effort of the medical crew, those that could be saved were saved and those that couldn't be saved were...well, best not to think about all that were lost.

I needed a distraction. I needed a few days rest. Nothing would delight me more than exploring Camelot. I'd missed most of the magic, but I still managed to catch glimpses of the castle rising out of what used to be the town square.

However, I was tired. Exploring would come later after I'd had some rest. Supposedly, I was now living in the castle. Normally my son probably wouldn't be too happy to have his mother come live with him, but in a castle that size I doubted he'd even notice I was there.

I needed a bed.

Walking up the street was an event. Everywhere I looked things were different. All the old houses were gone. Stone cottages had replaced them. Well, at least they were attractive, and probably an improvement, definitely safer.

I knew my old home had been altered in the same way. I wasn't too happy about that. Change wasn't something that interested me, but at least I wouldn't have to deal with that leaky roof any longer.

Merlin was waiting for me at the drawbridge. I hadn't seen him since he'd gotten home. He looked much better. There was even a bit of color in his cheeks.

"How are you feeling?" I asked.

"Much better," Merlin answered. "It was a much needed rest. In fact, I just woke up this morning."

"Have you seen Arthur?" I asked. "He hasn't left the castle since it grew out of the river."

"He probably needed some rest as well," Merlin answered as he took my arm and led me across the drawbridge.

"How did things go on your trip?" I asked. "Obviously you were successful."

"I know what you're getting at," Merlin answered. "Unfortunately, Arthur and I haven't patched things up between us. If anything, the wedge has been driven deeper. I'm failing him. I hate to admit it, but I simply can't reach him."

"He'll come around," I said.

Merlin had an expression on his face. I'd seen that expression from others. It always came when I told them not to give up on my son. It was a look of pity reserved for blind mothers the world over, but I wasn't a blind mother. I knew what my son was capable of.

"I think you'll love your new place," Merlin said, changing the subject.

"Will I?" I asked.

"Well, I know how you love the stars," Merlin said. "The castle has the best view you could imagine. It's time for you to live like the mother of the king. You've seen too much battle."

"I've seen too much of the results of battle," I corrected.

"Yes, you need a rest," Merlin said.

"Wait a minute," I said. "Are you trying to tell me something?"

Merlin came to a stop, and turned to face me.

"You're doing too much," Merlin said. "I want you to retire."

"People need me," I argued.

"They don't," Merlin said. "What you've done for them has been incredible, but now I'm concerned about you. You're sacrificing your own health."

"Absolutely not," I said.

"When's the last time you've eaten?" Merlin asked. "When's the last time you've slept?"

"Just stop," I said. "I'm not going into that castle to live a life of royalty while the rest of Camelot is out there risking their necks."

"The only ones in danger anymore are the soldiers that leave the safety of Camelot," Merlin said. "Camelot itself is impregnable. Dellia, this place is now safe. Not even Morgana herself could force her way beyond Stronghold Wall. Battles will no longer be fought here. We'll have to leave Camelot to rid the world of Morgana's forces."

"And you don't want me to go on these dangerous missions?" I asked.

"I do not," Merlin answered. "I want you to stay safe. I want you far away from danger. Think about what would happen to Arthur if he lost you."

"This isn't a conversation I want to have right now," I said.

"Fair enough," Merlin said. "Let me show you to your room. I hope you're okay with ghosts."

"Ghosts?" I asked, even though I was sure Merlin was only teasing.

Retiring—how could I retire? Our medical team was growing, but they still needed everyone they could get a hold of. Sadly, I wasn't as young as I used to be. I wasn't sure I'd be up for traveling. As much as I wanted to help, maybe Merlin was right.

Right now wasn't the time to think about retiring. I was too tired. I needed my rest. I could assess things later. I doubted I'd retire though. It wasn't in my nature to stay idle.

The castle loomed over us as we walked past all the shops and vendors. A few of the shops had already opened. The delicious smells of cooking meats filled the air. I was hungry. I was tired and I was hungry. I hoped there was something to eat in the castle.

The castle doors were closed and Merlin knocked politely.

"Is it normal to close the doors?" I asked.

"It's your home," Merlin answered. "Would you keep the door to your home open?"

"Shouldn't there be guards outside the doors?" I asked.

Merlin laughed.

"This is Camelot," Merlin answered. "Nothing can hurt Arthur here."

I shrugged as the doors swung open.

I then screamed when I saw the ghost.

Merlin thought that was pretty funny, and so did the ghost. The two of them laughed as I tried to catch my breath. I'd seen one too many horror movies apparently, because Wendell was quite a lovely deceased person.

"I'll have you escorted to your room, Lady Dellia," Wendell replied, "but perhaps you'd like something to eat first?"

"Yes," I answered. "That would be nice."

Merlin said goodbye, and left me in Wendell's capable hands. I wasn't used to having servants. I didn't know how to act around them. I did my best to be polite, but I'm sure they sensed how uncomfortable I was.

After I ate, I was taken to my tower. Yep, I didn't have just a bedroom, I had an entire tower to myself. It wasn't too shabby.

I slept like I'd never slept before. I felt safer than I had in a long, long time. By the time I had awoken it was mid-afternoon of the next day. Servants were there waiting for me. Food had already been prepared.

I ate at a table in my bedroom. I was feeling lonely.

"Has anyone seen my son?" I asked.

The ghosts shook their heads.

"Could one of you lead me to his room?" I asked.

The ghosts looked at each other guiltily.

Uh oh, what was Arthur doing? Their reaction made me nervous. Was my son already destroying the castle? Was he lying passed out drunk in one of the many rooms?

"How bad?" I asked.

Before they could answer, they were saved by Merlin who had appeared at the door. Merlin must have overheard me asking questions, because he had a polite smile on his face as he excused my ghostly servants.

"Arthur is indisposed," Merlin said.

"He's got a girl?" I asked.

"Something like that," Merlin answered. "You probably don't want to know. Regardless, you'll see him very soon. I'm going to retrieve him myself."

I gave a sigh.

"Some things have happened," Merlin said. "Some things that we need to meet with the others and talk about."

"Is it serious?" I asked.

"I'm afraid that it is," Merlin said.

"When you're dressed Wendell will lead you to the room," Merlin said. "It will be the only time you'll ever be allowed access."

Merlin left after that. I had questions for him, but they'd have to wait. I took a quick bath in a big tub of hot water, brushed my teeth, combed my hair, and got dressed. Wendell was waiting for me.

"Where are we going?" I asked.

"We're going to the war room," Wendell answered.

"What's so important about the war room?" I asked.

"Surely you know what lies in the war room?" Wendell asked.

"I have no idea," I answered.

"Then you're in for a treat, Lady Dellia," Wendell said. "Normally only the sworn knights of Camelot are allowed into this room, but an exception has been made on this occasion. Merlin wants everyone to be there."

Walking to the room took no less than fifteen minutes. We went down one flight of steps after another. There was something in the air, a reverence. I was about to witness something important.

Down a narrow stone stairway was an immense wooden door. Wendell opened the door onto a large room. I walked in, my shoes clacking on the marble floor. In the center of the room was an ancient round table. The table was close to twenty feet in diameter. It was polished a deep brown and scarred from years of use. In the very center of the table a dragon was carved into the wood.

My breath caught in my throat.

"Is this..." I struggled to ask.

"The Round Table," Merlin answered as he appeared out of nowhere, "Yes."

"Where are the chairs?" I asked.

"The chairs will appear when the knights are sworn in by the king," Merlin answered.

The door opened once again. Tristan, Wayne, Arthur, Bedder, Gwen, Reynolds, and a few others walked into the room. Their reactions were a lot like mine. For five long minutes the room was completely quiet.

"This is the war room for the Knights of the Round Table," Merlin finally said in a quiet voice. "Great men have met in this very place centuries ago. Great men will meet here yet again."

"What's the big deal?" Arthur asked. "It's just an old table. You guys need to get a life. I'm going back to my room."

"Arthur," Wayne said. "C'mon man. Show some respect."

"I don't want involved in any of your little games," Arthur complained. "If you want to play your little games in the castle, go ahead, but leave me be."

"Arthur," Merlin said. "One of the smaller villages that have sprung up in our vicinity over the last couple of years has fallen under attack."

"I'm sure you can handle things," Arthur said.

"Indeed we can," Merlin said. "I just wanted to give you the courtesy of an invitation before we planned things without you."

"Next time don't bother," Arthur said as he rudely walked away.

No one said a word after the door slammed shut behind my son. I knew they wanted to. I could tell by the way everyone looked at me. Tears threatened to burst from my eyes, but I held them back.

"Tell us what's happening, Merlin," I said.

"Our soldiers followed the forces of Morgana," Merlin said. "They left the area after giving up on the battle. When they crossed into a forest we typically don't monitor, our soldiers returned to the castle to report that the enemy had left our domain. It seems that the Death Reapers and the giants have now returned."

"Only this time they aren't attacking Camelot," Wayne said. "They're attacking one of the villages that should be under our protection."

"Why aren't we monitoring the woods through which they entered?" I asked.

"It's beyond what we typically consider our borders," Bedder answered. "That forest has been claimed by the Death Reapers. There's a rumor that they have an encampment there."

"We don't the manpower to protect the entire world," Merlin said. "Therefore, we've set up borders that we can easily maintain."

"And these villages are inside our borders?" I asked.

"Yes," Merlin answered.

"So since the Death Reapers and the giants can't attack Camelot, they're now going to attack the surrounding villages?"

"Yes," Merlin answered.

"These villages," I said. "Did they come into being so that they could have our protection?"

"They did," Merlin answered.

"Then it's settled," Gwen said. "We go out and defend the villages."

"It's not that easy," Bedder said. "This is the same army that was defeating us up until Merlin brought back the true Camelot. They still have giants with them."

"We have Merlin with us," Wayne said.

"Merlin," Gwen said. "Can you stop the giants?"

"Giants are relatively magic resistant," Merlin said. "It would impossible for me at this juncture to take on a group of them."

"Could you distract them?" Wayne asked.

"I'm sure I could," Merlin answered.

"What if you made a distraction," Wayne said. "And we attacked the Death Reapers during the distraction?"

"The distraction wouldn't last forever," Merlin answered. "Eventually the giants would be back in the fight, unless the distraction was painful enough...I think I have an idea. How many giants did the Death Reapers have with them?"

"I'd guess about thirty or so were left after they gave up the attack," Reynolds answered.

"It'll be pushing things with that many," Merlin said, "but I have an idea."

"Then let's prepare to ride out," Gwen said.

Everyone agreed and sprang into action. Gwen was a natural leader. She and Merlin made a good pair when it came to a battle. Merlin wasn't always much for inspiring people, but he could plan. Gwen was an inspiration to everyone. Soldiers would willingly die for her.

"Come with me," Merlin told me as he walked towards the door. "I'll need you to help me prepare."

We walked back up the stairs, down a hallway, down another hallway, and eventually found ourselves entering a secret passage hidden behind a tapestry of two jousting knights. Merlin immediately lit a torch and led the way.

"You know this castle very well, don't you?" I asked.

"Yes indeed," Merlin answered. "I spent a great amount of time discovering its secrets."

"I'm wondering if I'll ever get used to this place," I said. "It's impossibly huge."

"You'll get used to it," Merlin said. "You have all the time in the world to learn about the castle."

The passageway broke out into many different directions. Merlin never once got lost, and in no time at all, we came to a dead end. Merlin smiled, located a lever between two rocks of the stone wall, and pulled. A hidden door creaked on gritty railings, but rotated open. Merlin stepped out into the sunlight and I followed him. We were near his little cottage.

"We'll be needing some nets," Merlin said.

"Nets?" I asked. "Why?"

"Because we need to catch a bee," Merlin answered. "Actually, I'd prefer a wasp. Wasps are nasty little buggers."

Merlin went inside his home and came back with two nets. He handed me one of the nets and we went to work.

"Be mindful of my rose garden," Merlin said. "Toad has taken up residence there, and he wouldn't be too happy if you crushed his home."

"I'll be careful," I said, "but can you tell me why you want to catch a wasp?"

"I need a wasp to distract the giants," Merlin answered.

"How will one little wasp distract a group of giants?" I asked.

"It won't just be one little wasp," Merlin answered. "It also won't be very little. Trust me, it's not the best plan I've ever had, but it'll work. Like I said, wasps are nasty buggers."

We'd been looking for a good ten minutes, and I was starting to get rather cold. That's when it occurred to me that it was the completely wrong type of weather to be catching wasps. My palm went to my forehead, and I questioned my own intelligence.

"Merlin," I said. "It's wintertime. We're not going to find any wasps."

"I'd normally agree with you," Merlin said, "but Toad keeps the garden rather warm for his flowers. We should be able to find something if we look hard enough."

"Why don't you just ask Toad?" I said.

"We had a few drinks last night," Merlin said. "I doubt I'll be able to wake him up. Gnomes enjoy their alcohol like no other creature I've ever encountered."

"You've met my son, haven't you?" I asked.

Merlin laughed at my joke, and swung his net.

"Did you catch something?" I asked.

"Just a groggy bee," Merlin answered. "I'd prefer a wasp. Switch nets with me. You can hold onto this little fellow, and I'll continue the search."

Right before I could trade nets with the wizard, I saw what he'd been searching for. The wasp was black and yellow. Its wings were buzzing slightly as if it were preparing to take flight. Merlin saw what I was looking at.

"Can you catch it?" Merlin asked.

"Yes," I answered.

I prepared to swing the net, but the wasp took flight as I was pulling back for my swing. It didn't fly high, but it moved quickly as if it sensed my intentions. It took me three swings to catch the little critter.

"Good job," Merlin said. "Let's bring it into my cottage."

Merlin released his trapped bee, and I followed him inside his little home. The bright sunlight provided all the light we needed to see. A waist-high shelf ran along the entire side of the house. On this shelf were various instruments, potions, and ingredients I'd never be able to place. In the opposite corner was a small yet comfortable looking bed. In between the shelf and the bed was a closed door that I suspected of housing the bathroom. All in all, the home was orderly and comfortable looking despite having no architectural significance whatsoever.

"Why don't you live in the castle?" I asked.

"I prefer a bit of privacy," Merlin muttered as he searched for something on his shelf.

I looked at the walls of his home, curious to see where his taste would lie when it came to décor. Apparently, Merlin had no taste in décor. I couldn't find a single decoration on his walls. Everything seemed to have some type of use, even if the use of the object was unknown to me.

There was a nightstand by Merlin's bed. On top of the nightstand was a framed picture. I picked up the picture and turned it around. I recognized the artwork immediately. It wasn't particularly great, instead, it was rather sloppy looking. It had been drawn by my son when he was six years old, a present to his grandfather.

"Arthur gave me that when he was a boy," Merlin said looking a bit embarrassed. "He was the sweetest boy. I often miss those days. I had the picture framed. I've kept it with me ever since. I was so happy to have Arthur back in my life. The years had been a bit lonely without him."

"It seems as if you've given up on him," I said.

"We've had this conversation before," Merlin said. "I have nothing but the best wishes, but I can't seem to reach him."

"He'll surprise us all," I said. "I promise you. We've not yet seen the best of my son."

Merlin had the wasp inside a small glass tube. The little insect was furious. I watched its wings buzz and its stinger poke repeatedly at its prison.

Merlin smiled at me and went back to his shelf. He put a stopper on the glass tube holding the angry wasp, and rummaged through his many ingredients.

"What do you plan on doing to that thing?" I asked.

"I plan on using it to our advantage," Merlin answered. "Giants don't have a lot of natural enemies. They're too big and tough. My goal here is to create a natural enemy for them, but I need to make that same natural enemy safe and docile around other creatures so I don't upset the natural balance."

"I think I'm following," I said.

"I want a creature whose sole reason for living is to attack giants," Merlin said. "So, I'm creating two potions. The first potion contains a hair from an angry giant. This will irritate the wasp. The second potion will contain a fragment of a dead giant's skin. This potion will help the wasp grow to a large size. With the two potions combined, the wasp will be completely uninterested in all other creatures...in theory."

"Wait," I said. "You aren't positive how this will work?"

"Potion making isn't an exact science," Merlin answered. "It's my best guess. This is some intricate shit I'm working with here."

"You could be creating a menace," I argued.

"That's what I'm trying to do," Merlin said.

"No," I said. "You could be creating something that attacks people."

"Well if that's the case I'll just reverse the magic, and no harm done," Merlin said.

"It's that easy?" I asked.

"I wouldn't call it easy," Merlin said. "I doubt you'll find anyone else that can do what I do."

Merlin apparently found his ingredients, because two glass bottles began fizzling up with bubbles. I didn't like the smell they were producing. It smelled of harsh chemicals that burn the lining of your nose.

When the bottles stopped bubbling, Merlin grabbed a dropper, sucked up an orange liquid from one of the bottles, and dropped a drop on top of the wasps head. The wasp started growing immediately, and Merlin had to dump it out of the tube.

I watched the wasp roll and twist as it grew and grew on Merlin's shelf. The wizard paid it no attention at all. Instead, he gathered up another few drops of the second bottle into his dropper, and dropped a few drops of the new bright blue liquid onto the wasp's head.

"We'll need to wait a bit," Merlin said looking over to me.

"Do you have a cage or something for this thing?" I asked.

"We won't need it," Merlin answered, "but I will need a map."

Merlin began rummaging now through files of papers until he found a map of the area. He studied this map briefly for a moment, and the wasp just kept growing and growing. I found myself stepping away from the beast and moving close to the door, in case I needed to make a run for it.

Merlin scooped up a quill pen and marked the map just as the wasp finished growing. It was now a bit longer than my arm and including its legs twice as thick. The wasp turned its head and stared at Merlin as Merlin came closer.

I watched the crazy teenaged wizard kneel down in front of the giant wasp, and point to his map.

"Here," Merlin said as if the creature could understand him. "They'll be here. Gather more of your kind, find them and attack. Do so now."

With those words, Merlin poured more of both potions onto the wasp, walked past me and opened the door. The wasp walked outside as if it were a dog. I frantically moved out of its way, but it truly had no interest in me.

"Now watch," Merlin said.

The wasp moved in front of the flower garden. It buzzed its wings, and other wasps soon emerged. They flew towards the creature and the blue and orange cloud that started to puff up around its body. Wasp after wasp dropped from the sky and began convulsing on the ground as they grew and grew. In less than ten minutes over two hundred wasps flew up into the sky and took off in the same direction.

Merlin smiled as he watched his creation take flight.

"Merlin," I said. "I know he's gotten worse. I'm not an idiot, he's gotten much, much worse, but he's still my son. I still believe in him."

Merlin didn't meet my gaze, but he nodded in understanding.

"Let's go find the others, and see how things are going," Merlin said.

Everyone in the war room met towards the rear of the castle where a great army was gathering under Reynolds direction. Wayne, Bedder, and Tristan arrived in full armor. The rest of the soldiers were covered in chain mail and tunics. Not far away in the stables, I could hear Goliath complaining loudly that Arthur hadn't shown up to release him. The horse was made for battle, he enjoyed running out with the rest of the horses.

I looked back up at the castle as if I could see my son. No, I would not lose hope for him. I'd never do that. I could never do that. He needed help. That was it. He needed someone that could reach him. There was a good man lurking in there somewhere.

Weapons were sharpened. Arrows and bows were gathered. High at the top of the castle, horns blew out a triumphant sound and the forces of Camelot moved out.

"Well Dellia," Merlin said. "I'll suppose I'll see you when we get back."

Silly Merlin, he was the only person not wearing armor. Instead, he wore cowboy boots, blue jeans, and a green t-shirt. He didn't impress me.

"I saw your medical team move out," I said. "Not a single one of them is good enough."

"We already talked about this," Merlin said. "I don't want you endangering yourself."

"So instead you're going to risk the lives of those that become injured?" I asked. "I'm no child. With what right do you make these decisions for me?"

"I'm only thinking of your well being," Merlin said. "You're getting too tired. The strain and stress is catching up to you."

"Then get a better team of medics for our soldiers," I said, "because until that happens, I'll be riding out with the rest of you."

I didn't bother arguing any longer. Instead, I motioned for a horse and one of the stable boys quickly brought her over for me. I mounted up and stared at Merlin with a look that dared him to test me.

Merlin sighed, lowered his head, and trotted off without another word. I gave him some space and followed behind him.

We rode out of the castle to the cheers of the townspeople. They were proud of us. They were proud of Camelot and they were supportive of our desire to help others. I lived in a good place. The people of Camelot made me happy.

Four hours later, and we were nearing our destination. The small town was less than two hours away from our current position. Tristan took off alone to scout ahead. He was the quickest rider. Nothing but an arrow could catch him. Still, I worried. I worried and I was tired.

A soreness in my lower back began creeping up along my spine after the first hour of riding. I kept my mouth shut about the pain, but it was becoming almost unbearable. Would I be able to take it for another two hours? Silly question, I had to take the pain. I couldn't slow us up.

I shifted uncomfortably in my saddle for the umpteenth time. Merlin looked over at me as if he knew something. I glared at him.

Gwen and Reynolds rode over to talk to Merlin.

"What are things going to look like when we get there?" Gwen asked.

"As you know, the defenses on these little towns are pretty impressive," Merlin said. "They will have delayed the forces of Morgana."

"The Death Reapers will start the attack with archers," Reynolds added. "That'll give us some time as well."

"I'm just hoping we aren't riding out to save an already vanquished town," Gwen said.

"They definitely can't last for an extended period," Merlin said, "but we should be arriving just in the nick of time. The walls around this place are quite sturdy, and their archers are excellent."

"Anything magical about this place?" Gwen asked.

"Unfortunately no," Merlin answered. "Just solid construction."

An hour later Tristan came back to us.

"The way is clear all the way to the town," Tristan informed us. "The Death Reapers probably don't think we'll want to leave the safety of Camelot."

"That makes sense," Gwen said.

"What's the status of the town?" Merlin asked.

"Not so good," Tristan answered. "Most of their archers are down, and the giants are using a battering ram on the drawbridge."

"Well that's not good," Merlin said. "I was expecting them to hold out a bit better."

"It's their new leader," Tristan said. "That guy in the red armor, he knows his shit."

"I've seen him on the battlefield," Wayne added as he rode over to meet with us. "Who is he?"

"I'm not sure," Merlin answered with a worried expression on his face.

We picked up the pace, and arrived faster than we anticipated. Our foot soldiers were used to marching. They'd arrive to the battle fresh enough to fight. At least that's what Reynolds assured the rest of us.

I moved over to the rest of the medics. That was where I belonged. I couldn't stay with the warriors; I'd just be in their way.

I was terrified. I'd never ridden out to a battle before. I've always been relatively safe and away from all the danger. This was going to be dangerous.

My hands began to tremble as we heard the first signs of the fighting. Orders were being shouted, men were shouting, men were screaming.

I closed my eyes and concentrated on my breathing in an attempt to calm myself. It wasn't working. The pace suddenly picked up all around me. One of the other medics grabbed my horse by the reigns and moved me out of the way.

I looked at him with what I was sure was a very frightened expression.

"I'll take care of you ma'am," the young man said. "We can't have anything happen to the king's mother now can we."

I smiled and patted his hand in a thankful gesture as we entered a clearing, and the battle was suddenly raging in front of me.

The medical team moved out of the way and waited impatiently. The Death Reapers and giants had broken through the wall and were already inside the town. With the lack of opposition, our archers began to scale the defensive walls and fire from their elevated positions. The soldiers on horseback rode right through the broken drawbridge with the foot soldiers following closely behind.

The plan was to surprise and overwhelm the enemy.

A soldier had been placed in charge of the medical team for our safety. He watched our entire army enter the town.

"We're good to go," the soldier said. "You can't save anybody from out here."

We rode forward and entered through the drawbridge. I saw blood and bodies everywhere. A thick green fog hung over the entire area and contrasted greatly with the bright blue sky. I was too close to the battle. My entire body was shaking with fear.

My fear made me ashamed.

I needed to act. Instead, I was frozen. Actually, the entire medical team was frozen solid. Not forty feet in front of us was a mighty giant. He was swinging his powerful fists down at Wayne and Bedder as they rode around him in weaving patters and slashed at his hairy legs.

Over to my left, on top of a small, snow-covered, wooden building, Gwen and a few other archers were firing arrow after arrow into the Death Reapers. I watched her for a moment. She was shouting orders that I couldn't hear over the din of battle. How had she become so brave? How did all of them become so brave?

The fighting was close and terrible. Inside the defensive walls were less than a mile of open space, beyond that was the actual homes of the residents. It was clear almost immediately that we were outnumbered. It was clear that they'd been expecting us.

The giants thundered amongst our soldiers. They were unstoppable. Had it only been us facing the Death Reapers we would have stood a chance. The giants ruined that chance. Everyone was going to die.

We'd walked right into a trap.

A soldier fell not far from me. I dismounted my horse and ran through knee high snow to help him. The soldier in charge of our safety yelled for me to return, but I ignored him. The young medic that promised to take care of me came with me. Together we stopped the bleeding from the soldiers knife wound, and dragged him away from the field of battle.

The soldier in charge of our safety began yelling at me.

I yelled back.

"Everyone has a job to do!" I shouted. "And I'm going to do mine. You were told to keep us safe. Well, find a way to do that, and allow us to still do our jobs!"

The man looked confused, but the distraction was enough to drive the medical team into action. We administered help as swords clashed around us. We dragged the wounded away from danger when moments allowed.

My back was in terrible pain, but I ignored the throbbing ache and did my best to help the soldiers in need. I had no concept of time. The fight could have been going on for hours, or possibly it was only minutes.

Wayne was smacked from his horse.

The giant advanced towards him. It brought its foot up high into the air. Wayne wasn't moving. He was either unconscious or dead. I picked up a sword from the ground, judging by its rusty blade, it had once belonged to a Death Reaper.

I brandished the rusty sword at the giant, and the giant laughed. I screamed out, but I could barely hear my own voice over all the buzzing.

Buzzing?

I looked towards the sky. The wasps had arrived. In a great cloud, their black and yellow bodies descended onto the battlefield. They attacked as one, a great swarm that attached itself to giant after giant.

The giants began to scream out.

I watched as they flailed their arms around in the air, and swatted at the aggressive insects, but it was to no avail. The swarm damn near blotted out the sky. Certainly the swarm had grown tremendously after it had left the castle.

One of the giants fell down. Its body was covered with welts and bumps that I could see despite all the fur. I couldn't tell whether or not it was dead, but that didn't matter much anyway. As soon as it fell, Tristan ran over to it and slashed open the creature's neck.

Two more giants fell, and the rest began running away. I didn't know where they were headed; probably they had no destination in mind. I think they only wanted to escape the stinging pain of the wasps. They were out of luck. The wasps pursued them into the forest.

Our soldiers cheered as they fled.

I relaxed just a bit.

I shouldn't have.

From the opposite end of the town another wave of Death Reapers approached the battlefield. They moved slowly past all the houses. I could see their forms emerging through the green fog. I screamed out a warning. I screamed it as loud as possible, and I repeated it over and over again, but nobody could do anything. They were all still fighting against the previous Death Reapers.

I opened Wayne's helmet.

I slapped at his face until I saw his eyelids flutter and open.

"How bad is it?" I asked.

"What are you doing here?" Wayne asked.

"I'm saving your life," I answered. "Now how badly are you hurt?"

"I'm okay," Wayne answered. "I'm just a little bruised up. You need to get back towards the rear of the battle where it's safe."

Bedder appeared with Wayne's horse just as Wayne began rising to his feet. The man looked a bit unsteady, but that wasn't going to stop him.

The soldier in charge of our safety had arrived.

"Keep her out of the battle," Wayne said to him.

"I'm trying, sir," the soldier answered.

Another soldier fell towards our left. I ran out to help him just as the new wave of Death Reapers joined the battle.

I reached the fallen soldier right as he took his last breath. I held his hand and after he was gone, I closed his eyes and ran to the next person that needed my aide.

She was an archer.

She was standing next to Gwen when she fell. The arrow was in her heart. There was nothing I could do. Gwen was above me on top of the wooden building. She was firing bravely as arrows flew all around her.

"It's too dangerous here," the soldier in charge of our protection said. "We need to move."

"Go help the others," I snapped.

"The others aren't in any danger," the soldier snapped in return. "They haven't entered the battlefield."

"That's because they're useless," I said.

The poor girl was dying in my arms. I couldn't save her. I looked up and saw Gwen's beautiful face staring down at me for a brief moment. Her blue eyes were wide in fear. She wanted to know the girls fate. I shook my head sadly and Gwen immediately went back to firing her arrows.

I whispered to the dying girl. I told her she was brave. I told her that her pain was almost over. She smiled the sweetest smile, and died in my arms.

We were attacked.

Three Death Reapers came at us. The soldier protecting me fought them bravely, and managed to hold them off, but he received a deep cut on the inside of his left thigh. I could see the blood flowing freely from the wound.

Gwen fired three arrows in rapid succession and our attackers fell dead in front of us. I looked back towards Gwen, but she wasn't paying attention. She was once again focused on firing her arrows into the battle.

The soldier in charge of protecting me fell to one knee.

"How deep is the cut?" I asked as I put my arms around his shoulders and leaned him back on the ground.

"It's bad," the soldier answered. "I'm feeling weak. This is the worst I've ever been cut."

"Well, I've got you," I said. "I'll make sure you're okay."

"I'm the one that's supposed to be protecting you," the soldier said.

"It's a team sport, young man," I said. "Now let's get you out of here."

"I can't move with a wound like this," the soldier said. "I'll bleed out."

"I've already stopped the bleeding," I said. "Now let's go."

The soldier limped, and I helped him move towards the relative safety of the rear of the battle. The rest of the medical team was working busily on the wounded that were already brought to them.

I helped sit him down and ran back into the battle. I dodged blades and ran away from Death Reapers in an effort to reach the wounded. I needed supplies. I needed help. More and more of our people were falling, and I was the only one running out to help them.

I was wrapping a head wound when a group of Death Reapers found me. Their silver eyes smiled right along with their crooked lips, and I knew I was in trouble. Had I been foolish? Yes, I had most certainly been foolish, but I also saved people.

Merlin was going to be furious.

The ground erupted underneath the Death Reapers and they were thrown backwards only to be suspended in midair. I looked around and saw Merlin walking towards me through the green fog.

He was indeed furious.

"What the hell do you think you're doing?" Merlin asked as he neared me. "What if I hadn't seen you?"

"Should we just leave our own soldiers to die?" I asked.

"It's very clear to me that we need to improve our medical teams," Merlin said, "but we'll work on that later. Stop risking your damn life."

I wasn't listening to him. I was wrapping up the poor soldiers head. I wasn't sure if he was going to make it, but I wanted to provide him with the best possible chance.

"Help me get him to the rear of the battle," I said.

Merlin cursed, looked over to the group of Death Reapers he'd left floating in midair, raised a fist, clenched his fingers, and the Death Reapers all collided into one another over and over again until their lifeless bodies dropped to the ground.

After that, Merlin motioned with his fingers and the wounded soldier rose into the air. The two of us walked him back to the rear of the battle where Merlin gently set him on the floor.

"He's not going to make it," Merlin said. "You risked your life for a dying man."

"I'm doing my job," I said. "If I was anyone else, you'd let them be."

"You're not anyone else," Merlin said. "You're the king's mother."

More Death Reapers charged us, and Merlin used his magic to fend them off. I looked out towards the battlefield, and that's when I finally noticed what was happening. With the giants gone, our soldiers were able to push themselves towards the outer borders of the battle. Slowly but surely, they were beginning to surround the Death Reapers.

I felt a brief moment of happiness until I noticed more figures moving in between the houses on their way to the battlefield. Just when we were slowly starting to turn the tide of the battle and overcome our enemy, more began to arrive.

I motioned to Merlin, and pointed at the oncoming Death Reapers.

Merlin smiled.

The leader in red armor was emerging through the green fog. He was menacing. Something about him was just wrong. His reddish horse was angry and screaming. The Death Reapers all around him were large and wearing plate armor instead of the normal chainmail.

They attacked our soldiers.

There were only forty or so of them, but they moved together as a unit. They were elite and better skilled than we had ever seen. The leader got closer and I could see that his helmet had a metal snout with small slits for the eyes.

Merlin went into action.

With a grabbing motion of his fists, he caused a tidal wave of snow and dirt. Some of the elite group were knocked from their horses. Their leader wasn't among them. Alone, he rode to meet Merlin while the rest of his group continued their attack.

Merlin met the Red Knight slightly away from the main battle, in an open area of trampled snow and blood. The Red Knight drew his sword. Merlin stamped his staff into the ground and a wall of fire surrounded the Red Knight.

The Red Knight charged through the flames before Merlin could react. He swung with his sword, and Merlin was forced to use his staff to block the blade. The blade severed the staff, and Merlin began to look worried. It was a subtle expression; you'd have to know him very well to notice.

Merlin shoved his hands into the snow, and roots and vines shot up to wrap around the legs of the Red Knight's horse. The horse struggled violently, but couldn't free himself. The Red Knight jumped away from the horse and calmly walked towards Merlin.

Merlin held his ground.

The two of them came together in a flurry of steel and wood. It was too close for my comfort. Merlin didn't like to fight up close and personal. He preferred to use his magic from a distance. He also carried no weapons. All he had to defend himself with were the two broken pieces of his staff.

From out of nowhere, Wayne rode through the green fog, came up behind the Red Knight, and slashed downward with his axe.

At the last moment, the Red Knight stepped out of the way, and sliced upward into Wayne's side. The fight stopped briefly as Wayne continued riding for close to ten feet before falling from his horse.

The Red Knight's sword erupted in a black flame.

"What is your name?" Merlin asked the Red Knight.

"I am Death," the Red Knight answered. "I am Death to Camelot."

The two of them collided again. In the brief flurry of movement, one of the broken pieces of Merlin's staff went flying out of his hand.

The Red Knight's sword came to Merlin's unprotected side, and without another option, Merlin reached out and caught the blade. The Red Knight yanked it away in a fury, and the blade cut deeply into Merlin's hand.

The Red Knight began to circle Merlin. Drops of the wizard's blood dripped from his hand and became lost among the other splatters of blood on the trampled snow.

Merlin cast away the remaining side of his broken staff and brought his hands together. A ball of flame ignited between his palms. The ball grew bigger and bigger, and when it was the size of a basketball, Merlin sent it towards the Red Knight.

The ball of flame collided with the leader's chest armor in a mighty thump, and exploded in a shower of sparks.

"I was raised in the flame, wizard," the Red Knight gloated. "I grew to a man in a place of darkness and fire. Your magic is weak, and not a threat to me."

"I can see that," Merlin said. "Morgana must love you dearly."

The knight attacked.

Merlin evaded the attack, but lost his balance. I searched for a weapon, and found another rusty sword in the grip of a dead Death Reaper. I ran through red slush, and fell to my knees in an attempt to pick it up.

The Death Reaper's hand had frozen on the grip. Two fingers broke away as I finally pulled it free from his grasp. I ran back towards Merlin and the Red Knight.

I snuck as quietly as I could sneak. I came up behind the Red Knight, and swung the rusty swords downwards towards the area between his head and right shoulder.

The sword hit him with a clang of steel on steel, but didn't penetrate the red armor. The Red Knight spun around and slapped me away from him. His metal encased hand hit me on the cheekbone and sent me falling into the snow.

In a daze, I watched as the Red Knight looked down at me. Why was he staring at me like that? Did he know who I was? Would he kill me just to anger Arthur?

Merlin jumped on his back.

In another setting, it might have been comical. The knight thrashed around trying to dislodge Merlin, like a bull trying to knock a cowboy from his back.

I saw blue flashes of electricity gather around Merlin's hands as he shocked the knight over and over through his armor.

The armor must have been magical. The Red Knight refused to fall, and right as he finally got a grip on Merlin's leg, Wayne appeared once again. He was back on his horse and bleeding through his armor, but he somehow rode by the Red Knight with an outstretched hand and Merlin grabbed a hold of it. The two of them circled around blocking me from danger as I ran back to the rest of the medical team.

A horn blew loudly over the sound of battle. It rang out three times signaling the order to retreat.

I looked towards the battle. The foot soldiers were running towards me, while the soldiers on horseback covered their retreat. I couldn't find Merlin and Wayne. They were lost in the chaos. I couldn't see the Red Knight, but the way in which he stared down at me haunted me greatly. His eyes, there was something about his eyes.

Before I knew it, I was caught up in the rush of retreating soldiers. I was outside the town and someone was holding my horse still for me as I climbed up.

Our forces retreated as fast as we could, but our enemy didn't seem to be following us as we moved down the twisted trail through the winter forest.

In a far off clearing we gathered.

Order was called. Foot soldiers were assembled into groups. When the mounted soldiers arrived, they rode in and amongst the gathered foot soldiers as if creating a defensive line, but why weren't we moving?

"We're waiting for the archers," Merlin said as he and Wayne rode up beside me. "They covered the final retreat. As soon as they arrive, we'll head home."

"What happened to the people of that town?" I asked. "I never saw them."

"Massacred," Merlin answered. "That new leader of theirs is something else. His blade and armor are both enchanted. He fights like a demon..."

"He's also an incredible leader," Wayne interrupted. "His group of mounted Death Reapers must have attacked from the rear. I caught a glimpse of the bodies. I've never seen so many bodies. They were being carted away."

"More soldiers for Morgana," Merlin said. "I can't believe this happened. I can't believe we were so thoroughly beaten."

Gwen and the rest of the archers began to arrive. They seemed to be missing about half their number. Reynolds was riding next to Gwen and continuously looking over his shoulder.

"They didn't pursue us," Reynolds announced as the two of them met up with us.

"Let's use this time to bandage up the wounded," Wayne said. "We can get them stable for the ride home."

"That's a good idea," Merlin said.

"I'll get started," I said. "The medical team is near the foot soldiers, send the injured to us, and we'll do what we can."

The next few hours were a daze as I went to work. We rushed, but not because we were in danger. We rushed so that the wounded would sooner get the proper medical attention they needed.

We had lookouts all around us. Merlin himself was at the top of a hill surveying the area. I couldn't believe the Red Knight had gotten the better of him. Merlin's magic was useless against this new enemy. I couldn't get over that. Merlin had always been the unbeatable one in my eyes.

We'd lost a terrible fight. Too many of our soldiers died in the battle. Too many of them were dying around me. The wounded were beyond count. The injuries ranged from broken limbs, all the way up to severed limbs.

Everything would be better once we got back to Camelot. Camelot was safe. Once there we could rethink everything. Once there we'd figure out what went wrong.

I was covered in blood when all was finished, and we were ready to get moving. We should have been finished long before we actually were. Many of the soldiers needed care a lot sooner than they received it. In the future, I'd make it my business to improve the medical team.

I walked to Merlin as the wounded were being prepared to travel. The wizard looked worried at the top of his little hill.

"It freaks me out to see a teenager in only a t-shirt during winter time," I said. "It makes me want to shove you into a jacket."

Merlin smiled.

Something was bothering him, and I didn't need three guesses to figure out what it was.

"Do you want to talk about it?" I asked.

"Not really," Merlin said.

"Alright then," I said. "Are you ready to leave?"

"He beat me, Dellia," Merlin said.

"Yes he did," I said.

"My magic still isn't where it needs to be," Merlin complained. "I haven't reached anywhere near my full capabilities."

"You said it would take time," I said.

"We're running out of time," Merlin said.

"You just got over being severely injured by the Widow Queen," I said as a flash of red in the distance distracted me. "I think you're being a little hard on yourself."

"Well I don't like getting my ass kicked," Merlin said. "I much prefer being the ass-kicker."

I laughed at his little temper tantrum as my eyes scanned the tree's in the distance. I was sure I saw a flash of red against the white background of snow, but whatever it was had vanished instantly. Was it a wounded soldier? Was someone trying to catch up to us?

"I don't think it's funny at all," Merlin said.

"Have you considered that our opponents are getting tougher?" I asked.

"It doesn't matter what our opponents do," Merlin said. "I'm freakin Merlin. I should be able to handle anything...and what in the hell are you looking for?"

"I thought I saw something," I said.

"What?" Merlin asked, becoming instantly alert.

I pointed in the direction that I'd seen the flash of red.

"It came from over there," I said. "A flash of red and then it was gone."

"I don't see anything," Merlin said. "I don't sense anything."

I scanned farther along towards the right. Far away, on top of another hill I once again saw red against the white background of snow. The Red Knight was standing on top of a hill very similar to ours. He was pointing at me.

"Merlin," I said. "He's found us."

A saw a brief flash of movement, but I couldn't tell what it was. My chest was suddenly on fire. The pain was excruciating. I gasped for breath as I fell down the hill. Merlin was right behind me. He was stopping my fall. I couldn't breathe. Merlin was holding my head in his lap. Snow began falling all around us, and a crowd began to gather.

"What happened?" Gwen asked as she ran to me and grabbed my hand.

"The Red Knight," Merlin answered. "A single shot and then he was gone."

"Merlin?" I whispered in a quiet voice. "Why did I fall?"

"Shush, my dear," Merlin said as he brushed his cool hands against my forehead. "Don't try and talk. We'll take care of you."

Take care of me?

Why was I in so much pain?

I tried to lift my head. Someone told me not to move, but I ignored them and lifted my head anyway. I started crying when I saw the arrow sticking out of the center of my chest.

Merlin began shouting orders, and slowly I lost consciousness as I watched the blood flow from my body and begin to pool in the snow.

♣ MERLIN ♣

I shouted out my orders a second time, and everyone began to move. The medics did their best to stop the bleeding, but what I really needed was a horse. Not much could be done for Dellia out here in the cold. I needed to get her back to the castle.

"I don't think she should be moved," Bedder said as I lifted Dellia into my arms.

I ignored him, and walked towards my horse.

"Merlin," Wayne said. "What are you doing? We shouldn't move her."

"She'll die out here," I said as I trudged throw snow up to my knees.

Gwen stepped in front of me and held out her hands.

"Moving her will cause her pain," Gwen said. "We need to do what we can here."

I looked her in the face. Her expression shocked me. I looked at the faces of the others. They all wore the same expression. They'd given up. They didn't expect Dellia to live. They only wanted to ease her passing.

"I'm taking her to the castle," I said.

"What's so important about the castle?" Wayne asked.

"Toad," I answered. "He's a healer. If anyone can help her, Toad can."

"Merlin," Bedder said in a sad voice. "No one can help her. I'm sorry, but she's too..."

Bedder didn't finish. His emotions had overwhelmed him.

I moved around Gwen right as a soldier brought me my horse. A few twists of my fingers, and Dellia became as light as a feather. I mounted the horse,

156

grabbed a blanket from my saddlebag, wrapped it around her, and cradled my friend in my arms.

I left without another word.

Toad could save my dearest friend. That's why he stayed on. His healing magic would come in handy someday. We both agreed. Now was the day. I'd save Dellia.

I rode fast.

I whispered words of encouragement to the horse. I lent the steed my strength. Faster and faster we rode. The snow flew five feet into the air behind us, and I realized we could go even faster with a bit of magic.

I twisted my hands and focused my energy. My horse became lighter. No longer was he plunging through the snow on the trail, now he was running on top of it.

Snow.

When had it started snowing?

It must have happened after Dellia was struck by the arrow. Why would it snow after she was struck? Was it some sort of sign?

My eyes began to burn. At first I thought it was only the cold air rushing past my face, but I soon realized that I was crying. Dellia was so still in my arms. I pushed my cheek to her forehead, she was too cold. I felt for her pulse and found it weak.

In record time I was pounding through the gates of Camelot. People rushed to get out of my way as I rode to the castle.

At the drawbridge, I shouted for Toad. To my relief he answered almost immediately. I watched the little gnome rush over and climb on top of the horse.

He took a brief glance at Dellia.

"Get us to the infirmary immediately," Toad said.

I rode on.

Once again, I rode as fast as my horse could carry us. We crossed the drawbridge, and entered the castle. It was the shortest way to the infirmary. Inside the castle, I turned left and then right. We galloped down a long hallway, and entered the infirmary at the back of the castle.

I eased Dellia off my horse and set her down on the nearest bed. The working medical staff immediately ran over to help, but Toad chased them all back.

"This woman is beyond your simple skills," Toad said. "I'm the one she needs."

I began to pace as the gnome went to work. In a cabinet towards the back of the infirmary, his tools of the trade were waiting. I grasped Dellia's hand. My tears were freely flowing, and I didn't care who saw me weeping.

"Merlin," Toad said. "You must go."

"I need to be by her side," I argued.

"You need to leave," Toad said. "It'll get worse before it gets better. You're already emotional."

"I understand that, but..." I tried to say.

"Go alert the king," Toad said. "He needs to know."

Arthur.

I'd forgotten about Arthur. What was I going to say to him? What could I say to him? All of this was my fault. I should never have allowed Dellia come with us. She should have stayed in the castle. She'd have been safe in the castle.

I left the room just as Toad began issuing out orders to the medical staff. Dellia, my poor Dellia. The wound was so grievous I feared for the future.

"Where is Arthur?" I asked the nearest ghost.

"He's in his bath, I believe," the female ghost answered with a slight bow.

The castle was enormous and the king's bath was far away. I'd have to use all the shortcuts and hidden passageways. That wouldn't be a problem. I knew all of them like the back of my own hand.

I saw Wendell moving towards the infirmary. He looked frightened. I didn't blame him a bit. The news was spreading. I needed to reach Arthur before anyone else.

"Is it true?" Wendell asked.

"She's been seriously injured," I answered. "I need you to wait for the others by the main door. Many of them will be coming. Don't let anyone near the infirmary. Send them all into the waiting room. Provide them with plenty of drinks and refreshments."

"As you wish," Wendell said with a slight bow before vanishing through the nearest wall.

Back to Arthur, what was I going to tell him? How was he going to react? Was he sober? Was he sober enough to understand what I was about to tell him?

I touched a hidden lever behind a statue, and made my way into a dark passageway. With a snap of my fingers, sconces along the walls burst into small flames. Arthur's bedroom was located in the highest tower. This passageway and a few others would lead me to the hidden staircase behind his bookshelf.

Making my way to his bedroom took time. It was time that felt like a waste. I'd seen wounds like Dellia's before. I knew the outcomes of those wounds. I didn't want to think about it. I only wanted to believe that Toad could work his magic, and save my dearest friend.

I stepped through the hidden bookshelf, and wiped by eyes. I went to the nearest mirror in Arthur's room and cleaned my face. My tears had left streaks in the dirt below my eyes

After I was somewhat presentable, I made my way to the bath. It wasn't a bath by any normal means. To most people it would be considered a large shallow pool. There was a ghost guarding the door. Beyond the ghost I could hear the sounds of women giggling.

"I must have a word with the king," I told the ghost.

"The king is not to be disturbed," the ghost replied.

"Arthur's mother has been injured," I managed to say without cracking my voice. "Would you like to share that news with him, or would you like me to do it?"

The ghost looked slightly nervous.

He stepped out of the way.

I entered the hot and humid room.

Arthur was in the pool. He wasn't alone. I knew that from the giggles I'd heard earlier, but what I saw was shocking. There were numerous attractive women scattered about, and all of them were in various shades of undress.

Arthur had a woman in each arm. He was definitely drunk, but he wasn't completely senseless.

He looked up as I approached.

"I'm not to be disturbed," Arthur said with a sneer.

"We need to talk," I said.

"No we don't," Arthur said. "You need to clean yourself up."

"It's about your mother," I said.

The sneer instantly fell from Arthur's face.

"What about my mother?" Arthur asked.

"Perhaps we can talk somewhere more private?" I asked.

"What about my mother?" Arthur repeated.

"She's been hurt," I answered. "It's very serious."

Arthur stood up.

"What are you talking about?" Arthur asked.

"She came with us to the battle," I answered.

"You took my mother into battle?" Arthur asked.

"I tried to stop her," I answered. "I should have tried harder. We lost the battle. We retreated. We stopped to patch up the wounded and the Red Knight snuck up close enough to let loose with an arrow."

"An arrow?" Arthur asked. "Is she..."

"She's still alive," I interrupted. "Toad is working on her. He's an incredible healer, all gnomes are, but it doesn't look good."

"Where is she?" Arthur asked.

"She's in the infirmary," I answered.

Arthur leapt from the pool, and ran out of the room. He stopped by the ghost watching the entrance of the bath.

"Where's the infirmary?" Arthur asked.

The ghost tried to give him directions, but Arthur was too impatient to listen. Instead, he charged into the hallway dripping wet and naked as the day he was born. Ghostly servants began to follow him, begging him to dress. Many were offering towels. Arthur ignored them all, and demanded directions.

I watched from his bedroom doorway.

It was probably best that he rid himself of anger before he saw his mother.

"What's happening?" Lancelot asked.

I couldn't find the boy. He was getting pretty good at sneaking up on people. I assumed that he was in the dark wooden rafters above my head. I should have guessed that he'd be near Arthur and keeping an eye on him.

"Dellia has been injured," I answered.

"Is she going to be okay?" Lancelot asked.

"I don't think so," I answered.

A bit of dust fell from the rafters and Lancelot was gone. I went back inside Arthur's room, and grabbed some clothes for him. After that, I slipped back into the secret stairway. I'd meet him at the infirmary.

I didn't have to wait long.

Arthur came barreling down the hallway with an entire entourage of ghostly servants. He looked both angry and panicked. I stood before the doors to the infirmary.

Dellia was screaming in the background.

"You shouldn't go in there," I said.

"That's my mother!" Arthur screamed. "Get out of the way!"

"You shouldn't see her like this," I said. "And she shouldn't see you like that."

Arthur fumed for a moment.

Excalibur appeared next to him. One second it was just Arthur and then when I looked down, I saw the sword standing straight up from the floor. Arthur tilted his head as if he were listening to the weapon. I could only guess what the sword was telling him.

"Here, Arthur," I said. "I brought you your clothes."

Arthur looked at me.

His eyes were starting to redden.

"I won't fight you," I said. "If you really want to see her, I'll move out of the way. I only wish to spare the both of you."

Arthur shook his head as if clearing his thoughts.

"Why's she screaming?" Arthur asked.

"They were probably removing the arrow," I answered. "It's quiet now. I think the worst is over."

Arthur winced when I mentioned the arrow.

"I'm going in there to see my mother," Arthur said as he dressed. "This is the end of the conversation."

I nodded and stood out of the way.

He was going to attack me if I tried to stop him.

Arthur finished dressing and went into the infirmary. As soon as the door closed behind him, Lancelot spoke up.

"He's going to go crazy if anything happens to her," Lancelot said.

"I think he's too far gone to be too much of a problem," I said.

"You really don't know him at all," Lancelot said.

I gave another nod, and let my mind wander.

Arthur came out of the infirmary. He looked broken. I looked at his watering eyes questioningly.

"She's still here," Arthur said, "but there was poison on the arrow. She probably won't last the night."

Arthur walked away without another word. I should have hugged him. I should have said something to him. I shouldn't have let him just walk away, but I myself was overcome with grief.

I slid my back along the wall until I was sitting down, then I curled up my legs and hid my face. I should have gone somewhere private and gotten control over myself, but I just couldn't convince my body to move.

Eventually, Toad came out of the infirmary.

He sat down next to me.

"She's not in any pain," Toad said. "I was able to do that much for her. She's very tired, but no pain."

"Can I go see her?" I asked.

"She's sleeping," Toad said.

"Does she know?" I asked.

"Yes," Toad said.

We sat in silence for what seemed like hours. I probably would have sat there the entire night, but I heard voices coming from down the hallway.

Gwen, Tristan, Reynolds, Wayne, Bedder...they were finally arriving. They wanted to know about Dellia. I looked down at Toad and he looked up at me.

"You should say something," Toad said. "One by one, they can come in and say their goodbyes."

I got to my feet with an unnecessary grunt, and made my way to the others. Wayne locked eyes with me immediately upon entering their room. The big man read the look on my face, collapsed in a chair, and openly wept.

"The arrow was poisoned," I said in a voice unfamiliar to me. "She suffers no pain, but she won't last the night. If there's anyone that would like to see her, we can arrange for that to happen."

"How's Arthur?" Wayne asked.

"Not well," I said. "He left after seeing his mother."

"He left?" Gwen asked.

"Yes," I answered.

"Where'd he go?" Gwen asked.

"I couldn't say," I answered.

"His mother's in a room dying, and he just left?" Gwen asked. "What the hell is wrong with him?"

"Be quiet!" A sharp voice snapped from up in the rafters, causing everyone to jump. "Mind your tongue when it comes to Arthur."

Gwen looked at the rafters for a few seconds.

"I'm very sorry, Lance," Gwen said. "Now is certainly not the time."

Lancelot didn't reply.

"Well, like I said, if any of you would like to see her just let me know." I said.

Gwen was the first to go in. She came back weeping. Others followed her. I'm not sure who, the moment rapidly became a blur of moving shadows and indistinct voices. Day had turned into evening when I finally went in to say my goodbyes.

"There's a sea of candles right outside of the castle," I said to Dellia.

"I've heard," Dellia said in a voice so weak I wanted to scream.

"You've certainly made an impression on people around here," I said.

"I did my best," Dellia said.

"I can't even count how many lives you've saved," I said.

"Merlin," Dellia said. "You can't blame yourself for this. I had a job to do and I did it. We aren't responsible for this war."

Damn it.

Damn it.

Damn it.

My eyes filled up with water, and the tears broke through. I couldn't hold it back. I didn't want Dellia to see me cry, but I couldn't hold it back.

"You weren't supposed to get hurt!" I cried. "You were supposed to be safe. You were supposed to stay safe."

"That doesn't much sound like me," Dellia said. "And it certainly wasn't your decision to make."

"I don't want you to leave," I said. "I don't want you to..."

The sobs came. I was ruining this. I should have been telling her how much she meant to me. I should have been comforting her. Instead, it was her tired hand that reached for mine.

Dellia held me for a long time.

I didn't want her to let go of me.

I wanted to be a barrier against death.

I wanted to save her.

Arthur was in the doorway.

How long had I been standing there with my face buried in the nape of Dellia's neck, and my arms wrapped around her?

"Arthur," Dellia said.

"Hi, Mom," Arthur said.

"Come here," Dellia said. "Let me see you."

I moved out of the way as Arthur approached. He was clean, but smelled of alcohol. He held onto his mother's hand, and placed his palm on her forehead. Dellia could barely keep her eyes open, but she tried her hardest.

"Look at you," Dellia said to Arthur. "My handsome boy."

Arthur smiled sweetly.

"How are you feeling?" Arthur asked. "Does anything hurt?"

"No," Dellia said. "I'm fine. Toad is a wonderful doctor."

"Can I get you anything?" Arthur asked.

"I just want you to stay and visit with me," Dellia said. "Would that be okay?"

"Of course," Arthur said. "I'll stay as long as you want me to."

"It won't be as much fun as watching the stars with me," Dellia said. "I wish we could do that right now."

Without a word of warning, Arthur picked his mother up out of the bed. Nurses rushed forward, only to come to an immediate stop when they saw the look on the king's face. Arthur was not going to be denied.

"Arthur, what are you doing?" Dellia asked.

"I'm taking you to the stars," Arthur answered.

I helped wrap her up in a blanket and Arthur walked out of the room. The nurses and ghosts followed at a distance as Arthur walked towards his bedroom at the top of the highest tower. Wayne came forward.

"Where's he taking her?" Wayne asked.

"They're going to watch the stars," I answered.

"No," Wayne said. "They're going to say goodbye."

✣ ARTHUR ✣

My mother.

My mother was dying.

Her body felt light in my arms as I carried her up stairway after stairway. Her eyes were closed, but I could feel her breathing and I could feel the heat rolling off her in waves.

Don't leave me.

Please don't leave me.

I pounded through my bedroom, and took the circular stairs in the corner of the room to the top of the tower. There, in a circular area amongst the battlements of the castle, I brought my mother to the stars.

"Mom," I said. "We're here."

My mother opened her eyes.

"Wow," my mother exclaimed. "What a view."

I took a seat on the floor, curling in behind my mother and placing her back upon my chest.

"Your beard is rough," my mother said.

"I'll shave it off for you," I said. "I'll do anything for you."

"Don't be silly," my mother said. "You look very handsome with a beard."

"How are you feeling?" I asked.

"I'm very tired," my mother said. "There are some things I need to tell you."

"You can tell me later," I said. "Let's just watch the stars. I think I can see some of the planets."

"Arthur," my mother said. "I love you very much. You know that, right?"

"I know that," I said.

"Good," my mother said. "I've tried so hard to reach you. Everyone's tried so hard to reach you, but the thing is, you died the same night your wife and son died. I understand all of that. I know you were changed, and I don't blame you a bit, but I need you to come back to us now. I need you to take part in the world again."

"I'll do my best," I said.

"No," my mother said. "I need you to do even better than that. I need you to be the man you used to be. I need you to be a king."

"I will," I said. "Anything you want. Just...just...don't leave me."

"My sweet boy," my mother said. "I'd stay if I could. I love you so much. I'm so proud...proud...of...you."

A small gasp of pain, and I watched as her eyes slowly closed.

My mother.

My beautiful mother.

She was gone. She was gone forever. The emptiness crashed over me. The loneliness overwhelmed me. What alcohol was left in my system demanded more, but I didn't give into the demand. Instead, I held on tighter to my mother and cried into her shoulder.

My mother was gone.

My mother was gone.

I wasn't a good son. I was a horrible son, but she loved me anyway. She made excuses for me. She took care of me. How the hell was I going to continue without her? Why even bother? I could just stay out here forever. The cold would take me away sooner or later.

An hour or so later, I heard a door open and close.

Nurses and a doctor attempted to take my mother away from me, but I refused to let her go. Merlin was there. Wayne was there as well.

"It's okay, Arthur," Wayne said. "It's time to let her go."

Merlin was behind everyone and off to the side.

The ancient wizard inside the body of a teenager was crying so hard, he couldn't force himself to help Wayne.

Wayne grabbed my face, and looked me in the eye.

"I'm so sorry, Arthur," Wayne said.

His emotion overwhelmed me. I loosened my grip, and my mother was gently pulled away from me. As soon as she was gone, another wave of grief crashed over me. I'd never be able to hold my mother again.

Nurses were all around me.

Blankets were being wrapped around my shoulders. I was being led back into the castle. I felt warm hands on my forehead, and suddenly Wayne was carrying me.

I'm not the one who died.

I don't need to be carried.

I'm the one who outlives everyone he loves.

♣ GWEN ♣

My heart had broken. I couldn't believe Dellia was gone. I couldn't believe I'd never see her again. She was the strongest woman I'd ever met. How many lives had she saved? I saw her in the thick of battle running out there to save our soldiers.

She was a hero.

She was my friend.

In many ways, she was like my own mother.

All of Camelot mourned her passing. Gifts were brought night and day to the castle. Arthur was nowhere to be seen. Merlin and I accepted the gifts. Merlin and I consoled her many friends.

Arthur.

A mother couldn't ask for a worse son.

How could he not be here to honor her?

The funeral was on a Saturday morning. People came from all around. The neighboring towns must have emptied. The people braved the cold, grey sky, and stood outside in the snow as her body was laid to rest in the cemetery.

Arthur did not attend.

I looked for him in the services. I looked for him at the cemetery. Dellia's only child didn't even attend her funeral.

I was beside myself with anger. No one else made mention of it. They were too polite, but I was fuming. Dellia deserved better than that. She deserved a son she could be proud of, not some womanizing alcoholic.

After the funeral, everyone went back to the castle. Food had been prepared, but not many of us had an appetite.

I began to drink.

It wasn't something I normally did to excess, but I was angry. I was angry that I'd lost Dellia, and I was angry at her son for the way he treated her.

I doubted he even loved her.

He was probably in his room celebrating.

Day turned into evening, and the mourners slowly departed, one after another. Merlin made himself available for everyone even though grief weighed upon him heavily. I, on the other hand became distant.

I wanted peace and quiet.

I wanted to be away from this castle.

I wanted to hit something.

I wanted to kill something.

I left the ballroom. I couldn't stay. I meant to leave the castle, but instead I found myself marching up towards Arthur's tower.

What was I doing?

I knew very well what I was doing. I was going to tell him. I was going to tell him what a horrible person he was. I was going to ask him to leave the castle. He wasn't worthy of being a king. He wasn't worthy of being a son.

I was going to tell him every nasty thing I'd ever thought of, and he was going to listen. I'd force him to listen. If I had to chase him all around the castle, he was going to listen to what I had to say.

My legs were shaking as I climbed the last of the stairs. I was drunk. I knew I was very drunk, but I didn't care. The alcohol gave me the courage to do what needed to be done. I wanted to break him with my words. I wanted to wound him. To make him feel the pain he should already have been feeling.

There were ghosts guarding his doorway.

"You can't come go in there, milady," a ghost said to me.

"Are you ready to fight me?" I asked.

"We don't want to fight you, milady," the ghost said, "but we were given orders."

"Who gave you those orders, the king?" I asked.

"No milady," the other ghost answered. "It was the gnome."

That caught me slightly off guard.

"The gnome?" I asked. "Where is he? I'll have a talk with him."

"I'm right behind you, Lady Guinevere," Toad said. "What brings you up to the king's bedchamber?"

"I'd like to have a word with Arthur," I said.

"Now is certainly a bad time," Toad said. "Perhaps if you come back tomorrow?"

"I'll see him now, thank you," I said while turning around to face the ghosts and the door.

The ghosts stepped out of the way, and I entered Arthur's bedroom. The bedroom was empty. There was no wild party with nude girls running around. There was no laughter. The room instead gave off a sadness that took my breath away.

"He's left his bed again," Toad said. "You'll find him on the tower."

"Indeed," I said as I set out for the winding staircase that led to the top of the tower.

My rage was returning. So what if he wasn't having a party. I'd still find him deep inside a bottle. He'd still be the uncaring son that'd been nothing but disappointment to his mother.

I was going to have my day. I was finally going to unburden myself and tell our idiot king what everybody wanted to tell him, and should have told him a long time ago.

I opened the wooden door that led to the top of the tower. I walked outside into the cold and found him immediately. He was sitting on the stone floor, wrapped in blankets, and watching the stars.

There were bottles all around him, and not a single one of them had been opened. I was confused, but I was still angry. That is until he slowly turned his head to face me.

Anguish.

A profound sorrow that instantly broke my heart, that is what I saw on his face. He wasn't drinking. He wasn't partying. He was mourning.

I took a step towards him, and he put out a hand to stop me as if the force of his will alone would keep me away.

His beautiful face looked so sad, I couldn't help but weep. I grabbed the hand that attempted to stop me and held it to my heart.

I wanted to tell him something. I wanted to share his grief, to let him know that tonight alone I would be his friend. I'd be there for him. Beauty should never be broken.

I dropped to my knees and wrapped my arms around him.

"I should have been a better son," Arthur cried. "I disappointed her so many times."

"She loved you," I whispered. "She loved you more than anything in this world."

"I miss her," Arthur cried. "I miss her so much."

"I've got you," I said as tears ran down my cheeks. "I won't let you go."

Arthur wrapped his arms around me, and held on as if he were about to slide off the face of the earth. I ran my fingers through his reddish-blonde hair. I held him until he stopped shaking, and then I whispered things to him. I told him about my life. I told him about what I'd lost, and what I dreamed.

He listened, but never spoke a word. Occasionally, I caught his grey eyes looking out towards the stars, and other times his eyes would be closed. I understood how lonely he felt. I understood what he was going through.

As dawn came, so did the nurses. Toad came along with them, and motioned for me to wait as Arthur was carried back inside the tower.

"He stopped drinking when his mother died," Toad said when we were alone.

"That's good isn't it?" I asked.

"Now that we're through the worst of it, it is," Toad answered. "We almost lost him a few times. It's dangerous for an alcoholic to abruptly stop drinking, but that's exactly what he did. Fortunately he was discovered and I've been able to take care of him with the proper potions."

"He'll be okay, though?" I asked.

"Yes," Toad answered, "but his heart is broken, and that I cannot heal."

I left the tower. I left the bedroom, and in the hallway that led to the first set of stairs, I heard a voice.

"Is this what you wanted?" Lance asked from somewhere above me.

"What do you mean?" I asked.

"He's been broken," Lancelot said. "I've never seen him so bad. Does that make you happy?"

"Of course not," I answered. "My heart weeps for him."

"He'll come through this," Lancelot said. "There's been a change in him."

"I wish him the very best," I said. "I'm not your enemy, Lance. I promise you."

I continued down the stairs, and made my way to the opposite side of the castle where I had a room. I needed to collect myself. I felt off balance. I felt dazed.

I was freezing cold.

How long had I been up there on that tower? Poor Arthur, I couldn't get over his sadness. I couldn't move beyond the regret he was feeling. I kept picturing his face, and the grief that filled it. I should go to him again. I should help him through this.

No.

What was I thinking?

Going to that man, at this time would bring about my ruin. I had to keep my distance. I needed to keep him out of my thoughts.

Time went on.

Weeks turned into months.

There were more attacks on neighboring towns, but no battles. By the time we arrived to help out, the battle was already over.

We were bedeviled by our enemy.

A large group of us met about four times a week in the war room to discuss strategies. Something must be done, but none of had any great idea's. Build up our army. Train our soldiers better. Those were the only suggestions we had because we had no idea where the forces of Morgana were hidden.

We tried to bring people to the castle. They'd all be safe behind Stronghold Wall, but people didn't want to leave their homes and abandon their livelihoods, and truly Camelot couldn't support all of them.

The meetings continued. We shouted at each other. We agreed with each other. We tried everything, but we couldn't stop the attacks.

Arthur attended a meeting.

It was a shock to every one of us.

Arthur just walked into the room. I hadn't seen him for such a long time. To the best of my knowledge, no one had.

"Would it be okay if I sat in for this one?" Arthur asked Merlin.

"Of course it's okay," Merlin said. "This is your home."

Arthur nodded, but as the rest of us discussed tactics, Arthur never spoke a word. All he did was stare at a map like we weren't even there.

When the meeting was over, and everyone began to walk out, Arthur whispered something. All of us stopped and looked back at him.

"What's up, Arthur?" Wayne asked.

"What's this place here?" Arthur asked as he pointed to a spot on the map.

"That's an abandoned town," Tristan answered.

"It's located in between two other towns that have already been attacked," Arthur stated.

"One of those towns has been attacked three times," Wayne answered.

"Place our army inside the abandoned town," Arthur said. "Arm them with weapons that can also double as farming tools and construction tools."

"What are you thinking?" Merlin asked.

"We fill a town with our army," Arthur answered. "We make that town come back to life. We give the town a small contingent of soldiers to keep them safe, but not enough to worry this Red Knight. We let them attack us."

"Shit," Reynolds said. "That might just work. Can you imagine them attacking a town, and in turn being attacked not only by the soldiers, but by the farmers, and shop keepers, and stable boys as well?"

"A town full of trained soldiers just waiting to be attacked," Merlin said. "Very good, Arthur; very good indeed."

"Let's plan this out," Wayne said.

For the next four hours, we went over every detail of the plan. Arthur once again became quiet as the rest of us discussed things. I kept stealing glances at him, but he never once looked back. It was as if he didn't even remember the evening we'd shared at the top of his tower.

That was for the best.

Days later, we dispatched a group of five hundred soldiers to the abandoned town and went to work on once again making the place habitable.

Arthur was there.

The king kept to himself mostly. He spent most of his days fishing in the nearby stream. He never drank anything but water and coffee. He seemed calm and undisturbed by the inevitable attack.

I mixed in with all the other women. We did our own fair share of work around the town and in less than two weeks the place was looking rather nice. Surely it was at least looking good enough to attack.

I kept my bow hidden behind the counter of an inn that I pretended to run. I waited patiently for action, because I very dearly wanted to stop these marauders. I'd seen the mangled bodies of the men and women that were left behind after their attacks. Bodies too damaged to be resurrected to serve Morgana. I'd also seen the ruined bodies of the children that were too young to be of assistance.

I wanted payback.

I wanted revenge, and so did every other man and woman in this town.

The attack came one month later during a warm and dry evening. Most of the town was asleep except for the guard. When the alarm bells began to ring, everyone went into action.

Death Reapers were running everywhere when I stepped out of the inn, but this time instead of meeting innocent townspeople, they were confronted by trained warriors.

The Death Reapers were taken by surprise.

Their attack was sloppy, not something that would work on a trained army and they fell by the dozens.

I shot freely. Arrow after arrow brought down our shieldless adversaries. There was nothing the Death Reapers could do to change the tide of the battle. They tried, but as they regrouped we surrounded them.

It was over quickly.

We had prisoners.

"Where were the giants?" I asked.

"Yeah," Wayne agreed. "Why no giants?"

The question was put to the prisoners, and it was discovered that the giants had been having trouble with Merlin's magic wasps. They were currently making leather armor that would protect them from the savage stingers.

"That'll be easy enough to take care of," Arthur said as our soldiers celebrated. "We can burn them in their armor, what do you think Merlin? Something that'll burn hot enough to get their attention."

"I think I can come up with something," Merlin said.

"Excellent," Arthur said. "We'll be ready for them when they reappear. We should also keep some of those wasps of yours inside every town. Do these things use a hive?"

"Yes," Merlin answered. "I can make that happen. It'll take a bit, but it should be doable."

"One week," Arthur said. "I want to get these towns up to snuff. We can't expect to hide everyone behind Stronghold Wall. Nobody wants to leave their home and livelihood. Instead, we must go to them. We must make their homes safe."

Bedder grumbled something that I didn't hear.

"I also want more scouts," Arthur continued as he looked at a map. "I want to know when these attacks are coming well in advance. I want the people that live in these towns to have enough time to prepare. I want to give our soldiers enough time to help them out."

"Anything else?" Bedder asked.

"Yes," Arthur continued. "I want a group of fifty soldiers to stay out of the main fighting. These soldiers will have only one job, and that's to attack the wagons."

"What wagons?" Bedder asked.

"The wagons they use to carry off our dead," Wayne answered.

"Exactly," Arthur agreed. "Let's cut off their supply of fresh soldiers. From this day forward, our fallen people will remain with us."

"Wow," Tristan said quietly.

Arthur looked at him and smiled.

"This is just a start," Arthur said. "We'll do more as the need arises."

"That's all great," Bedder said, "but who put you in charge?"

Arthur looked at Bedder. He wasn't irritated; instead he seemed to understand Bedder's frustration. Merlin came to Arthur's defense.

"You forget your place," Merlin said. "Arthur is the king."

"Yeah," Bedder said. "I've heard that for a long time now, but I've never seen Arthur care about much more than himself. He's not my king. In this day and age we elect our leaders, and nobody in their right mind would ever elect him."

Everyone was shocked.

Except for Arthur.

"I understand how you feel," Arthur said. "I've made more than my fair share of mistakes. I've been a horrible person, but I made a promise to my mother. I'll do what needs to be done. All I need is for you to give me a chance."

"You don't deserve it," Bedder said.

Arthur drew Excalibur from its scabbard. It was at this time that I noticed all the blood on Arthur's clothes. I hadn't seen him fighting, but he must have slain many.

"I need you, Bedder," Arthur said. "I need all of you to win this war."

"You are no king," Bedder said. "You are no soldier. We've been fighting this entire time. You haven't."

"Then make me a knight," Arthur said. "All of you together. Make me a knight, and watch what I can do."

"I won't," Bedder said. "I can't...I don't know how."

"I do," Merlin said.

Arthur flipped his sword and handed the handle to Bedder. Bedder's eyes went wide as he grabbed the weapon.

"Everyone, grab the handle," Merlin said.

All of us moved forward to comply. Together we touched the handle of the magical sword and felt its power vibrate through us in waves. As one, our hands began to burn and blister as the sword heated up, but none of us let go.

Arthur dropped to his knees in front of Bedder. As one, we moved the tip of the sword to Arthur's left shoulder.

"IN THE NAME OF GOD, ST. MICHAEL, AND ST. GEORGE," Merlin shouted as we moved the tip of the sword back and forth between Arthur's shoulders, "I DUB THEE KNIGHT. BE LOYAL, BE BRAVE, AND BE TRUE!"

Arthur stood to his feet.

I looked around, and saw that all the soldiers had gathered near us. They watched with proud eyes. A moment had come. A great moment, and they had all been there to witness it.

The cheers rose up.

Arthur reached out his hand for Excalibur. Bedder gave it back instantly. Smoke was beginning to rise from his glove.

"I'll follow you," Bedder said.

"Thank you," Arthur said.

I looked towards Merlin. The wizard had tears in his eyes.

Someone handed me a drink. I don't know who it was. I was so caught up in the moment. It was if time had come to a stop. What had just happened? Was I the only one feeling this way?

Merlin came over and grabbed my hand.

"It's the magic inside of you," Merlin said. "You feel a little disorientated, am I right?"

"Yes," I answered.

"This is an important moment," Merlin said. "The magic is letting you know this. Arthur is coming into his own."

"I see," I said. "Listen Merlin, I've been meaning to talk to you about this..."

"You're ready to give up on magic?" Merlin asked.

"Yes," I answered. "It's not working out for me in a timely enough manner. I can better help out with my bow."

"What we need isn't another archer," Merlin said. "What we need is another wizard. I have a way to speed things up for you. Would you give me one last attempt?"

"I don't see how that'll make a difference," I said. "Unless it can fully give me something to..."

"Bring forth the magic," Merlin interrupted. "That is exactly what I intend to do."

"Alright," I said. "I'll give things one more chance."

"Excellent," Merlin said. "I'll let you know when the time is right."

Wayne patted Arthur on the back, and Arthur laughed. He looked so different without the alcohol. He stood differently, he had different mannerisms. I didn't know this person. Secretly, I wondered about him. Secretly, I had my doubts concerning his leadership, but I quickly resolved to wait things out and give him a chance. I clearly remembered the dream in which my father came to me. Following Arthur is what my father wanted me to do. Yes, I'd give him a chance.

"That was like a scene from a movie," Wayne said.

"I know," Arthur laughed. "I've seen that movie."

I smiled from a distance as the men joked around. A moving branch from a nearby tree caught my attention.

"Is that you, Lance?" I asked.

"Yes," Lance answered.

"How are you doing this evening?" I asked.

"Why do you stare at Arthur?" Lance asked.

"I'm...I'm not sure what you mean?" I answered.

"I don't think I like the way you look at him," Lance said. "And you're always watching him."

"I'm sorry," I said. "I didn't realize—"

"He's changed," Lance interrupted. "He's stopped drinking. He won this battle for us. You didn't see how many Death Reapers he killed."

"I hope you're right," I said. "He does indeed seem like a much different person."

"That's because I am," Arthur said from behind me.

I spun around. With the exception of the hidden Lancelot, Arthur and I were alone. His eyes were beautiful. I'd never seen eyes like his before. His hair had fallen into his face, and he was brushing it back with a casual motion of his hand.

"I'm sorry if I offended you," I said realizing that this was the first time Arthur and I had actually spoken since that night.

"You didn't offend me," Arthur said. "Everyone should be thinking the way you're thinking. I have a lot to prove."

He moved closer to me, and I suddenly had trouble catching my breath. He was handsome when he was a drunk, but that paled next to the man who stood before me now. There was vitality in him, a healthiness that drew people close.

Women were going to love this new king.

Men were going to envy him.

"Yes," I managed to whisper. "Well, I wish you the best."

I tried to move away, but Arthur gently caught me by the arm. He moved even closer to me and I could feel the heat of his body.

"I haven't forgotten what you did for me," Arthur whispered.

"It was nothing," I whispered back.

"No," Arthur argued. "It was everything."

He let me go, and vanished into the nearby crowd of celebrating soldiers. I stood there like an idiot just outside the celebrations wondering why my heart was beating so ferociously inside my chest.

"I told you he was different," Lance laughed from somewhere behind me.

"Oh shut up," I grumbled as I wandered away in search of privacy.

♣ LANCE ♣

I missed Dellia.

I'll always miss Dellia.

She was family, Like Arthur, she cared about me and accepted me. I'll never forget her, I'll honor her always, but life doesn't come grinding to a halt when we lose someone we love, it simply marches on.

That being said, after many months I finally realized that life wasn't half bad. Arthur had quit drinking, and a new Arthur had emerged. The death of his mother destroyed the drunkard, and left a king in his place.

It wasn't easy for him.

I was one of the few people that saw him rage and tremble inside his room each night, far from the prying eyes of others. I witnessed his struggle. I watched him come out on top, and every night since he emerged from his room brought out a new aspect of his personality that I'd never before seen.

He was a military genius. From his very first battle this was evident. He knew how to outsmart his opponents. In no time at all, we were winning battles. We were successfully defending our people.

Merlin concocted some sort of serum that was painted onto the tips of all the arrows. If the giants wore their leather armor, arrows were fired, and upon contact with the armor a green flame would ignite. These green flames were magical in nature. They therefore burned only the giant, and nothing could extinguish them until the giant had been reduced to ash.

Eventually, Arthur began sending raiding parties out after the Death Reapers. These parties were also successful. Unfortunately, the one thing we couldn't discover was the location of Death Reapers main base.

That's what Arthur wanted most of all. He wanted to go on the offensive. He wanted to bring the fight to the Red Knight and keep the battle far away from our castle.

The captured Death Reapers were of no help. The moment they tried to tell us where their hidden base was, they began to gag and froth at the mouth until they died. Merlin believed it was a curse, and set about trying to find a cure.

Aside from that however, everything was going well. People were happy. They'd cheer Arthur as he rode down the street. They brought gifts to the castle. More and more people joined his forces. More and more towns sprang up near our borders.

The soldiers loved him. He was a warrior king who rode into battle beside them. He had no peer. The things he could do with Excalibur defied explanation.

I was happy.

I was happy that my friend was no longer riding the lonely road of self-destruction, but was Arthur happy? I wasn't sure. He laughed. He had friends, but he threw himself into his new path without consideration for anything else.

While others celebrated and relaxed, Arthur pored over maps and gave out orders. He was constantly striving to stay ahead of the Red Knight, who was a military genius in his own right.

No, I wouldn't say that Arthur was happy. I could say that he was no longer self-destructive, but he didn't have a deep enjoyment of anything. Only thoughts of war and the safety of Camelot mattered to him.

I on the other hand had a wonderful distraction from war. Cindy was the love of my life and I was making progress with her.

We kissed.

I did it. It wasn't easy, I was scared to death, but once our lips touched... well, it was quite natural. I enjoyed kissing her, and she enjoyed being kissed by me.

I wanted her to see me. I wasn't exactly ready for that yet, but I wanted it and therefore knew it would be someday possible. Most importantly, Cindy was happy. I loved her patience and understanding. She meant the world to me.

I visited her as often as I could, and when I wasn't with her, or fighting some battle somewhere, I was exploring the vast castle.

Inside my new home I found countless tunnels and secret passages. There were so many nooks and crannies I didn't even need my power to vanish from sight. The castle was perfect for me. It was also perfect for Arthur.

Arthur rarely got any time to rest, but when those rare moments appeared he was up at the top of his tower watching the stars. I knew why he did this. I only wondered if it gave him a small amount of peace.

His life was going by at about a thousand miles an hour. Apparently, being a king doesn't mean you have life of leisure. Arthur was rarely left alone, and that proved especially difficult waters for me to navigate.

I was the king's protection. I now had to protect him during his many public appearances. I had to make sure all these new people buzzing all around him weren't assassins. Still, as difficult my job had become, Arthur had it much worse.

The endless fighting takes a toll.

He and the others had become battle-hardened. It's an inevitable conclusion to the life of violence that they lived. Unlike normal men, they never talked about what they were doing over the weekend. Instead, they spoke in terms of what they were going to do when the war was over.

That was their ultimate goal.

They wanted an end to the violence. They wanted to wipe the Death Reapers off the face of the earth, and Arthur was the one man that could help them get there.

The battles became fiercer and fiercer. Under Arthur's leadership, our soldiers had become crueler to the enemy. Mercy was never shown. Arthur wanted the Death Reapers to fear us. He wanted the very idea of us to chill the blood inside their stolen bodies.

Most of all, Arthur wanted the Red Knight.

Our king searched high and low for his enemy. He looked for him on battlefields and in the small camps of Death Reapers that roamed around the countryside. Arthur wanted the man who had killed his mother.

One day, during a break from the many battlefields, Merlin planned a knighting ceremony and invited not only the usual suspects, but many fighting men that I'd never seen before.

Upon accepting the invitation, all the would-be knights spent the evening alone thinking of all duties that would soon come their way once they were sworn in. I envied them. I could never be knighted, not in front of everyone. That would be too much for me, but I longed for it.

Arthur wanted to meet me in the throne room in the middle of the night. This wasn't especially odd. He often had little missions for me, and so I only expected another assignment when I entered the vast room.

The candles were few and far between. Arthur sat upon his throne, and Merlin stood off to the side. In the dim light, Arthur appeared the fierce warrior with his long hair and blazing eyes. Shimmers of red came from his beard in the flickering candles.

I hesitated to approach.

"Lance," Arthur said. "Is that you?"

His voice cracked through the silence of the room like a gunshot. Merlin came up from behind him and leaned against Arthur's throne.

"I'm here," I said in a voice that sounded too high in pitch.

"Come forward and stand before me," Arthur said.

This order panicked me. It shouldn't have, but something was going on. I forced myself out of the shadows. I forced myself to stand near the foot of the small flight of stairs that led to his throne.

"Tomorrow is a big day for everyone," Arthur said. "Being knighted means something. It's a great honor that is only bestowed upon the greatest and most loyal warriors. Some of them have always been considered the knights of Camelot, but tomorrow the title will be official. Here in this very room, legends will rise. Do you understand how important this is?"

"I do," I whispered.

"Then answer me this," Arthur said as he rose from his throne and made his way down the stairs. "How could I do this without you?"

"I don't understand," I said as Arthur drew forth his sword.

"Take a knee," Arthur said.

My heart jumped into my throat as I did what he asked of me.

"IN THE NAME OF GOD, ST. MICHAEL, AND ST. GEORGE," Arthur said as he moved the tip of the sword back and forth between my shoulders, "I DUB THEE KNIGHT. BE LOYAL, BE BRAVE, AND BE TRUE!"

Tears were streaming from my eyes. I was a knight. I was the very first of Arthur's knights. I could hardly accept what was happening.

"Rise Sir Lancelot," Arthur said.

I did as he asked.

"You have a young lady that would love to hear about what just happened," Arthur said with a smile.

"I do," I said with a cracking voice.

"I'm so very proud of you," Arthur said. "Now get out of here and don't get caught by Cindy's father."

I wish I could have hugged him. I wish I could have told him all that he meant to me, but that wasn't our way. Instead, I ran from the room, and made my way over to my girlfriend's house.

✤ ARTHUR ✤

I swore in my knights before the entire court. One by one they took a knee. One by one they rose a knight. People cheered. It was a good day. I gave them the ballroom to celebrate, and celebrate they did. Even Lance stopped by to watch the festivities from a hidden nook in the rafters of the room.

I made an appearance, but then I was back in the war room pouring over the many maps. The Red Knight, where was he? Had he left the area? Why hadn't I found him yet?

I took a moment to look at the Round Table. It was now filled with the chairs of the men I had knighted. The room seemed different somehow. As if it had only now come to life.

I made my way to the maps along the wall and circled a possible area to search, but I had no real faith in the fruitfulness of the area, it was too close to Camelot. I was frustrated. The Red Knight was frustrating me. Was that his plan? Yes, that had to be his plan. He wanted me to become reckless.

"Arthur," Merlin said. "What are you doing down here?"

"I'm working," I answered.

"Why aren't you in the ballroom celebrating with your knights?" Merlin asked.

"I have other concerns at the moment," I answered.

"Do you need any help?" Merlin asked.

This was the moment. I knew how badly Merlin was hurt when my mother died. Since that evening, we'd gotten closer and closer. He gave me his everything, but I still saw the pain in his eyes.

"Did you love my mother?" I asked.

"Yes," Merlin answered after a small hesitation. "She was the most wonderful person."

"I can still see your broken heart," I said. "Time hasn't dimmed your sadness."

Merlin sighed and took a seat.

"I have a personal goal," I said.

"Tell me about it," Merlin said.

"I'm searching for the Red Knight," I said. "I want to kill him."

"Yes," Merlin said. "That isn't exactly shocking."

"Will you help me find him?" I asked.

"I most certainly will," Merlin answered, but something in his voice worried me.

"Tell me," I said.

"Tell you what?" Merlin asked.

"Tell me what you're keeping from me," I answered.

Merlin looked at me and smiled sadly.

"It's about the Red Knight," Merlin said. "He's not reanimated. He's a living person."

This shocked me.

"Are you positive?" I asked.

"Yes," Merlin answered. "When he shot the arrow he was alone and without any of the green fog that marks the magic of a reanimated corpse."

"Where would...why would," I stammered. "Why would someone fight for such evil?"

"I truly don't know," Merlin said, "but he's powerful and skilled. He might have taken my life if things had gone only a little bit differently. My magic was useless against him."

"Well, Excalibur will not be useless," I said. "I'll cut him down just like I cut down the Black Knight. I only wish I knew who this new opponent was."

A small tap made both of us look up towards the rafters.

"Lance," I said. "Are you up for an adventure?"

"I am," Lance volunteered from somewhere up above us.

I pointed to the area of the map that I was interested in. It still wasn't a logical place to search, but I felt uneasy about the area.

"Give me a quick search of this area," I said. "If the Death Reapers are hidden there do not engage."

"I'll be back by tomorrow afternoon," Lance said.

"Excellent," I replied.

A tiny scraping sound later, and Merlin and I were left alone in the war room.

"We must take care that our vendetta against the Red Knight never compromises our agenda in defeating Morgana."

"That's the beauty of it all," I said. "In order to defeat Morgana, we must eventually defeat the Red Knight as well."

I patted Merlin on the back and left the room. I didn't exactly know where I was going, probably to my room. I hadn't slept enough in the recent days, but I instead found myself wandering around the castle.

The torches in the unused hallways and rooms had burned down to embers, but I didn't mind. I appreciated the shadows and the cool air of the castle.

I was restless.

The Red Knight haunted my every moment, and I should have found him by now. Why had he suddenly stopped leading his men into battle? I dreamed of fighting him. I dreamed of taking his life. I needed my revenge, but I also needed to control my rage.

I sighed heavily.

I was in a hallway that I hadn't entered before. On the walls were paintings of armored knights battling an assortment of different foes. Soldiers, giants, monsters, and Death Reapers were the most common of enemies, but the largest painting in the room had a knight in shining armor fighting a great dragon. The knight held a blue flaming sword.

I stared at the painting for a long moment while the sounds of the celebration lingered far off in the distance. I would become a great king. It may take time, but I would free this world of Morgana and all her forces.

The sounds of the celebration abruptly went silent.

I cocked my head in an attempt to hear what was going on, and I was almost instantly rewarded by the sound of a beautiful voice singing a lonely song about love and loss.

The voice was so exquisite that I abandoned all my morbid thoughts instantly. The voice touched me. It lifted my spirits, and made me care about the singer. What unknown person in my kingdom possessed such a voice? What sadness could have befallen her to elicit such pain?

Without a will of my own, I headed towards the direction of the voice. I had to know the singer. I had to meet with her. I had to...to what? What could I do for her? Still, I needed to know her identity.

I moved faster towards the ballroom, picked the wrong direction, and had to backtrack. I was getting nervous now. The song was going to end before I entered the ballroom. I was only a couple of hallways away, and I found myself running.

The song was coming to an end as I entered the ballroom slightly out of breath. No one noticed me enter the massive room and move along the far wall. They were too intent upon the singer of the song and all were turned in her direction.

I moved into the crowd and politely pushed past body after body just as the song ended. The applause was immediate. Some of the audience even wiped at their eyes. The band struck up, and the crowd departed.

I found myself standing in front of Gwen. She looked me in the eyes and blushed ever so slightly.

"Was that you?" I asked as her companions moved away from us.

"Did I disturb you?" Gwen asked kindly. "It wasn't my idea. I didn't mean to disturb the party."

"You didn't disturb the party," I said.

An uncomfortable silence passed between the two of us as people began dancing all around us. I was swimming in the deep blue of her eyes. I couldn't help myself. Gwen was the only dream that could force its way past my visions of revenge.

I grabbed her hand.

"Will you dance with me?" I asked.

Her brows furrowed in confusion for just a moment.

"I shouldn't," Gwen said. "I should get back to my friends."

I held her hand only a few seconds longer before releasing her.

"I understand," I said. "It was a silly idea."

"It's fine," Gwen whispered before turning away from me and rejoining her companions."

I stood there for a moment longer wondering if anyone had taken notice of my rejection, and then I decided that I didn't care. What was it about that girl? She always had an effect on me. I knew that from the moment I laid my eyes on her, but it was easy enough to keep away from her when I was drinking. Why couldn't I do the same now?

Because she was there for me when I needed her.

She didn't much like me, but she stayed with me all through the night because I was suffering. Did she know what that meant to me? No, that would be impossible. I saw her with new eyes, and even though I still tried to avoid her as much as possible, I was completely aware of my heart's secret desire.

I loved her.

It wasn't wise, and she obviously didn't share my feelings. Nothing would come of it. Nothing could come of it. To be with another would betray the love I had lost. I wouldn't allow myself.

What a joke.

If I had the opportunity, I wouldn't be able to stop myself. The only saving grace once again was that Gwen didn't share my feelings. She would be the gate that prevented me from entering.

I left the ballroom and made my way to my tower.

I climbed up and stared at the stars for a long while. They were so clear I could almost reach out and touch them. My mom should still be enjoying the stars. I wished she were with me. I wished I could tell her about Gwen.

I went to bed alone, as I had done ever since my mother had died.

I had duties in the morning, and as the light of dawn began to shine through my window I woke up still tired, but ready to start another day.

Wendell was waiting for me as I got out of my bath.

"Your knights are arriving, your majesty," Wendell said.

"Have them wait in the war room," I said.

"As you wish," Wendell said. "Would you like some breakfast before your meeting?"

"No time," I said. "I'll grab something to eat later on."

I dried quickly, donned a pair of jeans, a flannel shirt, some socks and shoes, and made my way to the war room.

Everyone was present by the time I got there. Gwen had a seat near the table and behind me. She was to be present during meetings, but she wasn't allowed to become a knight or sit at the Round Table. It was an old rule that needed to be abolished, but I had more pressing concerns at the moment.

"Anything new?" Wayne asked.

"I have Lance searching a new area of the forest," I answered. "I don't have high hopes of him finding anything, but the search for the Death Reapers base will continue until it's found."

"Here, here," Wayne said as he pounded his fist upon the table.

"How is everything going with training and recruitment?" I asked Reynolds.

"Everything is going extremely well," Reynolds said. "Nothing to complain about."

"Put a bounty on the Red Knight's head," I blurted out to all of them. "Anyone that finds the hidden base of the Death Reapers will become a rich man."

"Is that wise?" Merlin asked. "How many untrained men and boys will rush into the woods looking to become rich?"

"That's sort of the point," Tristan said.

"They aren't trained," Merlin argued. "They'll be killed if they happen to stumble anywhere near the hidden base."

"We're getting desperate," I said.

"We aren't that desperate just yet," Merlin said. "There are still plenty of places to look."

"There're about a billion places to look," I said. "That's the problem."

"It's a needle in the haystack kind of thing," Wayne said. "The forest is huge."

"I don't think we should involve the public just yet," Merlin said. "What if I send out word to mercenaries?"

"Are there mercenaries?" Wayne asked.

"Yes," Merlin answered. "They defend some of the towns outside of our borders."

"That might work," I said. "We could put them on our payroll permanently."

"Are they tough?" Wayne asked.

"Tough enough to still be alive despite their line of work," Merlin answered. "They also tend to understand the forest."

A small argument broke out around the table.

I raised my hand and slowly everyone settled down.

"We'll try Merlin's..." I said before a knock on the rafters above me let me know that Lance had arrived.

He was early, and it wasn't like him to call attention to himself like that. I looked over towards Merlin and he was as concerned as I was.

"Lance?" I called out to the rafters. "Did you find anything?"

"Yes," Lance answered from somewhere above our heads.

"Everyone wait outside please," I said to the room.

Lance wouldn't be able to speak freely in front of a room full of people. He'd need privacy. I understood that. It wasn't a big deal.

When the room was empty, Lance began to speak.

"I found them," Lance said. "I found the Red Knight and their entire base."

"How long will it take us to get there?" I asked.

"We can get there in about six hours," Lance said, "but there's a problem."

"What's that?" I asked.

"They've been very busy building up their defenses," Lance answered. "We won't be able to break down their walls easily. They also have many archer towers, and the land has been cleared an acre in every direction. Our best bet would be to surround them and cut off their supply lines."

"Wait a second," I said. "How fortified could they possibly be?"

"They have a castle," Lance answered. "They have walls of stone surrounding the castle."

"How's that possible?" I asked.

"Magic," Lance answered. "Dark magic, the land is covered in a green fog. The very air is chilled with evil. It's not a good place."

"In my domain?" I asked. "How could I not have known this? I had no faith in that area, I was just being thorough."

"Maybe the dark magic hid this from you," Lance said.

"Can you draw me a map?" I asked.

"I've already done so," Lance answered.

A piece of paper fluttered down onto the table. I opened it up and saw the layout of the Death Reapers base. It was exactly what I needed.

I pounded on the table and Wendell appeared.

"Invite the others back in," I said. "We've got work to do."

I was enlarging the map that Lance had given to me on the wall board as everyone re-entered the room. When I was finished, I took a seat and pointed at the map.

"This is the hidden base," I said. "It's only about six hours away from here if we take a shortcut. It's been right under our noses this entire time."

Everyone moved to take a look at the map more closely. I waited for them to get a good look and sit down once again before I said anything. Everyone was looking at me anxiously, but none of them said a word.

"We're going to attack tonight," I said. "Now who has an idea that will get us a win?"

The table damn near exploded. Attacking so soon was a bad idea. Their base was well defended. We couldn't hope to break through their walls. Magic was used in its creation. Magic was probably protecting this castle.

On and on the complaints went, along with the shock that the Death Reaper base was so close to us.

I raised my hand, but no silence came from the gesture.

I stood up from the table.

"I understand," I said. "It won't be easy. That castle will be almost impossible to enter, but we're going to try anyway. My question wasn't why we shouldn't attack. My question was how do we win?"

The room remained quiet.

"Very well," I said. "I'll tell all of you how we're going to win."

There was doubt and concern, but I ignored all of it. I went over the basic outlines of my plan. I went over the size of the army we'd need. I went over what materials we'd need.

"Now," I said. "Who has something to add?"

"This might work," Bedder said. "It'll be dangerous, but it might just work."

Merlin said nothing, but he was smiling.

"Merlin," Tristan said. "Could you deal with any of the spells protecting this place?"

"Probably not very quickly," Merlin answered honestly. "Protection spells by someone of Morgana's strength are almost impossible to remove. Just as she will never be able to penetrate Stronghold Wall, I'd have a difficult time getting through her walls."

"Your words make me curious," I said.

"I'd eventually be able to break through," Merlin said. "The spells become stronger the longer they live. The Red Knight's castle and the walls protecting it are new. I'd get through eventually, but I'd have to be relatively close, and it'd take too much time."

"Alright," I said. "Let's scratch that idea. I don't want a long drawn-out battle. I don't want a siege that lasts months. I want this done in one evening."

There was a collective sigh from the room.

"Now," I said. "Can anyone add to my plan?"

"I can," Gwen said from behind me.

"Tell me what you're thinking," I said.

Gwen had good ideas. After that, there were more good ideas. The minutes ticked by, and inside of four hours we had a plan.

"Reynolds," I said. "Get the troops ready. Everyone else get some rest. This will be a long and violent night. Make no mistake about that."

In moments the room was clear with the exception of Merlin. The wizard was still smiling. I looked over at him, wondering why he hadn't left.

"This reminds me of the old days," Merlin said. "You were just as tricky back then."

"So you think this will work?" I asked.

"I don't think it will be easy," Merlin said, "but the simplicity of it will confuse the Death Reapers."

"I'm not so concerned about confusing the Death Reapers," I said. "My only worry is the Red Knight. He's no idiot."

"He's no Arthur either," Merlin said.

I smiled as Merlin left the room, but I stayed where I was in front of the map. My mind was moving at a hundred miles an hour. I scanned everything. No stone was to be unturned. I wanted no surprises. This was my chance at revenge. I didn't want some blunder to rob me of the Red Knight's head.

When I was satisfied, I went back to my room and fell asleep until Wendell woke me up. I rubbed my eyes and once again hopped into the bath. I didn't know when I'd next get an opportunity to bathe.

The hot water relaxed my tense muscles. When I was ready, I went over to my armor in the far corner of the room. The armor had been cleaned and polished until I could see my reflection. It was beautiful. A true work of art, and despite all the protection it offered me, it was lightweight and comfortable.

Thirty minutes later, and I was outside in back of the castle. My knights were around me, and my soldiers were ready to march. The sun was lowering on the horizon. The air was cool, but dry.

"This is the moment we've been waiting for!" I shouted out to everyone.

Cheers went up all around me.

"We've found the hidden base of the Death Reapers," I shouted. "If we can take it out, we'll have struck our enemy a terrible blow."

More cheers were shouted.

"Now," I said. "Follow your orders. Listen to your commanders. Stealth and trickery will win this day instead of strength."

More cheers came forth. My army was ready. I was ready. Merlin was on horseback nearby. He was wearing his customary jeans and t-shirt. The wizard was smiling at me, but he looked nervous. Well, join the club. I was nervous as well.

Four stable boys were attempting to walk Goliath over to me, but Goliath was being his usual pain in the ass, and after one of those boys was bitten on the arm I gave him a loud whistle. The stable boys were noticeably relieved as the mighty horse pushed away from them and ran towards me.

"That horse is just as moody as you," Wayne said.

"He's probably even a bit worse," Bedder added. "I've never seen such an angry beast."

"He just likes everyone to know he's in charge," I said as I climbed onto Goliath's saddle.

I made myself comfortable, and after tying my helmet down, I gave Goliath a soft nudge to begin our journey.

We rode slowly through Camelot. People stopped to cheer us on and wish us well as they saw us ride along the road. My knights surrounded me as if they expected danger to pop out at any moment. I found this to be a bit funny. Was I not going to be fighting before the evening was over?

We rode slowly. Time was on our side. I didn't want to attack until the evening was late and sleep had claimed the majority of our enemy. The men joked all around me, but my mind had drifted to the Red Knight. Vengeance would soon be mine.

Before the sun sank too low, Lance took his leave of us. That was fine; I knew this was an eventuality. He'd be back after his change. We were on the trail and that was slower going than expected because it wasn't as wide as I'd hoped. Still, not a problem though, time was on our side.

When we finally entered the last legs of our journey, I called for a rest. I wanted everyone to be fresh, and we'd journeyed a relatively long way.

You don't want to go into battle with a sore ass?" Wayne asked.

"If that were true he'd of left you behind," Merlin said.

I laughed as I brushed Goliath and fed him an apple.

"You know," Wayne said to Merlin. "I've been wondering something."

"What's that?" Merlin asked.

"Why can't you use any of your magic to help us reach our destination faster?" Wayne asked.

"Magic doesn't really work that way," Merlin answered. "I suppose I could figure something out, but that'd leave me pretty exhausted afterwards."

"So?" Wayne said.

"Who's going to save your ass if I'm exhausted?" Merlin asked.

Everyone laughed.

Goliath was getting antsy. It was if he could sense that a battle was going to happen soon.

We rested for an hour.

When we were finished, word was sent down the enormous line of warriors that the time for silence had come upon us. In the distance, I saw Gwen with the other archers. She was wearing leather armor and a red cloak with a hood. Her beauty took away my breath.

"How many of us are there?" Wayne asked.

"Close to seven thousand," Reynolds answered.

"Why didn't we bring any more?" Wayne asked.

"These are the best and most disciplined," Reynolds answered. "They'll be more than enough to attack a single castle."

"Might even be a little overkill if things all go according to plan," Tristan added.

I didn't join in on their conversation. My mind was on the upcoming battle. I was going over the plan once again. I was also getting nervous. If the plan didn't work, we were going to be in trouble. Success depended upon my plan.

"Start breaking off into groups," Lance said from the trees above me as a way of announcing his return. "We're getting dangerously close."

I nodded to Reynolds, and he rode off to handle Lance's request.

The forest was eerily quiet. The trees were barren and lifeless looking. The moon was fortunately big and bright, so we were able to move without torches and lamps, but I didn't like this place. It was touched by evil and it made me uncomfortable.

Reynolds rode back to me.

"Everything's ready," Reynolds said. "I'll ride with the soldiers."

"Is that necessary?" I asked.

"No need to take chances," Reynolds answered.

"Be safe," I said.

"I'll lead them into position," Lance said.

"Fine," I said. "We'll wait for you here."

As quietly as possible half our army stepped into the forest surrounding us and disappeared from sight. I listened to them as they moved away, and I didn't like the noise.

"Merlin, can you do something about the noise?" I asked.

"I already have," Merlin said. "We can hear them easily enough, but the Death Reapers won't be so lucky. It was a simple spell that'll last until the battle begins."

"Tristan," I said. "Scout ahead. Take Izzy and a few others. Be careful and kill silently if you see anything."

Tristan nodded, pointed at a few knights and they all rode off.

"I guess now we wait," Wayne said.

"No shit," Merlin said.

"I hate waiting," Wayne complained. "I'd rather just get to the killing. This stealth shit is for ninjas. I'm a knight. I'm a warrior."

"You're an asshole blowhard is what you are," Merlin whispered.

A quiet laughter rose up all around us, and that was okay. The knights needed to let off some steam. We were soon to be in the thick of things and all of us were stressed.

"Arthur," Lance called quietly from the trees off to my left. "They're in position."

"Let's move out then," I said.

We rode silently until we met up with Tristan and his party at the foot of a marsh. The green fog hovered above everything.

"Any trouble?" I asked Tristan.

"Nothing at all," Tristan answered.

I found that rather odd. Why wouldn't the Red Knight have soldiers patrolling the area? They were just asking for a sneak attack. Something wasn't right.

"Beyond this marsh is another patch of forest," Lance said. "After that is where the land has been cleared in front of the castle."

"Did you cross over this marsh?" Merlin asked Lance.

"No," Lance answered. "I cut through the forest in the direction I led Reynolds."

"This is odd," I said. "There should be patrols."

"I don't like the look of this marsh," Merlin said as he dismounted from his horse.

"What're you thinking?" I asked.

"The green fog shouldn't extend so far from their castle," Merlin answered. "I sense dark magic in this area."

"Is it dangerous?" Wayne asked.

"Dark magic is always dangerous," Merlin answered. "What do you want to do, Arthur?"

"We don't have much choice," I answered. "We'll move forward."

Goliath gave a low rumble of unhappiness as we entered the marsh. The ground was soggy and wet. We managed to find a trail, but on either side of the thin pathway were bodies of stagnant water.

"Don't let the horses step into the water," Merlin cautioned.

"Why not?" Wayne asked with a slight tremor in his voice.

"I don't know," Merlin answered honestly.

Grassy plants came up to Goliath's belly, and they grew denser the farther into the marsh we travelled. Eventually, I had to get off the horse and lead him. It was the only way I could ensure that the two of us stayed on the path.

About midway into the marsh, Bedder, who was also walking his horse, slipped on the squishy ground and fell into a large puddle. Bedder cursed, but managed to find his feet almost immediately. The brown water came up to his waist.

Wayne moved towards him and offered his hand, but before Bedder could grab it, the water around him began to churn. Wayne reached for him, but Bedder was yanked below the surface before Wayne could aid him.

"This is it," Merlin said, by way of warning.

I pulled Excalibur free of its scabbard. The water near my feet began to churn. Goliath began to panic.

"Something's going on over here!" I shouted.

Tristan and Izzy were instantly by my side.

"What is it?" Tristan asked.

"No clue," I answered.

A doughy pale hand reached out and fastened itself around my ankle. I yanked my leg back, but the grip was strong. Tristan grabbed me around the waist as the hand began pulling me into the water.

I slashed out with Excalibur and severed the hand from its arm. I stood back up, just as the owner of the hand emerged from the puddle.

At one point the monster before me had been human. The silver glint in its milky eyes also told me that it had become a Death Reaper, but something was wrong with it. I wasn't facing a human intelligence.

Its clothes had almost completely rotted away. Its skin was waterlogged and sagging from its bones. It didn't speak, but it made a low gurgling moan, just as others of its kind also emerged from the deep puddles.

The light of Excalibur's now burning blade was like a beacon to these lost souls and they came for us hungrily.

"What the hell are they?" I asked as I slashed at the monster before me.

"The rotten ones," Merlin answered. "The ones too damaged to still be of use. The perfect defense, I knew this place was just wrong. The entire area is polluted. No wonder you couldn't sense the enemy so close to your doors."

As the rotten Death Reaper in front of me went down, Excalibur burned even brighter. In no time at all we were all surrounded.

"Cut them into pieces!" I shouted out. "Protect the archers. I don't want them using up all their arrows before the battle."

The knights hurried to follow my commands. Wayne had finally managed to pull Bedder from the water, but his attacker refused to let go. Frustrated, Bedder punched at its face. The soggy skin ripped free of the skull where his fist connected.

"Somebody, help Bedder!" I shouted as I slashed my sword around and around to prevent this new enemy from closing in on me.

Merlin unleashed a small fireball into the ruined Death Reapers face, and it moaned loudly before releasing Bedder and submerging once again into the water.

I went on the attack.

It wasn't a difficult fight. The creatures didn't like the flames dancing along the edge of my blade. They backed away as I came at them, but I didn't let that stop me. I slashed and hacked at their slow-moving bodies.

Tristan and Izzy did the same, but they couldn't get the ruined Death Reapers to back away. In no time at all, they'd be overwhelmed.

"Fire!" I shouted. "We need torches. Lots of torches."

The archers hurriedly went about following my command, but it wasn't easy. The area was wet, and the trees were few. We had to hold off our attackers until enough torches could be lit.

The ruined Death Reapers made no distinction between horse and rider. Either would fill their hungry bellies. I began to hear the cries of horses. I panicked and looked to Goliath. He was surrounded, but fighting valiantly.

I moved to help him, and cut freely at his attackers while standing behind them. I had to be careful to avoid the horse's powerful kicks.

A ruined Death Reaper grabbed a hold of me.

Where it had come from I couldn't say, but I was completely caught by surprise. I fell on my side, and the bastard landed right on top of me. He was climbing up my armored body just as I was attempting to climb away from him.

The angle was all wrong for my sword. I couldn't get the leverage to hack at him; so instead, I let go of Excalibur and spun around in the mud and muck. Now, the ruined Death Reaper was on top of me. I grabbed at its neck with my left hand, its skin came away in my grasp, but I still managed to keep its biting mouth away from my neck while my right hand reached behind my back and pulled free my dagger.

I slashed at ruined neck and brown puddle water leaked out with only the faintest traces of blood. I continued slashing until the head was almost severed from the body. The ruined Death Reaper went limp on top of me, and just as I pushed it away, another set of hands grabbed me by the shoulders.

I'd fallen too close to the water, and more and more hands broke the surface to grab a hold of my shoulders and arms.

I felt brittle fingernails breaking against my armor as I was pulled towards the water, and I struggled to get away from them. I reached out for Excalibur, but couldn't quite get my hands around the fallen sword.

I clawed at the ground, and I slashed with my dagger to no avail. In moments, I felt the water seep into the openings of my armor. I barely had time to register the coldness of the water when I was suddenly submerged.

This body of water was deeper than the one Bedder had fallen into. It was also deep enough to drown in, despite being only five feet or so in circumference.

I tried to scream, and water filled my lungs. I couldn't see anything, but I could feel the many hungry mouths chewing at my armor just searching for a bit of flesh.

My world starting growing black as spots danced at the edge of my vision. That's when I saw the blue light, no, not a light…a fire. Excalibur had appeared. Could I reach the sword? I tried, and my fingers came up short.

I only had seconds. Any longer and I'd fail everyone. I'd fail my mother. I reached once again, and this time Excalibur was in my hand.

I swung out, a weak and clumsy slash with my sword, but it was enough. I was released. I was free, and I began climbing up the muddy bank until I found the oxygen I so desperately needed.

I took a great gasp of air as I lay on my back. Ruined Death Reapers came for me, but Goliath was there. The great horse began kicking and stomping at them. The light of a torch came over to me.

"I found him!" Tristan shouted.

More torches came, and suddenly the ruined Death Reapers were retreating back into their watery dwellings.

Izzy helped me to my feet

"Well, that sucked," I said between coughs.

"We thought we'd lost you," Tristan said as he hugged Izzy tightly.

"Nonsense," I laughed. "I had Excalibur and Goliath to protect me."

"How does that sword burn under water?" Izzy asked.

"It's magic," I answered as I backed away from the body of water. "Are there any left?"

"No," Merlin answered. "The flames burn their eyes. We've created enough torches to keep them at bay, but we should move quickly through this marsh, regardless."

"No arguments here," I said. "Have everyone mount up. We're going to ride as quickly as possible."

"Is that wise?" Bedder asked. "The horses could stumble on this terrain."

"The goal is to be away from this marsh before the torches burn down," I said. "Now let's go."

Big words on my part, I'd never risk Goliath. We went as fast as possible, but we never endangered our horses. The torches burned down all too rapidly, and the ruined Death Reapers came at us once again, but we didn't stop or slow down. The best thing we could do was swing wildly from our horses until we'd made it safely from the marsh.

Once we'd entered the relative dryness of the forest, our large company relaxed and took stock of our damages. We'd lost a total of thirty-one archers, zero knights, and eighty-seven mounted soldiers. They were tough losses, but not nearly enough to slow us down or change our minds.

"Have everyone rest up," I said. "Then we'll get into position."

I sat alone with my back against a thick tree, and heard a rustling behind me.

"I almost got killed back there," Lance said. "Those things could sniff me out. I spent the entire fight buried underneath about ten of them."

"How'd you get out?" I asked while breathing a sigh of relief that Lance was indeed safe.

"Goliath kicked them off of me," Lance said.

"Are you injured?" I asked.

"Yes," Lance answered.

"Care to elaborate?" I asked.

"No," Lance answered.

"Lance," I said. "I need to know how badly you're injured."

"I'd rather not say," Lance said.

"Why the hell not?" I asked.

"I want to fight," Lance answered.

"You're out of the fight," I said. "If it's bad enough that you won't talk about it, you can't be fighting."

"I'm going to fight anyway," Lance said.

"You're a pain in the ass," I complained. "I'm getting a little pissed here."

Wayne heard me arguing.

"You're either fighting with Lance, or you're talking to yourself," Wayne laughed as he approached.

"Lance is injured," I said, "but he won't stay out of the fight."

"You're out of the fight, Lance," Wayne said. "It's as simple as that."

There was no reply.

"I don't think he's here anymore," I said.

"Little fucker," Wayne said. "Well, on the plus side, if he can move that fast and that quietly he's probably not too badly injured."

"I guess we'll find out," I said. "How's everyone looking?"

"They're looking pretty relieved to be out of that marsh," Wayne answered. "Reynolds is probably getting impatient about now. What do you think?"

"I think Reynolds is too good of a knight to get impatient," I answered. "Besides, he had a lot of setting up to do."

I got to my feet and someone handed me a cup of warm coffee.

I noticed Merlin walking in and among everyone. Gwen was farther away from me. I watched her as she tested and retested her bow.

"She's a looker," Wayne said. "That's for sure."

"You think so?" I asked.

"Definitely," Wayne said. "Too bad she hates your guts."

"She doesn't hate me," I said. "I just irritate her."

"I'm pretty sure she hates you," Wayne said.

"What the hell do you know," I grumbled. "You've been married forever."

"That's how I know," Wayne said. "A husband gets a sense of these things. Hey, are you getting sweet on her?"

I laughed out loud, and from somewhere above us, Lance laughed as well.

"Getting sweet on her?" I asked.

"It's an expression," Wayne said as he shrugged his shoulders.

"It's an archaic expression," I said.

"I don't know what that word means," Wayne admitted.

There was more laughter from above us.

"We found Lance," Wayne said.

"It's not like he can go too far," I said. "He's my bodyguard."

"I need to get a bodyguard," Wayne said, "but someone a little less annoying."

"Lance isn't annoying, not usually," I said.

Lance laughed a bit more, and that made me a bit more confident that he was fit to fight. I gave a soft chuckle and surveyed the area as my head got back into the game.

"I think it's about that time," I said.

Wayne shook off his usual mirth, and became deathly serious. Merlin looked over in our direction and I waved him over.

"You think we're about ready?" I asked.

"Yes," Merlin answered.

"From here on out, I want silence," I said. "Keep the archers in the middle, and the knights and soldiers on either side of them, just like we went over. Fan them out in two rows. Pick your way through the forest as quietly as possible. Let's not test Merlin's magic. We don't need speed. We need secrecy."

"I'll spread the word," Wayne said.

"As will I," Merlin said.

I nodded at both of them. I wanted to say more. I wanted to give more orders, so that everything would go according to plan, but I didn't. Our men and women were seasoned warriors. They didn't need to be reminded a hundred times of what we were going to do.

I watched as word spread out.

I had pride in these people. Together we'd seen some serious fighting. I recognized most of them by name. They were now my family, but I kept myself at a distance from them. Soldiers fight and soldiers die.

I finished the last of my coffee and noticed that my hands were shaking. I was nervous. Too many things could go wrong. There were too many ways in which we could lose this battle.

I threw away the cup.

I must not fail.

I must avenge my mother.

I will avenge my mother.

Tears rose up into my eyes as I thought about her. I missed her too much. She shouldn't have died. If I had been a better son, if I had taken up my leadership sooner...I could go on and on. The simple fact was that my mother was dead and it was as much my fault as the Red Knight's.

I mounted Goliath.

The horse gave a low snort to show his excitement, and I pulled free my helmet and placed it upon my head. Things were different when I wore the helmet. It was almost as if I could hide behind the metal and become someone else.

I often wished I was someone else.

I slowly rode around our people. I wanted them to see me. I wanted them to know that I was among them. They'd be fighting to the death very shortly, and I'd be right next to them.

Finally, we were ready.

We moved out slowly through the forest. The green fog became thicker and thicker as we neared the enemy castle. There must have been a lot of Death Reapers hidden away in this vile place. I planned on rooting them out and stomping them like rats.

We came to the edge of the forest.

I finally got my first look at the enemy castle. I saw the high black walls of wet stone. I saw their black banners with the white drawing of a dagger piercing a heart. Beyond the walls I heard raucous laughter and drunken singing. I heard the sounds of men brawling and women screaming.

"They seem to be having fun," Merlin said.

"You can see the sentries on the wall," I said. "Look at them. They aren't really paying attention."

"They've gotten used to being hidden," Merlin said.

"Well," I said. "They aren't hidden any longer. Are we ready?"

"Yes," Merlin answered.

"Then sound the horn," I said.

A loud horn blew out from somewhere down the line. A long and proud call to arms, and then a moment of silence.

The castle erupted into motion.

The laughter and screams died in throats. More and more Death Reapers appeared on the walls. Torches were lit in some areas but extinguished in others. The clang of metal could be heard all the way to the tree line as weapons were grabbed.

Another horn blew.

This one came from the side of the castle. It was Reynolds letting us know that they were ready. The Death Reapers were in a full panic. They couldn't figure out where the attack was going to come from.

They shouldn't have worried. It didn't matter where the attack was coming from. I had other things in store for them.

Hundreds of my soldiers ran into the open field in front of the castle from the left and right side. The Death Reapers made ready with their bows, but before they could fire, my soldiers banded together into groups with their shields held above their heads and before their bodies.

When the arrows came, my soldiers bravely surged forward as death in wooden shafts punctured, and splintered against, their shields.

"So far so good," Merlin said.

"It's a poor attack," I said. "Why would anyone charge from the sides to attack the front?"

"To you it's a poor attack," Merlin argued. "To anyone else it's the best of few options."

"It has to be believable," I said.

"It is," Merlin said.

We watched silently as soldiers continued to flood onto the battlefield and join into groups with shields. They pushed their way to the closed drawbridge an inch at a time. Occasionally, the shields would break apart and my men would fire back.

It was believable.

My attack was working.

Twenty minutes or so into the battle, and a great number of soldiers were amassed at the drawbridge with their shields still raised high above their heads.

"They should be getting into formation soon," Merlin said.

My answer was a silent nod.

My focus was on the battle. I didn't want conversation. I wanted results.

The mass of soldiers began to move in on one another. What at first looked like a chaotic jumble of soldiers without any idea of what to do, began to change. A line began to form, a long line that extended from the drawbridge to almost thirty yards into the open field before the castle.

The line then began to widen as soldier after soldier sought out an open space with which to reinforce the human and shield tunnel that was being created before the angry eyes of the Death Reapers above them.

The first of the battering rams took the field. It wasn't anything fancy, just a heavy wooden pole with a metal tip, and fifty men on each side carrying it forward over the uneven ground.

The battering ram was heavy, and the going was slow. Most of the men fell underneath the onslaught of arrows, and the ones that lived scattered back into the forest.

"There are plenty more," Merlin said.

The next battering ram emerged from the tree line. This battering ram was somewhat lighter than the first, and the fifty men on each side were able to travel considerably faster. They almost made it to the shield tunnel before the survivors were forced to drop the wooden pole and retreat.

"They're close enough," Merlin said. "The battering ram is lighter. We might have something here."

Another group of men broke from the tree line. These men were not encumbered by a battering ram. Instead, they carried shields above their heads and ran quickly in a loose grouping. When they reached the fallen battering ram, they each picked it up with one hand, while still defending themselves with their shields on their free hands.

They traveled quickly.

In just a few moments, they had reached the shield tunnel, dropped their own shields and charged forward with all their might.

I head the battering ram clang against the drawbridge of the castle, but with so many shields held aloft, I couldn't see the actual attack.

"They may be able to break through," Merlin said.

"I doubt that," I said. "The Death Reapers will upgrade their attack on the shield tunnel very shortly. If I really wanted to succeed, I would have created a wooden structure to protect the battering ram instead of a shield tunnel."

"I see," Merlin said.

I'd shocked the wizard.

"As long as it looks like we're really trying," I said. "That's all that matters."

The Death Reapers grouped together high on the walls above the shield tunnel, just like I expected. They threw down rocks and shot arrows on my soldiers.

These attacks only had limited effects. Sure, they'd take out a soldier or two as a rock or arrow made it past the roof of shields, but they weren't nearly taking out enough of my men to stop the battering ram.

I heard a loud crack about the fifth or sixth time the battering ram impacted with the drawbridge. That shocked me; I figured the drawbridge would have been of sturdier construction. Still, there was a long way to go, before my men were through.

The boiling oil was next.

This was what I was most worried about. The Death Reapers carried big vats of the hot liquid and cried out in triumph as they poured it over their castle walls.

The boiling oil succeeded where the rocks and arrows failed. Men fell screaming in agony as the oil gushed past their shields.

The shield tunnel fell apart on one side as more and more oil was poured. Others rushed in to repair the damage, and they were burned as well, but as their flesh bubbled and split another crack echoed out and a hole was made into the drawbridge.

A horn was blown from the shield tunnel, and more soldiers ran from the tree line. The attack was fully underway. This next part was crucial. Close to three thousand had taken the field. The charge towards the broken drawbridge was a sight to behold.

I listened to the sound of steel against steel as my men entered the enemy's domain. This was the time of my highest anxiety. The Red Knight's soldiers would be in formation beyond that drawbridge. My soldiers would be raging berserkers wanting to hack away at anything.

The battle only lasted another twenty minutes, and Reynolds blew his horn to signal a retreat.

The survivors, of whom there were many, could not stand against the Death Reapers in the tight confines beyond the drawbridge. My soldiers were forced to flee.

The interesting thing about their defeat wasn't that they so eagerly retreated. What was so interesting was the direction in which they retreated. Instead of running off to the left or right into the tree line on either side of the castle, the soldiers ran forward.

I waited patiently as I watched everything unfold before me. As soon as my soldiers were halfway across the open field, the Death Reapers rushed from the castle in great masses after them.

The scent of blood was in the air. My army was beaten and disorientated. They'd be easy to slaughter. Why let them go free?

"When you're ready," Merlin said.

I watched the Death Reapers get closer and closer to my soldiers. I saw a few of them go down as they were overtaken.

"Arthur?" Merlin asked.

"Now," I said.

Merlin gave the signal and the horn blew in two short bursts.

The retreating soldiers dropped from their feet as arrows filled the air. Death Reaper after Death Reaper fell to my attack. I looked down the line of archers as they fired their deadly arrows. My plan had succeeded.

We faked an attack. We lost the fake attack. We retreated, and drew the Death Reapers out of their castle. Now they were ours. Now we could pick them off one by one, and by the time we were finished, who'd be left to defend their castle?

It wasn't much of a fight.

The Death Reapers had no defense.

They fell from their horses and my soldiers cheered.

"I can't believe this actually worked," Wayne said.

"I can't believe they actually got through the drawbridge," Merlin said. "I didn't expect that."

"Get ready," I said. "We're going after them now. I want to take the castle as quickly as possible."

Word went down the line, and a number of our archers stopped firing their arrows. Those were the ones with questionable skill. There were other archers that could take out a bird in flight. I didn't worry about them. They could fire all they wanted, and I wouldn't be worried about taking an arrow in my back.

"We're ready," Merlin said.

I pushed down the face plate on my helmet, and nudged Goliath with my heels. The great horse bolted from the tree line just as I pulled Excalibur from its scabbard.

I hit the field of battle with twenty of my armored knights. The Death Reapers that hadn't been felled by arrows screamed out in fear, but we showed them no mercy. Today, we were the evil ones. Today, we were planning on finishing them once and for all.

Behind the armored knights came the rest of my cavalry and foot soldiers. It probably looked impressive. How could it not? In this, the final battle, I had unleashed pretty damn near the entire force of Camelot.

Horses thundered down the field of battle.

I was the first to reach the scattered Death Reapers. Excalibur swung freely taking lives. Goliath enjoyed charging into the horses of the enemy. He seemed to favor the crunch of his armor against their flesh.

In no time at all, my armor was splattered with blood and mud. Wayne was next to me, he looked almost as bad as I did. Merlin however, was as clean as if he hadn't ridden through a battlefield of corpses.

More Death Reapers poured out of the castle. They were desperate to stop us from gaining entrance. We charged into them and then past them. Nothing would stop us. Nothing could stop us.

"Arthur," Merlin said as the knights regrouped around me. "Perhaps you shouldn't be leading the charge."

"Why not?" I asked.

"It's getting pretty dangerous," Merlin said. "We can't afford to lose you."

"I won't be dying tonight, Merlin," I said. "I can assure you of that."

I charged Goliath forward once again. I was in a hurry to gain entrance into the castle. My knights scrambled to keep up with me. A final wave of mounted Death Reapers came for us, and after a brief scuffle, we'd reached the drawbridge.

I slowed Goliath down.

My knights spread out in a line to my left and right. Behind us, the battle continued to rage, but it was ending nonetheless.

"Should we wait?" Wayne asked.

"No," I answered. "We're knights for a reason. We'll clear the way. Let the danger be ours."

I was the first one through the damaged drawbridge. I had entered a large open courtyard. The green fog was much denser here than on the battlefield behind me. It made seeing anything somewhat difficult.

At the opposite end seemed to be a large grouping of tents, but I couldn't be sure. I saw no Death Reapers. Where had they gone? Surely not everyone behind the castle walls had entered the battle.

"What the hell?" Wayne grumbled.

"Be quiet!" Merlin said.

I kept looking as I rode slowly forward. Damn the fog, I couldn't see anything. Vague shapes all around me. Nothing was moving. It couldn't be that easy.

"Lance!" I shouted. "Where are you?"

I felt a slight weight hop on Goliath's back directly behind me.

"I'm right here," Lance said.

"Scout around as quickly as possible," I said. "Stay hidden."

The weight was gone. I pulled Goliath to a stop and raised my hand so that the others would stop as well. I wasn't in the mood to play games. Lance would soon root them out wherever they were hiding.

A few minutes ticked by, but those few minutes felt like an eternity.

"Giants!" Lance shouted out through the fog.

I hadn't expected giants inside the castle. This was unfortunate, and as the ground began to tremble with their footsteps, I feared I had made the gravest of mistakes.

Through the green fog, I saw them begin to take shape at the far end of the field. One after another they came forward from behind the castle walls.

Something was wrong with them.

They were hunched and limping. The clink of chains could be heard with each step they took. When they were finally close enough, I could see evidence of severe mistreatment.

I made ready to charge when giant after giant fell to their knees in front of us.

"We surrender," the first of the giants said. "Let us go, and you'll never see us in these lands again.

"What happened to you?" I asked.

"You happened to us," the giant said. "At first you came at us with the stinging insects, and after we were forced to wear leather armor you came after us with fire. We couldn't win. We wanted to leave, but the Red Knight is cruel. He made us suffer for our cowardice. He forced us to fight one another for his amusement."

"Well," Wayne said. "Looks like we finally took care of the giant situation."

"That'll be a huge blow to the Death Reapers," Tristan said.

"Please," the giant continued. "You are the great King Arthur. You've beaten us, and we are no liars. We'll leave this place forever. Mankind will no longer be troubled by giants."

"Where's the Red Knight?" I asked.

"I don't know," the giant answered. "We've been kept down in the cellars. We've seen nothing of the battle."

"Damn," I cursed.

"There's probably a back door somewhere," Wayne said. "He must have escaped when he realized he was losing the battle."

"Izzy," I said. "Escort the giants out of here. Line them up against the wall. I'll deal with them after I'm finished here."

Izzy nodded at me, rode forward a bit, and motioned for the giants to follow him. I watched the giants pass me by. The creatures were stupid and therefore terrible actors. They weren't going to be a problem.

"Well," Wayne said. "Let's tear this place up and head back home. It looks like we're done here."

I raised a hand at him for silence, and looked towards Merlin. The wizard was looking at the surrounding walls. He must have been thinking the same thing that I was thinking.

With the Death Reapers came the green fog. When the Death Reapers died, the green fog evaporated. We weren't alone inside these castle walls.

"Prepare yourselves," Merlin whispered.

The attack came from all around us.

The giants were but a distraction.

Hidden doors flew open along the walls, trap doors opened in the ground, and we were surrounded by hundreds upon hundreds of Death Reapers.

Almost instinctively, we formed a circle.

"Stay together!" I shouted. "Don't let them break the circle."

Easier said than done, we were grossly outnumbered.

I slashed and hacked from Goliath's back, as he in turn kicked and bit. I quickly realized that I couldn't maneuver enough and neither could the rest of my knights.

"Dismount!" I shouted and all of them obeyed me.

We moved closer to one another as we fought off the advancing Death Reapers. Soon, we were shoulder to shoulder. With the exception of Goliath, the other horses had run away from the battle. Goliath continued to fight, and I worried about his fate.

"Merlin," I said. "Give them something to think about."

Merlin smiled, and the ground all around us erupted forward knocking countless Death Reapers from their feet, but the wizard wasn't finished.

Bringing his hands together and twisting his fingers, he summoned up a ring of fire to encircle us.

"That won't hold them forever," Merlin said, "but it'll slow down their approach."

"That's all we needed," I said. "It's time to earn your titles boys!"

My knights cheered and made ready for battle. The Death Reapers climbed back to their feet or were trampled into the ground as their comrades rushed to take their place.

The flames slowed them considerably because they now had to leap through the fire to engage us. The clanging of metal against metal echoed off the walls.

Death Reapers were no match against knights. My only worry was that their sheer numbers would tire us out.

I shouldn't have worried about that.

Before they could overwhelm us reinforcements arrived.

Arrows flew over our shoulders striking down our attackers before they could get close enough to harm us. Soldiers rushed in to aide us, and Reynolds appeared next to me.

"This is the last of them!" Reynolds shouted. "Defeat these men, and we've won!"

I smiled underneath my helmet.

All together, we pushed against the remaining Death Reapers. It wasn't easy, they were numerous, but with victory so close to our hearts we managed to do the incredible.

I stabbed at a rushing Death Reaper. I saw his eyes go wide in disbelief as Excalibur easily punctured his chainmail and stole his life. Before he could fall though, I grabbed him by the collar and used him as a shield against the next attacking Death Reaper.

A short time later, two Death Reapers came rushing towards me at the same time as I pushed ahead of my knights and soldiers. Their eyes were mad with glee and visions of killing the king. I took both their heads before they even realized I was attacking.

Bodies began to stack up around me.

I had to be careful. I had to watch my step. A fall could be fatal under these conditions. From behind me, I saw no less than five Death Reapers fly through the air. That had to be Merlin's doing, but I had no time to think about it. More and more Death Reapers were charging towards me.

I had underestimated the numbers of our enemy inside the castle, but it was no matter. We were here, we were ready, and we weren't going to fail. This was no longer a battle of tactics and trickery. This was a free-for-all barbarian raid; may the strongest win.

The green fog began to drift and swirl around us as more and more Death Reapers fell. I saw a flash of red in the distance, and pushed my way in that direction.

More bodies fell around me.

More Death Reapers came towards me and me alone.

I had pushed too far ahead of my army.

I was in danger.

Arrow after arrow began to fly by me, giving me the space I needed to defend myself. I chanced a look over my shoulder and saw that the archer was Gwen. She had a look of determination on her face as if she were refusing to let me die.

Another flash of red.

Arthur

Turn back

Excalibur, the sword was speaking to me. The voice of the sword was loud and clear inside my head, but why was it telling me to turn back?

Turn away from this revenge

I ignored the sword, and continued to push forward. The green fog cleared around me, and up ahead I saw what I'd been hoping for. The Red Knight was at the top of the rear wall of the castle. He was shouting out orders to his men. At last, at long last I'd have my revenge.

I became a demon.

I moved even faster than before. My skill was born of instinct. Death Reaper after Death Reaper fell to my blade.

Merlin shouted out for me.

Someone else shouted out for me.

I ignored them, just as I ignored Excalibur.

I'd reached the far wall. I entered a stone doorway, and found myself facing a hallway full of Death Reapers. Their faces were almost comical as they looked from me to my flaming sword. I fell upon them before they had time to defend themselves.

From the hallway, I came upon a winding staircase. I took the stairs two at a time. More Death Reapers came running down the stairs as if they could slow my advance. I stabbed into their rushing bodies, and threw their lifeless forms from the staircase.

Soon, the stairs became slick with blood.

I moved from left to right, trying to find traction. I refused to fall, and then I fell. I cursed out loud as my body thumped down stair after stair. My free hand reached out, grabbed a bit of stone from the wall, and stopped my fall.

My helmet was crooked.

I yanked it from my head.

I glanced up the staircase, and saw no danger. I climbed to my feet, and still there was no danger. I was alone on the staircase. Below me, the moans of the dying echoed upwards in a morbid chorus of sounds.

I climbed the remainder of the staircase.

I exited the arched doorway, and took my first step onto the wall. This was the right place. Standing before me was the Red Knight, and he was all alone. So why hadn't he drawn his sword at my approach?

I took another step.

The clear air of the open sky was a welcome relief from the smells of blood and guts indoors. I breathed deeply, and celebrated my victory.

At long last, my moment had arrived.

I took another step.

The Red Knight still refused to draw his sword. This isn't what I wanted. I wanted the fight. I wanted to kill him slowly, to make him suffer.

I took another step, and the floor beneath my feet collapsed. I fell through the top of the wall, past the staircase, and down into the hallway filled with bodies.

I'd hurt myself, but somehow I'd managed to remain conscious. I scrambled to my feet, but I was slipping and sliding in all the blood and juices of the hallway.

I'd created a messy slaughterhouse, and I was trapped in my own designs. Merlin entered the hallway with Wayne and Bedder. They grabbed at my arms and helped me to my feet.

"The Red Knight?" I asked.

"He's gone," Merlin answered.

"I've been defeated," I moaned.

"Nonsense," Merlin argued. "You're the victorious one. You've taken his castle and sent him running."

Soldiers outside the bloody hallway were cheering as the last of the Death Reapers fell to their swords.

"Arthur," Wayne said as he removed his helmet. "This is a victory. You did it. You took the castle. This is incredible. Our greatest victory yet, now we can tear this place to the ground."

"No," I said. "We'll leave it as it stands."

"Why?" Bedder asked. "If we do that, they'll surely claim it again."

Merlin smiled.

"If they claim this place once again, we won't have to look for them," Merlin said. "I'll make sure to look for any magical traps, but surprisingly I don't believe any have been set. They merely relied on being hidden."

"Weaken the walls as well," I ordered. "Use magic; make sure they'll never discover what you did. I want them to take refuge in their own coffin."

"I can do that," Merlin said. "Give me an hour. This place will look safe to them, but we'll easily be able to break through their walls."

Merlin went off to do his thing, and I limped my way out of the hallway. The fresh air once again felt good to me.

My army saw me emerge, and a great cheer went up. I looked around and saw men and women clapping and screaming my name.

I raised my arm to them and waved.

Wayne came up behind me, and handed me my helmet.

"You don't want to lose this," Wayne said.

"Where's Lance?" I asked. "I haven't noticed him."

"No idea," Wayne answered.

The large knight had a cut on his cheek that was bleeding profusely.

"How'd you get that?" I asked.

"A dagger slipped underneath my faceplate," Wayne answered. "Damn near got my eye."

"You were lucky," I said.

"Well, I'm not the idiot that took off his helmet," Wayne countered.

"Even with my helmet off, I still didn't get cut."

"No, but you fell through a roof," Wayne said.

"Don't remind me," I said.

"Listen," Wayne said. "What you did was nothing short of a miracle. It was you that brought us this far. We may not have gotten the Red Knight, but we struck a blow to our enemy that won't soon be forgotten."

"That's what you don't understand, my friend," I said. "I'm only interested in the Red Knight. I'll not rest, nor be satisfied until I've taken his life."

Wayne fell silent, and I took the opportunity to move away from him. I went looking for the surrendered giants, but discovered that they'd fled during the battle. That was fine with me. It would save me having to order their execution.

Staring out at the open field, I watched as our wounded, dying, and dead were carried away. My heart went out for those unfortunate warriors that would never make it home to their loved ones.

I whistled for Goliath.

A few minutes later, the massive horse came thundering towards me. I checked him over for any damage, found that he was unharmed, and climbed up into his saddle.

"Lance," I called out. "Are you out here?"

I rode around the battlefield, careful not to step on any of my dead soldiers. I continued to call for Lance, and finally heard the weakest of whispers.

I rode in that direction.

"One more time, Lance," I called out. "Where are you?"

The cold fingers of panic grabbed a hold of my spine and travelled up to my shoulders. I'd hate myself if anything happened to my little bodyguard.

"C'mon, Lance," I called out. "I need your help."

"Arthur," Lance said in the weakest of replies.

I jumped off Goliath's back, and searched the ground on my hands and knees until I found the boy stuck underneath a large dead horse. Quickly, I pulled him free, and searched his body with my hands.

"How bad are you hurt?" I asked.

"I wasn't fast enough," Lance said. "I should have listened to you."

"That doesn't matter," I said. "Now tell me how badly you're hurt."

"The wound tore deeper when the horse fell on me," Lance said. "I'm so sorry I wasn't there for you."

"Merlin!" I shouted. "Merlin, I need you!"

Merlin came rushing from the castle, within moments the wizard was kneeling down next to me.

"He's hurt badly," Merlin said, "but it need not be fatal. You need to get him back to Camelot. Toad can fix him. I'm sure of it."

I wrapped Lance in my red cloak and climbed back into my saddle. Without any further words, I galloped into the forest, and headed towards home. I refused to allow the Red Knight another victim. Lance was going to live.

I pounded past Stronghold Wall in record time. People were forced to scatter out of my way. We should have taken Toad to the battle with us. The gnome could already have been working on Lance.

Over the drawbridge I rode, right up to the front doors of the castle. I screamed out for Toad, and heard his little voice answer me from one of the many rooms.

"Lance has been injured," I said. "Merlin sent me to find you."

"The infirmary," Toad called out. "Meet me there."

Toad was waiting for me when I got there. Behind him were a team of nurses and doctors ready to be of assistance. I placed Lance on the table, and stepped away.

Toad put on some strange type of goggles with a purple lens and inspected Lance for nearly five minutes. Lance didn't make a sound. I couldn't tell if he was awake or unconscious. All I knew is that he was too cold to the touch.

"The wound is not fatal," Toad said. "It's serious, but not fatal. I'll have him back on his feet in no time. You just leave everything to me."

I nodded and left the infirmary.

As soon as the door closed behind me, a massive sob burst forth from my body. I had lost my mother. I had almost lost Lance. So fierce were my emotions, I was forced to reach out a hand to grab the nearest stone wall or risk falling from my feet.

The wave of emotion passed quickly.

In no time at all, I was back in control of myself, and wondering what to do. That's when Gwen stepped from the shadows of the nearest hallway.

I looked at her.

She looked at me.

Both of us had tears in our eyes.

"He'll be okay?" Gwen asked.

"Yes," I answered.

"You'll be okay?" Gwen asked.

"Yes," I answered.

She came towards me, and I straightened myself up. Her small hands touched the breastplate of my armor. Her face was only inches from mine. I could smell her sweet breath. She kissed my cheek gently, an angel's kiss, and she walked away.

I stood there like a fool, breathless at being so close to her. The way I felt was almost painful. She stole a small piece of me each and every day. I'd never escape her, and I'd never have her. It was a fate I deserved for failing so many.

♣ GWEN ♣

Lance woke up four days later feeling rather sore, but nonetheless mended. I wasn't there when he woke, but Arthur was. Arthur rarely left his side. I worried about what would happen to our king if Lance should perish.

I worried about our king for other reasons as well. The look on his face after he left Lance in the infirmary haunted me. Arthur was a lost soul. He needed someone to care for him, but it couldn't be me.

The two of us would never be together. Of that I was sure.

After the news of Lance's recovery got out, the streets were alive in celebration. I allowed myself some fun as well. How could I not? I certainly deserved it.

I found my loyal friend Tara just outside of the castle with a large mug of ale. She smiled when she saw me approach, and I smiled in return.

"You're wearing a dress!" Tara exclaimed.

"Yes," I said. "It happens occasionally. Where can I get one of those drinks?"

"Steve," Tara asked the young man standing next to her. "Would you get my friend a drink?"

"Of course I will," Steve replied. "What's your name my dear...oh wow! It's you!"

"Don't embarrass her," Tara laughed, "It's hard enough to get her to have any fun as it is."

"I'm sorry," Steve said. "It's just that...well, you're Guinevere."

"Gwen is fine," I said while offering my hand. "It's nice to meet you."

"I don't suppose you could introduce me to Arthur, could you?" Steve asked.

That caught me by surprise. Why would I be capable of doing such a thing?

"I'm sure I can arrange that someday," I answered. "He's a very busy man though, so you'll have to be patient."

"Is it true that he took on an entire battalion when you raided that castle?" Steve asked.

"Yes," I said. "That's true."

By this time, some of Steve's friends had gathered around with interest.

"How'd he get so tough?" Steve asked.

"As far as I know, he's been training to fight since he was a child," I answered.

"Have you ever held Excalibur?" Someone else asked.

"Kind of," I answered. "Only Arthur can truly wield that sword, but I was there when he was knighted."

"Okay," Tara interrupted before more questions could be asked. "Gwen came over here to have fun. So, let's get her a drink and try and forget that she's a famous person."

At last someone was kind enough to bring me a drink, and I settled in to relax with the growing throng of people. It was a good day. I saw Merlin talking to a group of teenage boys that listened to his tales with wide open and wondrous eyes. Wayne was also nearby with his family. The big man was smiling as he held a child on his shoulders. He waved when he saw me.

I spent some of the day wandering around. Everyone was dressed in bright colors. There were streamers and signs all around. There was confetti and food. The celebration grew bigger and bigger. Sometime after the sun had set, Merlin used his magic to create fireworks over the castle. A massive crowd gathered for the show, and that's when I looked towards the river flowing past either side of the castle.

A man and a young girl were fishing a short distance from the castle. I wondered why they weren't joining the revelry, and I realized that the man was none other than Arthur.

I watched them for a bit. Both of them were laughing. Both of them were having fun. Who was this young girl? What was she to Arthur? I'd never seen Arthur have an interest in kids before, but they seemed to know each other.

I picked up my drink and set out to visit with them.

Why?

I don't know.

That's not true. That's not true at all. The truth was, I was curious. There was so much about Arthur that I didn't know. There was so much about him that was a mystery. Why was the man suddenly so mysterious? I could never tell what he was thinking. He rarely talked to anyone about anything.

"Hello," I said when I was in earshot.

Arthur and the girl turned to look at me.

Arthur looked a bit surprised to see me, and that was good.

"How are you?" Arthur said as he rose from his tattered chair.

The air was a bit cooler next to the river. Arthur and the young girl had lanterns set up next to them that gave off a pleasant light.

"I'm good," I said. "I saw the two of you down here and thought I would stop by and say hello."

"It's the three of us," Arthur said. "This is Cindy, Lance's girlfriend. The three of us thought we'd do a little fishing."

"Ah," I said. "Lance is here. I should have known."

"Hello, Gwen," Lance said from the nearby trees.

"Hi, Lance," I replied. "I'm glad you're feeling better."

"You're Gwen?" Cindy asked.

"I am," I answered.

"I knew it," Cindy said. "As soon as I saw how pretty you were, I knew you had to be Guinevere."

I laughed, but didn't know how to respond.

"I think you embarrassed her," Arthur said with a smile.

"Why aren't you out celebrating?" I asked in a complete subject change.

"I am celebrating," Arthur answered.

"By fishing?" I asked.

"It keeps me out of trouble," Arthur answered.

"I guess so," I said. "Well, I don't want to intrude. I guess I'll head back to the celebrations now."

"Why don't you stay?" Cindy asked. "We have plenty of fishing poles."

Arthur looked into my eyes.

I should leave.

I should get far away.

"Okay," I said. "I don't know much about fishing though."

"That's not a problem," Cindy said. "We can show you."

I took the seat farthest from Arthur, and before I knew it, I was lost in conversation and laughter. How often had I spent time with young people?

Almost never, I found Cindy to be a delightful young lady, and finally had the opportunity to see another side of Lancelot. He was certainly a very intelligent young man.

Arthur, well Arthur could charm the scales off a rattlesnake. He knew how to tell a story. He could put everyone in awe one moment, bring tears to your eyes the next, and leave you laughing at the end. He told stories of when he was a young boy. He told tales of his mother, and he also told tales of Merlin, when Merlin wasn't such a teenager.

I had an incredible time.

This is what it was like to have family. Different generations enjoying one another's company. I shouldn't have come.

Arthur was so charming.

I caught a fish.

Arthur himself helped me reel it in. He stood behind me, with his arms wrapped around me. I found myself leaning backwards just to feel the warmth of his body.

When the evening ended, I found myself walking back to the castle by myself. I told the little group that I wanted to find my friend, but the truth of the matter was that I needed to clear my head.

I had enjoyed myself too much.

Arthur was something special. I hadn't seen this side of him. Lately, he seemed obsessed with destroying the Death Reapers. I hadn't known there were these other parts to his personality.

That evening, I fell asleep in my warm and comfortable bed with a smile on my face. I'd had a wonderful evening, and the best parts were spent with Arthur.

#

A dream came to me.

I was standing on a grassy hill that was filled with flowers, and walking up that hill was none other than my father. He was wearing tan pants and a white button-up shirt. He looked so young, and he was smiling as he walked towards me.

I ran to him, and he enfolded me in his arms.

"You have no idea how good it feels to hold you once again," my father said with tears in his eyes. "I'm so very proud of you. You've done everything I've asked and so much more."

"I did my best, Daddy," I cried. "I wanted you to be proud. It wasn't easy, but I tried my hardest."

"And you succeeded," my father said with a smile. "I've never been more proud."

"It's so good to see you again," I cried.

"Yes," my father said, "but I don't have much time. I've come to tell you something."

"What is it?" I said.

"Leave," my father said. "You've found the reborn king, you've helped him find his way, but now you must leave him. You must leave Camelot."

I was shocked.

I was upset.

"Why?" I asked. "This is my home."

"Because the king loves you more than anything else," my father answered. "He loves you more than he realizes, and that is a dangerous thing."

"How could love be dangerous?" I asked.

"Arthur must not fall," my father answered. "If he should fall, all will be lost. You're a distraction that could prove to be fatal."

"I'll keep my distance," I said. "Surely I don't need to leave. Arthur's feelings for me haven't jeopardized anything so far."

"Arthur must not fall," my father repeated.

"I understand that," I said as my father started to fade from my dream, "but I don't need to leave Camelot. I can keep him at a distance. You asked me to find him. It's not fair that you now ask me to leave this place. Where would I go."

My father couldn't answer. Too much of him had faded away, and what remained drifted on the next soft breeze that stirred the pretty flowers.

I woke up in my bed feeling very alone.

♣ ARTHUR ♣

I woke up early, but I didn't get out of bed right away. For the first time in a long time, I felt somewhat content. I watched the sun rise through my window. I saw its pale light fill my bedroom little by little until the new day was fully upon me.

I smiled.

I could imagine a life like this. I could imagine a life without war. If only I could wake up like this every day for the rest of my life. If only my people could wake up like this every day for the rest of their lives.

I went into my bathroom and jumped into the gigantic warm bath. This wasn't so bad either. Relaxing inside a bath of hot water, it was so simple, yet felt so damn good.

I took my time getting out of the bath.

There wasn't anything on my schedule today. All of Camelot was still celebrating. A week or so off wouldn't hurt anyone. The forces of Morgana weren't going anywhere.

Fishing.

Yes, that was definitely on my agenda. I could spend the entire day fishing. Perhaps Lance would be interested in accompanying me again. Probably not, he'd probably want to spend some alone time with his girlfriend. She was a nice girl, I approved of her. She looked familiar though, I wondered if I had dated her cousin or something.

Wayne would probably be up for some fishing. He enjoyed it almost as much as I did. We were country boys after all. He'd spent yesterday with his family; surely they could spare him for a bit.

Yes, I'd saddle up Goliath and ride over to Wayne's. That sounded like a good plan. I finished toweling off, pulled on some jeans, a t-shirt, some boots, and a baseball cap. I looked in a mirror, and noticed how long my beard had grown. I truly did look like a king...well, except for my hat and clothes.

I went to the window and looked out at my kingdom.

A heavy yet natural fog had settled low over the ground. It looked impressive, especially around the forest. I wondered if Gwen would visit once again. Did I make any headway with her yesterday?

She seemed to have fun with me. She certainly wasn't her usual icy self. Well, that wasn't fair. She was only icy towards me. Except for that one night, she was beautiful that night. She was a dream come true, and I could never forget her soft touch. If only I could have that touch once again.

I wasn't such a bad guy.

I opened my bedroom door and found Wendell there waiting for me.

"Good morning, your majesty," Wendell said.

"Good morning Wendell," I said. "Did you manage to have any fun yesterday?"

"Of course, your majesty," Wendell answered with a smile. "Will you be having breakfast this morning?"

"That sounds like a great idea," I said.

"Excellent, your majesty," Wendell said. "What can I have the chefs prepare for you?"

"Call me Arthur, please," I said. "And surprise me on the breakfast. I'd like to eat in the library, if that's okay?"

"Of course, sir," Wendell managed.

"Nice," I said. "Now how do I get there?"

Wendell gave me directions. It wasn't too difficult to find, and I was there in under twenty minutes. I opened the twenty foot tall wooden doors and stepped into a bookworm's wet dream. The circular library was four stories tall and all the floors were jammed packed with books. A metal spiral staircase led to each floor. Rich rugs were placed all over the stone floor giving the place a warmth that made me smile. Scattered comfortable couches, and two ancient desks next to a crackling fireplace finished off the room.

I wasn't much of a reader, but that was going to change.

Merlin walked in from a hidden passage after I'd sat in a comfortable couch. He looked surprised to see me.

"What are you doing here?" Merlin asked.

"I live here," I answered.

"Indeed you do," Merlin said, "but I don't often find you in libraries."

"I just had an urge to check it out," I said. "I thought I might have my breakfast here."

"Maybe I could join you," Merlin said. "If I'm not intruding, of course."

"Feel free," I said. "What was that room you came out of?"

"That's essentially a storage room for ancient spell books and such," Merlin answered. "I doubt you'd be interested in that. What types of books are you interested in?"

I thought for a bit.

"I'd like to read up on magical creatures," I answered. "After encountering old lady spiders, giants, and Gods of the Forest maybe I should educate myself a bit."

Merlin laughed.

"Third floor, right over there," Merlin said as he pointed. "Many of the books also have illustrations. That tends to come in handy for identification purposes."

"You're such a nerd," I said with a laugh.

Merlin looked over at me and grinned sheepishly, and that made me laugh even harder.

"Did you expect me to deny it?" Merlin asked.

"Well, yeah," I said.

"What's the use," Merlin said. "You young people will think what you want."

"Young people?" I asked. "I'm older than you."

"I only look young," Merlin said.

"I've heard you argue with Wayne," I said. "You act as old as you look."

Merlin sat down on the couch opposite mine.

"Hey," I said. "What are your plans for today?"

"I don't have anything major," Merlin answered. "Why do you ask?"

"I was thinking about getting Wayne and going fishing," I said. "Would you like to come along?"

Merlin smiled.

"I haven't gone fishing since you were a boy," Merlin said.

"You were the one that taught me all I know about fishing," I said.

"I'd love to go," Merlin said. "Thank you for inviting me."

"Don't mention it," I said. "We'll have a good time. Just try not to light Wayne on fire or anything."

Wendell was at the door.

He looked nervous.

"Wendell," I said. "What's wrong?"

What would a ghost have to be afraid of?

"Sir," Wendell said from the doorway. "Sir Reynolds is looking for you. It seems that some riders have approached the gates of Camelot under a white flag."

"What's the problem with that?" I asked.

"The riders are Death Reapers," Wendell said.

"Send in, Sir Reynolds," I said. "I'll meet with him here."

"Of course, Sir," Wendell said as he vanished through the wall. "What the hell?" I said as I looked towards Merlin.

The young looking wizard seemed just as stumped as I was. The very idea of a Death Reaper arriving at the gates of Camelot under a white flag was unthinkable. Death Reapers as a rule didn't negotiate or talk things out.

Reynolds arrived, and walked inside the library.

"Four Death Reapers," Reynolds said. "They rode up to the gates under a white flag. They wish to speak to Arthur. All they'll tell me is that they were sent by the Red Knight."

"I'll meet them in the throne room," I said.

"Impossible," Merlin said. "The Death Reapers won't be able to pass through Stronghold Wall."

"Then I'll go and meet them at the gate," I said.

"Unheard of," Merlin complained. "You're a king. Such a thing is beneath you."

"How the hell do you expect me to get the message then?" I asked.

"They must give the message to the guards," Merlin said. "The guards can then pass it along to you."

"We've already tried that," Reynolds said. "They will only speak to Arthur."

"I'm going," I said as I rose to my feet.

"Arthur..." Merlin said.

"Enough," I interrupted. "I wish to get to the bottom of this, and I don't want to spend all day doing it."

"Wendell," I called.

The ghost rose through the floor in front of me.

"Have someone put a saddle on Goliath," I said.

"Right away, sir," Wendell said before vanishing through the floor.

"I'll never get used to that," Reynolds mumbled under his breath.

"You'd be surprised at what I've gotten used to," I said.

"I used to believe that Death Reapers were the strangest things I'd encounter," Reynolds complained. "At least they die if you stab at them."

"Fortunately, the ghosts are on our side," I said.

"I'm coming with you," Merlin said as Reynolds and I walked out of the library. "Where's Lance?"

"I haven't seen him yet," I answered.

"He should be here."

"It'll be fine."

"Have a guard formed for Arthur," Merlin said to Reynolds. "I want at least fifty men to ride out with him."

"So many?" Reynolds asked.

"I don't understand the situation," Merlin said. "Let's not take any chances."

"Very well," Reynolds said before sprinting away.

"You're making me nervous," I said.

"You should be nervous," Merlin said. "Your recent victories are making you arrogant."

"I'm not being arrogant," I said. "I just don't see any danger inside of Camelot."

Excalibur appeared before me the moment my gaze moved away from Merlin. I grabbed the sword without breaking my stride and strapped the belt around my waist.

Danger

The voice of the sword inside my head was unexpected.

Don't go

"Of course I'm going," I argued.

"What's happening?" Merlin asked. "Is Excalibur speaking to you?"

"Yes," I answered honestly. "Excalibur doesn't want me to go."

Merlin certainly didn't like that. He complained the entire way to the front door of the castle. It took me a bit to get there, but I only got lost a few times. Reynolds was there waiting with Goliath, Merlin's horse, and the fifty men.

All of them gave a great deal of space to Goliath.

"Did Goliath give you any trouble?" I asked as I climbed into the saddle.

"That horse has a demon inside of him," Reynolds said. "Shouldn't he know by now that I'm on your side?"

"Goliath has a bit of a temper," I said.

Merlin climbed into his saddle and with me in the lead, we rode out to meet with the Death Reapers. I took my time with the ride. I wanted them to wait. I refused to rush myself for a Death Reaper. I also thought about ordering their execution, but wasn't sure Merlin would allow such a thing since they approached under a white flag.

I'd bring up the idea once we arrived. It'd be an interesting conversation to have in front of the Death Reapers. I also began to wonder what the Death Reapers would do if the situation was reversed.

By nature, the Death Reapers were villainous and evil to the core, but what about the Red Knight? Did the man have honor? What about Morgana, did she have any sense of honor? I knew almost nothing about our enemy. I only knew their soldiers.

Moving into the town, I saw Wayne on horseback rushing to catch up with us. I smiled when I saw him. He didn't smile back.

"What's happening?" Wayne asked. "People are starting to gather at the gates. I heard something about Death Reapers. Are we under attack once again?"

"Some Death Reapers have arrived," I said. "They would like to speak with me."

"So, why are you going?" Wayne asked.

"That's exactly what I was wondering," Merlin said.

"They can say what they have to say to the guards," Wayne said.

"Never mind all that," I said before the two of them could build up too much steam. "Let's just get this over with."

The crowd of people that had gathered around the gate parted when we arrived. They looked nervous. I noticed that there were archers spread out all along Stronghold Wall. I smiled thinking about how nervous that must be making the Death Reapers.

I exited the gate.

There were four Death Reapers. Merlin, Reynolds, Wayne, and I rode up to them. My soldiers spread out around them until they were completely surrounded. The green fog swirled around all of us.

"Make the wrong move, and we'll kill you," I said.

"We are unarmed," one of the Death Reapers said. "We only bring you a message."

"And this message comes from the Red Knight?" I asked.

"It does," the Death Reaper answered.

I appreciated the tremor in his voice. I smiled to see that his hands were shaking. All of that let me know that my enemy had grown to fear me.

"Why can't the Red Knight bring me his message himself?" I asked.

"Such a thing is unheard of," the Death Reaper answered.

"What is unheard of is for a king to be disturbed by a lowly messenger," I growled.

"You won't be king for much longer," another of the Death Reapers purred.

Wayne pulled free one of his axes.

"Keep your tongue still," the first Death Reaper said to his mouthy friend.

"No," I said. "Say something else. Give me a reason to remove your tongue."

Merlin tried to say something, but I raised my hand to silence him. It wasn't something I'd normally do, but in the current circumstances I wasn't about to be interrupted.

I stared at the Death Reapers until all of them were forced to look away.

"What is your message," I said.

"The Red Knight wishes to challenge you," the Death Reaper said. "An honest fight between the two of you. He wants no trickery only a fair fight."

The message was unexpected.

"He's really challenging me?" I asked.

"He seeks to settle things between the two of you," the Death Reaper said. "He knows that you have a grievance with him."

My upper lip curled away from my mouth in an involuntary snarl. The man that killed my mother had challenged me to a fight.

"I accept," I said.

"No," Merlin said. "It'll be a trap."

"There will be no trap, wizard," the Death Reaper said. "The Red Knight needs no trickery to kill your king."

"A king must never accept a challenge such as this," Merlin argued. "The idea is ridiculous. Surely you and the Red Knight understand this. The king must be allowed to choose a representative."

"No," the Death Reaper said. "He will only fight Arthur. Your other knights will die too quickly. The Red Knight seeks the challenge of a master."

"I accept," I repeated.

"No," Merlin argued.

Once again I raised my hand to silence Merlin.

"It'll save us time," I said. "This way I won't have to chase him around anymore."

"I can't allow this," Merlin said.

"You can't stop this from happening," I said. "Where and when?"

"The Red Knight will be inside the graveyard at sunset," the Death Reaper answered.

Without another word, I rode back to the castle. Merlin was right behind me, and clearly agitated.

"Arthur," Merlin said. "I can't believe you accepted this challenge."

"Of course I accepted the challenge," I said. "I want my vengeance. If this fool is willing to make it easy for me, then so be it, I'll gladly show up and take his life."

"The Red Knight is no easy victory," Merlin said. "I've fought him personally."

"I'll kill him," I said. "And that'll be the end of it."

"What if it's a trap?" Merlin asked.

"I'll have you and my knights there to make sure I make it out alive," I answered. "Now stop trying to talk me out of this, and figure out some ways in which you can keep me safe if there does happen to be treachery involved."

I rode away from Merlin after that. I didn't want to hear anymore. I was too excited. Finally, I'd have him. Finally, I'd be able to kill him. I couldn't remember wanting to hurt someone so badly in my entire life.

Not an ounce of fear coursed through my body. Fear was the furthest thing from my mind. All I could think about was victory. My skill practically assured me of my success.

Lance found me just as soon as I arrived at the castle.

How he'd learned so quickly about my upcoming fight was a tad shocking, and he wasn't exactly happy when I confirmed that I was going.

"You can't go," Lance said. "Not at that time. You can't do that."

"I'm going," I said.

"Not at sunset," Lance said. "Pick another time."

"It's already been arranged," I said.

Merlin, Wayne, and Bedder gathered in the distance listening to the exchange. Gwen also arrived from a different hallway.

"Well, rearrange it then!" Lance shouted at me.

My friend was upset. If I had the duel at sunset, he wouldn't be able to go. I hadn't thought of that. I only considered the fight itself and an end to the Red Knight.

"Calm down," I said.

"I won't calm down!" Lance continued to yell. "You're needlessly endangering yourself for selfish reasons. Instead of me calming down, you need to grow up."

Lance was yelling at me in front of a gathering crowd. That was unheard of, but as proud of him as I was, I wasn't going to listen. Fortunately, Merlin came to my rescue.

"Lancelot!" Merlin said. "He is the king. You will not raise your voice to him."

I saw a flicker of movement, and Lance was gone without another word. I looked towards Merlin. The wizard's young face was distraught.

Everything would be fine once the Red Knight was dead.

I went to my room and told Wendell that I wanted no disturbances. Why could no one understand that this was a good thing? Yes, my main motivation was revenge, but I'd also fight the Red Knight if he hadn't killed my mother. Because killing the Red Knight would end his threat, and that would be best for everybody.

I took a nap.

When I woke up, I had a bite to eat, and then soaked in my bath. My mind was on the upcoming battle, and any problems I had with my friends were pushed away until the fight was over.

When the time arrived, I climbed out of the bath, dried off, and went over to my armor. It shined brightly in the sun from the window. The helmet was the most impressive piece. Without being overly large it was shaped into a dragons head. It was fearsome.

Wendell arrived silently and helped me put all the armor on. I didn't really need the help, but it seemed to make the old ghost happy.

"You haven't said anything, Wendell," I said. "Do you have an opinion on this duel?"

"You are the king, sir," Wendell said. "It's not my place to advise you. I only want you to return to us safely."

"If I somehow don't return," I said. "Look after Gwen and Lance for me. Would you do that?"

"I don't think you understand, sir," Wendell said. "You are the heart and soul of Camelot. If you fall in battle, the city will vanish."

"What?" I asked.

"Surely Merlin has told you this?" Wendell asked.

"No," I answered. "He left that one out."

It wouldn't have mattered if Merlin had told me. I would still be going out to kill the Red Knight. I'd still go out and fight in the battles besides my knights and soldiers.

When the armor was all situated, Wendell attached my red cape, and tucking my helmet under my arm, I strode from the room.

All the ghosts bowed to me as I passed them by.

Merlin and a group of my knights were waiting for me in the throne room. I went to join them. All of them were in armor. All of them were looking towards me and waiting for my orders. In the background, I saw Gwen. She wasn't wearing her leather armor, and that meant she wasn't going to be accompanying us.

She looked towards me but once and her features were far from kind, yet another person against me going out to fight.

"My job is to win the fight," I said to my knights. "Your job is to keep me safe. I know that many of you are against this duel, but it's too good an opportunity to pass up on. So let's move beyond any complaints. I trust all of you. I know that no treachery will end my days with you by my side. Let's move out."

Merlin and Wayne led the way to the stables. The rest of my knights gathered around me and kept me in the middle as if an attack could come from inside the castle.

Goliath was armored up and waiting for me. Excalibur had appeared next to the horse, and before climbing into the saddle, I belted the sword to my waist.

Do not have this duel

Even my magical sword was against me.

I ignored Excalibur. The opinions of a sword meant nothing to me. I was unafraid. I'd faced too much for a single knight to cause me any worry.

The ride through Camelot wasn't met with cheers. Instead, the people that had gathered along the streets looked solemnly towards our galloping band of knights.

I pulled my helmet on as if it could grant me a layer of privacy that would protect me from all the disapproval.

Nobody said a word as we rode out to the cemetery.

I remembered the last time I was here. I'd faced off against the Black Knight. I'd triumphed despite the overwhelming odds and my own injuries.

The Red Knight would fare no better than his predecessor.

I missed the Gods of the Forest. Their company would have been most welcome at the moment, but then again, I had with me over twenty of the greatest warriors in my kingdom. They were my brothers. They'd die for me if that was what was needed. How could they not let me assume the same risk?

The sun had finally begun to descend as we arrived at the cemetery.

From somewhere inside the gates, I saw smoke rising up into the sky. The Red Knight was already there. The smoke came from torches.

We rode our horses past the gate and into the cemetery.

I knew where the Red Knight would be waiting. I led my men, and followed the familiar path to the graves of my wife and child. My mother was buried here. She was next to my father, and he was next to my little family. This was my first time visiting her grave, how fitting that I would be killing her murderer so close to her resting place.

I couldn't think about that now. The rage and anger inside of me had to take a backseat to my skill and instinct. The Red Knight had to be good or he wouldn't be challenging me. I had to focus on the fight, and tune out everything else.

We came to the pond and the large square clearing before it. A battalion of Death Reapers had gathered on one side of the clearing. I sized up the offense, and realized that my group of knights would quickly be able to defeat them.

Not far away were the oak tree and the bench that I'd never sat on. The oak tree was still providing shade over the graves of my wife and child. The grass all around was a deep green.

The Red Knight stood before their graves with his back towards me. He wasn't wearing his helmet; it was tucked under his arm just as I had earlier carried mine. I could see his long black hair though. It hung almost to his shoulders in thick waves.

The sight filled me with rage.

I looked to Merlin.

"You know what to do if he cheats," I said.

Merlin nodded, and I dismounted Goliath. The horse wasn't happy about that, and let the entire cemetery know it with a deep bellow.

I entered the clearing as one of the Death Reapers went to inform the Red Knight that I had arrived. The gesture made me sneer. He was close enough to the clearing. He knew we had arrived. He was only trying to make me feel unworthy. I'd show him my worthiness.

I watched as he acknowledged his soldier, donned his helmet, and walked slowly to the clearing.

I stood with my back to my men. The Red Knight stood with his back to his men. There was nothing between us. Torches on poles lined the clearing, and it wasn't even dark yet.

The Red Knight's helmet was shaped like a boar's head, complete with a metal snout. Small spikes covered his shoulders. I couldn't see his eyes through the slits of the helmet. His blood red armor was spotless, not a speck of rust. All together, the effect was chilling.

"I underestimated you," the Red Knight said in a young man's voice. "I'd heard you were a stumbling drunk, and disregarded you."

"Your information is just a little dated," I said.

"I can see that," the Red Knight said. "What you've accomplished has been impressive. I especially enjoyed how you obliterated my partnership with the giants."

"I had help with that one," I said.

"You also prevented my men from recovering the bodies of our victims," the Red Knight said. "That proved most troublesome in the long run."

"That was me," I said.

"You've also beaten my forces," the Red Knight said.

"More than a couple times," I said.

"And I took your mother," the Red Knight said.

"You'll die for that," I said.

"I've been waiting for this moment," the Red Knight said. "A single one of my arrows has brought you to me. If only we could talk just a little bit longer."

"I didn't come here to talk to you," I said.

"Of course you didn't," the Red Knight said. "You came here to kill me just as I came here to kill you."

The Red knight drew his sword. It wasn't anything special, a metal cross-guard, a leather wrapped handle, and a double-edged blade. He held the weapon low in one hand.

I drew Excalibur.

I held the blade high.

"You're my guest here," the Red Knight said. "The first strike must be yours."

I stepped forward, and began to circle to my right. The Red Knight matched me step for step. I moved slowly, each step was measured. The Red Knight concentrated on keeping pace with me.

I attacked.

My strike was perfect. I aimed for his hip. I wanted to take away his movement, but I had to give him credit. He somehow managed to evade a damaging blow. My sword tore through his armor, but missed his flesh.

"Your skill has not been exaggerated," the Red Knight said, "but you're not as young as you used to be."

He came at me with a flurry of strikes. I dodged and blocked every single one of them, grabbed a hold of his armor near his neck, and flung him to the ground.

The Red Knight rolled away quickly and came back to his feet.

Stop play games

Finish him

Contrary to what my sword thought, I wasn't playing games. I was robbing my enemy of his confidence. That would make him hesitate and think too much.

I came at him again.

I sent a flurry of slashes towards different areas of his body. The Red Knight blocked them all. He was good. He had experience, but how good was he?

I slowed down my attack.

The Red Knight took advantage of the opportunity, ducked under a slash, and came up right next to me. He slammed the pommel of his sword against my helmet, and in turn I kicked out at his knee, dropping him to the ground once more.

This time when he rolled, I attacked.

I came at him, stabbing at the ground in an attempt to pin him to the grass. I was unsuccessful. That meant that I was fighting a highly skilled man.

It was my turn to be impressed.

I backed off, and the Red Knight got to his feet.

We circled each other once again.

"You truly are a master," the Red Knight said.

By way of an answer, I charged towards him with my sword held low. Of course, he swung at my head, and that was exactly what I wanted.

Excalibur struck out like an attacking snake and sliced through the armor on the Red Knights arm. My sword burst into flames.

"First blood goes to me," I said.

The Red Knight shook his arm violently as if the gesture would rid him of the pain. I heard a low growl of anger come from underneath his helmet right before he charged me.

Sparks flew from our swords as our battle grew more and more heated, more and more unforgiving.

I wasn't sure how much time had gone by, but the sky had grown darker. I barely noticed the change in lighting with all the torches, and a burning Excalibur.

An armored elbow crashed into my helmet.

The blow momentarily stunned me, so I slashed out in a wild pattern to gain some distance. My helmet was damaged. The Red Knight had dented the area around my right eye. I couldn't see properly, the helmet had to go.

I breathed a sigh of relief as my helmet came off, and my vision was restored. That was the Red Knights first decent blow of the entire fight.

We came at each other again.

I slashed at the outside of his leg only because I saw an opening, and managed to draw more blood.

The Red Knight cursed and backed away from me with a limp. I charged after him, and he blocked my blow at the last possible second. We traded attacks, and I sliced into his shoulder at the same time as he sliced into mine. His blade erupted in a black flame.

"Now I'm not the only one bleeding," the Red Knight said.

"Yes," I said. "You are."

The Red Knight didn't know that Excalibur's scabbard prevented me from bleeding, but the realization didn't deter him. He was enjoying himself. He wasn't worried about dying. It was as if he was playing a game he knew he was going to win. What was I missing?

Finish him quickly

Yes, I was missing something. Excalibur knew what it was. The Red Knight knew what it was, but I was in the dark. Surely his sword wasn't all that important. Obviously it was magical, but it couldn't compare to Excalibur.

I attacked again.

I went for his forward leg. If I could slow him down, I could finish him sooner. Apparently, the Red Knight had the very same idea and we ended up in a tangle of swords and arms.

Being so close to him frustrated me. I dropped Excalibur, and reached up under the Red Knights helmet. I yanked his head down, and started kneeing him over and over in the face.

I did this until he was forced to unlatch his helmet in an effort to escape me. I watched as he tumbled to the ground and rolled away from me.

I threw his helmet away as the Red Knight climbed back to his feet and brushed his hair away from his face with an armored hand.

He was older.

I couldn't explain that.

A young man stood before me, but I recognized the child he'd once been. I saw the light line of a faded scar by his left eye, but it did nothing to mar his looks. He'd grown into a handsome man.

The black hair came from his mother. I should've recognized it instantly. His eyes were a striking contrast. Those he got from me.

"Hello, father," the Red Knight said as he plunged his sword deep into my stomach.

It hurt like hell, but not nearly as much as the pain of my breaking heart. How was this possible? It had to be a trick, a cruel trick and nothing more.

In an act of pure reflex, I backhanded the Red Knight away from me. He stumbled from his feet once again as I in turn stumbled backwards.

I had no idea that I was so close to the gathered Death Reapers the Red Knight had brought along with him until I felt the long dagger being plunged into my back. I hated the sound it made as the metal of the dagger slide against the metal of my armor.

The ground erupted all around me.

That would be Merlin.

The Death Reapers had cheated. All bets were off. The battle erupted all around me, but I saw none of it. I only had eyes for my son. How had he grown up so much? I almost regretted hitting him. I'd swollen up his chin.

He came towards me, yanked me away from the Death Reaper that had stabbed me, and threw me to the ground.

I fell into a heap.

My body no longer responded to my commands. I only noticed that the dagger from my back had withdrawn because I saw it in my son's hand.

"You were told not to interfere," my son growled at the Death Reaper before thrusting the dagger into his neck.

One of my knights came after the Red Knight. I believe it was Tristan. There was a brief struggle, and Tristan fell to the ground.

"Stop," the Red Knight said calmly.

The battle continued.

"Stop!" The Red Knight shouted.

All together, his soldiers stopped fighting.

"I regret this treachery, father," my son said to me as he pulled his sword from my stomach. "I wanted only a fair fight between the two of us."

"You can't...you can't be...my son," I said.

"My name is Mordred now father," the Red Knight said.

"How is this possible?" I asked.

"My mother found me and brought me back," Mordred said. "You left me rotting in the ground. She's taught me all about you. I know what a selfish bastard you are."

"I don't understand," I said.

"Do what you can to survive your wounds," Mordred said. "I'll come for you when you're well."

My son made a motion with his hand, and he and his Death Reapers walked away. I called out for him. I didn't want him to leave. I had to see him. I called until my voice was hoarse.

Merlin was beside me, and removing my armor.

"Don't move," Merlin said. "I don't know how bad the damage is."

"Is that my son?" I asked.

"Stop struggling," Merlin said. "You can make things worse."

"Is that truly my son?" I asked.

"Yes," Merlin said.

"How bad is it?" Wayne asked.

"He has two stab wounds," Merlin answered. "One is to the stomach, and the other is in his back. He might have punctured a lung."

"What do we do?" Wayne asked.

"We get him back to the castle," Merlin said. "Toad is waiting. The damage is severe, but Excalibur's scabbard will prevent him from bleeding out."

I was in and out of consciousness during the journey back to the castle. I wasn't interested in my wounds. I had no time for the worries of my men. My son was alive. My son had returned, and he wanted to kill me. How was any of this possible?

Before I knew it, I was inside the castle, on a table in the infirmary. Toad was doing something to me. It hurt, but I didn't care. I called out for Merlin. Nurses and doctors did their best to hold me down, but I pushed against them.

"Arthur," Toad said. "Merlin isn't here. Stop struggling. I'm trying to close your wounds."

"Where's Merlin?" I shouted. "I need to speak with him."

"He's outside somewhere," Toad said. "You can speak to him after the danger has passed. Right now I need you to focus on you. Right now you're dying. I can save you, but I need you to help me."

"Bring me Merlin!" I shouted. "I need to know how. I need to find my son."

"Hold him down," Toad said to the nurses. "I'm going to put him under. I can't do anything for him until he stops struggling."

A cloth went over my nose and mouth. It had a funny smell, and I felt very light-headed. I fought against the blackness creeping in at the edges of my vision, but I was overcome despite my attempts to stay awake.

I awoke to the sun shining into the room.

Excalibur and the scabbard were leaning on the wall next to my bed. My body was sore, and I felt extremely weak when I tried to sit up.

A nurse came to the side of my bed. She gently placed her hands against my shoulders and guided me back down.

"You'll reopen your wounds," the nurse said. "If it wasn't for Excalibur and the scabbard you wouldn't have made it. It took us hours to patch you up."

"Where's Merlin?" I asked.

"He's not here," the nurse answered. "He's having a meeting with the other knights."

"Where are my clothes?" I asked.

"Your clothes and your armor were taken away," the nurse answered.

"Bring me something to wear," I said.

"I don't think I can do that," the nurse said. "You're not supposed to be moving."

"Listen to me," I said. "I'm not asking you, I'm telling you. Bring me some pants and a shirt."

"I...I...Don't know..." the nurse stammered.

"Now!" I shouted.

The nurse finally did as I asked.

Getting out of bed proved to be an interesting challenge, everything worked, but I was so weak and tired I couldn't tell if I wanted to pass out or just lay back down and sleep for a week.

Finally I asked the nurse to leave because her worried looks were becoming annoying. I got dressed, saw some blood staining the white bandages across my stomach, and quickly buckled Excalibur around my waist.

My throat felt like sandpaper.

I found a pitcher of water, and drank greedily. The water made me nauseated, but I managed to keep it down. I rested until the nausea passed, and then got to my feet once again. I was better this time. I felt a bit stronger.

The nurse came back with some more people. I didn't know if they were doctors or nurses, and I didn't care.

"Leave me be," I said.

All of them stopped in their tracks.

"We've sent someone to find the gnome," one of them said. "Can you wait for him, please?"

"No," I said as I walked out of the infirmary.

Some of my strength returned as I walked to the war room. It wasn't a lot of strength of course, but it was enough to keep me on my feet and moving. After a while I didn't even need to use the walls as support.

This is foolish

Excalibur wasn't happy with me, that wasn't a great shocker. Well, my sword wasn't going to stop me either. I wanted answers, and I wasn't going to wait for them one second longer. If Merlin wasn't intelligent enough to make himself available to me, then I was going to go to him.

I threw open the door to the war room.

Everyone got to their feet, astonished at the intrusion.

Wayne took a step towards me, and I put out my hand to stop him. I saw Gwen standing in the back of the room. Her eyes were bright and beautiful.

I looked at Merlin.

The youthful looking wizard refused to meet my gaze.

"My son?" I asked.

"Yes," Merlin answered.

"How?" I asked.

"The darkest most foul magic imaginable," Merlin said.

"He's too old," I said. "It has to be a trick."

"She only needed his body," Merlin said. "He was resurrected and raised in another dimension. The mortal clock ticks differently in other dimensions. Morgana raised and trained him there, so he'd be ready to lead her armies in the here and now."

"Impossible," I said. "I can't believe it. I buried my wife and child myself. The Gods of the Forest recovered their bodies."

Merlin was silent.

Red, hot venom began to drip into my veins. My mouth developed a tremor I couldn't control. The entire room full of warriors looked nervous and uncomfortable. They knew something I didn't.

"Merlin," I said. "Tell me."

"I never could have dreamed this would happen," Merlin said. "Arthur, I'm so sorry. I'm so terribly sorry."

Merlin was crying.

I could see the tears welling up around his eyes before they dripped freely down the sides of his face.

"What are you sorry for?" I asked.

My voice had taken on a darkness I wasn't familiar with.

"I told the Gods of the Forest to do what needed to be done," Merlin answered. "I knew that if we didn't recover the bodies of your family, it would destroy you."

"It wasn't my family that I buried?" I asked.

"No," Merlin answered. "You're family was not recovered."

I leapt towards Merlin, and grabbed him by the front of his shirt. The wizard still refused to meet my gaze.

"This is your fault!" I screamed. "You lied to me about my family!"

Merlin said nothing.

I shook him and screamed into his face. He had no reaction. Wayne came and put an arm on my shoulder. I turned my head and gave him a look that forced him to release me.

"Say something," I said to Merlin.

"I deceived you," Merlin said in a quiet voice, "but I did what I had to do for your sake, and for the sake of others."

I slapped Merlin away from me.

His young body crumpled and fell against the wall.

"My mother is dead because of you!" I screamed as I closed the distance between us. "My son has been perverted into my enemy!"

"It was necessary," Merlin said as I lifted him up.

"No," I said. "Your lies have done nothing but ruin my life."

I kneed him in the sternum.

I heard the breath go out of his lungs, and threw him away from me once again. I watched as he collided with the nearby chairs, and came back to his feet.

"Enough," Merlin said. "I appreciate your anger. I understand what you're going through, but enough."

"I'll let you know when it's been enough," I said as I drew Excalibur from the scabbard.

There was a commotion behind me. My knights were thinking about separating us. They were welcome to try.

"Stay back," Merlin warned everyone. "I can handle this."

"Can you?" I asked.

"Arthur," Merlin said. "Please, I don't want to hurt you."

Merlin's fingers began to twitch. Smoke began to rise from his palms. The wizard was getting ready to defend himself.

With my sword hung low, I closed the distance between us.

Lightning shot from Merlin's fingertips. I deflected the bolts easily with a casual swing of my sword.

"Is your heart not in this?" I asked. "With all the damage you've done to me, how could you not be willing to finish what you've started?"

"I've made mistakes," Merlin said, "but I've never wanted to hurt you."

I grabbed him by his tiny throat, and pushed him against the wall with one hand. Merlin choked and struggled, but my grip was too strong for him.

Kill the wizard

"Stay out of my head!" I shouted.

"Arthur," Wayne said from behind me. "This isn't you. Excalibur has gotten into your head."

I squeezed tighter on Merlin's throat. I watched as his face turned purple, and his eyes bulged from their sockets.

"Is that what you think, Merlin?" I asked. "You think this isn't me that's attacking you?"

Though it was difficult, Merlin nodded.

"Well I can assure you," I said. "This is all me."

241

I gave a final squeeze just as Merlin reached his slender hands to my face. A blast of heat and a wave of force pushed my away from him, but it wasn't enough to topple me over.

I was attacking the second my sliding feet came to a stop.

Another jolt of lighting came towards me. Again I easily deflected the blast. Another came after that. It was stronger, but nowhere near strong enough.

In essence, all of Merlin's celebrated magic was nothing to Excalibur. The wizard was in trouble, and he was only now beginning to realize it.

I could see the fear creep into his young face. I could see the situation growing out of his control as he struggle to come to grips with what was happening.

I grabbed him by his hair, dropped Excalibur and pounded my fist into his face. The first punch shocked him. The second punch shattered his nose. The third punch rendered him senseless, and the rest were meant to finish him off.

I felt hands against me, but they weren't enough to pull me away. I struggled against them, and continued my assault.

Without warning, I was released.

A gentle hand replaced the rough ones that gripped at me. A soft arm wrapped around my shoulder just under my chin. I felt her soft hair against my face. I smelled her sweet breath.

"I've got you," Gwen whispered into my ear. "It's okay now. Let him go."

I obeyed her without question.

With blank eyes, I watched my knights rush forward, pick up Merlin, and take him away from the war room. I was left alone with Gwen.

"My son," I said.

"I know," Gwen said as she held me tightly.

"My mother," I said.

"I know," Gwen said. "It's okay. I've got you now."

"My son," I said. "He tried to kill me."

"I'm so sorry," Gwen said.

"He tried to...he tried..." I stammered. "My son..."

I began to sob. It wasn't a silent expression of emotion by any means. All the pain of my entire life welled out of me.

To her credit, Gwen didn't run from the room. Instead, she held me tightly just like she did when my mother died.

After a while, I felt a hand gently hold on to mine. It wasn't Gwen, though she was aware of the new presence.

It was Lance.

♣ GWEN ♣

Arthur ended up back in the infirmary after he attacked Merlin. He'd opened up all his wounds, though it took us a while to realize the damage on account of Excalibur's scabbard preventing him from bleeding.

He'd been there for almost two months, and I hadn't visited him. I needed my distance. I needed to think things through.

Lance came to me within the first week. I'm not sure why he'd chosen me, but he was crying. I heard the emotion in his voice even though I couldn't see him. He blamed Arthur's injury on himself.

The poor kid.

I did my best to comfort him, but he wasn't really having any of it. In his mind, if he'd been there, Arthur wouldn't have been injured. He was questioning himself, and finding himself inadequate.

I told him that it wasn't his fault. I told him that the blame was on Arthur. A king should never have accepted a fight like that. Arthur jeopardized all of us by agreeing to that fight.

That's when it hit me.

That's when I understood why I hadn't visited Arthur.

I was angry with him.

What he did was stupid, and I was angry that he'd almost gotten himself killed. If it wasn't for Excalibur and the scabbard, he'd have been dead right now.

I didn't want Arthur to be dead.

What did I want?

Well, that was certainly the question, wasn't it? What did Arthur mean to me? Everything was happening so fast. I couldn't keep up.

And then there was the dream. My father told me to leave Camelot. He wanted me away from Arthur.

I needed to speak to Merlin.

I hadn't seen him since the attack either. I was pretty sure that had to do with what he'd done to Arthur. I understood his reason, but the result of his deception was ghastly.

I went to visit Merlin.

It was early in the morning when I knocked on the wizard's door. The air was cool, and there was a light fog drifting over the lake.

Merlin answered his door, and I was shocked to see that he looked as if he'd never been attacked. Even the teeth that had been broken out were replaced.

"Guinevere," Merlin said with a smile. "What a pleasant surprise."

"I need some advice," I said.

"I hope all is well?" Merlin asked.

"That depends on what advice you have to give me," I said.

"Come in," Merlin said. "Tell me what's going on."

I did as he asked. His home was cozy, nothing extravagant, but full of instruments and potions of various types.

"I had a dream about my father," I said. "He came to me and told me to leave Camelot. He said Arthur was too in love with me, and he seemed to think of me as a distraction. He told me that Arthur must not fall."

"How do you feel about what he said?" Merlin asked.

"I don't want to leave," I said. "This is my home. This is all I know."

"Ghosts often have wonderful advice," Merlin said. "They can come to us with the best of intentions, but in the end, they are only ghosts."

"What does that mean?" I asked.

"It means that most ghosts aren't any more intelligent than living people," Merlin said. "They certainly don't have the power to predict the future."

"Their advice isn't any more important than the advice of a living person?" I asked.

"Exactly," Merlin said, "but..."

"He's my father," I said. "My father never steered me wrong. What do you think I should do?"

"Young women rarely pay any heed to their father's wishes," Merlin said. "This place is your home. I can't imagine you not being here. I agree with your father that Arthur must not fall, but you've been nothing but a positive influence on my grandson."

"Have you talked to him?" I asked.

"Arthur?" Merlin asked to which I nodded. "Yes, because of my past deeds I will not be banished from Camelot."

"I couldn't imagine him banishing you," I said. "Are you angry with him?"

"Not at all," Merlin said. "I thoroughly deserved the thrashing he gave me. My actions proved disastrous."

"I understand why you did what you did," I said.

"I believe Arthur does as well," Merlin said. "Or perhaps he just felt bad about kicking my ass."

"So the two of you have made up?" I asked.

"I wouldn't say that," Merlin said. "He's still very angry with me. I'm not sure he'll ever love me again."

"You're his family," I said. "Time heals all wounds. Eventually he'll get over it."

"Eventually he'll have to face his son," Merlin said. "And that's my fault."

"Can we not talk to his son?" I asked. "Can we not show him the path to a better life?"

"I wish I knew," Merlin said. "All we really know right now is that Mordred seeks Arthur's death, and Arthur has no wish to fight his son."

"You're right," I said. "You deserved to get your ass kicked."

Merlin laughed out loud, and I joined him. I got the feeling that he hadn't laughed much in recent days.

"So what are your plans now?" Merlin asked as he wiped the tears from his eyes. "Will you be staying or will you be taking your fathers advice?"

"I'm staying," I said. "I'll be there for the tough times ahead, but I'll keep my distance from Arthur."

"So you won't pursue a relationship with the king?" Merlin asked.

"No," I answered. "I have no interest in that, but I do believe in him. I believe he's the leader we need. We'll win in the end, and my bow will be ready for the final battle."

"Your bow?" Merlin asked.

"Yes," I said. "My bow."

"Your archery skills aren't what Camelot desires from you," Merlin said. "Camelot desires your magic."

"That wasn't really working for me," I said.

"I realize that," Merlin said. "Now is the time to force things a bit."

"How so?" I asked.

"There is a small white flower that grows in the marsh near the Red Knights castle," Merlin said. "I saw it myself as we fought our way past the submerged Death Reapers. This flower has the ability bring forth magical powers."

"Then why didn't we grab one while we were attacking?" I asked suspiciously.

"This is an adventure you must undertake alone," Merlin answered. "The flower will know if you have help. I can give you a map and a description of the flower, but that's all."

"It'll be dangerous," I said.

"You can choose to reject my idea," Merlin said.

"How badly do you need another wizard?" I asked.

"I'm no match for Morgana," Merlin said. "I need help."

I had no real desire to become a wizard. I was more than proficient with my bow, and that had proved useful enough in the battles I'd been a part of.

Magic.

It was a pain. All the training I'd so far received involved a lot of frustration and very little results. I wasn't willing to dedicate my life to learning magic, but now I'd been offered a way to cheat all the long hours of study.

Two wizards would definitely be useful.

"I'll need to sneak out of here," I said. "There's no way anyone will let me do this on my own."

Merlin looked a bit worried.

"If anything goes wrong," Merlin said. "You'll be all alone. I want you to fully understand the dangers."

"We'll need the extra magic," I said. "It'll be worth the risk."

"Very well," Merlin said. "Meet me here at midnight, and we'll get you started on your journey."

I left Merlin wondering if I should be nervous. Arthur and Lance had gone on his missions, and they always came back with nightmarish tales.

I went to the stables.

Arthur was there with Goliath. He was drinking heavily, and laughing with the stable boys and a few soldiers.

He smiled when he saw me.

"Drinking again?" I asked.

"Well," Arthur replied. "A man's got to be good at something."

"You shouldn't even be out of the infirmary," I said.

"Nonsense," Arthur argued. "Toad did an incredible job of patching me up. He couldn't save my mother, but he did good things for me."

"You're angry," I said. "You're sad. You have a right to be both, but let's not lose sight of who you are."

"I'm not really interested in a lecture," Arthur said. "I appreciate everything you've done for me, but I'm good now."

"Arthur," I said. "You aren't good if you're drinking."

"It's fine, Gwen," Arthur said.

"Why don't you gentlemen give Arthur and I a few minutes to speak privately," I said to the soldiers and stable boys."

Arthur sighed heavily as they walked away.

"Don't put me in a situation in which I'll need to be rude to you," Arthur said. "I don't want to argue."

"We need you," I said. "All of us need you. Without you, we'll never win. Without you, hope is lost. You must not fall."

"I'm not interested in fighting anymore," Arthur said.

"Of course you're not interested in fighting anymore," I said. "You'll be fighting against your son. I can't imagine what you're going through, but your son is still in this fight, and he's coming after you whether you like it or not."

"What would you have me do?" Arthur asked. "Am I supposed to kill my child?"

"Yes," I answered.

Arthur looked at me, and the pain he was going through was evident on his handsome features.

"I can't kill my son," Arthur said.

"He needs to be stopped," I said. "And you're the only one that can lead us to victory."

"I need to talk to him," Arthur said as the tears welled up in his eyes. "I need to show him that we aren't the bad guys."

"Your son has been poisoned," I said. "He's been twisted and turned by Morgana."

"I won't fight my son!" Arthur growled as he climbed up into the saddle on Goliath's back.

I didn't say another word. I watched as he rode out of the stables, and wondered if Arthur's days of being a king were already over.

"He'll come back to us," Lance said from somewhere above me in the rafters of the stable.

I jumped about a mile high.

"Lance," I said. "You scared the hell out of me."

"Sorry," Lance said.

"Why do you think he'll come back to us?" I asked.

"He didn't take the bottle," Lance answered.

I looked, and sure enough, the bottle of whiskey that Arthur had been drinking was resting on top of a bale of hay.

"A momentary relapse?" I asked.

"Yes," Lance answered.

"Where do you think he rode off to?" I asked.

"The graveyard," Lance answered.

"Lance," I said. "I need to tell you something."

"I'm listening," Lance said, "but tell me quickly. I need to catch up to Arthur."

"I'm going on a journey tonight," I said. "I'll be looking for a flower that will help bring forth my powers."

"Where are you journeying?" Lance asked.

"I'll be heading off towards the enemy castle," I answered.

"Why the hell would you do that?" Lance asked.

"Because we need another wizard," I answered. "I can be a lot more beneficial with magic than I can be with a bow."

"You'll get yourself killed," Lance said. "Arthur will never allow you to go."

"Arthur has no say in the matter," I said. "I'm free to do what I will. I'm only telling you this in case something happens to me. I don't want Merlin being blamed."

"Merlin has done enough damage," Lance said. "You should stay away from him."

"Merlin has saved many lives," I said.

"He lied to Arthur," Lance said.

"Yes," I said. "He lied to Arthur, but his intentions were good."

"You shouldn't go," Lance said stubbornly.

I was about to try and explain, but a creak of wood told me that I was alone in the stable. Lance was apparently finished with arguing with me.

Fine, I had other things to do.

Not really.

The rest of the day went by extremely slowly. I was nervous, but I was also excited to be doing something. Could I really unlock my magical powers simply by plucking a flower from the marsh? The benefits far outweighed the potential dangers of the marsh.

I thought of all the ways in which I could help everyone. I'd still need practice, I understood that, but I'd also have access to the magic. That was what I needed. I could create a fire with only that one small spark.

At midnight, I made my way to Merlin's home. My horse was there waiting for me. I knocked on the door and the wizard let me in.

"I've cast some spells on this cloak," Merlin said. "It'll help you become invisible."

"Like Lance?" I asked.

"Yes, very similar," Merlin answered, "but make sure you don't move when you wish to hide. Movement will give you away."

"Okay," I said.

"Take these as well," Merlin said as he handed me a small map, and a glass orb filled with blue smoke.

"If you find yourself in trouble, shatter the glass," Merlin said. "I'll be alerted."

"Okay," I said. "Anything else?"

"Yes," Merlin said. "The flower blooms with the first ray of sunlight. Pluck it immediately. You'll find it growing abundantly on the bushes with the white thorns."

"I saw those bushes," I said. "I know what you're talking about."

"Excellent," Merlin said. "Now remember, I only need one. Take the flower and bring it instantly back to me. I don't want you out there longer than you need to be."

"Understood," I said. "What will you do with the flower once I give it to you?"

"I'll mix it with some other ingredients and make an elixir for you to drink," Merlin said.

"The elixir will bring forth my powers?" I asked.

"In small doses at first," Merlin said, "but it'll definitely open the doorway for you."

"Then I'll leave at once," I said.

"Have a care," Merlin said. "Magic doesn't always cooperate when you take shortcuts. This task may become more difficult than it needs to be."

I left Merlin before I lost my nerve.

I was almost shaking when I left Camelot. Behind me was my home. An impenetrable fortress, ahead of me was only danger.

The things we do for others.

I carried a short sword and my bow. I had water, but no food. I didn't expect to get hungry until I was safely home. Currently, I didn't consider anywhere else to be very safe, especially at night.

The forest closed in around me.

I jumped at the first sound I heard. This made me laugh. I had a bit of a journey. I needed to calm down. The forest was dark and cool. I had trouble seeing the way, but my horse seemed as if it had been programmed with the directions, and I rarely had to look at the small map.

With nothing else to do except overreact when I heard a noise, I started to become sleepy. I hadn't rested properly. I'd tried, but sleep wasn't always my friend.

My eyes began to close involuntarily. I fought against them, but it was a pointless battle. Eventually, I drifted off into a light sleep.

I awoke easily enough when the horse came to a stop near the edge of the marsh. I could smell the marsh, but I couldn't see it. I checked the sky. It was lightening. I needed to reach one of the bushes before the first ray of sunlight hit them.

I dismounted from my horse.

I moved quietly through the trees.

When I entered the marsh and the green fog that covered it, I became extremely careful with my footing. I didn't want to disturb the water. That would prove fatal.

Off in the distance, I heard arguing. I wasn't alone. I pulled the hood of the cloak over my head and became very still. Across a body of water, I saw three Death Reapers dragging a fourth.

"I can still be useful," the Death Reaper being dragged pleaded.

"You were useful three weeks ago, mate," the lead Death Reaper said. "Now you're just in the way."

"Just kill me then," the Death Reaper being dragged pleaded.

"You still have a duty to fulfill," the lead Death Reaper said. "Now get in the water."

"Please," the Death Reaper being dragged said as they shoved him into the water. "Please...not this..."

It was over. A booted foot shoved his head under the water, and there the Death Reaper remained.

I waited while the remaining Death Reapers passed around a flask of whiskey. They were laughing as if what they did to their comrade was something to laugh at.

I would never get used to the cruelty of our enemy.

Even to one another they were cruel. What kind of oath did they give to Morgana? Who would want to live as they live? They were from another time, maybe that was it. Possibly the world was crueler back in medieval times.

Surely Camelot was different. Surely Camelot was a good place. Why would they choose a path other than Camelot? It didn't make sense to me.

Arthur could have shown them...Arthur.

Why must my thoughts drift back to Arthur?

He had probably sobered up by now. What would he make of this little adventure? Probably he'd think as highly on this as I thought on his fight with the Red Knight.

The Red Knight, how low was Morgana willing to go? To resurrect Arthur's dead son and turn him against his father was about as evil as evil gets.

Poor Arthur.

The Death Reapers wandered away from the edge of the water. I watched them as they left, and much to my surprise, I saw them walk right past that which I was searching for.

The bushes with the white thorns.

I made my way over to them as quietly as possible. I knew now that I wasn't alone in the marsh. Did that mean that the Death Reapers had reclaimed their castle? Arthur predicted that'd they'd do so.

At some point, I'd lost track of time. The sun was just now casting out its first rays of the morning.

I heard movement through the trees.

Quickly I replaced my hood and froze.

The movement became louder, but I still saw nothing.

I heard laughter from behind me. I couldn't turn around. I wasn't supposed to move. Another group of Death Reapers or perhaps the same one I'd seen just a bit ago. They were talking about women.

They seemed to be walking straight towards me.

Their footsteps were ridiculously loud in the quiet marsh.

I placed my hand on my short sword.

They were right behind me.

I heard a slight thump on the ground, followed by a quick series of slicing sounds. I spun around, and drew my sword.

Three dead Death Reapers were on the ground behind me.

"Lance," I whispered. "Was that you?"

"Be quiet," Lance said. "We need to leave."

"I need to wait until the flower blooms," I said.

"It's a trap," Lance said. "This area is flooded with Death Reapers."

The flowers began to bloom.

"I've come too far," I said as I reached out to touch the bush.

"Don't touch that," Lance said.

He was too late on the warning. The moment I touched a blooming flower, a low moaning sound echoed over the marsh.

It was a trap.

The dirty water rose and bubbled. Wet corpses rose from the muck and mire. Shouts rose up around us. Commands were being issued. Footsteps could be heard.

"I'll hide," I said.

"They'll find you," Lance said.

I freed up my bow and took aim at a nasty looking Death Reaper crawling out of the water not far away.

I pierced his head with an arrow, changed my stance, and took out a group of three that had emerged from the forest on the other side of the body of water.

There was movement behind us now.

The sun was rising higher into the sky.

Lance went into action. He was a blur of lethal movement. A grotesque art, that left only corpses in his wake.

He cut so fast, most of his victims never even had a chance to cry out. I was glad he was on my side, but even he wasn't going to be enough to get me out of this mess.

The glass orb.

My mission was a failure. It was time to admit defeat, but I still had options. I reached for the orb deep in my cloak. My fingers wrapped around its cool surface, and then I was tackled from behind.

The glass orb rolled away from me.

Rough hands sought to pin my arms behind my back, but I was already in motion. I yanked my short sword from its scabbard and went to work.

I sliced up and down, and then I thrust out the tip of my sword. I'd drawn blood from two of my four attackers, but no fatalities.

No problem.

I just needed the space to draw my bow.

I dropped the short sword, the Death Reapers came at me, and I brought all four of them down when they were only a couple feet away.

I turned and shot out more arrows. My aim was perfect. One arrow meant one kill. I was on fire. Bodies were dropping all over the marsh.

I looked over to the last place I'd seen evidence of Lance. All I saw now was a struggling group of Death Reapers, and the group seemed to be thinning out rapidly as more and more of them dropped to the ground.

I looked to the horizon.

The sun was higher in the air.

Another thought occurred to me, and my heart sank like a rock.

Lance.

He was about to go through his change. Very soon, I'd be left all alone.

The group attacking Lance was no more. I shot more arrows at the advancing Death Reapers on my side. The Death Reapers from the water were by far the worst. They seemed without fear, and I had no fire with which to chase them away.

"Gwen!" Lance shouted from somewhere. "Run! Run Now!"

"I can't just leave you!" I shouted out.

"Just go!" Lance shouted. "Get away from here!"

I fired another arrow. I claimed another rotten life, and then I ran. I felt like a coward for running, and leaving Lance, but I understood what was happening.

Lance himself needed to leave the battle.

The young knight wanted to make sure I was safe before he vanished into the forest. Okay, I understood it, but I hated it. Lance was a young man. I shouldn't be leaving him. He should be leaving me.

Never mind that Lance was one of the fiercest warriors that we have. Never mind that the only reason I was currently alive was because of his intervention.

I just hated leaving him.

I ran as fast as I could, and I fired arrow after arrow as I ran. Death Reapers were all around me. If they got too close, I let them have it. I didn't need to pause in my running to aim. I needed less than a second to find and pierce a target.

I didn't worry about where I stepped. Everything evil was already alerted to my presence and chasing after me. I splashed freely, and hoped that I didn't step into a puddle that was deeper than anticipated.

The Red Knight stepped out of the tree line directly in front of me.

I shot an arrow, and just like in a movie, he snatched it out of the air. I drew another arrow, and the Red Knight went into motion.

It was unbelievable.

He covered the space between us in the blink of an eye. He ripped the bow from my left hand easily, so I tried to stab his eye with the arrow.

No luck, he turned his head slightly and my arrow broke against his helmet. He pushed me backwards, and I fell.

The Red Knight.

Mordred.

The son of King Arthur.

"He loves you," I said.

"Does he?" Mordred asked.

"You know he does," I said.

"I know nothing of the sort," Mordred said. "Death is often only a temporary condition. Where were my father and his wizard when my body was rotting in the ground?"

"Morgana used dark magic to bring you back," I argued. "Merlin would never use magic like that."

"Merlin will ultimately do what his king asks of him," Mordred said.

"It was never considered," I said.

"It was considered," Mordred said. "It was considered by my mother."

"Morgana isn't your mother," I said. "Your mother died, and mercifully, she wasn't resurrected with foul magic."

"Is that right," Mordred said. "Well perhaps you should meet the dark queen, and see for yourself."

255

♣ LANCE ♣

Gwen ran, and I watched her go.

She was being pursued, but I quickly dispatched the bulk of her pursuers.

The change was upon me.

I felt the tingling along my spine. I could hold it back no longer. It was my turn to run. I could only hope that Gwen could make it to safety on her own.

A noise from behind.

Eight Death Reapers were busily searching for me. Well, I wasn't exactly expertly hidden. If they searched enough, they were sure to find me.

I let them get a little closer, and I attacked.

I sliced at them, and the blood flew...at first.

Before I knew what was happening, I was surrounded. The Death Reapers knew exactly where to thrust their swords, and it was all I could do to avoid them.

I was losing my camouflage.

My anxiety hit the roof.

I went into a full panic.

I slashed out sloppily. I dodged clumsily. After I was cut deeply on my hip, I decided to flee the area.

I leapt high into the air, or at least I should have. I could no longer leap to great heights. Instead, I was left clinging to a tree branch not ten feet above my attackers.

One of them threw his sword at me.

The weapon hit me in the back, but did no damage.

I climbed up the branch and looked at my arms.

They were visible. Not completely, but visible enough to make my escape infinitely more difficult. I scurried higher into the tree.

Once I was high enough, I leapt to another tree.

I barely made it.

I climbed even higher in the new tree, and mapped out my route. That's when I saw Mordred. He had captured Gwen.

I wanted to chase after the two of them, as they moved deeper into the forest, but I was weakening by the second.

I jumped to another tree. I landed on a lower branch, and surveyed the area. I was looking for the glass orb that Gwen had dropped when she'd been tackled.

I finally found it in the hand of an unsuspecting Death Reaper. I took aim with a spike. I could hit it from here, but it wouldn't be easy.

I threw the spike.

My aim was off. Right as I let go of the spike, the Death Reapers that had been after me started shaking my tree.

My spike ended up hitting the Death Reaper holding the glass orb in the middle of his back. He cried out in pain, and dropped the orb.

The orb hit a rock.

The glass shattered, and the blue smoke drifted lazily about before darting away towards Camelot.

I'd done all I was capable of.

I climbed higher into the tree, and leapt into another one. Fortunately for me, the forest was dense. In no time at all, I'd lost all my abilities, and could only hide as the Death Reapers searched for me from below.

Merlin would be warned, but Gwen was still lost to us. I didn't expect her to live. How would Arthur handle the news?

I started crying.

Once again, I'd failed Arthur.

The waiting was hard. Two hours a day, I could do nothing but wait. It doesn't seem like much. Heck, it isn't much, but those hours kept landing when I was needed the most. I could run from my debilitations, but I couldn't hide.

When the sun was good and risen, my powers returned just like they always did. I was gone in a flash. I heard shouts from the ground. Perhaps they'd seen a blur of movement. It didn't matter much. I was long gone.

I made the trip back to Camelot in two hours.

I made a rapid search for everyone, but found no one. That meant they had already gathered in the war room.

I made my way there through a secret passage that led into the rafters. Everyone had gathered. All of them were arguing, except for Arthur. Arthur was sitting in his seat, petting a white kitten that playfully swatted at his beard.

"I don't understand how you could send her into such dangerous territory," Reynolds was complaining to Merlin. "Haven't you done enough damage around here?"

"She wanted her powers," Merlin said. "The choice was hers. She knew the risks."

"You speak as if you don't have any feelings on the matter," Wayne said. "She was dear to all of us."

"I'm broken hearted over her kidnapping," Merlin said.

"We need to get her back," Reynolds said. "If they took her in the marsh, they've definitely reclaimed the castle. We must attack."

"Many of our soldiers are injured," Bedder said. "We haven't completely recovered from the last battle."

"What are you saying?" Reynolds demanded.

"I'm wondering if she'd want us to risk so many lives for hers," Bedder answered honestly.

"We must rescue her," Wayne said.

The arguing started all over again. Everyone was talking at once. Arthur watched them all with a blank expression on his face, but he never said a word.

"What if I go?" Tristan asked.

"What do you mean?" Merlin asked.

"What if I go alone," Tristan continued. "I could sneak in, grab Gwen, and run. Once I get to my horse I'm unstoppable."

"I don't like that idea," Izzy said. "It's a risk. You don't even know where they're keeping her."

"We have a pretty good idea," Wayne said.

"It might be a good idea," Reynolds said. "A small group of us instead of an entire army."

"It shouldn't be too hard to dig up some of the Death Reapers' rusty armor," Wayne said. "We could go in disguise."

"It won't work," Merlin said. "Surely there will be protective spells against such a thing. You can't forget about magic."

"Well, we need to do something," Reynolds said as he pounded his fist on the table. "Arthur, you're the king. What do you say?"

The room became deathly quiet.

Arthur looked at Reynolds.

He stopped petting the kitten, and set the animal down on the floor.

"Camelot isn't ready for another drawn out battle so soon," Arthur said. "If we attacked now, we'd surely lose."

"Merlin has already weakened the walls," Reynolds said. "We'd have easy access this time."

"I will not send my people to another major battle without proper preparation," Arthur said. "We have no idea how many of them there are, and we have no idea what changes they've made to their defenses."

"What if we send Lance to find out?" Bedder asked.

"That'll take too long," Reynolds said. "Gwen will be dead by then."

"We'll definitely investigate what we're up against," Arthur said, "but there will be no rescue attempts. The risk is too great."

Reynolds stood.

"Is this because she rejected you?" Reynolds asked. "I've seen you mooning all over her, and I've seen her reject you."

Arthur looked calmly at Reynolds, but something sinister crept across his features.

"My heart goes out to Gwen," Arthur said in a measured voice, "but I'll not risk everyone for one."

"Then let me go," Reynolds said. "I'll do it alone."

"No," Arthur said. "You're too important here. We need you to rebuild the army."

"You're killing Guinevere!" Reynolds erupted. "You are sentencing our queen to the death."

Merlin, Wayne, and Bedder stood immediately.

"This is not the way to speak to our king," Merlin said.

"He's no king to me," Reynolds said.

"You must retract those words," Merlin said. "Or risk being banished from Camelot."

"I'll not..." Reynolds tried to say.

"Stop," Arthur said as he stood up. "No doubt emotions are running high. Reynolds spoke without thinking. In time I'm sure he'll come to agree with me. As for now, this matter has been settled. Gwen chose her own path. Merlin put the damn idea into her head, and all of us must make peace with it. Now feel free to talk behind my back. I have things to attend to."

Without another word, Arthur left the room. Something was wrong. Arthur wasn't acting like Arthur. He wasn't drunk. I was sure of that. I knew his drunken mannerisms better than anyone. Something else was going on.

"Gentlemen," Wayne said. "The argument is over. Our king has made his decision. Let's all go find something with which to occupy our time."

I watched as Wayne ushered everyone out the door.

Merlin sat back down in his chair, and watched all the knights file out of the room. Finally, the two of us were alone.

"Something's wrong," I said.

"Lancelot," Merlin said. "I'm not surprised."

"Something's wrong," I repeated.

"Everything's wrong," Merlin said. "I've failed again."

"I'm not talking about Gwen," I said. "I'm talking about Arthur. There's something wrong with him."

"Of course there is," Merlin said. "He's lost his one chance at ever finding happiness."

"I think it's more than that," I argued. "Stop feeling sorry for yourself, and do something about it."

"You expect me to meddle once again?" Merlin asked.

"I expect you to make sure your king isn't about to do something foolish," I said. "Everyone is so absorbed in their grief that they haven't noticed how Arthur is acting very unlike Arthur."

Merlin looked towards me.

"What could Arthur do?" Merlin asked.

"I wouldn't even hazard a guess," I said, "but I think we need to keep an eye on him."

Merlin began to walk around the table.

"Leave me with my thoughts," Merlin said. "I'll summon you later. Try and keep an eye on Arthur."

I moved back into the secret passage and came back out onto a wide empty hallway. I searched for Arthur, found Wendell, and asked him about Arthur.

"You gave me a fright, Sir Lancelot," Wendell said. "Arthur's in the library."

"Which library?" I asked.

"The library on the second floor," Wendell answered.

As luck would have it, I knew exactly where that library was. I moved at full speed. The stairs and distance were nothing to me.

Arthur was sitting at a table skimming through a book when I entered the room. I was silent, but somehow he still knew I was there.

"I've been wondering where you've been," Arthur said.

"I was with Gwen when she was kidnapped," I said.

"I know," Arthur said. "We saw parts of the fight with that blue smoke stuff. I guess it came from a glass orb that Merlin had given to Gwen."

"Yes," I said. "I was the one who broke it. I did my best to send a warning to you."

"Well," Arthur said. "It worked."

"Arthur," I said. "This is my fault. I failed Gwen. The rising sun...it drove me away. I wanted to help her, but I couldn't. I'm so sorry. I tried. I really tried, but I can't help it. I can't control myself."

I was crying.

Arthur turned in my direction.

"Lance," Arthur said. "This isn't your fault. You aren't responsible. I ask that my knights do their best for others, and you have done so time and time again. I'll never blame you for this. I know you did your best."

I ran to Arthur and hugged him around the waist. It shocked him for a moment. I rarely ever touched anyone, but soon he was hugging me back.

"Go get some rest," Arthur said after a long while.

"What about Gwen?" I asked.

Arthur didn't answer.

✤ ARTHUR ✤

I waited.

Time was what was important.

I needed to bide my time.

Everyone was dealing with their grief. The only two people that would really pay any attention to me at the moment were Merlin and Lance.

I needed them to relax.

The moment came late at night when a drunken Reynolds tried to ride out with only a few men. His brothers in arms had to restrain him.

I slipped into a secret passage that led to the front of the castle. From there, I crossed the drawbridge, and made my way into the shopping district.

A feed store held my armor. The owner of the store was more than happy to help me out. I'd met him earlier in the day while he was visiting his son, who was a soldier in training.

The store owner led an angry Goliath out of the stable, to his shop, and tied him to the nearest post. Goliath was happy to see me. A few snorts of acknowledgment in my direction put a smile on my face. He was already wearing his own armor.

I fed him an apple for behaving so well. I half expected him to eat the poor store owner. I went inside the store, and donned my armor.

"What's going on?" The store owner asked.

"Nothing you need to be concerned about," I said.

"I would hope that my actions for the king would in no way endanger the king," the store owner said.

"I won't lie to you," I said. "What I'm doing now I'm doing for my own selfish reasons. I'm doing what I'm doing because I can do nothing else."

"You're going after Guinevere," the store owner said.

"Thank you for helping me," I said.

I climbed on top of Goliath's back, and rode slowly out to the main cobblestone road. I looked towards the castle. No alarms had gone off. They probably wouldn't for a while, but sooner or later somebody was bound to check on me.

I rode towards the main gate, still moving slowly so as to not arouse any unwanted attention. That would come soon enough.

Camelot was awake even at this late hour.

My home was in mourning.

Gwen was loved by all, and the news of her capture spread like wildfire.

I summoned all the guards at the main gate once I'd arrived. I told them to hold their tongues until my knights came looking for me. I also gave an order that I shouldn't be followed.

Once I was past the gate, I rode fast. I wanted to cover as many miles as possible. I wanted to eliminate any possibility of my knights catching up to me.

I would risk no other life.

This battle was for me.

I didn't expect to win.

I only knew that I had to try.

Goliath moved as if he shared my urgency. How great it felt to be riding with a purpose instead of waiting impatiently in the cool rooms of the castle.

What would I find once I'd reached the castle of my enemy? I had no idea. Would Gwen still be alive? I hoped so. I felt that she was still alive. In my mind, the world would become a much darker place if she was no longer here, and I didn't feel that sort of darkness just yet. It was coming though. I had to hurry.

Mile after mile flew by me. I didn't get tired. We only rested once. I drank some water. Goliath drank from a stream.

Dawn would break soon.

I heard a noise.

It sounded like branches shaking from somewhere behind me. A small bit of panic travelled up my spine. I wheeled Goliath away from the stream, and charged forth along the trail.

I was being followed.

The great horse moved faster and faster, but he couldn't outrun the source of the sounds that were following us.

I looked towards the sky.

It had lightened ever so slightly.

My son's castle wasn't very far away. I couldn't believe how far I'd travelled. It seemed as if I'd only been riding for an hour or so.

Whatever was following me, was gaining.

I was riding through green fog and marsh. Waterlogged Death Reapers crawled towards me from their wet graves, but I was too fast and they were too few.

I hit the patch of forest, just as the sun began to peek out over the horizon. I was through the forest and running towards the enemy castle over the open field when I heard a voice calling my name.

"Arthur!" Lance called out from the trees behind me. "Don't do this! Wait for me!"

I wheeled around, and saw Lance's outline through the trees. He was rapidly becoming human, which meant that I had at least an hour before he'd leave the safety of the forest.

I didn't say anything to him.

There was nothing to say. He wouldn't change my mind, and I had no words of comfort to share.

I wheeled Goliath back towards my son's castle. I saw mounted soldiers riding towards me, and I charged out to meet them.

I pulled Excalibur from its scabbard. The blade shone brightly in the morning sun, and as I passed by the four mounted Death Reapers, the magical sword ignited as their bodies dropped to the ground behind me.

I saw that the drawbridge was open.

They weren't expected an attack, and they surely were going to be alarmed by a single mounted knight.

More mounted Death Reapers came for me.

Goliath charged into them fearlessly. As I hacked and slashed, my horse bit and kicked. More Death Reapers fell to the ground.

Goliath roared out a loud growl that couldn't have been very common in horses, and I saw the fear creep into my attackers' eyes. That was good. I wanted their fear. I was here to do them harm.

A head flew over ten feet in the air. A horse's body crumpled from a savage kick. My attackers began to scream.

In no time at all, they began to flee. I chased them down. I struck out at them from behind. More bodies fell.

I was only beginning.

More mounted riders came for me out of the open drawbridge. This time it was a group of ten. Excalibur was burning. The approaching riders could see the carnage behind me, but still they came.

Goliath ran straight at them, until they were forced to scatter. The Death Reapers tried to surround me, but I was too quick for them. The ones I couldn't reach with my sword fell prey to Goliath's kicks.

I yanked left and right on the reins.

I stabbed and cut.

Blood was splashed all over my armor. My red cape was billowing behind me as if I were facing a fierce wind.

More bodies fell to the ground.

I only had one thought in my mind...Gwen. Let her be alive. That's all I wanted. I didn't care about what happened to me. I only wanted Gwen to live.

More mounted soldiers.

I came for them immediately, and I noticed that they were finally hesitating before they engaged me. Good, they now understood what they were facing. I was death in armor. I would kill them all.

A sword found its way to my flesh right under my left arm. The pain was shocking. I gasped out loud. The wound was deep, but it wasn't enough. I killed the Death Reaper for the insult.

More and more bodies.

Archers appeared on the walls of the castle.

Goliath was pacing back and forth as I sized them up.

I was a lone knight on a field of the dead.

I could feel their fear.

I rode closer to the drawbridge. The strings of the bows were pulled back. My upper lip was curled in a snarl. I wanted so desperately to charge past the drawbridge, but I couldn't risk Goliath getting hurt. This was my mission. My horse had come as far as I'd allow him.

I dismounted.

Goliath nudged at me. He didn't want me to leave him. The horse's eyes were wide with worry, and he was making desperate sounds. I grabbed his reins, and whispered into his ear. My voice calmed him, he stayed put as I walked towards the drawbridge, but he called after me as if I'd broken his heart.

I looked up at the archers along the walls. They were watching me, but they weren't firing. I entered the drawbridge.

Inside the castle walls, I was surrounded by my enemy, and they were many. Death Reapers everywhere, a massive army of them, and the mounted riders I'd just killed were only a single drop in a very large bucket.

I was right not to lead my army here for a battle. Even if we'd somehow managed to win, our losses would be catastrophic. No doubt that was what my son was hoping for.

Gwen.

She was alive.

My eyes took her in. She was wearing a white dress, and standing on a wooden platform. She was tied to a pole, and my son, the Red Knight was standing next to her with a small dagger in his hand.

Gwen was looking at me. Her face went through a wide range of emotions until finally the tears began to fall.

She was only fifty yards away from me, but the space between us was filled with swords and hatred. The thick green fog of so many Death Reapers hung low on the ground. It chilled my legs.

I attacked.

♣ GWEN ♣

I was in a dark cell when I awoke. I could see the night sky from a barred window high on the wall. It stank of disease and misery. Where was I? No doubt I'd been taken to the Red Knight's castle. Was I to be a prisoner? Would they bargain for my life?

I was wearing a flowing white dress. I vaguely remembered rough hands undressing me, and shoving the dress over my head. When I fought back, I was beaten. Everything else was too foggy to remember clearly.

I saw movement through the bars.

"I'm glad you're awake," Mordred said.

He'd been sitting there on a stool and watching me. He still wore his armor, but not his helmet. A scar on the left side of his face drew attention to the color of his eyes. He looked very much like his father.

"I'm your prisoner now?" I asked.

"Not for long," Mordred said.

"You're using me to bargain?" I asked.

"No," Mordred said. "You're to be executed."

I said nothing.

Mordred approached the bars of my cell and grasped them with both of his hands. His face looked almost sweet it was so perfect. How could someone so beautiful be so full of evil?

"I know who you are," Mordred said.

"I'm just a girl trying my best to do what's right," I said.

"You are Guinevere," Mordred said. "Your beauty is legendary. It's no wonder my father loves you. A mere glance from you would have the power to bring men to their knees."

I stayed quiet.

"This isn't personal," Mordred continued. "I'd rather not kill you, but your death is invaluable. Imagine what will happen to my father when I claim your life. I thought taking his mother would be enough to bring him down, but I was wrong. I need to eliminate all the loves in his life. I need to leave him with nothing."

"Why?" I demanded.

"I've already explained that to you," Mordred said.

"You hate him because he didn't bring you back to life," I said, "but you don't understand how much he suffered when he lost you and your mother. Your deaths almost killed him."

"My resurrection will be what kills him," Mordred said. "Don't try and convince me not to hate my father. I was raised to hate that man. I enjoy hating that man, and most importantly I'll enjoy taking his life."

"He'll kill you," I said. "If you force his hand he'll end your life."

Mordred began to laugh. It was a soft laugh, a sweet laugh. Everything about him was deceptive.

"I almost had him in the cemetery," Mordred said.

"Only because he knew who he was fighting," I countered. "You've lost the element of surprise."

"I don't need any tricks," Mordred said. "I'm the greatest swordsman this world has ever seen."

"No," I said. "You aren't."

More laughter.

"I appreciate your devotion," Mordred said. "I'll feel sadness when I cut your throat. Such a beautiful woman you are. I'll not let you suffer terribly."

Mordred left the dark room, and I was left to fully absorb what would soon be my fate. I was scared. To die in battle at any moment was expected. The idea of it was frightening, but nothing compared to awaiting your execution.

I closed my eyes and leaned back against the stone wall. I needed to center myself. I needed to be brave. I wouldn't give them the satisfaction of seeing my fear. A single tear fell from my eye, and I roughly wiped it away.

Soon I'd be reunited with my mother and father.

For hours I sat against the cold stone wall and listened to my breathing. I couldn't sleep. I didn't want to sleep. I wanted to experience every bit of life that was left to me. I wanted to be brave.

I stared at the stars through the barred window. I was still staring at them when the sky began to lighten with the coming of dawn.

Death Reapers came into the cell. None of them spoke to me. They unlocked the door to my cell, and tied my hands behind my back. I kept my face as impassive as I possibly could. I'd show them no fear. I'd give them no emotion.

My trembling breaths gave me away. I was breathing too loud and too fast. The truth is, I wasn't ready. I hadn't been able to steel my nerves. I was terrified, and in my terror I prayed for a miracle.

Surely I was missed. Where was my rescue? Knights in shining armor should have already been attacking...yeah, right.

There would be no rescue. I knew it. Camelot wasn't ready for another major battle. To attack would be suicide. I was going to die.

One face kept appearing in my thoughts. Arthur, where was he? Did he know? His revenge would come, and it would be unstoppable and fierce.

Arthur.

I couldn't stop thinking about Arthur. In my final moments I was thinking about Arthur. What did that mean?

I was led up a short flight of stairs to a wooden platform in the center of the vast courtyard. The entire Death Reaper army was laid out all around me. Their sickly green fog drifted slowly over the ground.

I was pushed roughly against a wooden pole that rose out of the center of the wooden platform. My arms were tied behind me to the pole. This was it. The moment had arrived. I clenched my eyes to hold back my tears.

Mordred began speaking to his Death Reapers. He was talking about striking a blow to the heart of his enemy. I heard my name, I heard Arthur's name, but I couldn't follow what he was saying.

I was looking to the sky. My mind was drifting away from the horrific scene. I could just barely see the faint glow of the far off stars.

Mordred walked towards me to the cheers of his army. I couldn't look at him. My eyes remained focused on the sky above me. I smelled his hot breath as he slowly entwined his fingers in my hair and pushed my head backwards.

My breathing sped up once again.

A small blade danced at the edges of my vision.

A warning bell sounded out.

Mordred released me and stormed to the edge of the platform.

I looked around.

All eyes were focused on the drawbridge. Soldiers were mounting horses and riding out. Mordred was shouting orders.

Was this the rescue? What was happening?

Archers climbed up and took position on the battlements. Mordred hadn't been expecting whatever was happening outside the castle walls.

"Who could be this stupid," Mordred said as he paced along the platform. "What man is this brave?"

More riders went out, and more followed after that.

"Allow him entrance!" Mordred shouted as the screams of the dying echoed from outside the walls."

Faintly, I could hear the sounds of metal striking metal, and then all was silent. The army of Death Reapers before me parted, and I had a clear view of the drawbridge.

A lone knight with a flaming blue sword walked into the courtyard.

Arthur had come.

I panicked. Where was his army? Where were his knights? Why was Arthur all alone? Arthur must not fall.

This couldn't be happening. Why would he come? What was he thinking? He couldn't help me, but my God...I was relieved to see him.

Arthur must not fall.

I wanted him to leave. I could hear Goliath complaining outside the walls. I wanted Arthur to turn away, mount his horse, and ride off to safety. Don't sacrifice your life for me. What are you doing?

I was crying now. No, I was sobbing. I wanted to scream out to him that he should leave. Things must not end in the way they were ending.

Instead, Arthur came towards me.

A Death Reaper tried to stop him, and Arthur's burning sword removed his arm. More came after that. One at a time, sometimes five at a time, Arthur cut them all down, and continued towards me.

Something strange was happening. The Death Reapers could easily overpower him if they attacked as one, but it seemed as if they were afraid to do so. Did Arthur inspire that much fear in them?

I spoke too soon.

Several of them came for him. Arthur killed two of them instantly, but another managed to pierce Arthur's arm with the tip of his sword. Arthur screamed out, and stumbled away. That moment of weakness broke whatever spell the Death Reapers had been under.

A blow from an axe hit Arthur's helmet.

The great king fell to his knees.

I wanted to scream out, but it wouldn't have mattered. I was helpless. Mordred looked at me, and smiled.

Arthur struck out, and severed the leg of the nearest Death Reaper. He got to his feet quickly, and deflected another sword strike.

I watched as he yanked away his damaged helmet with his free hand, and defended himself with the other.

Blood sprayed out in a crimson wave as Excalibur cut through the neck of the Death Reaper that stabbed him.

A burning torch was thrust in Arthur's face. Arthur screamed as his hair caught fire, and slapped at his head. Another Death Reaper capitalized on the distraction, and thrust a knife into his back.

Arthur spun around, cleaving the Death Reaper in two. Our enemy involuntarily took a step backwards when they saw that.

Mordred jumped from the platform as if he himself would be the one to kill Arthur. I watched as his red armor vanished amongst a sea of bodies.

Arthur continued walking towards me, as the full force of Mordred's enormous army swelled around him.

It was too late for escape now. The enemy was upon us. All we could do would be to die bravely. My poor Arthur, I could only watch as he was battered and cut. He killed all that stood in his way, but the injuries were taking their toll and he'd never had the chance to fully recover from his last fight with Mordred.

Finally, Arthur reached my platform.

I watched him climb up, and then he was standing before me, blocking out the image of all those Death Reapers standing behind him.

"Why have you come?" I cried.

"How could I not come," Arthur said.

My king, my handsome king, he was so battered and bruised. His hair was burnt on one side of his head. There was a laceration on the other. I could see how deep it was, because the wound refused to bleed. He was having problems catching his breath, and I saw the punctures in his armor, but still he smiled at me.

His hand came up and gently touched my face.

"Arthur," I said. "You must not fall."

"I fell a long time ago," Arthur replied.

I cried as he wrapped his arms around me, and kissed my cheek. I felt his heavy hands upon my bound hands. I felt his warmth, and for only a brief second my fear vanished. I was home. I was safe, and then it was gone.

"Be brave," Arthur said as he pulled away from me. "In this life you'll never walk alone."

He turned to face the Death Reapers. Excalibur was waiting for him. Arthur gripped the sword, but he was moving too slowly. His injuries were getting the better of him.

I cried out from the depths of my soul as he leapt from the platform into the midst of the Death Reapers, because I had finally accepted what I'd been fighting for so long.

I loved him.

Enough of my games, I loved him totally and completely. He was a missing piece of my soul. Our love withstood the centuries and I could no longer deny it.

I screamed as I saw the Death Reapers converge on him. He hacked at them, he sliced at them, but there were too many. He was taking more and more strikes. Some of them found their way past his armor, but most of them were only a wound of impact.

My beautiful king fell more than once. Each time he was able to get back to his feet, but I knew the time of his final fall was quickly approaching.

I cried out.

To whom I was crying I don't know, but I cried out for someone to help him. That's when the crowd of Death Reapers all around him broke away and spread out. That's when Mordred the Red Knight came forward.

Arthur was limping horribly, but the two of them circled each other. I pulled against my heavy bonds. I'd rush to Arthur if I could. I'd take his place and fight Mordred myself if only to prevent my love from suffering any longer.

My bonds felt tighter than ever.

The two knights came at each other.

Their blades whirled so quickly I couldn't keep track of them. The two of them became entangled. Arthur hit his son in the face with his elbow, and Mordred's nose began to gush. In return, Mordred threw Arthur to the ground and cut open the back of his leg. The Red Knight's sword sparked alive with a black flame.

Arthur cried out.

I struggled even harder. How could the rope around my wrists have become tighter? It didn't make sense. With my fingers, I searched the tight coils.

Arthur's dagger.

Arthur had shoved his dagger between the coils of rope for me to find. That's why my bonds were heavier and tighter. He'd given me an escape.

I stretched my fingers and grabbed the handle of the knife. From there I managed to move the blade up and down against the rope. It wasn't easy, my bonds were tight.

Arthur was back on his feet.

Mordred came towards him in a clumsy lunge. Arthur sidestepped, and sliced him along the ribcage. Mordred's armor opened up like butter, and his blood began to flow.

"Very good, father," Mordred said. "That wasn't an easy cut to make."

"Stop this," Arthur said. "I've no wish to fight you."

"You don't seem to understand," Mordred said. "My dream is to end your life. I give you no choice in the matter."

Mordred lunged again.

This time his burning blade managed to pierce Arthur in the hip. Again my king screamed out in pain. Mordred took a step back as if he were shocked that'd he'd managed to stab his father.

Arthur limped backwards. I could see the pain etched across his face. I could hear his wheezing breath.

Finally, the first coil of rope around my hands came away.

Mordred twirled his sword.

Arthur raised Excalibur weakly in defense.

Mordred slashed, and Arthur blocked.

The Death Reapers were cheering wildly all around us.

The two combatants became entangled once again. This time Arthur was too weak to defend himself. Mordred slashed him deeply across the back as if Arthur's armor didn't exist.

Another coil of rope came away.

Arthur fell to the ground, and struggled to right himself.

I was screaming.

Mordred approached his father slowly as if he were enjoying the moment. His handsome face had turned maniacal in his murderous glee.

I saw my poor Arthur. He looked tired and pale. He never should have come. His image blurred through my tears as Mordred raised his sword for the final blow.

My hands came free.

An energy poured through my limbs. I heard a crackle of electricity, and the hairs along my arms stood up on end.

I looked at my hands. They had erupted in a blue flame of magic, and I went on the offensive.

"NO!" I shouted from the platform. "YOU CANNOT HAVE HIM!"

Mordred looked at me. He saw the flame of magic in my hands, and his eyes grew wide in astonishment.

I scratched at him with my nails as if I was close enough to touch him, and the ground below him erupted in a small explosion.

The roots of trees long since dead wrapped around his legs, and I realized that I could control them. I moved my fingers back and forth, and the roots grew tighter and tighter.

Arthur struggled to stand.

Mordred slashed at the roots around his legs.

The Death Reapers moved in. Quickly they struck out at Arthur, and I lost focus for a brief moment. I sent my power towards the Death Reapers. The ground erupted around them in tidal waves of earth that pushed them far away.

Arthur was barely standing.

Mordred had freed himself.

I summoned up another push of magic, but I was too late. With his evil sword, Mordred pierced his father's sternum all the way to the hilt.

"NO!" I screamed as I lost control.

The ground began to explode as if dynamite were buried in the soil. The Red Knight was blasted away from Arthur. The Death Reapers were thrown here and there by the moving earth.

I had no focus.

I only had my rage.

It was all I needed.

I took on the entire army of Death Reapers. I watched as they attempted to rush me. The earth swirled around them in a miniature tornado. It picked them up and tore them apart.

I discovered the gift of fire. The attackers that I focused on began to burst into flames. I could hear their screams, and that only served as fuel. Before long, great jets of blue flame were shooting from my hands and enveloping all that sought to reach my love.

Arthur wasn't moving.

Mordred had vanished in the chaos.

I didn't care. There were still Death Reapers, and I'd make them all suffer.

Great gouts of flame rose from the ground as if volcanoes were erupting all around us. The flames shot out in burning clouds, I had very little control. This was magic brought forth by raw emotion.

And then, a black fog came.

It invaded the entire courtyard. It suffocated the green fog of the Death Reapers, and stilled my magical flames.

The air grew colder around me. Quickly, the land became a place where love and kindness could not exist. I didn't understand what was happening, but I knew it was evil.

I leapt from the platform, and ran to Arthur's still form.

I wrapped him up in my arms, and I saw him breathing. My love, my king was still alive.

"I'm here," I cried. "I'm here, and I'll never let you go."

Arthur reached up an armored hand and touched my arm. I saw a smile appear on his pale face.

"I love you," Arthur whispered.

"I love you," I said. "Don't you dare leave me. I need you. We all need you. Please, stay with me. We've only just begun our journey."

Arthur looked at me as the black fog grew denser and denser. The remaining Death Reapers, of which there were many, bowed their heads and backed away. I held tighter to Arthur, and looked around.

Through the fog came a woman in a black dress. Her hair was dark like Mordred's, and she was beautiful and flawless. I stared at her face. Her arched eyebrows and her black eyes were without compassion.

Arthur saw her and groaned.

I understood at once.

Morgana had come, and she was using the body of Arthur's deceased wife.

I watched as the fog swirled and danced around her. Like a sentient being, the fog caressed her and held her. Finally, she stood before us and smiled. The smile was bone-chilling and unearthly.

"Little Guinevere, playing with magic," Morgana said.

My hands ignited with the magical flame, and I stood slowly away from Arthur. I moved to face the evil queen, and her smile grew larger.

"Today we will walk free," I said.

"No, my dear," Morgana said. "Today I'll eat the both of you."

I lashed out at her with a jet of fire, but my attack was deflected with a casual flick of her wrist. The black fog swirled and churned as her black eyes and blank face watched me with something similar to amusement.

I clawed my hands and the roots of the dead trees swirled around her legs. I twisted my fingers and arched my wrists until the roots covered her hips, but Morgana never stopped smiling.

The black fog came in and wrapped around her, and with a slow blink of her eyes the fog savagely ripped away the roots.

Another flick of her wrist sent me flying into the wooden platform. I lost my breath with the impact, but Morgana wasn't yet done with me.

The black fog grabbed hold of me, and lifted me into the air. It squeezed tightly around my body as if I were in the coils of an immense snake, before slamming me into the ground.

I couldn't catch my breath.

My lungs were making an obscene sound as they tried to function once again, and I found myself crawling over the burnt bodies of the Death Reapers I'd slain.

Morgana looked to Arthur.

"You were a fool to come here," Morgana said. "You should have let her die."

I watched as Arthur tried to rise from the ground.

"You're not her," Arthur said. "You've stolen her body, but you're not her."

"I am your darling wife," Morgana said. "Just ask your son. I was there for him after you abandoned him. I raised him as my own."

"You turned him into a killer," Arthur said.

"Yes," Morgana said. "I did."

The black fog swirled and twisted. Mordred appeared behind Morgana. He walked forward until he was standing beside her.

Again, that horrible smile appeared on Morgana's lips. She put her hand on Mordred's armored shoulder, and trailed her fingers across his back as she walked behind him.

Mordred drew his sword.

Arthur continued his struggle to rise, but his legs were no longer working. He'd suffered too much damage. I was certain he was dying.

I stood up amongst the dead bodies, focused my power, let it build up, and released it as Mordred came for Arthur.

The earth rippled below me. It traveled to my enemy, and burst from the ground in sharp rocks that threw Mordred to the ground.

"Guinevere," Morgana said as the black fog rushed towards me. "I thought you were already dead."

The black fog seized me in its fierce grip, and raised me into the air. The grip grew tighter and tighter. I saw Morgana watching me calmly. She was taking her time, and toying with me. Mordred was already back on his feet.

"You won't win," I said. "No matter what you do to me, you won't win."

"I've already won," Morgana said. "You're just too blind to see it."

The fog squeezed me tightly, and I felt my arm snap. I screamed out in pain, and saw Arthur finally rise to his feet.

"No," Arthur said as he swayed unsteadily.

"The fallen king rises yet again," Morgana said.

"I'll kill you," Arthur said.

"You can't kill me," Morgana said thoroughly enjoying herself.

"I know who can," Arthur said.

Morgana began to laugh.

"Your little wizard has grown weak," Morgana said. "I'll kill him as easily as I kill you."

The fog swirled around Arthur and lifted him into the air next to me. Arthur struggled against its mighty grip, but he couldn't win.

"Any more threats?" Morgana asked. "I'd love to hear them."

"Just one," Arthur said.

"I can't wait," Morgana said.

"MERLIN!" Arthur shouted. "I NEED YOU!"

Morgana laughed.

A section of the castle wall blew forward, and the armored knights of Camelot rushed through the ruined section. Without warning a full scale battle began inside the courtyard.

Morgana looked around angrily, Arthur and I dropped from the sky, and Merlin stepped through the black fog to face Morgana.

Merlin.

A mighty wizard trapped in a teenager's body. His black hair was mussed. He was wearing jeans, a t-shirt, and an old hoodie. I was glad to see him.

"How?" Morgana asked.

"I knew Arthur would come for Guinevere," Merlin shrugged. "We followed as quickly as we could."

"You'll die with him," Morgana said.

"Not today," Merlin said.

Morgana lashed out with her hands, and her black fog took on the shape of a great snake that rushed towards Merlin.

The young-looking wizard plunged his hand into the ground, and a great fist rose from the earth to grab the neck of the snake and crush it.

"I'm stronger than you expected," Merlin said.

"Yet still not strong enough," Morgana said.

The two of them circled each other.

Reynolds appeared at my side, and lifted me to my feet.

"Are you well?" Reynolds asked.

"I'm hurt," I answered.

"Let's get you out of here," Reynolds said.

"We can't leave without Arthur," I said.

"Arthur's already being looked after," Reynolds argued.

I looked over towards Arthur. I saw Wayne and Tristan lifting his body over Wayne's shoulders.

There was movement all around us. Mounted knights were pouring into the courtyard. Death Reapers were attempting to stop them, and the battle was raging on.

I saw that the sun was low in the sky. Morning had arrived and I hadn't noticed it with all the black fog swirling around.

Goliath came charging towards us. The large horse was trampling any Death Reaper foolish enough to stand in his way.

"I need a bow," I said.

"What?" Reynolds asked.

"A bow," I said. "Do you have one?"

"I can get one," Reynolds said as he waved over a mounted knight, "but your arms broken. How will you shoot the damn thing?"

"That's my worry," I said. "We're outnumbered. You took them by surprise, but soon our enemy will regroup."

Indeed, in the distance I saw Mordred. He was standing on the platform, and shouting orders which his Death Reapers were rapidly obeying.

A thousand blades rose into the air all around us. Collectively the battle halted as all the combatants watched them rise.

I looked towards Morgana. She was twisting her arms. The blades all gathered together in a great cloud that moved through the air picking up speed before charging towards Merlin.

Merlin used his power to gather hundreds of shields, and forced them to cocoon his body as the blades rained down on top of him.

I gasped as some of the swords pierced through the shields, and then the shields exploded outwards towards Morgana. The evil queen stumbled backwards as she used her black fog to block the attack.

Merlin smiled.

Reynolds shoved a bow in my hand, and dropped a quiver of arrows at my feet. My arm was shaking as I drew the bow.

The pain was too much.

I couldn't pull the string back far enough.

I saw Wayne lifting and shoving Arthur's body over Goliath's back. He and Tristan then led the horse away from the battle while other knights converged around them in a protective circle.

A knight composed entirely of rock rose from the ground. It faced off against another; a fanged and clawed monster composed entirely of black fog. Merlin and Morgana stood on either side of their creations. Their arms were waving around, and their fingers were in constant motion.

Merlin's knight struck out with his stony blade, and cleaved a great wound into the monster's seemingly solid hide.

Morgana screamed out in pain.

Her monster clawed at Merlin's knight, and scratched it across the face. Merlin bore the wounds. He was soon bleeding heavily, and wiping at his eyes to keep his vision clear. His knight began to shudder and slow down.

I wanted to help him, but I didn't know how. That magic was far beyond me, and the pain in my arm wasn't my only injury. I was positive I had some broken ribs. The sides of my chest began to lance me with pain. I was soon seeing double and having difficulties concentrating.

"Gwen," Reynolds said. "It's time. We need to go."

"Not without Arthur and Merlin," I argued.

"Arthur is safe," Reynolds said. "Look for yourself."

I looked, and beyond the broken wall I saw Goliath being led down the open field. Arthur was still on his back, and Wayne and Tristan were riding next to him along with a grouping of knights.

Morgana attacked again.

This time her monster struck against the knight's leg, and Merlin fell with the impact. His knight froze solid, and then began to crumble into pieces.

With a wave of her hand, Morgana caused her monster to vanish. That sickly smile was back on her face. She'd beaten Merlin.

I tried my bow once again, and this time, despite the pain I took my shot. The arrow flew, but I was off target. Instead of piercing Morgana's heart, the arrow pierced her shoulder. Regardless, Morgana screamed with pain and fury as she ripped the arrow away.

Reynolds fearlessly ran to Merlin, and scooped him up as Morgana screamed and thrashed nearby him.

The black fog went crazy. It tore apart the platform I was to be executed on, and assaulted friend and foe without discrimination.

Somehow, against all odds, Reynolds managed to escape unharmed. As my friend was running towards me with Merlin over his shoulder, he pointed behind me. The look on his face was unforgettable.

I turned around.

A great number of Death Reapers were closing in on me.

I dropped the bow, and held Arthur's dagger. Reynolds was rushing to me, but he wasn't going to make it in time.

A blur of motion came from nowhere and sliced its way into the heart of the advancing Death Reapers. I watched as their limbs detached, and their heads rolled. I was soon splattered in blood, but alive.

Lance had arrived.

His spikes flew out, and his wicked little blades cut through bone. Reynolds came up and reached his arm around me. Before I knew what was happening, he was pulling me along, and shouting orders to the remaining knights.

We were soon surrounded in a protective circle and being led to the broken section of wall. I couldn't see past the armored backs of our protectors, but I could see them fighting furiously to keep me safe.

Outside the wall were horses. Reynolds shoved me on top of the nearest one, and helped Merlin climb up behind me.

"Can he even hold on?" I asked.

"I'll be fine," Merlin said.

Reynolds slapped the flank of my horse and we were off.

All around me I saw retreating Knights as Reynolds blew a horn that signaled our retreat. Each step of the horse brought a wave of agony to my injured body. I wasn't going to be able to keep this up for long.

"Are you okay?" Merlin asked.

"No," I answered honestly.

Merlin flattened out his hands against my stomach, and the pain lessoned greatly. I was able to ride, and ride I did. I followed my comrades deep into the forest, and headed towards Camelot as fast as my horse could take us.

Somewhere past the dangerous swamp, we all regrouped. Arthur had been placed on a primitive wagon, and the little gnome was furiously working on his wounds.

I dismounted against the protests of Merlin, and rushed to the wagon. Toad was shocked to see me.

"What are you doing?" Toad asked.

"I'll be riding with Arthur," I said. "How is he?"

"Horrible," Toad answered. "It's hard to work on him like this. He's suffered a lot of damage. The scabbard is once again the only thing keeping him alive."

We were moving again in less than a minute. Reynolds rode up next to us and handed me another bow, and a large quiver of arrows.

The pain was coming back to me, but I was going to defend Arthur with my dying breath if that was what was called for.

I felt a soft thump behind me.

"How bad is he?" Lance asked.

"He's bad," I said, "but he's still alive."

"Then let's keep him that way," Lance said.

Merlin rode nearby. He'd fully recovered his senses despite his bleeding face and leg. He was positioning all the knights in our traveling caravan.

"Our enemy will soon be upon us!" Merlin shouted. "Our only goal is to keep our king safe. Do not move from your positions, and make them suffer terribly for every inch they gain."

I looked to our knights. I couldn't see any of their faces due to their helmets, but I understood the posture of their bodies. They weren't about to fail. They were ready to fight until their death.

I laid out a bunch of arrows by poking their tips into the wood of the wagon. I was ready, to hell with the pain.

We rode down the trail, and around a corner. The way ahead of us was free and clear, but when I turned around once again, I saw our enemy.

There were too many of them.

We had forty maybe fifty knights, it was difficult to say. The mounted Death Reapers seemed to number in the hundreds.

Arthur reached out and touched my hand.

I looked down at him. Most of his armor had been removed as Toad worked on his body. I saw the brutal cuts and slashes that refused to bleed. I saw his old scars, and wondered how he was still alive.

So many wounds, too many wounds.

He smiled at me, and I placed my hand on his forehead.

"I won't leave you," I whispered. "I'll keep you safe, just focus on staying with me."

Arthur nodded, and I let the first of my arrows fly. I dropped the nearest Death Reaper, and the battle began.

We fought savagely, as did the Death Reapers, but we never stopped moving. Bedder was in the lead, and he made damn sure that our caravan never even slowed down.

My arrows dropped any Death Reaper that got too close to our wagon. I took care of one side, and Lance handled the other with his many spikes.

At one point, we were in danger of being overwhelmed, and Merlin and Wayne appeared. Wayne swung one of his axes, and Merlin assaulted the Death Reapers with a large ball of blue fire that ignited whatever it touched.

When we were safe once again, both of them dropped back towards the rear of the line where the danger was greatest.

I soon ran out of arrows, and Reynolds quickly rode up with another quiver. The pain in my arm and ribs stabbed at me with every movement I made, but I wouldn't stop. The wagon jerked and bounced along the trail, but I kept on fighting.

Far away, I saw Mordred on his red steed.

Merlin was using his magic against him, but the wizard's best efforts barely seemed to slow the Red Knight down.

"Faster!" Merlin called out. "We need to move faster."

The driver of our wagon looked over his shoulder. It was Izzy.

"I can't go any faster!" Izzy shouted. "It'll upset the wagon!"

Merlin cursed in frustration, but kept on fighting.

I was getting worried. We'd been at this for too long. Our knights were beginning to tire. Some of them had been slain. Our pursuers were overtaking those of us in the rear.

"Do not let them claim your lives," Merlin shouted. "We fight for Arthur. We fight for Camelot."

With a deep collective breath, all of us found our second wind. I stood up in the wagon, and fired towards the rear of our caravan.

My aim wasn't the greatest, not with a broken arm and broken ribs, but it was good enough. I dropped Death Reaper after Death Reaper.

I shot an arrow at Mordred, but it bounced helplessly off his armor. I watched in horror as he rode past Merlin, and came straight for our wagon.

No.

No.

I shot more arrows at him. They were useless. I looked around, I saw the blur of movement that was Lance, but he was busy defending his side of the wagon.

Excalibur appeared.

I looked at the magical sword, and then I looked towards the Red Knight. Without a second to spare, I picked it up just as Mordred came upon us.

He swung out his sword towards Arthur, and I blocked his blow with Excalibur. The two of us then began a series of back and forth attacks. It was abundantly clear that Mordred was the far better swordsman.

I was fighting a losing battle. I could barely keep up, and sooner or later he was going to get the best of me.

A spike flew out and bounced off his armor. Another spike came afterwards, and it bounced away harmlessly as well.

A blur of motion passed me and leapt into the air.

I watched as Lance landed on the back of Mordred's horse and attacked him from behind. Mordred wasn't prepared for Lance. In moments, the two of them tumbled from the horse and vanished into the forest.

The wagon never stopped moving.

Excalibur finally became burning hot, and I was forced to release the sword.

Toad looked me in the eyes.

"He's going to be okay," I said. "Lance is always okay."

"We can't stop," Toad said. "You know we can't stop."

Tears began streaming down my face.

"He's going to be okay," I repeated.

An armored hand grabbed a hold of the wagon. Quickly, I retrieved my bow and shot an arrow in the face of the Death Reaper. More of them came after that. We were being overtaken and it was happening quickly.

I fired arrow after arrow, praying that I wouldn't run out, hoping against hope that I wouldn't miss.

Out of the corner of my eye, I saw Merlin speed past us as we headed towards a vast clearing. The wizard was shouting something, but I couldn't understand him. Did he have a plan? Was he asking for more speed? I was clueless.

We entered the clearing, and found the soldiers of Camelot waiting for us. They attacked with long spears, and no hesitation.

The odds were suddenly in our favor.

I continued to fire my arrows, but the Death Reapers all around me had been driven away. I watched as our soldiers rushed into battle. I watched as the tide turned.

The wagon came to a stop at the far end of the clearing. Our remaining knights surrounded us as our soldiers continued their attack.

Merlin rode up to us.

"How is he?" Merlin asked.

"Not good," Toad answered. "He hadn't even healed up completely from his last fight."

"Can you save him?" Merlin asked.

"Not if we keep moving this damn wagon," Toad answered.

Merlin nodded, and fell from his horse.

Wayne immediately dismounted and picked up the fallen wizard.

"What happened?" I asked.

"He's exhausted himself," Wayne answered. "He'll be fine; I'll get him patched up."

I sat exhausted and in pain as Toad continued to work on Arthur. Reynolds rode up and placed his warm hand on my shoulder.

"We should take care of your wounds," Reynolds said.

"I won't leave Arthur," I said as I reached out for Arthur's cold hand.

"I understand," Reynolds said. "I'll bring someone to you."

I watched the battle rage in the distance. I saw the green fog become fainter and fainter. We were winning. It wouldn't be long until it was over. I was surprised to see that the Death Reapers were still fighting, and then

I remembered that somewhere in that forest behind them was their leader. He'd kill them all of they retreated.

Lance.

Where was Lance?

He saved us. He was so brave. Had we lost him? I couldn't bear the thought of losing him. How would I tell Arthur?

A woman came up and examined my arm. It hurt when she set the bone and wrapped it up, but she reminded me of Dellia.

"Can I give you something for the pain?" The woman asked.

"No thank you," I said before falling asleep.

I woke a few hours later. I was lying next to Arthur in the wagon and looking up into the clear blue sky. I watched the pure white clouds drift lazily for long minutes before realization came back to me.

We were moving.

I sat up, and it hurt like hell.

I felt Toad's tiny hand on my arm, and looked at him.

"Everything's fine," Toad said.

"Arthur?" I asked.

"He's alive," Toad said. "He'll have a long road of recovery ahead of him, but if he listens to me, I think he'll survive. We, of course, have that scabbard to thank for his life."

I looked at my injured love. He was sleeping and his forehead was sweating. I placed my hand on top of his forehead and found that he was burning up.

"There's an infection racing through his system," Toad said. "I can clear that up when we get back to the castle."

"It doesn't look good," I said. "He's so pale."

"It isn't good," Toad said, "but there's nothing I can do about it out here."

"I'm worried," I said.

"That's only natural," Toad said, "but he'll get the best of care. I'll bring him back to us. I promise you."

"We lost Lance," I said.

"I saw," Toad said.

"We need to go back for him," I said.

"That would be suicide," Toad said. "No doubt those woods are now crawling with Death Reapers."

"He might still be alive," I said.

"If he is," Toad said. "He'll come back to us. That kid has all the tools he needs to survive in a hostile environment."

I didn't like it. It wasn't right to leave someone behind. It wouldn't sit well with Arthur either. I knew that. We'd do something. We'd find Lance, and dead or alive we were going to bring him home.

I saw Camelot in the distance.

It was a welcome sight. I needed to rest. We all needed to rest. I closed my eyes and woke up in the infirmary. I wasn't alone. There were many of us in the room.

I slipped out of my bed. My bare feet hit the cold floor, and I padded over to Arthur's bed. I touched his forehead, and sighed with relief that it was much cooler than earlier.

♣ EPILOGUE: ♣
TWO DAYS LATER,
LANCE

Mordred and I tumbled away from his horse, and into the low bushes along the trail. His armored body landed on top of me, and I hurt something in my hip. It wasn't a serious injury, but movement wasn't going to be easy for a few days.

The Red Knight came to his feet quicker than me. His sword was in his hand and flashing dangerously as he sought me out.

I was careful not to move and give away my position.

"Lancelot," Mordred said. "I was hoping that we'd get a chance to fight. They say you are the greatest of Arthur's knights."

With quick movements, I bounded deeper into the brush.

"Are you afraid to face me, Lancelot?" Mordred asked.

Of course I was afraid to face him. From everything I'd seen of him, he was a monster and with my injured hip, I'd never stand a chance against him.

Mordred walked deeper in the brush. His sword scraped against the bushes as he poked and prodded for me.

Not far away I saw a tall tree with low hanging branches. With a quick look back at the advancing Red Knight, I rushed towards the tree.

Mordred pursued me.

Actually, he nearly cut me down, but somehow I managed to reach the tree and climb high before his blade could touch me.

"We'll meet again, Mordred," I promised. "Someday soon I'll come for you."

"I look forward to it," Mordred said.

I froze against the tree. Mordred couldn't see me, but he waited there for what seemed an eternity. Finally, his men began to call him from the trail. With a grumble, Mordred sheathed his sword and left me alone.

In the distance, I heard him telling his men to search the forest.

I leapt to another tree, and after that, another one.

I hadn't gone far, but I'd gone far enough to be safe.

I waited there until nightfall, and after my change, I headed off in the direction of Camelot. I was forced to walk. My hip was hurting furiously.

Eventually I found the clearing where our soldiers had been waiting. I found that odd. Everything about what had happened was odd.

I had questions, but they'd have to wait. I climbed a tall tree, and rested until my hip felt better. After that, I made my way home with only a slight feeling of discomfort.

Cindy was probably worried sick about me, but I first had a stop to make.

It was late at night when I crept inside the window of Merlin's little home. The wizard noticed me immediately.

"Lancelot," Merlin said. "We've been worried sick about you."

"I'm fine," I said. "How's Arthur?"

"He'll recover," Merlin said, "but it'll take time."

"I have questions," I said.

"Hopefully I have answers," Merlin said.

"Why send Gwen to such an incredibly dangerous place?" I asked.

"It was Gwen's choice," Merlin said. "I only presented her with the option."

"You sent her into danger with the promise of magic," I said, "but that little flower didn't give her any magic. The magic came from her emotions. She was worried about Arthur."

"That's true," Merlin said. "Her love of Arthur and her worry for his safety forced her magic to emerge."

"I'm also wondering how you were able to follow so closely behind Arthur when he went out to rescue Gwen," I said. "It's almost as if you'd planned for all of this. You even had our soldiers waiting at the clearing."

"You don't trust me," Merlin said. "I deserve that after what happened with Mordred. I made a mistake, but everything turned out all right in the end. Gwen has her magic. She was rescued, and the two of them are together and in love."

"You haven't explained yourself," I said.

"I'm not going to," Merlin said. "You're only thinking of the individuals you care about. I have greater concerns than that. I'm fighting for the entire world. I've aligned my pieces when need be. I wish things could be different, but like I said, I'm fighting for the world."

"You've endangered our king," I said.

"I was hoping that Gwen's powers would emerge in the swamp," Merlin said. "It was never my intention to endanger Arthur."

Finally, the truth.

"I understand what you're doing," I said, "but Arthur is under my protection. If you endanger either him or Gwen again, I'll kill you."

"I understand," Merlin said. "And I hate myself for what I've done."

"I can see that," I said. "I can see the pain in your eyes, and that's the only reason you're still alive."

"We have a truce then?" Merlin asked.

"For the greater good," I answered.

"Good," Merlin said. "Now we must prepare. Morgana has revealed herself. The final episode of this war will be coming soon, and we must do whatever it takes to win."

ABOUT THE AUTHOR

Michael Clary was raised in El Paso, Texas. He is the author of The Guardian Interviews series (*The Guardian, The Regulators, Broken,* and *Scratch*). He is an occasional practitioner of Mixed Martial Arts, and collects bladed weapons of various types. Before he wrote novels, he wrote and directed Independent films. Currently, Michael is living in Temescal Valley, California with his wife, family, and three Pit Bulls. You can follow him at www.michaelclaryauthor. com

BOOK

IS COMING

PERMUTED
PRESS

PERMUTED PRESS
needs **you** to help

SPREAD (THE) INFECTION

FOLLOW US!

f | Facebook.com/PermutedPress
🐦 | Twitter.com/PermutedPress

REVIEW US!

Wherever you buy our book, they can be reviewed! We want to know what you like!

GET INFECTED!

Sign up for our mailing list at
PermutedPress.com

PERMUTED
PRESS

14

Peter Clines

Padlocked doors.
Strange light fixtures. Mutant
cockroaches.

There are some odd things about
Nate's new apartment. Every
room in this old brownstone has
a mystery. Mysteries that stretch
back over a hundred years.
Some of them are in plain sight.
Some are behind locked doors.
And all together these mysteries
could mean the end of Nate and
his friends.

Or the end of everything...

PERMUTED
PRESS

THE JOURNAL SERIES
by Deborah D. Moore

After a major crisis rocks the nation, all supply lines are shut down. In the remote Upper Peninsula of Michigan, the small town of Moose Creek and its residents are devastated when they lose power in the middle of a brutal winter, and must struggle alone with one calamity after another.

The Journal series takes the reader head first into the fury that only Mother Nature can dish out.

PERMUTED
PRESS

Michael Clary
THE GUARDIAN | THE REGULATORS | BROKEN

When the dead rise up and take over the city, the Government is forced to close off the borders and abandon the remaining survivors. Fortunately for them, a hero is about to be chosen...a Guardian that will rise up from the ashes to fight against the dead. The series continues with Book Four: *Scratch*.

Emily Goodwin
CONTAGIOUS | DEATHLY CONTAGIOUS

During the Second Great Depression, twenty-four-year-old Orissa Penwell is forced to drop out of college when she is no longer able to pay for classes. Down on her luck, Orissa doesn't think she can sink any lower. She couldn't be more wrong. A virus breaks out across the country, leaving those that are infected crazed, aggressive and very hungry. `

The saga continues in Book Three: *Contagious Chaos* and Book Four: *The Truth is Contagious*.

PERMUTED
PRESS

A PREPPER'S COOKBOOK
*20 Years of
Cooking in the
Woods*
by Deborah D. Moore

In the event of a disaster, it isn't enough to have food. You also have to know what to do with it.

Deborah D. Moore, author of *The Journal* series and a passionate Prepper for over twenty years, gives you step-by-step instructions on making delicious meals from the emergency pantry.

PERMUTED
PRESS